THE CURSE OF AGGIE MULDOON

Nadia Kehoe

This is an IndieMosh book

brought to you by MoshPit Publishing an imprint of Mosher's Business Support Pty Ltd

PO BOX 147 Hazelbrook NSW 2779

indiemosh.com.au

First published 2016 © Nadia Kehoe

Cataloguing-in-Publication entry is available from the National Library of Australia: http://catalogue.nla.gov.au/

Title: The Curse of Aggie Muldoon

Author: Kehoe, Nadia

ISBNs: 978-1-925447-92-7 (paperback)
          978-1-925447-93-4 (ebook – epub)
          978-1-925447-94-1 (ebook – mobi)

Cover layout by Ally Mosher at allymosher.com
Images licensed from Adobe Stock.

Dedication

I dedicate this book to my husband, David Kehoe, your love for your ancestral land has inspired me to write this story.

To my daughter, Madeleine Kohar Kehoe, you are my best creation and I am lucky to be your mother.

Acknowledgements

The road to publication is a lengthy one for all authors and when one reaches that point, it's the result of many people who are involved helping to make the author's dream come true.

I owe a debt of gratitude to several people who have helped me on this wonderful journey to realise my dream of becoming a published author.

First and foremost a huge thank you to Jenny Mosher and her talented daughter Ally Mosher, from IndieMosh publishing, for taking on my work. I thank both of them for their professionalism, humour and patience with my waffling conversations. This mother and daughter team have been an absolute delight to work with. In particular I wish to thank you Jenny for putting up with my endless questions, answering them with so much detail and coming up with ideas to create a professional print and eBook. I also wish to thank Ally for designing the cover which not only captures the elements of the story but delivers my vision for the cover.

Many thanks also go to my brother Ara Nalbandian, editor extraordinaire! How lucky can a writer be to have a professional editor in the family. You have lovingly devoted many precious hours to help me with this book.

I also deeply appreciate the hard work of professional assessors, Joy Aimee and Catherine Hammond, in assessing my manuscript. Your advice and encouragement has kept me going and focused on improving my writing.

Thanks also go to my gorgeous cousin, Juliette Afarian, my lovely sister-in-law Jill Kehoe and dear friend Steve Gerakiteys for being my beta-readers, giving your honest and valuable opinions.

How can I leave out my husband, David Kehoe, my talented daughter, Madeleine Kohar (Kehoe) and my mother, Sylvia

Nalbandian who have always been there for me. Your support and encouragement has meant the world to me.

My heartfelt gratitude goes out to the late Cleo Pozzo, Literary Agent, who was ready to take me on as her client but sadly passed away. Her encouraging emails were a Godsend to me to continue my writing journey.

Finally I would like to thank you, my readers. I hope you enjoy my story as much as I enjoyed writing it. If you liked this book I would really appreciate if you could write a review.

Thank you all.

Nadia Kehoe
July 2016

CHAPTER ONE

A carved slab nailed on Fionnbharr Kavanagh's bleak and unwelcoming door read 'SIOTHCHAIN AGUS FAIRSINGE'. Later, I established this Gaelic motto meant 'Peace and plenty'. Ironic, considering the brutal history of the inhabitants of the dilapidated mansion for over a century.

Wrapped in my favourite scarlet coat and struggling against the fierce wind and rain, I fumbled through my cluttered handbag. Finally producing the key, I opened the ten-foot hardwood door.

'Damn,' I muttered under my breath as I inserted the unpolished key in the keyhole. I chastised myself for not organising the keys while in the comfort of my warm rental car.

The downpour of rain totally saturated me; it was so cold that it felt as though someone had massaged my entire body with a bundle of icicles.

That travel agent lied. She said the southeast of Ireland enjoys more sunshine than elsewhere in the country. Just my luck this rule doesn't apply today. For God's sake, who the hell secured this latch? There's no one living here.

With considerable effort, I pried open the latch. My hands ached from the hard work. At least, I had to be thankful I had a flashlight with me, as I took the first step into my ancestral home.

A chill went through me as I walked headlong into a cobweb. 'Ugh. Christ Almighty! Oh, yuk.' I jumped back, working fiercely to remove the creature's tattered snare from my face. I hate spiders with a passion.

This sentiment was hardly surprising since I'd grown up in Sydney. After all, Australia is home to some of the world's most venomous arachnids.

Casting a dim light, the torch I carried guided me down the dark hallway and I tiptoed into the first room on my right. At a glance, I hazarded a guess that generations of Kavanaghs would've congregated in this sitting room. These Kavanaghs were the side of the family whose unenviable reputation hardly ranked high in my father's esteem.

The first thought that entered my mind was to question my sanity, or as the case may be, my insanity to venture out here on my own. To think I was game enough to enter a house that for almost 150 years people considered haunted.

The reason for my lack of caution was my insane need for adventure. My family and friends, on the other hand, found it hard to understand this insatiable need and often said they wished I just led a secure, ordinary existence.

I admit I enjoyed the rush of adrenaline coursing through my body.

A few weeks ago, descending hair-raising cliffs to photograph Nepalese honey hunters doing their dangerous work was my main preoccupation. The likelihood of plunging down to a sure death was far greater than a swarm of bees stinging me.

My partner of four years, Dylan Turner and I are freelance photographers and were on assignment in Nepal. I'm a journalist by profession and Dylan is a first-class photographer. We make a good team. Dylan's incredible passion for his work, not to mention his artistic flair and my journalistic background, land us in some amazing places and give rise to some astounding experiences.

I met Dylan in England just over four years ago, when I was on a much-needed holiday. At the time, the pressures of the cutthroat world of journalism in my hometown, Sydney, stressed me so much I decided to tour the English countryside. As a fan of Jane Austen, I'd always wanted to visit the quaint villages so lovingly described in Austen's novels.

Dylan intrigued me from the day we met at an art gallery in Southampton where his photography was on display. I knew from the first moment I struck up a conversation with him he was the right man for me.

At this moment, however, all I felt was disappointment. Dylan didn't even offer to accompany me to Ireland to solve the family curse, which has passed down from generation to generation. I made excuses for him, such as the pressure of his creative work consuming him, and I shouldn't entertain such selfish notions that he should've been with me. Deep down, though, I knew things weren't right between us.

I shrugged and thought it was best not to deal with that issue now. *I should only think about solving this family mystery. It beats me why have they chosen me for this impossible task. I'm a journalist, not an amateur sleuth.*

Three weeks ago, on September 12, a letter arrived when I was in the middle of writing up an article for the assignment we undertook in Nepal.

Someone had addressed the envelope to me, sealed, and stamped it "highly confidential". It had come to my office, which is above Dylan's studio. The postmark on the envelope read Kildare & Co., a legal firm in County Wexford, Republic of Ireland.

I wasted no time and opened the envelope with the aid of a solid 18ct gold, ivory-handled letter-opener, a sentimental reminder of my maternal great-grandfather who had lived for a number of years in the prolific greenstone belt of West Africa making pots of money excavating gold.

The letter was brief. It simply stated that I, Kathleen Kohar Kavanagh, was the sole heir to my Great-Uncle Fionnbharr Kavanagh's fortune and estate. He'd died suddenly in the first week of July, at the grand old age of ninety-six.

A Mr Ambrose Kildare, undoubtedly one of the partners of the firm, had signed the letter with great flourish. He urged me to make a trip to Ireland. He stated there were legal requirements and certain conditions set that I would need to satisfy, before I could receive the inheritance.

Baffled, I sat there for a while wondering. *Why am I the one to inherit all this fortune? After all, Great-Uncle Fionnbharr has children, grandchildren and even great-grand-children of his own.*

To make matters even more complicated, I'd never set eyes

on my apparently pugnacious great-uncle. My only link to him was my limited knowledge of his eccentric reputation and the fact that he was my great-grandfather's second-generation cousin.

I wasn't exactly next of kin to Great-Uncle Fionnbharr, so I'd certainly never expected he would leave his entire wealth to me.

I read the letter six times before it dawned on me this was not a simple matter. There was much more to this bizarre request than was expressed in this otherwise ordinary legal letter. Frankly, I didn't care to have any part of his estate or his fortune.

Nevertheless, my usual curiosity overtook my senses and won the battle against my better judgment and here I was, three weeks later, flashlight in hand, walking through a haunted house.

***

When I arrived in Dublin three days ago, I wasted no time in hiring a car. I drove on Route N11, 90 km to northwest of County Wexford.

This was Kavanagh country and we were most proud of it. For centuries, the "Coamhanachs", the Irish Gaelic name for Kavanagh, have dominated the nobility, politics, the military and the arts in this county.

It's no wonder my father is proud of not only being Irish, but of having come from such a distinguished lineage. The only grey area that worried my father was Great-Uncle Fionnbharr and the transgressions of his side of the family.

Trouble had struck the Kavanagh family a few hundred years ago, when Cormac Padraig Kavanagh, a prominent and respected merchant, had lost his heart to a pretty and highly flirtatious young woman named Honora O'Rourke. She had been twenty-five years his junior and had the reputation that many men of her county admired her.

After a brief courtship, they had married and had four children, three boys and a girl. They had named the eldest boy Muiris, followed by Tiarnan; the girl they had called Ursula and the youngest boy was Cailean. They were handsome children except for the youngest, whose dark and brooding looks and nature were vastly different from those of his siblings.

The year was 1865. On a stormy day, Cormac Padraig Kavanagh had made haste to return home to his young family when tragedy had struck; he had been away at sea for three months, to establish a successful trade route.

Upon his unannounced return to his estate, he had discovered his wife, whom he had adored, in the arms of a young gangly man not much older than herself.

When he had witnessed their treachery and deceit, the story goes, Cormac had stirred to such heights of despair that, in a moment of madness, he had slaughtered them both.

The young lovers had died with their faces distorted so horribly by the frenzied attack of a wronged man that they had been almost unrecognisable. Although the public had pitied Cormac Padraig Kavanagh – for he had been a man driven to this gruesome act for reasons of crime of passion – the law had found him guilty. A few months later, they had sent him to the gallows.

Because of that fateful evening, townspeople had gossiped and the house of Cormac Padraig Kavanagh never saw peace. The tortured souls of the young lovers had stayed on to haunt ensuing generations of Kavanaghs.

To make matters worse, according to the story passed down through time, Aggie Muldoon, the mother of the gangly young man whom Cormac had murdered, upon hearing of the senseless death of her youngest son, had placed a curse on Cormac Padraig Kavanagh's family and his descendants.

CHAPTER TWO

Like lustrous blue on a canvas, aqua skies greeted me when I arrived in the town of Wexford. I headed straight to the Bed & Breakfast I'd chosen from a travel brochure. It was a charming guesthouse and close to my uncle's estate.

A middle-aged couple, Mr & Mrs Doherty, were the owners. The room was a decent size, with a four-poster bed. It had a sunny north-easterly aspect, overlooking a lovely cottage garden.

The décor was elegant with various pieces of period furniture; the Doherty's didn't spare any detail to make the room comfortable and homely. They even provided a generous basket of fruit with a card welcoming me to Wexford. Irish hospitality down to a tee, I acknowledged with a smile.

The warmth of the hypericum-scented water soothed me as soon as I immersed myself in the bath. I needed to soak my tired body. Each bubble that exploded spattered drops of silky water on my skin.

I closed my eyes to relax and empty my mind. Instead, a misty drizzle of memories started to trickle in.

His hungry lips greedily explored my body with the intensity of a wild beast devouring flesh. He wanted to possess every inch of me, even the crevices, which had previously been unexplored. No gentleness, he was uncompromising, even cruel. He was the mysterious stranger who sometimes interrupted my thoughts and invaded my dreams. He came uninvited, lurking like a dark shadow. Then he left and the deep silence that followed cocooned my despair.

When I opened my eyes with a start, I was still in the bath, but the warm water had turned cold. I shivered. The headache, which had developed on the flight from London to Dublin, had intensified. *I've to get him out of my head. I must relax. I'll take deep breaths and he'll disappear.*

Dylan's chiselled and handsome face replaced the wild-looking stranger from my nightmares and I immediately felt better. Dylan was the one person who made things right.

Once more, disappointment rose in the pit of my stomach when I reflected on how he wasn't keen on the idea of coming to Ireland with me, if for nothing else than to spend some quality time together. We lived and worked together, but our schedules were so hectic we hardly had time to speak, let alone anything else.

As I clambered out of the slippery cast-iron bath, my mobile phone played its hip-hop tune. I made a mad dash to hunt for the phone, buried deep in my bag.

'Hi, precious,' I answered, sounding out of breath.

'I missed your call before.'

'I rang you from the airport as soon as I arrived, but Paulette said you were on the other line.'

'Yeah. I was talking to Karl Redfield. You know, the guy we met last year in the States.'

'The Senator?'

'That's the one. Well, apparently they're trying to promote Cherokee culture on the reservations, probably a lucrative money-maker for the government. Anyway, he wants me to do some photo-shoots in Minnesota. Something about some tribal members harvesting wild rice at a festival.'

'Sounds quaint.'

'I didn't listen to all he said, but I remember him going on about conservation issues as this wild rice apparently is a food source for muskrats, waterfowl and deer. He's e-mailing me the details. The money is going to be good.'

'That's wonderful, hon. Keep me posted. Do you know when you're leaving?'

'No. I told you, I don't know the details. Probably in the next few weeks.'

'Why don't you come up here for the weekend? At least we can spend some time together before you head off to the States. It's magic here.' He gave no response, so after a few seconds I asked, 'Are you there, Dylan?'

'Yeah. I'm busy, I'm testing some equipment. What did you say?'

'Oh, nothing. Don't worry.'

'OK. I've got to go.'

'Bye honey. I love you.'

'Ditto.'

I felt crushed. *Can't he even bring himself to say those three simple words anymore?* I had a niggling feeling Dylan was preoccupied. He worked long hours. He was an artist and was prone to unpredictable mood swings probably attributable to his genius. Apart from being a brilliant award-winning photographer, he was also a painter, mostly abstract style.

We never talk about the future. Is the relationship going to progress to the next level? I certainly want it to develop into something more concrete. I'm thirty-three; my biological clock is ticking away. Besides, I want to experience the same contentment and happiness my parents have in their marriage. That's coming up to forty-three years. God, that's incredible! These days' people don't seem to cherish the sanctity of marriage.

As I squeezed the excess water out of my hair, I decided I shouldn't be so negative. *I'm exhausted and overreacting to everything.*

I felt confused as more pressing issues hit me. *The relatives won't be welcoming me with open arms. I'm a perfect stranger as far as they're concerned. After all, my great-uncle's estate and fortune should've gone to them, not me.*

The blow dryer worked furiously as I looked at my reflection in the bathroom mirror. The process of styling my hair usually took me a good ten minutes.

Although my hair was shoulder length, it was thick and had a certain kink, which annoyed me to no end. A drastic change of hairstyle was well overdue. I was tired of the auburn colour too. My eyebrows puckered up when I noticed, much to my horror, some renegade strands of grey jutting out from my skull. 'I'm too young for my natural colour to turn grey,' I said to my reflection. 'But, it's in my blood, in my genes.'

Nana and her siblings all had snow-white hair by the time they were in their forties. No, I'm not going to worry about it. With that resolution, I abandoned styling my hair and put the dryer back in the suitcase.

I returned to the bathroom to perfect styling my hair with some hairspray and considered my dilemma. *Every time I make a suggestion for a radical haircut, Dylan objects profusely. What's men's fascination with women's hair anyway? I should take the plunge, have a bob-style cut below my chin, and even go blonde or maybe jet-black. You never know, Dylan might even approve. Hey, what century am I living in? Why should I allow Dylan, or anyone for that matter, to dictate how long or short or what style I could wear my hair?* Then I softened. *No, Dylan would definitely not approve.*

The mobile rang again. I placed the hairbrush on the washbasin and went to answer it, hoping it would be Dylan to tell me he would join me for the weekend.

It was a male voice, which sounded quite mechanical.

'Ms Kavanagh, this is Ambrose Kildare. I thought I'd call you before our designated meeting tomorrow.'

'Oh, hello, Mr Kildare.' I was surprised. I didn't expect to hear from him before our meeting. 'I was going to ring to confirm our appointment. My flight got in earlier than expected.'

'I trust your flight was comfortable and the accommodation is satisfactory?'

'The flight was fine and the accommodation is very cosy, Mr Kildare. Quite charming, in fact.'

'Very good, Ms Kavanagh, then we shall expect you at eleven in the morning. The directions to get to our offices should be straightforward.'

'I'm sure I'll find your offices without any difficulty. I look forward to meeting you tomorrow, at eleven.'

'Have a good day, Ms Kavanagh,' Mr Kildare said and abruptly hung up.

He sounded peculiar. Even though I'd not yet met him, I'd already formed a picture of him in my mind. It would be interesting to see if he was anything like what I imagined him to be. I left the room.

The air was pleasant outside, perfect for a stroll around the fine grounds. Varieties of cyclamen, snowdrops, foxgloves and feverfew danced in the gentle zephyr. These plants filled the neat rows of cottage garden. I followed the stony trail that led to the rear of the quaint nineteenth-century neo-Tudor-style home to discover an ancient canal leading to some pebbled pools.

A small mound aroused my curiosity. It looked like a pet cemetery. When I approached the area, I confirmed from the eulogy on the granite tombstone it was the resting-place of a most beloved cat named, Freya.

A little further along, a sundial stood conspicuously among an assortment of herbs. I swirled around, like a ballerina, taking in the entire picture, noticing the minute details that made the atmosphere so charming.

I looked high up to the hundred-year-old trees, which gave the twenty-acre property its romantic setting. *It would undeniably be the perfect place if Dylan were beside me. I miss him and it hasn't even been a full day of being apart. The penitence for being in love, as my nana always says.*

All of a sudden, clouds started to gather ominously, taking over the blue sky and threatening a downpour.

I decided to venture back into the house and warm myself in front of the inviting fireplace, in the well-positioned sunroom. The Dohertys certainly had spent a lot of money to preserve the old-world charm of the place without making it appear too imperious.

Looking through a bay window, I appreciated the intensity of the rustic autumn colours of the surrounding countryside. Wexford, the county of my ancestors, was stunning. It was hard to believe I was here.

Although my father was born and bred in Australia, he feels fiercely connected to his Irish roots. He always describes Ireland as the lush green land that is the home of heroes and martyrs, poets and thinkers. Everything I've read about Ireland suggests it's an ancient country of contrasts, full of mystery, rituals and myths – a truly enchanting place.

The smell of freshly baked bread wafting into the room, made me realise I was ravenous. *I've had nothing since coffee and a cinnamon muffin this morning. I hope they'll serve dinner early.*

The sunroom held an interesting mixture of Victorian, Edwardian and 1920s furniture. I admired the Moorcroft vases and fine china collectibles. The wooden fire-surround was a contrast to the fresh mint-green walls and was the room's focal point.

A black and white photograph on the mantelpiece captured my attention. A young girl in a fairy costume sat on the lap of an intense-looking elderly woman. The gold writing engraved on the frame read, 'To my precious Aggie, on your fifth birthday, Grandmother Muldoon'.

My body immediately went rigid as though venom surged through my veins. I couldn't remove my eyes from the name 'Aggie Muldoon'.

Since childhood, I'd heard that name countless times and feared it. My father always referred to it by saying, and never in jest, 'Our Kavanagh clan has been cruelly afflicted by the curse of Aggie Muldoon'. Each time she heard the name, my mother, a religious Armenian Orthodox, made the sign of the cross and said some evil undoing-incantations in her mother tongue.

I didn't know what to make of this incredible coincidence. I certainly intended to question the Doherty's at the first chance and my wish came about sooner than I anticipated.

Not five minutes had passed since I'd put the photograph down on the mantelpiece, when Mr Doherty popped his head around the doorway and said, 'Waat are ye at, me blade? Ye comin' for a bite ter ayte? Me struggle an' strife has cooked up a storm.'

Sweet Jesus, what a thick accent. It took me a few seconds to get the gist of what he said. Nonetheless, I forced a smile and followed him in the direction of the enticing smells.

We entered an enormous country kitchen, a blend of classical style and up-to-date technology. The room didn't only look good but it also smelt heavenly.

Mrs Doherty wore a bright, honeydew-coloured apron, with generous vertical splashing of gold, which accentuated her long and thin torso. Somehow, her physique didn't blend in harmoniously with the timeless kitchen.

She took a large tray out of the oven. The smell of roast pork and bacon made me feel even hungrier. When she noticed her husband and I had come into the kitchen, she chastised him in a high-pitched voice, 'Honestly, Angus, why did you bring the girl into this messy kitchen? The rest of the guests are already seated in the dining room.'

'Please Mrs Doherty, your husband isn't to blame. I must say it smells great in here.' In order to defuse the situation I tried to flatter her by praising her culinary talents.

'Weemen, waat lashing an' fuss yer all make.' Mr Doherty motioned me to follow him as he shook his head, bemused by female logic. 'Com' on blade, I'll take yer ter de dinnin' 'all.'

'Maybe this isn't the right time. I can see you're very busy Mrs Doherty,' I said quickly before he took me out of the kitchen. 'I noticed a photograph on the mantelpiece in the sunroom. Is the little girl, Aggie Muldoon, related to you?'

'I'm Aggie Muldoon.' Not even a hint of emotion could I detect in the woman's husky voice.

'Oh.' I pressed on. 'By any chance, did you have a great-great-grandmother named Aggie Muldoon?'

'Yes, I'm named after her.' Mrs Doherty continued to baste the pork with its own juices.

'Have you heard of Cormac Padraig Kavanagh?'

'Of course I have. He was responsible for the premature death of my great-grandmother, Aggie Muldoon's youngest son. Kavanagh murdered the young man in cold blood.'

'This might come as a shock to you, Mrs Doherty, but I'm a descendent of Cormac Padraig Kavanagh.'

'It's not a shock to me. I know exactly who you are, and why you're here. Now if you'll excuse me, I have many mouths to feed.'

Her aloof and shrewd response stunned me so much I didn't recall how I got to the dining room and how I came to sit next to a good-looking man. My mind was in total disarray from the events that had just taken place.

'Of all the B&Bs I could've chosen, I had to pick this one. Why in God's name has this happened? It is unthinkable, a Kavanagh under the same roof with a Muldoon.' I suddenly felt cold as I muttered these questions under my breath.

'Are you all right?'

I looked up quite stupefied and stared into the man's face. I blinked. I felt confused. 'I'm sorry. Were you speaking to me?'

'Yes, I was wondering if you're OK. You look rather upset.' He repeated the question and then added, 'Would you like some water, or perhaps something stronger?'

'No, thanks. I'm fine.'

The serious look on the man's face made me think that I hadn't convinced him.

'Well if you're sure – we haven't been introduced, I'm Josh. Josh Abbott. Perhaps you've heard of Abbott & Sons? Well I'm the son,' he said with a broad smile, showing off his pearly white teeth and at the same time extending his right hand.

'I'm Kathleen.'

'Pleased to meet you Kathleen. So do most people call you Kathleen or Kath, perhaps Kathy?'

'A mixture really, anything from Kitty, Kat, Katyg to Katya to name a few. But you can call me Kathleen.'

'You never told me your surname.'

'Is that important?'

'I like to be well informed,' he said with a smile.

'Really. Once you know my surname, you will ask for my middle name.'

'So what is it?'

'What is what?'

'Your middle name.'

'Kohar.'

'Pardon?'

'Kohar,' I spelled it out slowly. He didn't have a clue.

'Haven't heard that one before. Is that a Celtic name?'

'No, actually it's Armenian. My mother is Armenian and my father is of Irish origin. Therefore they came to the conclusion it would only be fair to give me a name taken from each culture.'

'How fascinating. But I still don't know your surname.'

'Kavanagh.'

'That's definitely Irish.'

I looked away trying to discourage his prying but it didn't seem to dissuade him.

'So, do you live here in Ireland? Although before you reply, I must add I can detect an Aussie accent, am I correct?'

'You *are* perceptive, Mr Abbott.'

'Please, call me Josh,' he said. 'So tell me, what are you doing here, so far away from Down Under?'

'Well, that's a long story.'

'I'll let you in on a little secret,' he said as he moved closer. 'It's been my lifelong dream to visit Australia. Plenty of sunshine, great beaches and open spaces really appeal to me.'

'Well, then you must make a point of visiting my country. We're a friendly bunch, you know.'

'So I've heard. And judging by you, I can safely say the rumours are quite true that Australia is full of beautiful women.'

You're smooth, aren't you? I smiled.

He opened his mouth again, perhaps to continue his line of puffery when Mr Doherty interrupted. The older man's mission was to extract from his patrons their choice of soup: potato with fennel, roast baby turnip, or watercress and lemon. This was not an easy task, as not only did we have to contend with interpreting what our host was saying, but also in the background, Sir Arthur Sullivan's symphony in E minor was fast moving to its crescendo.

'I find it exceedingly hard to understand that man,' Mr Abbott confided when Mr Doherty was out of hearing range. 'I come to Ireland often on business and I must say I seldom have a problem understanding the locals. But in his case – for God's sake, it's not as though he's speaking Gaelic, it's English.'

I gave an all-knowing smile and was about to elaborate on the disparity of the English language, when Mr Doherty brought an elderly couple to our table.

'I am Doctor Hipolito Alfonso De Silva and this is my wife Ida Betriz. We are visiting here from Lisbon,' the older man began the introductions. 'We are here for the autumn Wexford

Opera Festival.'

'How wonderful. Indeed, this is a pleasure Doctor and Mrs De Silva. This lovely lady is Ms Kavanagh and I'm Josh Abbott.'

After the exchange of pleasantries, the soups arrived. It was quite comical to watch the interaction between Mr Doherty and the newly arrived tourists from Portugal. Between us all, we managed to order the desired choice of meals on offer.

The dinner was delicious; the food was wholesome and satisfying. The company was delightful too. Both Mrs De Silva, who lacked the confidence to speak much English, and I were quite happy to sit back and enjoy the entertaining chatter of the men, which became even livelier after they'd consumed numerous glasses of strong Irish whiskey.

It was well past midnight when I excused myself and retired to my room to prepare for the following day. I still felt uncomfortable about spending the night in the same house as Aggie Muldoon. I went to the door several times to check the lock. I seriously considered changing my accommodation, but the thought of uprooting bothered me; this place was just perfect.

***

The following morning I woke up in a state of consternation. I'd tossed and turned all night. At one stage, after finally falling asleep, I'd woken up with a jolt as anxiety had set in. It was distressing to feel this way.

I hadn't felt anxious like this for a long time. I shuddered when I thought back to a time when I suffered severe depression and felt anxious almost every day. That was when I was with my long-time partner, Jimmy. *What a bastard he turned out to be, sleeping around behind my back. I'll never forget that day when I caught him in bed, our bed, with my so-called best friend. The ultimate betrayal. Those two deserved each other. Why am I thinking about all that now? I've been so happy since Dylan came into my life. But I can't help feeling so edgy. Maybe, when I'm back home, I should see Jenny again and have some more cognitive therapy.*

I showered, dressed in a light woollen business suit and pulled my hair back. Putting on some dark sunglasses, I left the guesthouse without bothering to have breakfast, although I felt hungry. *I'd rather eat at a coffeehouse than run into that unpleasant Aggie Muldoon Doherty. Nasty bitch!*

***

The hot cup of tea and the raisin toast satisfied me.

As I was about to leave the coffeehouse I noticed Josh Abbott sitting at a booth, in deep conversation with two other people. I walked towards him to say hello when I saw his companions. One was Aggie Muldoon Doherty, dressed in black like a wicked witch, nursing a permanent scowl on her stern face. The other person sitting next to her was a tall, handsome man, about my own age or perhaps a few years younger.

Although I'd never set eyes on him before, I had a distinct feeling there was an air of familiarity about him. Taking long strides, I practically bolted out the door. *I should count my lucky stars they didn't notice me. Mighty interesting. Why is Abbot having breakfast with that horrid woman? Then again, it's not that great a surprise, considering he's a guest at her B&B. I wonder who the other guy is?*

Nonetheless, just seeing Aggie Muldoon Doherty made me more than nervous. The woman's cold, emotionless stare the previous evening had left me with an uncomfortable feeling, though I think I've enough intelligence not to allow old superstitions to affect me. Then I remembered the sheer terror in my father's eyes every time someone mentioned the name "Aggie Muldoon".

There was still another hour before my meeting with Ambrose Kildare. I walked around, not even taking any pleasure in the beautiful displays in the numerous tempting shop windows in this busy part of town.

A wooded area in a park facing a small lake was the perfect place to sit and rest. The water's gentle movement and the ducks' playful antics had an instant calming effect on me. I sensed my late grandfather was around. He would've loved this charming scene.

When I was a little girl, every Saturday afternoon, rain or shine, my grandfather and I would go to the local baker and buy two loaves of bread. It was our secret ritual. Hand in hand, we would make our way to the park where a small artificial lake was the sanctuary of a flock of ducks and geese. We would spend the afternoon feeding them and enjoying carefree hours in each other's company.

As the gentle breeze caressed my face, a tear ran down my cheek. I clutched the gold heart-shaped locket I'd worn since my seventh birthday when my grandfather had put it around my neck. I'd placed his photo in it, that way he always stayed close to my heart.

It was unbelievable he had died fifteen years ago; it seemed like yesterday. Not a day went by I didn't think of him, or miss and crave his company. He was such an extraordinary human being – kind, generous, and compassionate. He never had a cross word for his fellow beings or for me, for that matter. I missed his fine mind. He'd been my mentor, my teacher. I know that even in death, as he had been in life, he was my guardian angel. *Precious, precious man, where are you? Please protect me from the evil forces that surround me on this uncertain and ill-omened adventure.*

***

The door opened and a young, attractive secretary ushered me into Mr Kildare's office. She was tall and lanky, with abundant Titian curls, which she waved about indifferently.

The skimpy blouse and the excessively short skirt hugged her curvaceous body. *It doesn't leave any room for the imagination – hardly the image you'd expect from someone working for a solicitor.* The secretary's main preoccupation was her immaculately kept nails, which protruded grotesquely from her fingers like gargoyles from an old cathedral. She made an incessant sucking noise while chewing her bright blue bubble gum.

After assessing me with that peculiar disdain only a woman

can show another she motioned me to a chair. As I sat there, I could see that I didn't measure up to her standards, but then I was grateful I didn't look like a pole dancer in a nightclub.

'My boss is held up at the Supreme Court. Some important case. He'll be late.'

Wonderful. I picked up a magazine from the coffee table. While I engrossed myself in an article in the National Geographic about African marriage rituals, Mr Ambrose Kildare marched in as though he was the commandant of a battalion. He fitted perfectly the mental picture I had of him. He was short, slight, and with a receding hairline complemented by a bland face, and yet he possessed an air of absolute confidence.

Without a word of apology for making me wait for more than an hour and a half, he impatiently waved his arms about for me to sit opposite him.

'Firstly, congratulations are in order. You shall soon be a very wealthy woman, more than you bargained for Ms Kavanagh.'

'Pardon me for my lack of enthusiasm, Mr Kildare, but I believe I've no business in acquiring this fortune.'

'Your Great-Uncle Fionnbharr obviously thought it was your business.' He paused. 'Now look Ms Kavanagh, this sort of thing happens all the time. A favourite of the deceased ends up with the entire lot, naturally disgruntling the remaining doting family.'

'Well, that may be the case for some families. However, in this instance, you can hardly argue I was Great-Uncle Fionnbharr's favourite. He had never even met me and I for sure didn't know him.'

'Your great-uncle knew a lot more about you than you give him credit for. I can go as far as to say he admired your tenacity and courage. In fact, he thought that out of the whole clan of the Kavanaghs, you're the only one who deserves his vast fortune.'

'This is bizarre, Mr Kildare,' I said as I uncomfortably crackled in the barrelled-back brown leather wing chair. 'I'm very far removed in the genealogy of his side of the Kavanagh clan. I know very little about these relatives, but I can safely say

I do know Great-Uncle Fionnbharr had children, grandchildren and great-grandchildren of his own. Tell me, didn't he like any of them?'

'He used to refer to his family as "a pack of vultures" and those were his exact words, Ms Kavanagh,' he answered readily. 'I think he strongly felt they were earnestly awaiting his departure so they could have it all. Needless to say each one of them was astounded by the unexpected outcome of events.'

I gave an irritated laugh. 'I don't doubt that, but how can I feel anything but agitated, knowing only too well these people resent me. Furthermore, I've never met them before.'

'You'll get over it. It is, after all, a small price to pay for a fortune that is as vast as your uncle's. Your long lost-relatives are the least of your problems, Ms Kavanagh.'

Then, with a dramatic air, Mr Kildare announced, 'In order for you to inherit your uncle's fortune, you must first reverse the curse of Aggie Muldoon.'

CHAPTER THREE

The steaming shower was just what I needed after spending the morning in my uncle's 'haunted house'. It was comforting to be back in my safe haven.

I could still feel the impression the enormous cobweb had made on my cheeks. The soft face cloth helped remove this irrational fear of the spider's intricate dwelling.

I hadn't seen or learned much from my 'snooping' around the property.

It annoyed me at first that Mr Kildare had just handed over the keys and said, 'Although the estate hasn't been officially transferred to you, Ms Kavanagh, I think you would find it useful to inspect this fine house at your leisure. You never know what secrets are harboured there, which might prove to be useful for reversing the curse of Aggie Muldoon.' With that amazing assertion, he'd ushered me, rather briskly, out the door and hadn't even bothered suggesting he accompany me.

Therefore, without a friend or any support, I'd gone to the house on my own.

Apart from the darkness and the dilapidated state of the property, the experience hadn't been as daunting as I'd anticipated. Admittedly, for some inexplicable reason I wasn't nervous. I strongly felt the answers I needed to solve this mystery were at my uncle's haunted house.

***

Following the unpleasant encounter with Aggie Muldoon Doherty, I checked out of the B&B and sought alternative accommodation.

The new B&B was an old sandstone cottage. Mrs Whelan, an

elderly woman, owned this delightful place. She was a petite lady, with delicate features complemented by a small upturned nose. Her skin was smooth and remarkably devoid of anything other than light character lines.

However, her gentle, attractive demeanour was in stark contrast to her boisterous and determined character. I was sure no one would dare to upset this waif-like woman.

After unpacking, I decided to go for a walk. I slipped on my joggers and headed out into the garden. I was dressed casually in comfortable jeans and my favourite turtleneck cream jumper that my maternal aunt, Nairi, had knitted.

The grounds were neither as vast nor as fine as the Dohertys' property; nevertheless, they were peaceful and picturesque.

A gentle breeze greeted me as I made my way down an ancient path that led to a rose garden. I was just about to admire the various varieties of flowers, when a gate opened and in came Mrs Whelan, her smile wide and generous. She held in her arms a large cabbage. It looked quite comical, as the leafy green vegetable was almost the entire size of the old woman's upper body. It was as though she was carrying a big lump of rock.

''Ullo dear. Oi 'ope I didn't startle yer!'

'Not at all, Mrs Whelan. I was just admiring your beautiful roses. How do you manage to keep this garden so immaculate?'

'Ah, Oi get a young fella ter 'elp me. His name's Lochlan, a local boy. He's a gran' young'n, certainly 'as a green thumb.'

'But I'm sure most of the credit goes to you. It's so serene here,' I said as I took a whiff of one of the sweet-scented blooms, which was blood red. 'I'm sorry Mrs Whelan, how rude of me not to help you with that cabbage. It looks quite heavy.'

'Oh no dear, it's not 'eavy at all. Oi jist picked it from me vegetable patch. Me dear Aidan, that's me dear departed 'usband, well it was 'is favourite pastime, yer know, growin' 'is vegetables.' She sighed. 'Oi, of course, canny keep up wi' it as well as me man used ter. But, de Lord decided ter take me man from me, what could I do?' she continued, her voice growing more melancholic. Then she looked at me with her feisty eyes and said, 'I'm makin' Colcannon, t'nite. Oi 'ope yer will dine in an' try it.'

'That's a potato and cabbage dish, isn't it?'

'To be sure, 'tis one of our popular Oirish dishes an' I'm makin' 'ome-made sausages ter go along with it.'

'Then how could I possibly contemplate dining elsewhere, Mrs Whelan! It all sounds heavenly.'

'Well den lovey, I'll see yer at seven. It will be jist yer an' Oi t'nite. De Forbishers, de elegant tourists from Englan' an' Mr Morgan who is 'ere on business from Wales, well they are gonna sum fancy restaurant in town.' She shook her head. 'Oi better get back ter de kitchen — dem spuds are on de cooker — before Oi burn de place down — Oi'm such a forgetful, foolish old woman'. She looked up at the sky. 'I 'eard on de radio, dey expect storms t'night. Good thing yer dinin' in, me dear.'

'Really? There's not a single cloud in the sky, Mrs Whelan. It's a perfect day. I never believe the weather man.'

'Yer should believe it. As blue as it might be now, it can turn into a grey squally day.'

I stayed in the garden for the remainder of the afternoon, lazily stretched out on a hammock and absorbed in a book on Druid magic, called *The Lost Books of Merlyn*, which I'd taken the liberty to select from Mrs Whelan's small collection in the sunroom.

It was only when the sun mellowed and the light faded rapidly that I decided to retreat indoors. As I entered the cottage, I thought I was right not to believe in the weatherman; there would not be a storm tonight.

The smell of fresh wood burning in the inviting embers of the fireplace rekindled childhood memories; my winter school holidays in Australia.

I used to spend them in the cottage my paternal grandparents owned in the Blue Mountains, just outside Sydney. Snuggled cosily on my nana's rocking chair for what seemed to be hours on end, I used to stare into the fireplace. My vivid imagination used to create little people of different sizes and shapes. They would dance around and talk to me from the hearth. Then my nana would bring in piping hot Milo to drink and my pop would roast marshmallows in the fireplace.

They would tell me tales of the Celtic fire goddess Brighde, who guarded the fires of the hearth, smith and life. The rest of the evening, we would spend laughing and sharing spooky stories.

How I missed those idyllic days! My eyes stung as I fought back tears. The simplicity of my childhood, the inexplicable thrill my young mind experienced from the basic things in life resurfaced; but alas, I couldn't turn back the hands of time.

Mrs Whelan interrupted my reverie when she called me to the kitchen to share the rustic meal she'd taken so much care to prepare.

It was a modest country kitchen. Pots, pans and bunches of lavender hung low from the ceiling. The refrigerator and the furnishings looked as though they'd seen better days. Yet so much life and warmth radiated from every corner of the tiny room. I suspected my host's vibrant energy created the earthy and welcoming atmosphere.

The more I spoke to her, the more I realised Mrs Whelan was one of those rare individuals who couldn't be faulted. I could sense she was all goodness with no trace of malevolence.

It was nice to sit back and enjoy a good country-style meal, accompanied by excellent company. Mrs Whelan kept me in stitches of laughter with her roguish tales of her upbringing in a good but strict Catholic family. It was only when our tongues began to loosen, as we let our guard down after the second mug of hot toddy, that she raised the subject of Aggie Muldoon.

'So me dear, Oi hear yer met our town's sorceress.'

'Who do you mean?' I raised my eyebrows, somewhat taken aback by the sudden change of subject.

'You know who Oi mean. The Doherty woman.' Mrs Whelan made the sign of the cross. 'Oh that one is pure evil. Everyone in our town is downright terrified of 'er. Some folks call 'er the she-devil.'

Before I could say anything or even ask a question, Mrs Whelan quickly continued with her story. 'A few years ago, Donegal, me neighbour's nephew was takin' 'is girl home. It was a full moon and they were crossin' the moors, an' what d'ya think they witnessed?' The old woman's vivacious eyes held a mixture of terror and excitement.

'I've no idea.'

'In the pitch of the dark, only the moon guidin' them on their trail, they come to pass the most abhorrin' of sights.' She stopped and took in a deep breath. 'The Doherty woman was standin' over the corpse of a deer when within a blink of an eye, this she-devil shape shifted. One minute she was a woman, the next she became a beastly wolf. Her eyes were yellow and her demeanour ferocious. Without much commotion, she gave out the most chilling of howls in the still of the night and then devoured the dead animal before 'er.'

'My God, what you say is incredible, Mrs Whelan,' I interrupted, my mouth wide open in disbelief. 'Those kids must've imagined it all. I mean it was dark as you say. It's very easy to conjure up shapes and figures in one's mind, which is far removed from reality.'

'Aw no, those kids didn't imagine anythin'. For sure, they saw that devil become a werewolf. Those kids never came right after that night. Aye that poor doll. She never talked again and Donegal, well the poor lad hung himself within months of that 'orrifyin' experience.' She stopped speaking, then with a curious gleam in her eyes she went on, 'I'm surprised me dear that yer, of all people – the descendent of Cormac Padraig Kavanagh – can doubt this story. What with generations of yer family 'aving suffered immensely from the curse of Aggie Muldoon. I thought for sure, this story would intrigue you.'

'You know about the curse?'

'Everybody in this county knows about the curse of Aggie Muldoon.'

A knot took hold in my stomach, a mix of anticipation and dread. 'Please tell me what you know.'

'Well, let me tell yer ...'

CHAPTER FOUR

It was suddenly pitch black. Darkness encompassed the room as though a black hole had swallowed us.

'What in heaven's name is goin' on?' Mrs Whelan cried out. 'There are some candles in the second drawer, I'll ...' She never finished her sentence.

It all happened in a matter of seconds. The clatter and clamour of thunder sounded just as the lights went out and then there was a terrifying strike of lightning, so forceful the solid house shook as though a powerful earthquake had hit it.

The kitchen window, which I distinctly remembered Mrs Whelan locking before we sat down to dinner, burst open. The only way I can describe what happened is a swishing sound and an incredible commotion like a tornado twirling around, sucking up and destroying everything in its path.

In the confusion, I fell to the floor and took cover under the kitchen table my hands over my head, to protect myself. The pots and pans that had been hanging from the ceiling clashed like musical cymbals in an orchestra as they fell to the floor around me. I could hear china smashing as if a sledgehammer was pulverising every piece simultaneously.

During the course of these events, Mrs Whelan said her Hail Mary's and invoked the saints to protect us. Her incantations became louder and louder until they reached a shrilling pitch. Then her voice went dead.

I blurted out, 'Are you OK Mrs Whelan?'

Silence followed. Simmering fear stirred in the hollowness of my stomach. The blast of the thunder and lightning subsided.

The cold air was the only distinct force as with slow movements I crawled out from under the table and made my way to where I thought the door was. I knew the light-switch was next to the wooden frame. I buoyed up as though I surfaced from the dark floor of the ocean and with quivering hands attempted to find the light-switch. Feeling my way up the wall I finally located the large, old-fashioned switch and tried to turn the light on.

Nothing happened. The impenetrable darkness remained. Once more, I cried out to Mrs Whelan. No answer.

Moving slowly forward, my heartbeat was uneven but I could hear my heart thumping loudly. *God knows what's happened to the poor woman. Surely, if she's OK she would respond. Maybe she's passed out from fright. That's possible. It happens when people are under extreme, stressful situations. Mrs Whelan is an old woman after all. It wouldn't take much for her to suffer a heart attack, just from sheer shock!*

It was dark in the kitchen. The window was open and the wind blew in at such speed that it nearly knocked me back to the floor as though a freight train had rushed toward me.

I felt my way around, like an animal crouched down on all fours, to locate the dear woman. 'Mrs Whelan,' I kept calling out. No response.

A piece of glass pierced my palm. Pain shot up my hand. 'Damn,' I blurted out. It stung. I moved my hand to my mouth and tasted the tartness of my own blood. An unsettling feeling nestled in me as in the distance I heard a chilling howl.

I thought of Aggie Muldoon.

The lights came back on. I couldn't believe my eyes. A massive fir tree had crashed down, destroying everything in its path. Mrs Whelan's limp body lay face down on the cold floor, trapped underneath a thickset branch.

I ran to her, almost falling over broken objects that were scattered on the cheap linoleum. The room was like a rubbish dump, litter everywhere. With great effort, I removed the branch off her. It didn't take much effort to roll over the petite body.

Blood covered Mrs Whelan's pretty face, the side of her head crushed as though someone had driven an axe through it.

At times of crisis, there must be divine intervention, because I put aside the need to scream. Instead, I quickly checked the woman's pulse, to find she was miraculously still alive. I had no time to panic, so I looked around for my mobile and was finally able to call an ambulance.

It seemed like an eternity until the emergency services arrived. After a long time of stabilizing Mrs Whelan, the paramedics finally rushed her away to hospital.

***

'Are you the person who reported the incident?' a baritone voice barked behind me.

I jumped to attention at his commanding question and faced a tall and rather severe-looking man. He stood rigid, as though he was a military sergeant. I looked at him closely. The man was perhaps five, maximum ten years older than I was. Though handsome, he looked stern. He reminded me of my pop's friend who had been a Colonel in the Australian Army and a decorated veteran of the Korean War.

'Yes, I am.'

'The woman is a total mess. What happened?'

I felt like screaming at him. *Isn't it obvious what has happened?* Instead, I just kept looking at him as though I was oblivious to what was happening around me. I was in shock.

'Did you or didn't you witness the incident?' Before I could open my mouth he turned to where the body of Mrs Whelan had been and spoke out aloud, 'Terrible business, she's lucky to be alive.'

'It was incredible,' I finally spoke. 'Mrs Whelan and I were sitting here at the table, chatting away after we'd finished our dinner when lightning struck. At the exact same moment the lights went out and all I could hear was the sound of destruction as though an explosion had taken place.'

The military-looking man, whom I assumed was with the police, listened intently but didn't say anything.

'That's the only way I know how to describe what happened tonight. In the darkness, all I could hear was the cabinet doors opening from the sheer strength of this cluster of wind. China and glassware were lifted as if being sucked up by some powerful vacuum and then they shattered everywhere,' I relayed the horrifying scene in my tired mind. 'Then as quickly as it had come it died down — that's when the lights came back on and I discovered the tree had come down through the roof, trapping Mrs Whelan underneath.' I looked up with a bland expression and stared into the harsh-looking, brooding eyes of the police officer. 'But before the lights came back on, I heard the wolf.'

'What?'

'Like I said, it was definitely a wolf howling.'

'What wolf?'

'I don't know. I mean I couldn't have imagined that chilling howl.'

'I'm sorry to say that you did imagine it. I can assure you, there are no wolves or wild creatures in Wexford. It was probably a dog.'

'No. What I heard was not the howling of a dog.'

The police officer ignored me and moved about the room, examining the broken wares. I think he thought I should have my head examined. Only I knew what I had heard.

'We need you to come to the station to make a formal statement.'

'I want to go to the hospital to be with Mrs Whelan.'

'Are you a relative?'

'No, I only met her yesterday. I'm staying here at the guesthouse.'

'Where are you from?'

'I live in London.'

'On holidays?'

'No. Not exactly.' The whole mess made my mind feel cloudy. 'I'm here because my uncle has left his estate to me.'

'Oh, right, and who might that Uncle be?'

'Fionnbharr Kavanagh.'

'Then let me welcome you to Wexford, Ms Kavanagh. I'm Inspector Sean Muldoon.'

***

The next day I got up early and went to the hospital to visit Mrs Whelan.

I could only stay a short time. They had sedated her. She didn't know I was there. Her bandaged face reminded me of the 'mummies' I saw in London at a recent exhibition of 'death and burial' in Ancient Egypt.

A nurse who was looking after Mrs Whelan in the intensive care unit patiently answered my barrage of questions. The nurse explained the injuries Mrs Whelan had sustained were extremely severe and she was on the critical list.

'She's lucky to be alive. We have contacted her next of kin. I just hope she can last until they arrive.'

I was so upset I hadn't even asked about her family. *Lord, please let her live.* I left the whitewashed walls of the village hospital behind.

An hour later, I stood in front of a part-Georgian, part-Victorian Manor. This was my new accommodation. It was a large establishment. It buzzed with human activity. I was so unsettled after the incident that I hoped I'd be safer in a busy environment. A log fire blazed in the reception area.

The room commanded a good view of the coast. *I love looking at the sea – nature always helps settle my rattled nerves.*

The sun from the east threw abundant light through the large window as I sat quietly in the room and gazed out, my thoughts taking me back to the terrifying events of the previous evening.

That chilling howl. I can't erase it from my memory. Is there some truth to the story Mrs Whelan was telling of her neighbour's nephew, witnessing Aggie Muldoon Doherty turn into a werewolf right before his eyes? Could the howl I heard be Aggie Muldoon Doherty's? What am I thinking? It's ridiculous, there are no such things as werewolves in real life. Nevertheless, Mrs Whelan had been in the process of telling me about the curse of Aggie Muldoon, when the catastrophe took place. It was as though she really believed the story she'd been telling me. Is this all a coincidence or is it more sinister? Could this be a sign of the curse? Here I go again! These irrational thoughts are becoming a constant companion.

Then I tried to be practical, to rationalise by thinking how it would be possible for some ancient curse to control the weather. Besides, only that morning, Mrs Whelan had mentioned a brewing storm. As though I'd just stepped into a butcher's freezer, a cold feeling went through me. This time I knew I was out of my depth.

I tried to think of the curse. Did it involve werewolves? Like most people, I'd heard of werewolves and shape-shifters in mythical or legendary tales, and I'd seen entertaining movies about them. Who could forget classics like *The American Werewolf in London*? I'd seen it at least half a dozen times, mostly at the university cinema. I always thought these sorts of mythical lore were yet another aspect of man's vivid imagination. Now, I was confronted with perhaps the most intriguing and bizarre challenge of my life.

I sat alone, my left leg shaking uncontrollably. My leg always shook when I was anxious or nervous. And at that moment I was both.

The Inspector's stern face suddenly popped into my head. *Not bad looking. No, definitely good looking. But, stern, like he'd be always cross with you.* I gave out a nervous laugh as I shook my head. *Fancy that, he's the son of Aggie Muldoon Doherty. Is it coincidence or what?*

***

This was the reason they summoned me to Ireland, to remove the curse Aggie Muldoon had invoked – a curse so terrible it had lingered in the lives and minds of every member of the Kavanagh family for over a century.

The irony of the situation was that even though I feared this curse I didn't know anything about it. Here I was, a 33-year-old woman, and I'd never questioned my parents about the power of this curse, or for that matter, what it was.

Sure, I know the history, which goes back almost 150 years, but what does that have to do with the present? On the surface, my family appears ordinary and close knit. I can't think how 'the curse' has affected us and why my parents and the entire family are downright terrified each time the name of Aggie Muldoon comes up.

Late morning I rang Dylan. I missed him and I wanted to hear his voice. I told him about Mrs Whelan's injuries and that she was in hospital fighting for her life.

Dylan didn't say much, almost as though he hadn't listened to what I'd said. Nor did he sound concerned about what I'd gone through in the past few days.

He made no mention of coming to Wexford, even just for the weekend. Reverse the roles I would've jumped on the next flight to be with him. Especially, since I could've been seriously hurt. I guess he doesn't see it that way since I am all right. I'm being selfish. Dylan has a lot on his mind. He has a number of pressing projects to finish before he heads off to the States. Only if I could go with him!

Another telephone call I made was to my father in Australia.

'Hi, dad.'

'Well hello, my darling. How are you?'

'I'm fine. How are you and how's mum?'

'I'm well and so is your mother. Bless her lovely soul; she's not here at the moment. She mentioned going to Paddington with her sister. As we speak, she's undoubtedly doing some severe damage to her credit cards.'

'Dad, you know us girls, shopping is our favourite pastime.'

'Um – it seems paying bills is my favourite pastime.'

'Daddy!'

'I'm joking, my princess. So, tell me, how's Dylan?'

'He's well. I spoke to him a few minutes ago. I miss him terribly.'

'Oh? Has he gone somewhere for business?'

'No, I'm the one travelling.'

'Where are you, princess?'

'I'm in Wexford.'

Silence. I knew this revelation made my father nervous. 'Please tell me you don't mean Wexford, Ireland.'

'I do mean Wexford, Ireland. Dad, it's such an overwhelming and wonderful feeling to be in the country of my forefathers.'

'Kat, darling, I pleaded with you not to pursue this matter.

Nothing good will come out of it, love. You must get out of Ireland.' I could hear the agitation in his voice.

'It's all right dad I know what I'm doing. I promise you, I won't place myself in undue danger.'

'You mightn't seek danger, but danger will seek you.' He sounded all choked up. 'Princess, why are you doing this? Is it the damned fortune? I've always taught you that wealth is inconsequential. I cannot believe you, of all people, have fallen prey to the allure of money.'

'Dad, please calm down,' I said. 'I can assure you this has nothing to do with money. Both Dylan and I make enough to be very comfortable. I'm doing this to stop the curse of Aggie Muldoon'.

'You know nothing about this curse and its power. Get out of Ireland before it's too late.'

'I can't do that. I must find out what the Muldoons have over us Kavanaghs. This nonsense about curses must stop.'

'Nonsense?' he shrieked. 'Do you actually think this is nonsense? You are indeed mistaken. This curse is so powerful, no one will ever be able to reverse it, and if you continue to persist, it will destroy you. And I cannot allow that.'

'Then help me understand it. Tell me what the curse is.'

'I won't go into it over the phone. I'm going to come over to Ireland. You can't possibly deal with this on your own.'

'No. Dad, please, I can handle this.'

'I'll phone you as soon as I can and let you know of my flight details. I must go now. I have a lot to prepare.'

'Dad, please ...'

'My mind's made up, I'll be in touch.'

What've I done? I'm an idiot. I shouldn't have called him. I should've anticipated his reaction, and I should've shielded him from all this. Shaking my head, I let out a frustrated sigh. *My Irish determination and my Armenian stubborn streak always gets me into trouble.*

Making an impulsive decision to pay another visit to my Great-Uncle Fionnbharr's 'haunted house', I grabbed the torch and thrust it into my handbag. I slammed the door behind me and headed for my car.

CHAPTER FIVE

The door creaked as I forced it open. As I made my way into the house, the familiar musty smell greeted me as if it was a long-lost friend. I recalled my unpleasant encounter with the cobwebs the last time I was in the house, so I took great care not to walk into another one.

I began my search for clues in the dark, my torch being the only sense of security. Strangely enough, with each step I took, I felt a peaceful aura encompassing me. *My dead relatives don't mind me being here, wait till they get to know me.* I clung onto humour to keep me sane.

As I peered into the labyrinth of cavernous rooms, I realised in some parts of the vast mansion the temperature dropped considerably.

'I've got to buy some woollen underwear and wear a ski-jacket when I come exploring again,' I said out loud, my voice crackling. 'I can imagine this place to be chilling even on a summer's day.'

Twenty minutes later, I came across a doorway behind the small enclave of the stairs in the north-wing.

A half-torn blossom of crab apple-patterned wallpaper covered its exterior. When I lifted the latch, the door opened without much effort on my part. Torch in hand, I took the step over the threshold. My heart was palpitating. I felt like a burglar in the thick of the night aware of the danger I faced, but willing to take all risks.

A narrow and craggy stone staircase led me down to a basement. When I reached the bottom, I discovered it was a T-junction. Both sides of the corridor led to numerous chambers.

A quick look and I could just make out that the walls were of quarry stone. The musty smell was even stronger down here than in the main house. I decided to make a right turn at the T-junction and entered the first chamber.

It was a storage area. Old furniture crowded the room. I brushed past a Victorian walnut tapestry screen. *Wow, mum would love this. It would look great in her sun room.*

A hand-carved, wooden rocking-horse caught my attention. I caressed its head. Certainly, it was well preserved. It looked just like the one I'd longed for when I was seven years old and the family had taken a trip to South Australia. We'd visited the Hills district and a magnificent wooden rocking horse had been in the display window of a specialty toyshop.

I still remember shedding a few tears as my parents told me it was impossible to take such a large item on the plane back to Sydney.

Although, my parents always indulged me with abundant toys, I pined for that particular rocking horse for a long time.

'Enough nostalgia,' I murmured under my breath.

I moved around the room in fascination as though I was a child running wild in a toy store. My surroundings captivated me; I didn't pay much attention to where I was going. As a result, I knocked my knee on a rundown oak coffer. Howling like a wounded dog, I examined the source of the throbbing pain. The wood had grazed my left knee, leaving behind beads of blood that emphasised their vivid colour against my pale skin.

As I turned around, I forgot the pain. I could have sworn the rocking horse had moved.

A gentle breeze brushed past my flushed cheeks at the same time I heard the soothing melody of a harp. It felt like time stood still and I was looking into a room from a window outside.

A little girl of six or seven gently frolicked on a majestic rocking horse, the very same rocking horse I had just caressed. Laughter filled the room and the harp continued to play its repetitive tune. A beautiful young woman, tall and elegant with long trusses of golden hair, wearing a bright floral dress, gently rocked the wooden horse, while the little girl laughed with pleasure.

The melody of the harp changed pace, intensifying the force

of the breeze. The young woman's carefree mood altered when a young boy of perhaps twelve entered the room. There was a tremor in his voice as he cried, 'Mama, mama, you must come to the forest quickly. Cailean has drowned Pip in the wishing-well. He has murdered my squirrel.'

Like a sweeping vacuum, the whole scene disappeared before my eyes. My heart pounded in my ears. I felt cold as though a supernatural force had taken over me. I pulled at my coat, sinking further into it as though the action might protect me. My stomach felt as though a tight corset had been constricting me, making it hard for me to breathe.

My God, this is the first time in my life I'm experiencing such vivid visions, I know I've got great intuition but do I have psychic powers? Are my dead relatives trying to contact me? Creepy.

In the next chamber, I only found shelf after shelf of old wares. There were kerosene lamps, old tins, a hatchet, a dudeen – which I recognised as an old Irish tobacco pipe – boxes of rusty nails and other useless wares. These were all collectibles of an eccentric old man.

I continued inspecting the chambers and entered a smaller room, which had a wooden bed against the wall. I went by the bed, when the gentle breeze wafted past me once more. Laughter and giggling filled the small room. There was dancing and frolicking, as two young people whirled in each other's arms. One of them was the same beautiful young woman. The young man was lanky and didn't take his eyes off her. They appeared to be in love as they waltzed around the room, until they fell on the bed and made passionate love.

I felt overwhelmed. *I think it's time I leave. It's getting too eerie for my liking. Although, I'm intrigued how and why I'm having these incredible visions.* I fled. I had no business being in this haunting subterranean place.

***

The light from the torch became dimmer, so I started to head towards the stony staircase, otherwise sudden darkness would surround me. For some inexplicable reason, I decided to take a quick detour and have a peek at the only chamber that had a closed door.

It was strenuous turning the old-fashioned clamp. Nevertheless, because I was determined to get into the chamber I was eventually successful.

Fear gripped me as I entered the chamber. In the centre of the room lay two pairs of solitary shackles.

The breeze struck again, but this time it was more vigorous that I started to shiver. Deafening screams filled my ears. Immense torture and agony lay before my eyes. Sadness and anguish, lamenting, torment and regret – these were the harrowing feelings that overpowered me. Restrained in the shackles, I could make out the shadow of the beautiful young woman and the gangly young man as they emitted their final chilling screams. Side by side they lay naked, their faces and flesh torn to pieces, almost as though clawed by a ferocious, wild animal. I watched on in horror as the young lovers took their last breath.

For a split second, I thought I had stopped breathing. I had to get out. I had to escape from the room.

Highly distressed, I ran up the stairs as though I was running for my life. My horror turned to shock when just before I reached it, the door to the basement slammed shut. Someone secured the lock. I screamed and called out. With all my strength, I banged on the door. No amount of pushing would budge the thick piece of wood.

This is madness. Who is here? Why are they doing this to me? My God, this place is renowned for being haunted. Are the ghosts trying to destroy me? That's ridiculous, I don't believe in crap like that. Ghosts. What nonsense! But who is here? Locking me away. Wanting to get rid of me. Maybe it's my distant family – uncle Fionnbharr's descendants. No! I can't believe that. Surely these relatives don't want me dead. Or do they?

I was terrified and confused. As if the spooky visions weren't enough to contend with, the realisation someone quite menacing was in the house and wanted to harm me rattled my nerves even more.

I sat crouched on the stairs.

'My mobile phone. Thank God.' I fumbled through the handbag. The momentary excitement faded as I realised I couldn't receive or make calls from this underground dungeon. My worst nightmare was realised. The dim light from the torch died, leaving me in total darkness. Trapped, hopelessly trapped.

I pounded on the door. What use was it? Who would hear me? Exhausted, I prayed to God to rescue me from this startling dilemma.

'I must do something. If I sit here and do nothing, I will slowly perish. What choice do I have? I must crawl down the stairs and feel my way from room to room. There might be a way out.'

It took me some time but I reached the bottom of the stairs. This time I turned left. I hoped I wouldn't encounter more ghosts. *What ghosts? I'm just conjuring images in my head, because of the bloody history of my family. I don't believe in ghosts.*

Guided by the wall, I walked along until I reached what I thought was the end of the corridor. A few more steps I felt my way and reached a doorway. I opened it. Darkness lifted. I could see. Tucked away from the other chambers, it was a small room.

A faint light found itself through a tiny window, high up, almost at the edge of the ceiling. The size of the window didn't matter. It opened up fresh hopes for me. *If only I can somehow break the glass of the window, I might have half a chance of someone hearing me. What am I thinking? Who's going to hear me out here on this desolate 60-acre property? No, I mustn't give up like this. Just concentrate on the task on hand and then worry about the next step.*

I examined the window. Even if I managed to break the glass, how was I going to get up there to crawl through the small opening?

One step at a time. I somehow have to break this glass. How? How in the hell am I going to break it? I threw the torch but aimed badly. As it fell back to the ground, it shattered into smithereens.

'That was a bloody useless exercise.' Furious at myself, I rummaged through my handbag.

'Mobile phone, wallet, bunch of keys, tons of tissues and some make-up. Great! I need a heavy object to break the glass. The hatchet!'

I'd seen it in the second chamber. I didn't want to go back there, not in pitch darkness. *Kathleen Kavanagh, you aren't born to be a coward, you are a journalist and have been exposed to spine-tingling experiences before this. For goodness sake pull yourself together*.

I took a deep breath and tiptoed out of the room.

Darkness. Total darkness. Not a pleasant feeling. My heartbeat accelerated as if a racing car was negotiating a bend. Using the walls as a guide, I felt my way towards the chamber. Using my heightened senses, I finally arrived at the chamber where I thought I'd seen the hatchet. Bumping my knees along the way, I finally found the object I sought.

Cradling the hatchet, as one would a baby I left the room and headed back to the small chamber.

The trip back was even more challenging, as I relied totally on my sense of direction. Each step I took I felt as though it was the most arduous thing I'd done in my life.

I mustn't be negative. I know I'm going to get through this.

Along the way, I chanted incantations and prayers to ward off evil, which my mother had taught me in Armenian. Although I claimed not to be superstitious, I wasn't going to take any chances.

I arrived back at my refuge, without any harm. A great sigh of relief was all I could manage.

My arms ached from carrying the hatchet. It was much heavier than I'd anticipated. Then I set to work and went back to the first chamber where I'd noticed a sturdy-looking table. With considerable difficulty, I dragged it back to the tiny chamber. This whole process, took me just over an hour.

My knees felt unsteady, but I managed to stand on the wooden table and lugged the hatchet in my arms. *At least, this way I'm a bit closer to the window. I hope this works*. It took many attempts to gain strength enough to throw the hatchet, aiming directly at the window. Finally, the impossible happened. I successfully sent the hatchet through the window, shattering all the glass.

To my greatest astonishment, I heard a male voice, 'What the hell!'

'Please help me,' I yelled.

'Is someone down there?'

'Yes. I'm trapped down here.'

'How do I get you out?'

I sighed, and gave the man directions on how to rescue me.

Once more, I groped my way around through the corridor, and with great determination got up the stairs.

The lock opening was the sweetest sound to my ears.

A flashlight thrown on my face blinded me. The voice asked in amazement, 'Kathleen?'

As I blinked to get used to the torch's piercing light, I recognised the handsome face.

'Josh!'

CHAPTER SIX

Rain was pelting when I picked up my father at Dublin airport. As soon as he stepped out of the arrival lounge, I rushed to him and gave him a warm hug. I'd missed him so much during the past two years.

We decided not to waste time and headed back to Wexford. Although, I toyed with the idea of spending a few days in Dublin, I knew my father was here on a mission. The curse was heavily on our minds.

I made a concerted effort to avoid mentioning the dreaded subject and my father didn't say anything either. We caught up on each other's news on the road from Dublin to Wexford. I felt nervous as the rain kept coming down harder and harder almost blotting even the road out of sight.

'I see some things never change,' my father said.

It was only when we arrived at the hotel and back in the comfort of my familiar room that I broached the subject of the curse.

'Dad, please tell me all you know about Aggie Muldoon and this curse. This so called curse has plagued our family for generations and we should get to the bottom of it.'

My father, a handsome man, carried a vacant expression on his face. He looked unusually gaunt. By nature an easy-going man, he seemed withdrawn and fragile. A lump formed in my throat. My father was my rock, my mentor. I hadn't seen him for two years. I wondered if he had some health issues, which he kept from me. Maybe it was the strain of the curse and the long flight from Australia.

He paced the floor. 'Kat.' My father's pet name for me. 'Sweetheart, you're my daughter, my only child. I can't begin to tell you what you mean to me. I'm well aware, you are a determined and strong-minded girl – and yes, you're still my little girl. But, on this occasion, I wish you'd left this whole ghastly matter well alone.'

'It's too late for that, I'm already involved. Tell me all you know, Dad. I must have the truth.'

'All right, I'll tell you what I know. But mark my words, nothing good will come of all this.'

After a frustrated sigh he said, 'You already know about the gruesome history of our family. You know the story about Great-Great Grandfather, Cormac Padraig Kavanagh. Some 150 years ago, in a moment of rage he murdered his wife and her lover. The law sent him to the gallows for the ghastly crime he committed. Before his death, the mother of the murdered young man placed a curse on the bloodline of Cormac Padraig Kavanagh. Aggie Muldoon was that woman. However, what you don't know is what the curse is all about. And by God I've tried all my life to shield you from it.'

He stopped and placed his hands over his eyes and at the same time shook his head. Guilt consumed me. My father looked defeated at that moment.

***

'It's OK, Dad, you don't have to shield me from all this,' I said as I placed my arms around his neck and kissed his forehead.

He looked at me. His eyes sad, he cradled my chin in his warm palm. 'You and your mother are my life. I couldn't bear it if anything were to happen to either of you. I've feared this curse all my life and rightly so.'

'I know this is hard for you, but I must have the truth. We can work through this together. I don't believe in the saying, "ignorance is bliss". On the contrary, as you have taught me, "knowledge is salvation". We can only conquer the curse if we know the source of its power.'

I held his hands in mine.

'In a moment of madness Aggie Muldoon invoked the vilest of curses. The evil woman with her potent witchcraft cursed every first born of Cormac Padraig Kavanagh's bloodline, to die a horrible death.'

'What do you mean by a horrible death?'

'The first-born child of each generation would never reach his or her first birthday. The baby would die horribly, under tragic circumstances.'

'That's awful.'

'Yes my love, that's putting it mildly.'

Something was not right. My mind was in overdrive. My father was keeping something vital from me. It was obvious.

'Then how did I survive? After all, I am your only child.'

At this point, my father openly wept. I tried to comfort him. Nothing worked. He was inconsolable.

Then he blurted out a statement which was the most startling revelation to me, 'That's because you aren't the first born.'

***

It was no wonder I woke up with an intense headache. The previous day was one of the most emotionally charged days of my life. Discovering that I had an older sibling who had died before his first birthday both saddened and baffled me. I had so many questions to ask my father. I didn't know where to begin.

My father had been quite hysterical with all the pent-up feelings of sorrow and anger, so I'd decided not to pursue the matter any further, at least for the time being. I'd encouraged him to go to bed as grief had overcome him. His face had started to become paler and I had feared he might fall seriously ill.

Although he was only in his early sixties, my father suffered from high blood pressure and mild angina. It dawned on me his ill health was largely due to what he must've endured after the death of his first child. My eyes were misty. I felt for my parents at that moment. It was only through their goodness and their immense love for me that they'd kept this secret for so long.

Quickly getting out of bed, I placed my heavy head under the steamy shower. I could feel the tension melting away, as the water massaged my tight neck and shoulders. I lingered on taking comfort in the sensation the jet stream created on my skin.

Reluctantly, I left the shower and as I draped a large bath towel around me, the telephone rang. I thought it might be my father from the next room or Dylan. I was wrong. The authoritative voice of Inspector Muldoon greeted me.

'I hope I'm not disturbing you, Ms Kavanagh.'

'Not at all, Inspector. What can I do for you?

'I've some rather unpleasant news.'

'Oh?'

'Mrs Whelan passed away at 4 this morning. I just thought you might like to know.'

'Dear God. Oh that poor woman. This is awful. But why? I mean, I thought her condition was improving.'

'I don't have all the particulars yet, but I believe she suffered a brain aneurysm. As I said, I thought you'd like to know.'

'Yes, of course. Thank you.'

'Ms Kavanagh, I'd appreciate it if, over in the course of the next few days you'd pop into the station. We need to go over your statement. Particularly now that Mrs Whelan has died. I won't keep you any further. Good bye.' He spoke quickly and before I could respond, he hung up.

My head spun, as though I was on a roller-coaster. *Why? Why did this have to happen? This is all my fault. If I hadn't been there and we hadn't discussed the ill-fated curse, none of this would've happened. I'm being ridiculous. What happened that night was a freak act of nature. A sheer coincidence. I can't blame the incident on the curse, or can I?*

I went back into the bathroom, looked at myself in the mirror and stared angrily at what I saw. Stubborn, determined, curious and impulsive. These were four simple adjectives that described my character, the flaws in my personality that always got me into trouble. 'My father was right all along,' I said out aloud. 'This is only the beginning. Why didn't I listen to his advice?'

There was a knock on the door. I felt bewildered and my palms were clammy. 'No, I refuse to have a panic attack I can breathe and it's all in my mind.' I splashed some water on my face to cool down and went to answer the door.

It was my father, looking thin and weak.

'Were you asleep, sweetheart?'

'I just had a shower. Come in.'

'Are you sure you're all right? You look pale.'

'I'm fine, really. More importantly, how're you feeling?'

'The rest did me good.' He looked deeply into my eyes. 'Something has happened, Kat I know when you're keeping something from me.'

I walked to the window, my back to him. I needed to collect my thoughts. Looking down, I tried to concentrate on what was happening in the street below, the buzzing activity of daily life. The last thing I wanted was for my father to witness one of my panic attacks. *My parents must never know the kind of depression and anxiety I've endured for years. They always admired me for my strength of character and easy-going nature. They've already had such painful disappointments; they don't need to worry about me as well. I mustn't burden my father with what goes on in my head.*

I needed to take long breaths to control my shallow breathing. Licking my lips and inhaling deeply, I turned around and told him all that had happened in the past few days. I held nothing back.

'So the poor woman is dead and I feel responsible,' I said.

'Darling you're not responsible. Put that idea out of your head. But what you say about a wolf is incomprehensible.'

He came up to me and embraced me. It felt good being in his protective arms. I just wanted to break down and cry, to be his little girl again. Years ago, I could do that. Now, all that had changed. I was a grown woman and I felt that I was the one who should protect him. It was my turn to nurture him; the roles had reversed. For my father's sake, I must appear strong.

'Are you sure Mrs Whelan said the Doherty woman had turned into a wolf?'

'Yes, and just as she was going to tell me about the curse, the lights went out as lightning struck. The force of the massive tree coming through the roof created such noise and havoc I thought an earthquake was taking place.'

My father drew in a deep breath. I could hear his heavy breathing, almost gasping for air. It worried me immensely.

'Thank God you didn't get hurt. I couldn't go on living if anything ever happened to you.' My father chocked-up, took in another breath and said, 'I thought my life had stopped when your brother died. When our son was nine-months old, your mother and I decided to holiday in Ireland. Our baby died while we were on a camping trip near Lough Muckno, in county Monaghan.'

He gazed in the distance. His face was ashen. I recognised the anguish behind his eyes. 'What does it all mean, Kat?'

'Dad, I know this is extremely painful for you, but please tell me about my brother's death and about the other Kavanagh babies. It's vital I've all the information.'

My father sat at the edge of the bed, looking despondent.

'Since I was a young boy I knew about a curse. I knew it was something to fear and never to mention in our household. But I never knew what the curse entailed. Five years before you were born, a baby boy had blessed our lives. We named your brother Gregoire, after my mother's father. At around the same time, my brother Frank and Brenda had their first child, Jonathan.'

'What?'

'I'm sorry, Kat, I know this is an incredible shock for you. After 33 years you find out you had a brother and now I tell you that you also had a cousin.'

I felt pressure on my chest as though a thousand hands were squeezing my heart. Rehashing this tragedy tortured my father and that knowledge made me even more anxious.

'When our babies were close to nine months, the four of us decided to go to Ireland for a holiday.' His eyes filled with tears. 'We thought it would be fun, as us men folk were keen to do some pike fishing. It was a summer's evening. We'd set up the tents and your mother and Brenda were busy lighting the campfire while Frank and I cleaned the fish. The little ones were asleep in one of the tents.' My father produced a cotton handkerchief from his pocket and dried his tears. 'It was such a clear night. I remember distinctly your mother saying, "What a glorious sky, thousands of shimmering stars dancing alongside the moon!" You know how poetic she is.' He drew in a deep breath. 'Anyhow, it was indeed peaceful. The only sound we could hear was the crickets' chirping. The four of us were gathered, cooking the fish and talking about what we'd do the following day, when the stillness of the night broke. A sudden gust of wind gathered strength rapidly. Simultaneously, we saw flashes of spectacular lightening and heard the groan of thunder. As we began to gather our belongings to take shelter, a massive tree limb crashed on the tent where our precious little ones slept. From the tents, we heard the most agonising screams. Screams that will continue to haunt us for the rest of our lives.'

My father wept openly.

'It's OK, dad. Stop talking now. This is too much for you,' I said as I jumped up and grabbed a glass of water for him. 'Please drink this. Take a deep breath.' I cradled him. We cried together.

'No, I want to tell you everything I owe you the truth.' He stood up to drink the water. 'The tents were only a few feet away as we ran madly towards them, but it was too late. Our babies lay on the ground, their cots overturned. It was as though someone had come along and flipped the portable hammock-style cots over. The babies lay side by side, their faces to the ground. There was so much blood. We picked them up frantically, fearing the worst. They never woke up again. As we came to the horrible realisation that we had lost our darlings, all four of us just stared at one another in disbelief for what seemed an eternity. Then we started to sob uncontrollably until we were interrupted by the most chilling howl...'

'Come and lie down. You look so pale.' I helped him to the bed. 'I'll call the doctor.'

'No love, just get my tablets. They are called Nitrostat – in my toiletry bag.' He grew more breathless. I raced to his room, ran back within seconds and placed the tablet under his tongue. I called reception to contact a doctor.

***

Terror, indescribable terror. He was chasing me in the dead of the night. I ran, lost in the woods. It was icy cold and the fog made visibility almost impossible. I was breathless, my chest heaved as I kept running.

Where was I going? I knew I ran around in circles, hopelessly lost. He was cunning; he knew these woods. He lived in them. He gained on me. I could sense it and my terror rose. I couldn't run any more. I looked behind me. He was there, his hypnotic yellow eyes about to consume my soul. I screamed, such pain, such agony. His abominable claws began to shred my face ...

I opened my eyes. My pulse thumped like the beat of a djembe drum. Groping my way through the dark, I managed to turn on the bedside light. Beads of perspiration covered my forehead. It was hard to catch my breath.

I got up to go to the bathroom and flung the light switch on. Dare I look in the mirror? Finally I turned to face myself. I ran my fingers gently around the contours of my face. The dark bags under my eyes were telling. It was a nightmare and yet it felt so real. I turned the tap on, half-expecting blood to pour out of it. The cold tap water was refreshing since my mouth was parched as though I'd been walking in the desert for hours without a drink.

Back in the bedroom, I hurled myself onto the soft mattress. Burying my head in the luxurious pillow, I cried until the rays of the sun invaded my room blindingly.

***

It was early afternoon when my father resurfaced from bed. The Doctor had sedated him the previous day, sending him into a deep sleep.

'I came here to support and protect you, Kat. Instead, I've become a burden.'

'How can you say such a thing? You're never a burden. I love you.' I said as I hugged him 'But, at the same time I'm concerned about you. This whole mess has taken its toll on your health. I won't allow anything to happen to you.'

'Don't worry Princess, your old man is going to stick around to keep an eye on you.' The twinkle I knew so well was back in his eyes, but I had no doubt that rehashing the past had adversely affected my father's already delicate health.

That evening, we enjoyed a lovely meal together in a charming pub in the centre of town. It was a cosy place, dimly lit with dark wood panelling. The crowd was a bit bohemian but that added a sort of carefree buzz to the atmosphere.

The excellent performance of traditional musicians entertained us. I didn't once mention the subject of the curse, and my father was happy just to sit there enjoying the sounds of the various flutes, violins and the distinctive beat of the bodhran that created some lively Irish music.

His face was calm as he sipped some Guinness. At least his expression was devoid of the pain it had clearly shown for the past few days. Inspector Muldoon interrupted our relaxed mood when he came over to our table.

'Good evening, Ms Kavanagh, I'd a job finding you.'

'Inspector.'

'And you, sir, are?' The Inspector asked my father as he extended his hand to him.

'Stephan Kavanagh, I'm Kathleen's father.'

'I see. I wasn't aware you had family with you here in Wexford,' Muldoon said as he looked intensely into my eyes. A shudder went through me as his piercing gaze lingered.

'My father arrived yesterday morning from Australia.'

'Well I hope your stay is a pleasant one, Mr Kavanagh.' I thought his smile was crooked. 'Although, your daughter has some explaining to do.'

I really disliked him. He was so forceful.

'What do you mean?' my father asked.

'There's to be an inquest on Wednesday morning.' Inspector Muldoon turned to me. 'Ms Kavanagh, you're hereby summoned to be the only witness to the events leading up to Mrs Whelan's death. Please don't leave town before that date.' Opening his leather briefcase, he placed a subpoena in my hands. He looked hostile, as though we were enemies about to go into battle. I was lost for words as I watched the Inspector go out the door, his long, tawny-coloured raincoat making him appear quite dapper.

'What's this all about?' my father asked. His face looked

flushed. 'Who the hell is he to speak to you like this? Why, he practically accused you of the woman's death!'

'Calm down, dad. I'm not worried. For Heaven's sake, Mrs Whelan died as a result of an enormous fir tree coming through the roof and trapping her underneath.'

'How can I not worry, my love? What with everything else you have to contend with, this is the icing on the cake.'

The Inspector's attitude towards me had obviously agitated my father. The tiredness was back on his face.

'I knew nothing good would come of this whole mess,' he said.

***

'Did you hear the thunder last night?' asked my father as we sat on a wooden bench in the sterile corridor outside the coroner's chambers.

It was the day of the inquest. The weather outside was as bleak as the atmosphere in the courthouse. People marched in and out of offices; severe expressions dominated their faces as they went about their daily duties.

'Yeah, they're predicting storms for the rest of the week.'

The dark wooden door of the chamber opened and a guard came toward us. He ushered us into the courtroom.

The room was small, but it was well lit, almost cosy.

There were six other people already seated in the room. We both knew one of the six. He was sitting all rigid. He reminded me of a mean looking stuffed animal on display at a museum.

The Coroner's introduction commenced the proceedings. He explained the deceased's three sons lived in the United States. As they lived overseas, they'd made an application for the matter to be resolved quickly so they could bury their mother as soon as the inquest was over. The Garda Siochana, the Gaelic name of the Irish police, also requested a speedy inquest. Thus, the coroner saw fit to bring the matter forward. The Coroner explained that normally it would take at least six to eight weeks before a post-mortem report got sent to the Coroner's office from the pathologist.

I heard my name being called as though from a faraway place. As I walked to the witness box, I felt the all-to-familiar palpitations in my chest and prayed I wouldn't get an anxiety attack.

After I'd taken my seat in the witness box, the Coroner said, 'Tell us in your own words, Ms Kavanagh, what happened on the evening of the 26th, when Mrs Whelan sustained her injuries?'

I drew in a deep breath and began my account, 'I was staying at Mrs Whelan's guesthouse. She asked me to join her for dinner.' My mind drifted off to that fateful evening. 'We were sharing a hot drink together and having a good time exchanging stories. Then she talked about a local woman, whom she believed dabbled in magic.' Automatically, my gaze shifted in the direction of Inspector Muldoon.

'Who might that local woman be?' asked the Coroner, his thickset eyebrows puckered obtrusively on his furrowed forehead.

'We were speaking about Aggie Muldoon Doherty.'

'Do you know Aggie Muldoon Doherty, Ms Kavanagh?'

'I met her briefly when I stayed for a night at the Bed & Breakfast that the Doherty's run.'

From the corner of my eye, I could see the Inspector. It was obvious the line of questioning agitated him. He stirred nervously in his seat. However, I was determined to tell the story as it happened, not withholding any information.

The Coroner paused for a few seconds and inquired, 'Why did you find the need to change your accommodation? After all, the Doherty's property is one of the finest in these parts.'

'It was for personal reasons, your Honour.'

'I'm afraid I must ask you what those 'personal' reasons are.'

I found that question very difficult to answer. Where would I begin? The Coroner leaned towards me and said, 'Well, Ms Kavanagh, are you going to enlighten us with your response?'

'It has to do with the Curse of Aggie Muldoon, your Honour.'

At that moment, I felt the Inspector's intense stare piercing my body like a sword.

CHAPTER SEVEN

'My word, the inquest was harrowing. Thank God it's behind us now,' said my father as he loosened the tight knot of his Alice-blue tie.

We sat at a coffeehouse near the courthouse.

'Good thing the Irish police don't carry guns, otherwise from the look on the mighty Inspector's face I thought he would shoot you on the spot. I admire your bravado, my sweet. Publicly airing the Muldoon's skeletons in the closet is no mean feat,' my father said. 'So where do we go from here?'

I shook my head. 'Back to square one.' I felt bad for involving my father in this complicated situation. 'I've been here for several weeks and still haven't managed to learn much. I think the answers lie in Great-Uncle Fionnbharr's house.'

'You never told me much about that guy, you know, the one who saved you from Uncle Fionnbharr's basement?' my father said as he lit up his pipe. The coffees and a platter of sandwiches arrived.

'Dad, honestly, how can you go on smoking, especially with your heart problems,' I said in frustration. 'It's a vile habit.'

'You sound just like your mother, Princess. This is good for my soul. Don't you worry, I have good genes. They run in the family. Uncle Fionnbharr is an excellent example. My sources tell me he smoked a pipe right up until his demise. I say ninety-six is certainly a good innings.'

I crossed my arms, not impressed with my father's logic. I cleared my throat as I leaned closer to him. 'You asked about the man who saved me from the dungeon, as I call it. Ooh, that place is creepy. Anyway, his name is Josh Abbott, from Abbott and Sons.'

'Who are Abbott and Sons?' my father inquired as he made a

sucking noise on his intricately carved pipe.

'Apparently they're a large real estate firm, based in London. He's the son of the CEO. He claims he often comes to Ireland for "interesting" property deals.'

'So what was he doing on Uncle Fionnbharr's property?'

'No doubt investigating "interesting" property. But, he'll soon realise he'll get more than he bargained for with that place.' My eyebrows arched upwards as I thought about my soon-to-be "haunted house". 'Just as he gallantly came to my rescue, he had a call on his mobile phone and without so much as an explanation, he ran off. All too baffling, if you ask me. I haven't bumped into him since that awful day.'

'Most odd.' Little rings of smoke floated around my father's handsome face.

After lunch, we headed to the local library to see if there were any records on the history of the Muldoons. It was frustrating, as our search proved fruitless.

'What I want to do is visit the Registrar of Births and Deaths tomorrow. It's important we map out our family tree. I want to find out exactly how the other little ones died. Do you think you're up to it?' I said.

'Of course, I'm keen to see our family tree.'

We returned to the hotel.

I made some tea and my father sat down on the bed. I could detect dark shadows under his eyes. He looked despondent.

'You know, Kat, my parents brought up my brother and me in a similar way as we brought you up. They told us to fear the Curse of Aggie Muldoon. But our parents never explained what the actual curse was. I guess they wanted to protect us, just as we tried to protect you. That was a mistake. I know that now. This treachery must stop.'

'I'm so sorry you and mum went through such a soul-destroying experience I can't begin to imagine how it feels to lose a baby. But I'm glad I now know I had a beautiful baby brother. I want to be there for you and mum whenever you want to talk about him.'

'Thank you my sweetheart. You have every right to know the truth. I have to admit, a huge load is off my shoulders. It hasn't been easy keeping something as significant as this from you.'

The phone rang. 'Kathleen.' I could barely hear Dylan's voice.

'Honey, what's the racket I hear in the background?' My voice was decibels higher than normal.

'It's chaos here.'

The line went dead. I hung up feeling concerned. I jumped when the phone rang again.

'Hi, it's me again. Can you hear me?'

'Yes, I can hear you. What's happened?'

'The unthinkable, that's what's happened.'

I could hear the piercing sound of drills in the background. All I heard was my partner saying the word explosion.

'Dylan, did you say explosion? My God, what's going on? Are you all right?'

'Yes, I'm all right. There was an explosion here at the studio,' he shouted, as the background noise intensified. 'It was just incredible,' is all he managed to say before the line went dead again.

'This is unbelievable. Something terrible has happened at the studio and we keep getting cut off.'

My father stood next to me, trying his best to calm me down. I kept trying to phone Dylan on his mobile, but couldn't get through. After pacing the floor like some raging bull, for more than fifteen minutes, I jumped when the telephone rang.

'Bloody phone lines. I've been trying to ring you back all this time. It's mayhem here.'

'Are you sure you're all right? I'm going to get on the next available flight.'

'No, don't do that. There's no point.'

'What's going on?'

'This morning at about 9:30, a car exploded in front of the building. The impact from the blast shattered all the glass in the downstairs window. Luckily no one was seriously hurt. Poor Paulette and a client received some superficial cuts and bruises, mainly from shattering glass and debris. Some display cabinets are destroyed.'

'My God. What caused a car to explode?'

'Who knows? Rumours are circulating it could be an act of terrorism.'

'What? For Heaven's sake, there are no government buildings or any prominent businesses in the area that terrorists would want to target. It's just a street full of boutiques, cafés and other small businesses.'

'Look, I don't know. I'm pissed off. I've got to go running around chasing up repairmen and insurance claims and so on, not to mention everything I've got to organise for the trip to the US. Honestly, Kathleen you sure picked a right time to be away.'

'How was I supposed to know something like this was going to happen? Like I said, I'll be on the next flight.'

'No. Paulette will take care of everything, like she always does.'

'What's that supposed to mean?'

'The Investigators and police are motioning to speak to me. I must go.'

'I'll call you later. Take care. Are you sure you don't want me to come back?'

'I told you I have to go, Kathleen.'

He hung up before I could even say goodbye. I knew he was snappy because the situation frustrated him. Dylan was a perfectionist and a slight change to his organised life made him irritable. Not only was I worried for Dylan, but his coldness troubled me.

***

My father looked terrible. His face appeared sapped. I noticed he hadn't bothered to shave. That was unlike him. He always took pride in his grooming. This whole unsavoury situation took its toll on his enervated emotions. Like most men, he internalised everything – he struggled gallantly to conceal his feelings, although, his eyes betrayed his mind-set. Regret and sorrow had replaced the spark in his eyes.

'Let's have some breakfast before we head off to the Office of Births & Deaths.'

No response came from him. He stood by the window, gazing

out, as motionless as a statue.

I joined him. We watched the raging sea currents. When I looked at him, I saw tears in his eyes.

'What's wrong Daddy?'

He drew in a deep breath, unable to hide his pain. 'I was tortured last night. Damn it! You think you go to bed to rest; instead, you enter a worse nightmare. Your brother came to haunt me all night. I felt the agony he felt.' He stopped all choked up. 'I think he blames me for not protecting him.'

Those last words were almost inaudible. I was at a loss as to how to react but thought an aggressive stance would snap him out of his state of depression 'Stop it dad. Just stop it. Stop this guilt. You're not to blame for your son's death. It was Aggie Muldoon who murdered your son.' Although that was a calculated response, vengeance boiled in my blood as I thought of that wicked woman.

We wept together, tears mingling as we embraced each other, neither wanting to let go.

'Most of my life, Kat, I've been trying to block it all out, as though it never happened. It was too painful. But now, being back in Ireland, I realise once and for all, I have to face my demons if I'm to have any chance of attaining inner peace.'

'I promise you, we'll get through this together,' I said. 'Come, let's go downstairs. We both need a change of scenery.'

Breakfast was a forced requirement, neither of us in the mood for enjoyment of food. I hated seeing my father in this state. It was the first time I noticed signs of ageing on his gentle face and a tight lump formed in my throat. I had to be strong. He needed me. I forced a smile.

'If you aren't up to it, we won't go to see the Registrar of Births and Deaths today. How about we take a well-earned break and drive to the Wicklow Mountains. There's so much to do in the region.'

'Perhaps you're right, we do need a break.'

***

The rugged wilderness was breathtaking. We were in awe of

Nature's beauty, which flaunted itself in the spectacular scenery before us. Verdant forests, rocky glens and the violet colours of the heather cloaked the boglands. It was virgin land – untouched, untainted. Humankind's greedy destruction was not apparent here.

The outing was the best distraction for my father – for us both, in fact. He appeared relaxed as we explored this fascinating area. We came across the delightful valley, which Thomas Moore had painted such a charming picture of in his poetry. This was the Vale of Avoca. We visited the picturesque hamlet where the hand-weavers produced the most vibrantly coloured tweeds. The mill itself had been operational since the 1700s and was the oldest hand-weaving mill in Ireland.

After lunching in a small pub, we moved further northwest to Glendalough known as 'valley of two lakes'. This place was just as spellbinding, the perfect retreat in an ancient monastic site.

By the time, we returned to the hotel, it was already quite dark and we were both tired. We decided to order a light meal from room service. We were relaxing, making small conversation of the day's events, when the phone rang. I assumed it was Dylan. To my surprise, it was my cousin Laura's musical voice.

'Hi Kat, I've been trying to get a hold of you all day.'

'Laura, hi, this is a pleasant surprise. What's up?'

'Is your father there with you?'

'Yes, he is. Did you want to speak to him?'

Something was not right. Laura spoke in a strained tone. I asked, 'Is everything all right?'

'Now don't panic. Your mother is fine but she's had an accident.'

'What? When?'

By now, my father was next to me, almost trying to grab the receiver from my hand. 'What's going on?'

'You won't believe what happened. Your mum had a nasty fall down the stairs this morning and has broken her leg and left shoulder. She had a bit of concussion but she's doing fine.'

'Is she in hospital?'

'Yes, and she's been asking for your father. May I speak to him?'

My father and Laura spoke at length. When he got off the phone the strain in his face was unmistakable.

'Mum's going to be fine. Please calm down.' I embraced him. He hung onto me for a long time.

'I must go back to Australia. I can't bear the thought of your mother going through this on her own.'

'Of course, you must go.'

'I'm sorry, Princess. I don't want to leave you to deal with all this by yourself.'

'Dad, I'm a grown woman. I know how to look after myself.'

He paced the floor. 'This is unbelievable! Your mother has never had a fall in all the 41 years we've been married.' He struck his clenched hand on the table. 'First you get trapped in that basement, Mrs Whelan dies tragically, Dylan narrowly misses getting hurt in the explosion and now your poor mother. What's going on, Kat? Can that wretched woman's curse be so powerful?' He seemed at a loss for words for a while but went on as I stood silently before him. 'I think we can safely deduce that all these nasty incidences are tied in with the power of the Curse of Aggie Muldoon.'

***

It was late afternoon when I arrived back in Wexford, after dropping my father off at Dublin Airport. All I could think about during the drive back was my father's conclusion the curse was the source of these bizarre events. *Is he right? Can it be all pure coincidence or is there a sinister connection?* I felt vexed.

That evening, I decided to dine out because I needed a change of air. The affable concierge informed me there was a popular bistro within walking distance to the hotel. The brisk walk refreshed me. It gave me a chance to clear my head. Once inside, the art deco surrounds struck me. It was slightly overstated but there was a buzz in the atmosphere, which brightened me up considerably.

As I perused the menu, I couldn't help but feel that someone was watching me. Not even five minutes had passed, when a familiar voice boomed, 'How nice to see you, Kathleen.'

I looked up to find his charismatic ocean-blue eyes looking at me. 'Hey, Josh, we meet again.'

'Yes, indeed and once again it's lovely to see you.' He smiled and pulled the chair and sat opposite me. 'You won't mind if I joined you? I hate to eat alone, especially when I can enjoy the company of a beautiful lady.'

'The consummate flatterer, aren't you? Must come in handy, in your line of work.'

'How so? After all, I'm only in the real estate game.'

'I rest my case. You're a salesman.'

'You're teasing me. I can see it in your cheeky, loquacious eyes. Tell me, do you think I approached you to sell you some property?'

Go on Kathleen, strike while the iron is hot. Loquacious. That's a novel way to describe my eyes. I gave him a brilliant smile. 'Not sell, I suggest you want to acquire the property I'm about to inherit.'

The man sat looking uncomfortable, avoiding my gaze. After a few seconds, he broke the silence. 'What makes you suggest such a thing?'

'Simple. Remember that fateful afternoon you charged in on your white horse and rescued me from my uncle's dungeon? If it weren't for you, I would have perished in there. My harried spirit would roam about aimlessly in those bleak chambers, my only company being the other tortured souls who occupy the "haunted" mansion.' I enjoyed teasing him. 'You never told me what you were doing on my uncle's property?'

'You have caught me out. I have to confess. I'm very interested in acquiring your uncle's property. I was merely snooping around that day,' he replied. 'But it's only fair that I demand an apology from you.'

'How so?' I chortled.

'You narrowly missed killing me that day. It's not everyday I'm attacked by a hatchet. This calls for retribution. I suggest in order to absolve your errant deeds, you must give me first option to purchase your property.'

'You seem to forget or perhaps you're not aware my uncle's property has not yet been transferred to me. There are conditions to be met before I inherit anything.'

I could tell from his expression that what I said surprised Josh. He stared into my eyes long enough for me to start feeling uncomfortable. Much as I was curious to find out what else he had to say, I thought it was time for me to leave. He was being too forward and I didn't care for his directness. I was about to get up and leave when he asked bluntly, 'Conditions? Is someone contesting the will?'

'I'm not at liberty to discuss it.'

'I apologise for overstepping the mark. But tell me, do we still have a deal?'

'You're incorrigible and you certainly don't waste time.'

'I'm the best at what I do,' he replied.

'So you say.'

'Then I just have to prove it to you.'

***

The rain pelted down as though Heaven's reservoir had burst its banks. The galoshes I was waddling in made an annoying squeaky noise, like a hideous rat gnawing at some rope. I flung myself into the office of the Registrar of Births & Deaths.

A stern looking woman, hiding behind some slim spectacles, looked up from her desk. I got the impression she viewed me with disdain as she noticed the droplets of water surrounding my feet. Probably it changed the balance of her otherwise organised and sterile looking room.

I braced myself and approached her.

'Excuse me, I wonder if you could help me?' I sneezed just as I finished my sentence.

'Bless you.'

'Thanks.'

'How may I help you?'

'I'm doing some research on my family's history and I wondered if I may be able to have access to some records.'

'Well, first I need to see some identification and your own

birth certificate.'

I had come prepared, so I produced my ID card and my birth certificate. She took a long time examining the documents. Then she cleared her throat and at the same time wiggled her glasses, which were perched on her beak-like nose at a precarious angle. She leaned over the desk, her tiny body struggling to keep straight as she said, 'You're Fionnbharr's relative to inherit it all. Aren't you?'

'Yes, he was my great uncle. Did you know him?'

'You could say that.'

Taking advantage to find out as much as I possibly could, I prodded for more information. 'Can you tell me a bit about him? What was he like?'

'You're different from the rest of them. I can see why the dear man chose you to be his sole heir.' Her mood changed, she became distant. 'Look, I'll get into trouble if I talk too long with customers. I have a lot to do.' Her eyes softened for a moment. 'I'll get the records of your family but don't ask for anything else.'

The woman must have read my mind, as though she'd anticipated the forbidden request.

'Thanks,' I said. 'Can I also see records on the Muldoons?' I knew I was pushing my luck, especially considering she just told me not to ask for anything else.

'Wait here. I'll see what I can do. But you mustn't tell anyone,' she said. She acted nervously and headed out to a back room where I assumed they held the records.

She is scared even of her own shadow.

Five minutes later, the woman resurfaced, bearing in her slender arms a pile of documents.

'The library is just through those doors. When you find the relevant information I shall make copies of whatever you need.'

'You've been so helpful, thank you. May I know your name?'

Her eyes twinkled suddenly. 'Molly,' she hesitated. 'I'm Molly O'Rourke.'

'Really? What a coincidence. My great-great grandmother six generations back was an O'Rourke. We might be related.'

'I have to get back to work. I hope you find what you're

looking for.'

'Thanks. I really appreciate this.'

Molly quickly disappeared behind some shelves.

The Births & Deaths library was surprisingly large and smelt of wood polish. There was no one around and I suddenly felt very lonely.

I sat down at a desk by one of the two large windows that dominated the room and started to examine the documents.

Absorbed in my task, I wasn't aware several hours had passed until I'd looked at my watch. I'd been jotting down notes on both the Kavanagh and Muldoon families. Once I collated the relevant information, I intended to return to the hotel and commence compiling the family tree.

It astounded me to learn that in each of the five generations that came after the children of Cormac and Honora Kavanagh, the first-born child had died before his or her first birthday.

Armed with this information, I was ready to leave. I was content I'd accomplished quite a lot in the one day. As I returned the documents back to Molly I said, 'I can't thank you enough for all your help. I know what you did was beyond the call of duty. I was wondering if we could meet for coffee. I've got some questions to ask about my Uncle Fionnbharr.' I handed her my business card.

'Well, I don't know. I want to help, but I heard about Mrs Whelan.' Molly looked startled. 'I'm sorry, I have to attend to a customer.' She was abrupt and moved on to look after a woman who had entered the office.

I turned around to leave and came face to face with Inspector Sean Muldoon, whose black eyes were full of scorn.

'I see you've got nothing better to do than stir up trouble. Listen carefully, Ms Kavanagh, if you continue to spread slanderous rumours about my family, you'll answer to me.'

'Are you threatening me, Inspector?'

'Call it what you want. I'd read it as a warning.' With those intimidating words, he left the office, slamming the door behind him.

I was stunned. The aggression in the man's voice troubled me considerably. I left after a few minutes, the bundle of notes under my arm, braving the weather.

***

It was dark. I felt exhausted and cold. I ran for hours. He was everywhere. With each shadow created, he lurked behind every tree, looking at me through the dense forest. He was cunning like some big hunter. I was his prey and he enjoyed the chase. He knew the woods well; he lived in them. His hypnotising yellow eyes followed my every move. I ran, not knowing where to go. I knew I was going around in circles.

I could hear my own heaving and heartbeat in the stark night. No, I must not give him satisfaction. He must not sense my fear. Too late. He gained on me. I had no strength left. As I fell to the ground, I felt his hot breath on me. Such pain, such agony, blood and flesh mingling together as he stripped me of my skin. I let out the most chilling of screams ...

Confusion. I couldn't concentrate for a while. My eyes were wide open. Slowly reality set in. I had experienced the same nightmare a few days ago. I sat up in bed, shaking, my mouth parched; I was in desperate need of water.

Reluctantly, I got up to go to the bathroom and washed my face. The cold, still water from the minibar quenched my thirst. Looking at my watch, I saw it was 4:45 a.m. I paced the floor for a while. As I knew it would be impossible to get back to sleep, I decided to go to work on the family tree.

After relentlessly working for several hours, I finished compiling the family tree.

CHAPTER EIGHT

'Take a seat, Ms Kavanagh.' Ambrose Kildare QC looked harassed as he ushered me to my chair. 'You're probably wondering at the urgency to have a meeting this morning.'

'Yes, I must admit I'm curious. You didn't reveal anything on the phone.'

'I do apologise but I'm not one to discuss important matters over the telephone.' He sat behind the Chippendale partners' desk. The central piece on the desk was a malachite rectangular inkstand, with a gilt-bronze bell flanked by urn-shaped ink and pounce pots. With a cheeky grin, I postulated Mr Kildare would perhaps jingle the bronze bell for his secretary to rush to his side or to bring in some tea.

As though reading my thoughts Mr Kildare reached out and picked up his stylish fountain pen from the inkstand. He produced from a green leather stationary box a blank piece of paper and commenced writing. Not once did he speak to me. I sat, waiting patiently, my hands crossed on my lap.

I took in minute details of my surroundings. The man had discerning taste, judging from the expensive pieces that decorated his office. A 19th century Russian icon depicting the Virgin of Vladimir, in a gilt metal and enamel Riza, adorned the otherwise bare wall behind him. A piece like that was certainly a rare find and was worth a considerable amount of money. *With his hefty fees, he can afford it.*

I scrutinized the funny little man sitting opposite me. He had tiny white specks on his black woollen suit jacket. *Dandruff. Mr Kildare isn't as perfect as he makes out to be. I mustn't be mean – the man can't help having a dry scalp.*

After a long five minutes, he put down his pen and gazed into my eyes. He cleared his throat and said, 'We have a problem on our hands, Ms Kavanagh. Your long-lost relatives are contesting the will.'

'I'm not surprised. In fact, I thought they would've done it much sooner. I keep telling you that I shouldn't be the one inheriting the wealth. They're entitled to Fionnbharr Kavanagh's estate.'

'You're too generous, Ms Kavanagh. However, you will find your distant cousins don't share your sentiments. They will play dirty, in order to meet their objectives.' He stopped to make further notes. 'Shortly, we'll leave to go to Judge Malone's Chambers. I wanted to brief you about the proceedings. I don't want you to get a nasty surprise.'

'I'm not afraid of them. I've done nothing wrong. In fact, I'm going to say I wish to share the fortune. It's the fair thing to do.'

'Don't go charging in like the seventh Cavalry, Ms Kavanagh. Under no circumstances are you to mention such an intention. It's a preposterous idea. They'll go for the jugular and leave you with nothing.'

Like most people, I had a deep distrust of legal counsel. Perhaps that's unfair since some of my friends have ended up as lawyers and they're all wonderful people. But, I knew what I proposed didn't suit my uncle's lawyer.

***

The Judge's Chambers were not far from the offices of Kildare & Co.

The courthouse was a blend of the old and the new. The bright external stonework of various textures and colours was striking. The interior, however, was more subdued – a mishmash of Victorian and modern styles. I didn't feel at all comfortable in this building.

Mr Kildare led me down a long and wide hallway. He motioned me to take a seat on a bench as he went to confer with another Barrister of the law. In the ten minutes I sat there facing the courtroom, I forgot the discomfort I'd felt earlier and admired the Irish white oak woodwork and the classical cornice of the courtroom entry. As I had studied Classical Greek Art and

Architecture in my Arts Degree days, I appreciated the patterns of the classical Greek motif of triglyphs and metopes. The Parthenon in Athens has the same patterns.

My admiration of the fine architecture ended when my lawyer said, 'I hope you're ready to encounter your greedy relatives, Ms Kavanagh. And I beg of you, do let me do all the talking.'

The courtroom was expansive with its symmetrical continuity. The judge's bench was of matching oak as that of the doorways and was perched on a dais. Behind it lay Judge Malone's Chambers.

Mr Kildare gave a curt knock and ushered me in, as he opened the door. As soon as I entered the room, I had an overwhelming feeling of malice. There was complete silence as six pairs of intense eyes stared at me. It was one of those rare moments where I wished the ground beneath me would give way and swallow me up, so that I could escape the pure evil that surrounded me.

Mr Kildare introduced me to Judge Malone. The judge was a man of past-retirement age. He had an air of the old school but curiously enough, his eyes held an impish sparkle. A small burgundy bow tie awkwardly decorated the tight collar, which threatened to burst open any moment from around his plump neck. He had a silvery white mane. It struck me as odd that a man of his age should have such an abundance of hair. To my surprise, he rose from the massive leather-coated executive chair and extended a hand.

'A delight to meet Daithi Kavanagh's granddaughter,' he said. 'Your grandfather and I were the best of pals at school. Ah, yes I still remember the day when he broke the news his folks were moving to Australia. I cried all the way home from school. My word, he was a spirited young lad,' the Judge reminisced almost as though he was talking to himself, unaware of the people around him.

I smiled at him and took my seat. My attention totally directed at him, I avoided looking around the room at all cost. Despite my efforts not to look at my relatives, I felt the burning stare from those six pairs of intense eyes, as though my skin, like a leaf, conflagrated in a sizzling blaze.

'Well, I believe you've not had the pleasure of being introduced to your cousins, Ms Kavanagh,' Judge Malone said. I thought he placed a distinct emphasis on the word 'pleasure'. 'Over to your right is Conan Kavanagh – Fionnbharr Kavanagh's son and cousin to your grandfather, Daithi.'

My guarded smile failed to impress the eighty-plus man. He sat rigidly at the edge of his chair, hanging onto his wooden walking stick. For a split second, I felt sorry for him. He looked frail; his hands trembled, causing his walking stick to sway from side to side. However, when I concentrated on his face, the dangerous look in his eyes left me with a cold feeling.

'This fine gentleman over here is Meallan Kavanagh. He is Conan's son and is your own father's second-generation, cousin.' Judge Malone introduced me to the tall man who sat by the window. He was handsome and it overwhelmed me how he resembled my own father.

Meallan, at least, gave a curt nod of his head, slightly more acknowledgement than his father had given me. Like his father, his captivating eyes held a hint of wickedness.

Then the Judge introduced me to the younger generation, all four being more or less around my age. The introduction was, I assumed, in the order of their age: Seanan, Frainc, Vanessa, the only other female in the room apart from myself, and Donahl. The last face, I recognised immediately. Donahl was the one who had been in intense conversation with Aggie Muldoon Doherty and Josh Abbott at the coffeehouse the day I checked out of the Doherty's B&B. *What is the connection there? A meeting between a Kavanagh and a Muldoon is unthinkable considering the feud between our families.* I decided I'd ask Josh Abbott if I bumped into him again.

An unfamiliar feeling of sadness overcame me when I realised that under normal circumstances, I'd be delighted to meet a relative for the first time. Instead, I felt despised and cursed. It was not a pleasant feeling at all.

'This is an informal meeting, counsellor,' said the judge as he adjusted his awkward bow tie. 'I wanted Ms Kavanagh to meet Fionnbharr's family in my chambers before this matter goes any further. We might be able to work something out amicably. I don't want this to get ugly, Ambrose. I was very fond of Fionnbharr.'

'My client isn't the one making things ugly, your honour.'

'You expect us to hand everything over without a fight, Kildare? If so, you're sorely mistaken,' shouted Conan Kavanagh. 'Bullocks, you don't care about fairness and are only after a fat fee.'

'Now calm down, Conan,' ordered Judge Malone. 'One thing you can be certain of your case will be heard without fear or favour.'

'I've been around a lot longer than any of you put together. I know how the system works, Gereard,' the old man spat out with venom. He fixed a ferocious stare on me.

'I don't know what you think you know about the law, Conan, but I can assure you in my courtroom I run things justly without any bias or prejudice.'

The proceedings commenced, as one would expect of a preliminary hearing of this nature. It lasted almost an hour and it was vocal and heated. Often Judge Malone threatened to stop the hearing, unless Conan and his son conducted themselves with civility. For once, I listened to my lawyer's advice and didn't contribute in the proceedings. I clearly saw that these relatives were greedy and circumvent. And all this pent-up rage is for money – I felt shame that we shared the same bloodline.

'You won't get away with this. I'll see to it if it's the last thing I do,' Conan burst out as Mr Kildare and I left the Judge's Chambers.

***

The gushing wind roared, like a ferocious animal. The windows shook from the sheer force as though a cataclysmic event had gripped the planet. I tossed and turned, feeling disconcerted. I couldn't sleep. Frustrated, I switched on the night-light. I headed straight for the minibar and rummaged through the contents as if I was a homeless person bent on finding some scraps. Finally, I decided to munch on some salted cashews and washed them down with some ginger ale. The finest ginger ale in the UK read the label.

'I couldn't care less about the quality of this beverage. I'm not a connoisseur of ginger ale. This certainly isn't a good idea at two in the morning. I know I'll regret it later, when indigestion rears its ugly head.'

The after-hours snack had a mission to accomplish; at least my grazing action might calm my shaky nerves. I switched the TV on to distract my thoughts. That didn't work either. My mind insisted on reminding me of the unpleasantness of the previous day. I paced the room and then peeked through the curtains.

The room was on the third floor and faced the town, not too far from the ocean. The street below was like a ghost town, so deserted that a feeling of loneliness came over me. If not for the wind swooning the street lamps backwards and forwards, it would look as though life had never existed out there.

I pressed my nose against the glass, leaving an impression, as I used to do when I was a little girl. The lamp cast a shadow on the footpath.

I concentrated on the shadow. The dim light became more luminous until it formed into a distinct shape. It was him. He was out there, sitting proudly like some noble knight! The magnificent creature looked directly at me. With a regal air about him, his snow-white fur cloaked his wildness. His bewitching eyes locked into my own. I blinked and looked again.

The wolf was gone.

Impossible. What madness am I concocting in my mind? How can a wolf be in the middle of town? I must be imagining it.

It was now even more difficult to sleep but eventually I somehow managed to dose off for an hour or two.

The twittering of sparrows woke me up at the break of dawn.

A hot, invigorating shower revived me and I felt ready to face the new day. The steam completely covered the large mirror. I opened the bathroom door to let in some cool air. With swift, circular movements, I wiped the mist off the lower half of the mirror. Finally, I was able to glance at my tired face. Another bat of an eyelid and those golden eyes hypnotically gazed at me again. As I glared at my reflection, he was behind me, gallantly perched on the carpet. I swung around but he was no longer there. I moved forward. *Is he hiding somewhere? Will he suddenly pounce on me? Will he attack and kill me? He's cunning.* There was nothing unusual about the room except the window was moving back and forth, making a clanking sound as it hit the wooden frame. I went over and secured the window shut. *Funny, I don't remember opening it in the first place. What's happening to me? Am I becoming that unhinged? I have to pull myself together.* This imaginary wolf obsessed me.

***

It was an overcast day when I stepped outside. I looked at the sky; the fluffy clouds sprawled out like a sea of mother of pearl. An old woman carrying a basket of groceries went past me. She smiled. It was a sweet kind of smile as though she was saying, "good morning."

A pang of sadness set in as she reminded me of Mrs Whelan.

I was about to enter the coffeehouse, where I'd been going most mornings for breakfast, when a strong male voice called out, 'We meet again, cousin.' He prized the door open for me and I stepped inside the cosy room, glad to be out of the bitter cold.

It was Donahl Kavanagh, the youngest member of Uncle Fionnbharr's grandchildren.

'Would you care to join us?' he asked as I followed him towards the back wall, where an attractive, young woman sat immersed in a book.

He smiled at me and said, 'I'm in double trouble. I'm conferring on two counts with the enemy.'

'How so?'

'Well, you're considered enemy number one at the moment. This lovely creature,' he pointed to the young woman, who looked at me with a vacant expression, 'is enemy number two. She's my fiancée.'

He stirred my curiosity, so I asked, 'Why is your fiancée considered the enemy?'

'Well cousin,' he paused for a few seconds and with a grin on his face said, 'I'd like to introduce you to Eliza. Eliza Muldoon.'

I was speechless.

'Don't tell me you don't approve either, Kathleen.' He flipped off his sunglasses and placed them in his crisp-white linen shirt pocket.

'What right do I have to approve or disapprove?' What else could I say except try to be diplomatic? I slid down unobtrusively and sat on the wooden bench.

'You do seem rather astounded.'

'Just surprised, that's all.'

'So tell me, what's your impression of my old man and grandfather?' he asked as he stretched his long arm and picked up the menu from the next table.

I felt awkward speaking my mind. 'They are harbouring a lot of anger, but that's understandable.'

'Huh. Why should they harbour anger? They were downright awful to great-grandfather. I too would've cut them out of the will.'

'So you don't have a good relationship with your father and grandfather?'

'I tolerate them because they are my flesh and blood, but I don't have to like them.' His bright disposition became clouded. 'As they say, you can choose your friends, but you can't choose your family. So it seems I'm stuck with them.'

A sound startled me and I swung around to see what it was.

'What the hell is she doing here?' barked the woman. Aggie Muldoon Doherty wore an angry expression. Like the other day, she was dressed all in black and hid behind a pair of black sunglasses.

Oh great, here's trouble. Is she trying to be incognito?

'Mum,' blurted out the young woman. It was the first time Eliza opened her mouth.

'This is my cousin, Mrs Doherty,' Donahl faltered as he stood up ineptly.

'Sit down Donahl,' ordered the soon-to-be-mother-in-law. 'I

know who she is.' She scowled at me. 'You have the gall!'

My alarm turned into anger. 'You've got no right to speak to me like that.'

'Speaking about rights, are we? I shall have my day,' the woman shrieked as her face turned a shade of plum red. Abruptly, she left the coffeehouse.

Eliza sobbed and Donahl, unprepared for this sudden outpour of female emotion, looked simultaneously crestfallen and embarrassed.

'It seems like everyone in this town loathes the sight of me.'

'Rest assured, I for one don't loathe the sight of you.' Donahl tried to cheer me up.

***

'Connan, Uncle Fionnbharr's son, is a wicked old man,' I complained to Dylan.

'Doesn't sound like a nice character.'

'I wish you were here with me.'

'I can't get away, you know that. The insurance investigators are coming on Friday and I'm having meetings with Colin Hitch and his assistant editor for the unpublished archival photography of Everest. I can't find your notes for the article. Do you know where you've put them? This is such a mess.'

'I took those notes home. They're in my tawny briefcase in the walk-in robe. Please take it easy, honey.'

'That's easy for you to say, Kathleen. I'm under a lot of pressure.'

'I know that. I am too. It just worked out this way. We've to handle it as best as we can. I've got to go. Someone's knocking at the door. Love you,' I said. I loved Dylan dearly, but sometimes I found him difficult and unsympathetic to the point where I'd start to wonder whether we were suited. When things didn't go his way, he would rave and rant until all his frustrations left his body. Unfortunately, I felt I was always at the receiving end and at times, I felt drained as I did at that moment.

I opened the door. No one was there, but someone had left

behind a parcel the size of a shoebox. I picked it up. Addressed to me, it bore no return address. I was just about to open it when the phone rang.

'Hello darling.'

'Hi dad. What a lovely surprise! I was about to give you a call. How's mum?'

'Much better, but the poor love is still finding it hard getting around on her crutches.'

My father sounded calmer than he had been a few weeks ago. 'Unfortunately, her shoulder is really giving her a lot of trouble. She might need to have some cortisone shots.'

'Oh, no. Isn't that a painful injection?'

'I don't know, love. She's been having physio but that's not helping much. And the doctor suggested this treatment, so she wants to give it a go.'

We spoke for over an hour. I told him of my day in court but downplayed some parts so as not to worry him. My father had his own problems to contend with. 'So there's nothing to worry about. Everything is progressing as per schedule. I will speak to you in a couple of days. Look after mum and yourself. Lots of kisses to you both.'

'Coffee sounds nice,' I said aloud. I made one, even though it was instant and worse still, freeze-dried. 'I shouldn't complain. I'm after all staying in a hotel.' The hot liquid comforted me as it travelled down my throat. I sat at the edge of the bed and started to unravel the parcel. 'Maybe it's a surprise from Dylan. But it can't be, it's hand-delivered, without a stamp or a postmark.'

Someone had sealed the parcel well. I got a knife to cut through the tape. The programme on the TV distracted me. It was a documentary on Maria Edgeworth, one of the first Irish female novelists of the 18th century. Many years ago I'd read one of her novels Castle Rackrent, a provocative work attacking the Irish landlord class to which Edgeworth belonged.

Half an hour later, I switched off the TV. I felt flushed. The room temperature was too hot for my liking. I opened the window and took a lungful of the sea air. I watched a flock of swallows swoop past; they were probably migrating to a warmer place, to get away from the approaching winter.

Calm and peace reigned over the whole area.

Then I remembered the parcel. An unremarkable small box wrapped in brown paper. Scrutinising the bold, almost child-like writing of my name and address, I placed the box on my lap. *I love surprises*. The knife cut through the tape with precision. I prised the lid open.

A small item wrapped in black satin material sat in the middle of the box. Crunched up newspapers held it in position. I carefully picked it up and unfolded it.

My excitement turned to revulsion.

In the warmth of my palm rested a headless rat. I gave a startled scream and dropped the corpse onto the carpet. There was a note attached to the feet. It read, "A deserving end to a rat."

This act was unpardonable. What had I done to deserve such vindictiveness?

It was a warning from either my relatives or the Muldoons. Suddenly I felt ill.

It took me a good ten minutes, but finally I found his business card. With shaking fingers, I pressed the ten digits. The call went to a message bank. I hung up without leaving a message.

I kept staring at it. Repugnance. That was one way to describe my feelings. I couldn't bear to touch the rat. *What am I going to do? Maybe I should call someone from the hotel to clean it up.* Not wanting to create fuss, I decided against it. Besides the hotel staff might start rumours and I certainly wanted to avoid attention. I let out another scream when my mobile phone started to ring. I jumped up to answer it.

'Sean Muldoon here. I believe you have called on my number?' spoke the Inspector with an impatient tone.

'Hello Inspector, this is Kathleen Kavanagh. I'm sorry to trouble you.' My voice was subdued. 'I was wondering if you could stop by my hotel. I need to discuss something with you.'

He cleared his throat. 'Is this police business, Ms Kavanagh?

'Very much so, I'm afraid. I'm in room 306.'

Forty minutes later, I faced the stern-looking Inspector at

my door.

'Please come in.'

There was an awkward silence for a few seconds, as the Inspector glanced around the room. Like a magnet attracted to a metal object, the corpse of the rat immediately drew the inspector's attention and he swung his solid body towards it.

'Charming,' he blurted out. 'You must have a devoted fan out there.'

He sounded smug and I felt the urge to punch him.

'I thought it was important I report this deplorable act to the police.'

'You did the right thing. Any idea who might be playing a practical joke on you?'

'I don't consider this as a practical joke, Inspector, but a direct threat to my well-being,' I answered icily. 'I think you've a good idea who's responsible.'

'Ah – I was waiting to see when you'd get around to accusing my mother.'

His eyes were thunderous black. I felt afraid of him. *Damn. I shouldn't have contacted him. What's the point? He too is hostile towards me.*

The Inspector deftly bent down and put the dead rat back in its box. He shot a sharp glance at me. 'Look after yourself.'

***

They were the most beautiful roses I had ever seen: wine red and in perfect bloom. Set in a clear round vase, the two dozen roses were a welcome sight when I entered the room after having spent a gruelling day at the courthouse.

Impromptu, Judge Malone had summoned me to appear before him.

I went over to the arrangement and searched for a card. I found the small, green envelope camouflaged by the lush foliage. It read, 'I would be delighted if you would dine with me tonight. If I don't hear from you I shall pick you up at seven. Regards. Josh Abbott.'

The invitation astounded me and there was only half an hour

before he would be on my doorstep. What was I supposed to do but accept the dinner invitation? My head throbbed. I felt hot and clammy even though it was a cold day. I had a quick shower and put on some comfortable jeans and the new Aran jumper I'd bought a few days ago. I was happy to dressing casual since I was in no mood for a formal dinner. 'Let's hope my dinner companion shares my mood.'

It was exactly seven when there was a brisk knock on the door. Josh Abbott stood there, a wide grin on his face. He too was in jeans and wore a linen shirt with a tweed vest over it. He was striking.

'You've made me a very happy man by not refusing to dine with me,' he said. He knew how to turn on the charm at every opportunity.

I was about to tell him the truth that I only just found out about the invitation, but I changed my mind. Instead, I replied, 'I wanted to thank you in person for the gorgeous roses.'

'It's my pleasure. Beautiful roses for a beautiful lady.'

I felt heat rise in my already pink cheeks.

He drove his sleek black X-type sports Jaguar as though he was competing in a race and in no time, we arrived in Kilkenny. Josh said in the south-east people claimed Kilkenny was the pub lovers' paradise. The pub he chose was a historic coach inn.

'I thought, what with your bloodline, you might enjoy this place. In the 1300s a witch ran it.'

His comment astonished me. 'What do you mean witches run in my bloodline?'

'Witches and wizards. Your Uncle Fionnbharr was one.'

'That's ridiculous. Where do you get your information?'

'I thought it was common knowledge.'

'What nonsense. I agree he was eccentric but it's ridiculous to suggest he was anything else.'

Josh changed the subject. The rest of the evening went quickly. We had a lot in common. I was pleasantly surprised at his rich knowledge of ancient history. He was particularly keen and well read on Celtic mythology.

'I'm amazed you have such a remarkable grasp of Irish history,' I said.

'Why? Do you think English people aren't capable of knowing history outside England?'

'No, of course I didn't mean that. It's just that I find it intriguing you've such an acute interest in Ireland and its past.'

'I suspect I have Irish heritage somewhere along the line.'

'You suspect? You don't know?'

'I was adopted, so I really don't know anything about my background. I've always felt my adoptive parents knew something, but they kept it from me.' He shrugged and said, 'For some reason I feel akin to Ireland, particularly to Wexford. That's why I come here so often. It's almost as if I'm searching for my past.'

He had a sad look in his eyes. Just to lighten his mood, I said, 'And I thought you came out here for lucrative business prospects.'

'That's my guise to appease my father for my extended and frequent visits to Ireland.'

'Are you close to your adoptive parents?'

'Yes, they have both been doting parents. Sometimes, I must admit, I've felt smothered. But I guess that goes with the territory.'

'Didn't they have other children?'

'Not biological ones, but they adopted Timothy and Nicholas, Mum's nephews, when the boys were four. My brothers are identical twins. The story goes mum's sister Georgia and her husband were missionaries posted in some remote part of south-western Africa. During a violent skirmish between guerrilla fighters and the local military, the natives slaughtered all the missionaries. Lucky for the young boys, a local woman took them to safety and they survived the gruesome tragedy.'

'What a horrific story!'

'Indeed.'

Silence crowded us as we sipped on some herbal tea.

'I've been meaning to ask you, have you known the Muldoons for long?'

He looked up suddenly with a quizzical look. 'I met them a few years ago, on one of my visits here. Why do you ask?'

'Do you know them well?'

'As well as you'd know an acquaintance. Each time I'm in Wexford, I stay at the Doherty's B&B. As I recall that's where we met.'

'Yes, I do remember that night very well.' My mind drifted off to my emotions that evening when I discovered Mrs Doherty was Aggie Muldoon.

'I gather you don't care for the Muldoons much.'

'To tell you the truth, I don't know them at all. My prejudice is wholly based on generations of bad blood between our families.'

'Yes, I've heard of the infamous story of your great-great-grandfather murdering the youngest son of Aggie Muldoon. And in retribution the grief-stricken mother had apparently cast a powerful curse on your family.' His face was animated. I couldn't help but notice how attractive he was.

'You seem to be well informed.'

'People just seem to open their hearts to me. What can I say, I'm just that kind of guy.'

We were the last patrons to leave the pub. Josh was quiet during the drive back to Wexford and I sat back enjoying the telematics technology of his luxury car.

When Josh parked the Jaguar in front of the hotel, I was almost asleep.

He escorted me to my room.

'Well thank you, Josh, for a lovely evening.' I stretched up and planted a playful kiss on his left cheek.

He faltered, almost frowning. Then his expression softened. The fair skin on his face looked flushed. He reached out and gently touched the side of my face with his long fingers. They felt cool and soothing. He studied my face for a long time with scorching intensity. His ocean blue eyes were shades darker than I remembered. His fingers meshed into my hair as he tugged me to him and with passionate savagery brought my lips to his.

A delirious quiver shimmied down my spine. Time stood still, as though a vortex had trapped us in its path. All I wanted was to surrender to him. A surge of wantonness took over my senses. He was relentless in his ardour, almost wild with desire. When he released me, he looked physically shaken and blurted out, 'I'm sorry.' He rushed down the long corridor and disappeared.

I tend to fall asleep easily, but not on that night. I lay awake the imprint of his kiss still burning on my lips.

CHAPTER NINE

The kettle weighed my arms down as I poured the boiling water into the geometrical design mug. I took a sip of the full-flavoured liquid of Arabica and felt slightly better, until I thought back to the previous night.

The cold air was raw, bringing with it a sense of wretchedness. I felt tired, unwilling to face the day. *Maybe I should go back to bed, close the curtains and only resurface when I can face myself again.* I was still in shock and laden with guilt. Guilt of deceiving Dylan.

Looking dolefully at the ground, I heaved a great sigh. *I'm not the one who initiated the kiss. In fact, I didn't even have enough time to react to it. This is ridiculous! The blame can't rest squarely on my shoulders.*

The second mug of coffee tasted bitter, as though I was drinking black tar. *This is insane!* I sprang up from the armchair, determined to rid myself of this uncharacteristic black mood. Two hours later, the taxi dropped me in front of the gates of my soon-to-be estate.

The mansion was set on 60 acres of dense woodland. Shrubbery and overgrowth swallowed up the property. It would be a perfect haven for wild animals. A heavily wooded area caught my attention. I entered it. Like a young girl in a fairy tale, I followed the obscure trail, which led me into the thick of the wood. I continued on, even though I knew it could be dangerous. The mighty trees transmitted their collective energy. Their ancient wisdom humbled me. It felt exhilarating.

Shuffling my feet, I enjoyed crunching the dried leaves. The forest made me feel protected from the outside world. The outside world wasn't always a pleasant place. In fact, it was sometimes harsh and unforgiving. I felt sheltered here, but I didn't know why. Maybe, it was because I felt a sense of peace, a place where I could be true to myself a place where I could make the rules. There was no one here to judge me or force me to conform.

My inner serenity was shattered, when I became aware of a pair of burning eyes. They stared into my own so intensely that I thought I was about to smoulder out of existence. They were the same powerful eyes, those hypnotic golden eyes that followed me everywhere, not giving me a moment's peace, intruding even on my dreams.

Am I the trespasser? This is his home and I've come unannounced. My heart pounded, as fear took hold of my body like wildfire. I started to run. *Is he chasing me? I'm lost.* The trees, which I'd felt akin to, appeared to have abandoned me, almost as though they feared him too. I stopped, spun around and surveyed the dense vegetation. He was nowhere in sight and yet I knew he was ubiquitous. I began to run again, not knowing what path to take.

Each route I took was like the one I'd just left. Trapped. Defenceless. Vulnerable, like some animal caught up in a snare. These overwhelming feelings consumed my thoughts.

Then I imagined I was a delicate butterfly fluttering about, heading straight into a net. Visualising my wings pinned down on some board, I felt exposed, the world scrutinising me behind a glass casing.

Panting heavily, I decided I mustn't appear apprehensive. I must penetrate his mind, think like him. It was the best course to take. That might be my only chance of survival. With great concentration, I allowed my intuition to guide me on the right path. With slow steps, I meandered through the wood and finally found myself in a clearing.

***

The house was Gothic in design. The exterior with its steeply pitched roof, pointed windows with decorative tracery and proud pinnacles left a hostile feeling on an approaching visitor. It was a mysterious structure – one that gave the impression that much treachery and suffering had taken place in its solemn and eerie grounds. Perhaps that was only my preconception, because of what I knew about the tragic past of its inhabitants. The massive grey-stone walls with an abundance of chimneys appeared centuries removed from the modern age. It was bleakly desolate but as I walked through the wind-rattled grass, I appreciated its haunting beauty.

When I approached the house, I was still shaking. *I shouldn't have come here on my own, let alone enter a dense wood. What choice do I have, considering I'm somehow to attempt to change my family's unfortunate history?*

Dense clouds started to form, marring the pleasant morning. Circling around the house, I stopped underneath an oriel window. I admired the unusual design, the window projecting from the wall as a porch would. Intricately carved battle scenes highlighted the stones. *Building something so solid in today's terms would cost a fortune.* I continued to look at the window when I could swear a shadow of a figure wandered past inside the house. *Perhaps there's someone in there. I hope not.* Against my better judgement, I decided to go in and explore the unknown.

I climbed thirty stairs to reach the first floor. The corridor was long and narrow. Mould and salt damp stained the walls. There were six closed doors and another staircase, which led to the floor above. I decided to head to the second floor, and then work my way down. The stairs creaked and groaned. The banisters were broken in places. The floorboards were in a shocking state. Parts of light fittings lay shattered here and there. There was much dust and cobwebs about the place. It was obvious my great-uncle had neglected the estate for a very long time and left the place to go to ruin even well before his death.

The bleak corridor led to six rooms.

I hesitated then pushed open the first door and shone my torch around the room. It was quite a large room accommodating a massive four-poster bed. Tattered royal blue velvet curtains remained closed. On closer inspection, it was obvious moths and silverfish had feasted on the limp material.

Could this have been my uncle's room?

81

The only other furniture was an 18th-century Regency armoire in walnut, which stood awkwardly in an otherwise shabby-looking room. The wall paint had pealed and there were large mildew stains. The high ceiling carried patches of stains too. The floorboards were unstable under my feet as they squeaked and moved. I decided to leave the unremarkable room and move onto the next one.

The adjacent room was brighter by comparison. Paisley wallpaper with dominant purple hues adorned the mould-reeking walls. Tiptoeing, I moved towards the window and flung open the heavy purple drapes. Instantly, the natural sunlight emitted its warmth into the room.

Someone had stacked two dozen sealed boxes against one of the walls. A bulky dark-wood blanket box hid behind the door. My excitement escalated as I hoped these cases might hold a treasure-trove of information pertinent to the curse. I would come back to this room to look through them.

The third room was surprisingly smaller than the other two. Pushed against the wall was a single poster bed. The only other furniture was a three-door wardrobe. Suspended on the wall above the bed was a rifle with a fixed bayonet. For some inexplicable reason this small room made me feel nervous.

About to move into the next room, I noticed a small spiral staircase leading to an attic. I began to mount the awkward steps cautiously, my heart pounding as the timber under my feet swayed.

Just as I was about to release the latch, a door slammed. I jumped in fright, almost tumbling backwards.

I felt unsettled. There was no doubt in my mind, someone was lurking about the house.

More than anything else, I hoped I wouldn't encounter the apparitions of dead relatives as I did in the dungeon.

With apprehension, I pushed open the attic door. It was a dilapidated and cluttered room; cobwebs decorated the ceiling cascading down like delicate lace.

I slowly moved forward and looked around in fascination at all the old wares, trinkets, clothes and books, which someone had haphazardly stored in the small attic. A cold metallic hand brushed my arm; I swung around to face a display of 15th-century suit of armour.

'Wow, this place is a haven for keen antique collectors.'

Rummaging through some boxes, I screeched with delight when I came across a bundle of letters. I undid the pale blue ribbon that held together the fragile papers.

Holding the torch close to the first letter, I began to read the graceful cursive writing:

To my darling, cherished wife, Honora,

> *As I sit here in my chair, I see your exquisite face in the window of my mind. Oh how I miss you. I am by the fire, gazing at the mother-clock counting the hours till I leave to return to you.*

> *I wanted you to know that even at midnight while entering the doorway to the world of dreams I stopped myself in order not to lose sight of you. I am engulfed by such feelings of love that I feel like a little lake over-flown by the depths of the ocean. Oh tortuous love, reunite me with my love so that I feel whole again!*

> *My dearest darling, my exquisite, incredible woman, I love you, I love you, I love you.*

Cormac Padraig Kavanagh
18 December 1848

Tears flowed down my cheeks; my eyelids felt gritty and heavy. Deep emotions stirred in me as I read my great-great-grandfather's passionate words to the woman he adored. The devotion and ardour of the fragile man had survived; no one could ever take that away from him. His sincere words touched the depths of my soul. Even though I didn't condone my great-great-grandfather's final desperate act, I understood how in a fleeting moment, he'd decided to destroy his own heart.

Placing the bundle of letters under my arm, I started to leave the cluttered attic when I noticed a hefty Edwardian oak dressing chest with a long mirror and drawers. It was a striking piece. It needed a bit of work to restore it to its original splendour. I knew just the spot where it would fit; it would be perfect in my bedroom. There was a lot of grime and cloud accumulated on the mirror. With vigorous movements, I wiped the dirt of time away.

The reflection of my face in the mirror startled me; it was particularly gaunt and pale, making me look twice my age – so pale that a stranger would think I'd never set foot outdoors, never seen the sun. The more I stared, the more I realised the charcoal-grey jumper I wore made me look even more insipid.

What I needed was a dominant fiery colour. These silly thoughts caused considerable tension in my body. *What if my dead relatives' spirits trap me eternally in this great mausoleum? I'd never be able to set foot outside again. I would end up looking like Miss Havisham, the ghostlike woman from Charles Dickens' novel, Great Expectations, who never stepped outside after the day her lover jilted her at the altar. Why am I thinking of Charles Dickens, at a time like this?* Then I thought how Dickens's prolific writing had introduced me to the classics. I remembered at age thirteen I had an immense appetite for great literature. I'd read voraciously, borrowing books from my school library.

From those impressionable years, I knew I would one day become a writer.

My career in journalism stemmed from my passion for the written word. Thoughts of the classics distracted my mind from the gloomy surrounds of this dilapidated estate. When I came back to reality, I continued looking at my mirrored image and noticed the defined lines of exhaustion creeping under my eyes. It felt as though I'd looked into this mirror a thousand times before.

Black, burning eyes swallowed up my senses. Their powerful intensity scorched every part of my body. He looked wild, suiting his temperament. His striking face, at the same time, held immense remorse that had carried for perpetuity. Now, he was back to haunt me. Nothing had changed; those brooding heavy eyebrows, the jet-black hair and wild in its abundance stood proudly on his masculine shoulders. I turned around but he was not there.

I must flee. My life depends on it. How am I going to get away? I almost tumbled down the spiral staircase. Such pain, as the metal railing scraped the epidermis of my leg. The stinging flesh mingled with blood was agonising. The only sound I could hear was my heaving and my hammering heartbeat. *I must get out, otherwise he'll destroy me.* I reached the front door. Opening it, I fell straight into his arms.

***

'Whatever is the matter? You look like you've seen a ghost,' he remarked as I fought hard not to collapse.

'Please take me far away from here. I beg of you,' I managed to plead as it dawned on me into whose strong arms I'd fallen.

He drove fast, intermittently glancing at me, to make sure I was alert.

My mind was a blur, but I could still taste the fear.

He helped me upstairs to the room. For that, I was grateful. We didn't speak until after I had a chance to throw cold water on my face. When I came back into the room, he was busy making me a cup of tea.

'Thanks,' I said.

'You shouldn't go out to your uncle's property alone. You could get seriously hurt.'

'I'm searching for something, Inspector.'

'What are you searching for?' Before I could answer, he said, 'I would prefer if you called me Sean. Inspector sounds so formal.'

He actually had a nice smile.

'Only if you call me Kathleen.'

He smiled again and said, 'Deal.'

He made another cup of tea for me and another coffee for himself. 'What did you see in there that scared you senseless, Kathleen?'

I told him everything, even describing the apparitions I'd encountered in the dungeon on the previous occasion. He was silent. I got the impression that he was quite troubled. 'Promise me you won't go back there on your own.'

'All right. I won't go back there on my own.' I knew I wouldn't be able to keep that promise. I would go back there. It was the only way I could help my family end the curse of Aggie Muldoon.

'I must get back to the station.' To my surprise, he walked over where I sat, cupped my chin in his fingers, kissed my forehead and left without another word.

I was astounded. The Inspector had done a 360 degree turnaround. Then it hit me. Why was he at my uncle's house?

CHAPTER TEN

'I'll see you in damnation before I let you have it all,' growled the old man.

Such hatred! He was shaking. Upset as I was, I pitied him. *All this unnecessary negative emotion, and what's it for? Money. If only he knew, I would gladly share the inheritance.*

'You're as pathetic as your grandfather, you greedy slag.' He was furious. 'Mark my words, you'll pay. I shall make sure you don't enjoy a penny. Harlot.'

With that degrading outburst, he crossed the street, leaving me to deal with my humiliation in silence. I walked on, but I was aware of the whispered gossip. By the time I reached the hotel, I was trembling. The old man's crudeness exasperated me. I headed to my room.

It goes to show human nature where money is the object of the game. Absolutely pathetic.

I'd gone for my usual morning walk through the town centre, when I'd run into the embittered old man and his equally inimical son. I'd acknowledged the two men with a brief nod. No sooner had I done so, Conan Kavanagh had raised his walking stick high up in the air and had hurled his uncouth insults at me.

Making a well-deserved coffee, I sat on the bed and picked up the phone. As I dialled the overseas numbers, I thought of the bitter words the old man had uttered and realised he must hold a grudge against my grandfather. *The plot thickens. Maybe my father can shed some light on this.*

'Hello.'

'Hi Dad.'

'Well hello my darling, I was just thinking of you.' He sounded happy and relaxed. 'I hope you're not up to any mischief.'

'Come on Dad. What sort of an impression do you have of your only daughter? You're more likely to get into mischief than I am!'

We loved teasing each other. We were more like close friends than father and daughter.

'You know very well, Missy that I'm talking about your insatiable thirst for adventure.'

'My conduct has been exemplary. I've been leading a very dull life.'

'Good to hear it,' said my father as he chuckled.

'How's mum?'

'She's right next to me, anxious to speak to you.'

'Before you go Dad, I want to ask some things about granddad's cousin, Conan.'

'What do you wish to know, my love?'

'Do you know anything about bad blood between Pop and Conan?'

'I really don't know any specifics. However, I do remember my father mentioning that when they were young boys, Conan used to bully and harass him unashamedly. Has he threatened you my sweet?'

'I bumped into Conan and his son in the town centre. He accused me of being as cowardly and greedy as my Pop.'

'How dare he!' My father raised his voice. 'Huh! That must've incensed you. I hope you gave him a piece of your mind.'

'You know me, dad. I know how to look after myself.' How could I tell my father the truth?

'Anyhow, I'll ask your Pop for the story and get back to you,' he said. My mother was keen to speak to me and we had a nice conversation for the next half hour, talking about her health and her friends.

I finished the cup of coffee after I hung up. My mind wandered back to the ugly incident in the street. I concluded it was not just the matter of the inheritance. Conan harboured ill feelings towards my grandfather, stemming from childhood days. The man obviously had a spiteful nature. It would be interesting to find out more about his character.

***

'Sláinte!' the drinking glasses clinked as he pulled a chair next to mine. 'In Gaelic, it means "To your health".'

'To yours too.'

Donahl's warm smile matched his iridescent personality. *Now why can't the rest of the clan be like him?*

'Isn't this a grand place? I'm here so often, it's like a second home to me,' he said cheerfully as he scanned the room.

It was a dimly lit pub, full of character. Apparently the building was once a warehouse now cleverly converted with the extensive use of dark-wood panelling and a wealth of old wooden furnishings. The intimate atmosphere, coupled with a variety of entertainment, drew in large crowds. That night, the haunting melody of the centuries-old harp soothed us.

'A few nights ago the place was buzzing with the eclectic mix of rock and roots. What a contrast this music is, tonight.'

'I'm enjoying the enchanting sounds of the Irish harp, Donahl. It's placed me in an esoteric mood.'

'I'm surprised, cousin, given your educational background, you would be preoccupied with such thoughts.' He raised his arched eyebrows, further animating his gorgeous baby face.

Just as I was about to reply that one's educational background didn't necessarily influence one's ideologies, Josh Abbott interrupted our conversation.

'I'd no idea this place was the watering hole for the Kavanagh Clan.'

'Ah Josh, me man. Where have you been hidin'?' Donahl asked.

'I went back to London, just got back today,' Josh replied. He was not his usual relaxed self and didn't even look at me.

'Hello, Josh.'

He turned his head, his eyes void of warmth. I felt confused. *Why is he so angry with me?* I couldn't understand his changed attitude towards me.

He forced a grunt-like hello.

'What will you be drinking, my friend? Another one for you, Kathleen?'

'I'm still going with this one, thanks Donahl.'

'I'll have a Jamesons, thanks,' said Josh.

'One comin' right up.' Donahl headed for the bar.

Although the room buzzed with activity and there was plenty of conversation, I felt as though total silence surrounded me. Josh's uneasiness in my company was obvious. I wasn't in the mood to make small talk either. I felt awkward in his company. Donahl returned with two drinks.

'Cheers.' My cousin drained the contents of his glass in one breath. 'I must be off. I'm going to sneak around to see my sweetheart. Be good, you two.' He laughed making a gurgling sound and disappeared into the crowd.

There was undeniable tension between Josh and me. It was as though we were total strangers, wary of each other. I was determined he should initiate conversation. He wasn't in a hurry to do so. Instead, he had a vacant expression, as he sipped his whiskey. A striking looking young woman was playing the harp. 'You deceived me and tore my soul out and tortured me for infinity'. The gloomy words of the ballad flooded the room fusing with the accompaniment of the harp. Tears formed in my eyes, my emotions intertwining like climbing ivy. All I wanted to do was flee the room. *I must get away from here – from him.*

The last thing I remembered was rushing out in the cold of the night. Intense pain followed as something hit me and I found myself hurling high up in the air, only to come crushing down into the sea of darkness.

***

Minute cells of light bombarded my eyes. My head felt as though it was pressurised. I was convinced I had sunk into the dark abyss of the ocean, ready to explode. What was that chomping feeling? My insides were churning like a mincing machine.

He looked at me, marked concern in his dark, fiery eyes. I had no energy. The spots of light were back, irritating my eyes. So were those midnight black eyes. I stirred. He came closer and placed a warm hand on my shoulder.

'Welcome back.' I thought that was what he said. Confusion reigned in my mind. I had no idea what was happening to me. The gnawing feeling in the pit of my stomach was also back. I opened my mouth to speak but no words came out. *Trapped*, my mind insisted. They were holding me as a prisoner against my will. Perhaps, I was in a cauldron of rebirth. Was this how it should feel? My head was cloudy but slowly the agonising pain became a distant memory.

***

As I flipped my eyes open, it felt as though I had been asleep for several nights. I lay in a hospital bed. It wasn't surprising, I cried out as panic set in. A matronly nurse told me I was the victim of a hit and run.

'Good morning, Ms Kavanagh. I'm Doctor Byrne. How are you feeling?' a stocky woman in a white coat spoke loudly, slowly enunciating every word. Did she think I was an imbecile? She drew the curtains around the bed. 'You have severe concussion and multiple bruising and contusions. Really it's a miracle you are alive,' she continued in her monotonous tone, still making sure that I didn't miss a single syllable.

The Doctor's pager beeped. 'I shall be back in a minute, Ms Kavanagh.'

When she came back, I said, 'I can't remember anything. How long have I been here? What day is it?'

'Today is Monday the 1st of November. They brought you in two nights ago, on Saturday night.' The Doctor's tone now sounded detached as she prodded me with a cold instrument.

'I don't remember anything.'

'You weren't driving a car nor were you a passenger. It appears someone knocked you down when you were on the kerb trying to cross the street. Apparently, according to the statements of some witnesses, a dark car came from nowhere, swerved, hitting you. He or she failed to stop.'

'What? Why didn't they stop?'

Doctor Byrne's round face held a concerned expression. 'I *am* sorry. No one can explain why he or she did *not* stop.' The emphasis she placed on certain words irritated me, but I tried to concentrate on what she was saying. 'I shall check on you later. We need to do some scans this morning. By the way, you have a *visitor*. I shall send him in,' she continued ceremoniously. Why hadn't they already done scans or whatever else needed to be done if I'd been here for two whole days?

Sean Muldoon held a breathtaking bunch of coloured tulips in his arms. He handed them to me.

'We need to put them in a vase.' I sounded self-conscious as I could feel my colour rising. 'How did you know tulips were my favourite flowers?'

'I make it my business to know everything.' He left in search of a vase.

When he returned he found me sitting up in bed trying to untangle my messy hair.

'You gave me a bit of a scare yesterday. You were in and out of consciousness,' he said as he walked towards me. He looked concerned. 'That must be sore.' His fingers lightly brushed over what I assumed to be a bruise on my forehead.

'I didn't know you were here yesterday. Everything is a blur. The last memory I have of that night is leaving the pub.'

'That's understandable. You've been unconscious. Whoever the bastard is placed you in an extremely traumatic situation. I'm sure the events will become clearer in a few days.'

He sounded like a police officer again. He paced the room like a caged boar, his dark looks brooding. Then he came close to the bed and said, 'I've reason to believe this was not an accident caused by a wayward drunk, but a calculated act to murder you.'

'Oh!' was all I could manage to utter before his beeper went off.

'Duty calls,' he said. 'I'll call in this evening.'

I nodded, too flabbergasted to speak.

For the rest of the day, they subjected me to prodding and prying. They foisted every unimaginable scan on my battered and aching body. To my relief and owing to the ingenuity of modern technology the doctor diagnosed I hadn't suffered serious damage. They released me from the hospital. The intern on duty reassured me I was well equipped to nurse my own bruises. For that, I was grateful. As I'm fiercely independent, I dislike people fussing over me.

Back in my hotel room, I prepared for bed. I was exhausted. Wanting to hear a familiar voice, I decided to call Dylan. His strong voice was the only medicine I needed. I dialled the digits but when the phone started to ring at the other end, I abandoned the call. Dylan mustn't know about my accident; he was far too busy to have to worry about me.

The knock on the door startled me. I slowly put on my dressing gown, feeling sharp pain with every movement and opened the door. I immediately noticed a large wreath on the floor. With great difficulty, I picked up the card attached to it. I gasped as I read the ugly scrawl on the card, "Next time it'll be a trip to the cemetery".

I stood there for some time, too shocked to move.

'What's wrong Kathleen? What the hell ...' Inspector Sean Muldoon bent down and picked up the wreath. 'When did this arrive?'

'I don't know.' I felt bewildered. 'I guess just a few minutes before you got here. There was a knock at the door. When I opened it, this was lying here. Did you see anyone go past?'

'No, whoever it was must've taken the stairs. They'd be well gone by now. Anyway, what are you doing here? I went to the hospital and found they had discharged you. I'd have given you a lift if I'd known.'

'I didn't want to bother you.'

'This confirms what I said to you. Someone means business to harm you.' He ran his fingers through his bountiful dark hair. For a split second, he reminded me of the stranger in my visions. I shivered.

'I think for your own safety you must move out of here.'

'No. I'll not allow them to scare me witless. It only proves they are succeeding.'

'This is no time to be a hero,' he snapped. 'Look I've a spare bedroom, you can stay with me.'

His offer astonished me. I didn't want him to play the role of protector and at the same time, I was nervous to be around him. 'I don't think it's appropriate.'

'I don't have dishonourable intentions, Ms Kavanagh,' he replied. 'It's not as though I'm asking you to share my bed. It's just the sensible thing to do. I can keep an eye on you.'

'What about your mother?'

'Oh please! You're not still harping on about this damned curse, are you?' His tone was terse. 'And I hope for your sake you're not suggesting she had anything to do with this. Look, get a good night's sleep and I'll pick you up in the morning.' As he was about to leave he said, 'Remember, don't open the door to anyone.'

I was furious. Who did he think he was to order me about? Determined not to move into his place, I went to bed fuming.

***

It was a small apartment – a typical bachelor's pad with spartan furnishings. Practical. Functional. The sound system and TV were state-of-the-art and the main focal point in the open living area. He showed me to the guest room, which consisted of a fold-out bed and a glass side-table with a lava lamp perched in the middle. There was no cupboard. Two large hooks at the back of the door served as the only means to hang up clothes. Still astounded how I'd allowed this man to get his own way and bring me here, I followed him as we took a short tour of the apartment.

The bathroom was small and dark. Above the hand-basin was a wooden shelf. On it, he had lined sequentially bottles of aftershave lotion, talcum powder, deodorant, shaving cream and other paraphernalia for male grooming. I took my time washing my hands under the warm water and looked on curiously at the brightly coloured underwear hanging from a rope stretched across the bathtub. I smiled. The Inspector hid a different personality under his usually rigid bearing and sombre-coloured clothes.

I returned to the sitting room and glided into the comfortable black leather recliner.

Sean was busy putting on the kettle.

'Coffee or tea?' he asked.

'Tea, thanks.'

'You've a choice of Ceylon, Earl Grey, Orange Pekoe, Cinnamon Chai, Moroccan mint, or green tea.'

'I'm impressed. I'll try the Moroccan mint. It sounds rather exotic.'

'It's refreshing.' He sounded relaxed.

He used tealeaves instead of tea bags and served the sweetly perfumed tea in delicate china. He also cut some rich-looking fruitcake. We had morning tea in the sun-filled sitting room.

'I advise you to stay put and rest today. I've a good collection of DVDs and CDs, as well as an assortment of books to keep you occupied.' He picked up his keys from the table and said pointing a rather long finger at me. 'Remember what I said, you're not to leave the apartment.' He left, slamming the door.

'Am I your helpless prisoner, doing time? I'd better find something to do, otherwise I know I'll go stir-crazy, confined in this small apartment.' I circled the room looking at the books. I picked out one to read. 'A man after my own heart. It's nice to see the Inspector has a keen interest in murder mystery.' I arched my eyebrows at the catchy title, "Cold is the Grave", an Inspector Banks mystery.

Before settling down on the comfortable sofa, I couldn't resist having a peak in his bedroom. It was slightly larger than the guest bedroom, but as sparsely furnished. There was a double bed with a single 19th-century walnut Wellington commode and a seven-drawer matching chest. *The Inspector certainly has expensive taste; these two items alone must be worth around 20,000 Australian dollars.* Not long ago I'd done a feature for an antique magazine, so I was moderately familiar with prices of world-class antique furniture and objects. *Not bad on a policeman's salary.* There was an in-built cupboard near the door. The Inspector hadn't closed its door, so I could see a few pieces of clothing hanging on a rack. Sealed boxes were stacked on the top shelf.

A black and white poster hung on the wall above the bed head. The poster portrayed a wolf suckling Romulus and

Remus. It intrigued me why he'd chosen the symbol of the wolf to decorate his bedroom. Perhaps it was because the wild animal represented protection and nurturing, instead of cunning and treachery.

A popular tale in Celtic mythology told of the wolf swallowing the sun every day, causing night to appear. In a village mentality, it wasn't surprising people despised and feared someone like Aggie Muldoon, as they associated her with the dark side of nature.

The shrill ring of the phone startled me. Peter Robinson's multi-layered mystery landed on the floor. Who could be ringing at 10 in the morning? My first thought was Sean – he must be checking up on me. I slowly made my way to the kitchen, limping from the pain in my injured leg.

'Hello.' Pause. 'Hello?' Another pause. 'Is anyone there?' I asked, quickly becoming uncomfortable. They hung up quietly. I fell back on the island bench stool. *Who knows I'm staying here? Could Sean have let it slip that I'm staying at his place perhaps to his mother? I hope not.*

The phone rang again. I hesitated. It stopped after three rings. Droplets of perspiration formed at the nape of my neck. I snatched a tissue out of the box and pressed onto the dampness. Ten minutes later the phone rang again. I picked it up and said hesitantly, 'Hello'. Again no answer, but I could hear laboured breathing, as if it was someone with respiratory problems.

'You're beginning to bore me,' I said, trying to sound calm.

Eerie silence followed. I heard the click of the phone. He or she had hung up. Exactly ten minutes later, the telephone rang again. I let it ring ten times. Finally, I grabbed it. 'Oh how predictable, but didn't I just tell you this is becoming tedious?'

'What the hell,' Sean sounded annoyed. 'Is this how you usually greet callers, Kathleen?'

'I'm sorry. I thought you were the prankster.'

'Prankster? Has something happened?'

'Someone called three times and didn't speak when I answered the phone. You're the fourth.'

'I'll be right over.' He hung up before I could say I'd be fine and not to worry about me. Fifteen minutes later, I heard the rustling of keys. Could it be anyone but my host? I heaved a sigh of relief when I saw Sean Muldoon opening the door.

'You should've called me straight away.' He held a worried expression on his face and paced the floor. 'This worries me. Whoever it is knows you are here.'

'Have you told anyone I'm staying with you?'

He puckered his brow. 'Not a soul. Not even any of my colleagues.'

'Maybe it's some kids messing around. Simply a coincidence.'

He flinched. 'No, this is a private number. Highly unlikely. I don't like this one bit.'

I was lost for words and the pain in my ribs increased, causing me to wince.

'Are you still in a lot of pain?'

'I'm all right.'

'Don't try to be a martyr. Your eyes are telling me otherwise.' He walked to the kitchen cabinet and took some analgesics out of a small tin container. 'Here take two of these. I bet you the hospital didn't give you any.'

'No, they didn't. Anyhow, I hate taking medication.'

'Medicines have their place.' He handed me a glass of water. It took me a while to swallow the pills. 'It's unacceptable they just discharged you. I'm no doctor but I think they should've kept you at least another day. But hospitals are run by accountants these days and we as patients don't seem to have a say in the matter.'

The phone rang again. We looked at each other.

'Hello. Mum. Did you ring here a while ago?' He listened intently. 'I see. No, there's nothing wrong. I won't be dropping by tonight. I'm working on a case. No, I won't forget. Bye now.' He appeared pensive. I didn't dare ask about his mother's response.

'You can be rest assured my mother didn't make those calls.'

'Oh.' *As if she would tell you.*

'Let's eat.'

How convenient you change the subject, I wanted to say.

He was methodical in the kitchen and quickly produced an

elaborate salad made from fresh greenery, herbs, nuts and vegetables. To accompany this crisp blend, he made a divine-smelling omelette, which he served with a white chardonnay.

We ate the delicious lunch in silence.

'That was scrumptious, but I ate too much,' I said as I massaged my stomach.

His eyes lowered to my chest and navel. 'Glad you enjoyed it.'

I blushed and tried to search for words to hide my embarrassment.

Before I could say anything, he asked, 'How involved are you with Abbott?'

'What?'

'I said how involved are you with that Abbott character?'

'I know what you said. You're unbelievable.' A nervous laugh escaped my lips. The guy was acting like a jealous husband. 'Are you accusing me of having an affair?'

'Don't get so defensive. I just want to know where he fits in the picture.'

'Picture?' I raised my voice. 'There is no picture, Inspector. For your information, I've got a boyfriend back in England whom I love very much.'

'Glad to hear it.' The smug expression was back on his face.

We ignored each other in prickly silence for the rest of the afternoon. I kept myself busy, pretending to read the murder mystery, while Sean occupied himself by writing up reports on his NoteBook computer.

'What would you like for dinner?' he asked as he switched off the computer.

'I'm not hungry.' I lied. I was still furious with him.

'Look, I'm sorry for my remarks. Call it a truce?'

Arms folded, I kept silent. I was determined not to make it easy for him.

'Okay, I guess I deserve the cold shoulder.' He chuckled. His arrogance incensed me.

I picked up the shaggy fleeced pillow and threw it in his direction, aiming badly knocking down an ornament. He looked surprised at my childish action and picked up the ornament. I ran to my room, slamming the door.

For almost half an hour, I sat on the bed, hands laced under my chin, sulking. I was unable to move, ashamed of my behaviour.

He knocked on the door. 'Kathleen,' he said. 'I've been called away, a homicide. I'll be back as soon as I can. Don't open the door to anyone or answer the phone.' Silence. 'Did you hear me, Kathleen?'

'Yes.'

'I'll see you later and remember what I said.'

As soon as I heard him leave, I came out of the room. I didn't want to be alone.

When I went to the window to pull the blind down, I noticed him. The hypnotic yellow eyes pierced through the glass. Jumping back, I bolted to my room, securing the lock with shaky hands. I grabbed my mobile phone to call Sean but the battery needed charging. I swore under my breath.

What with the accident and the death threats, I knew my mind was not rational. 'Why do I keep conjuring up the image of the wolf?' I took in a deep breath and went back to the sitting room.

It was late evening and my stomach was growling. I was hungry. Rummaging through the refrigerator, I found Croghan, an organic goat's milk cheese, cherry ripe tomatoes and crusty rolls. This would have to do. I had no idea when Sean would return. As I placed slices of cheese and tomato on the roll, I remembered Sean saying something about attending a homicide. *Poor soul, whoever it was. What a horrible ending to his or her life. Probably, not the sort of thing you would expect to happen often in Wexford.* A cold shiver went through me.

I enjoyed the simple meal, which I completed with a hot mug of orange Pekoe tea.

It was a cold evening, without any rain. There was nothing of interest on TV. By ten o'clock, I decided to go to bed and read the intriguing mystery. However, I found I couldn't concentrate. Another hour went by, no sign of Sean. *Now I'm acting like an anxious policeman's wife. It's ridiculous.*

I felt thirsty, so I went back into the kitchen. The sink was dripping, like the precision thud of a heartbeat. *That's odd. I remember securing the faucet tightly when I finished washing up the dishes.* A rattling noise came from Sean's room. It unnerved me. I couldn't move although I wanted to know what the noise was and where it had come from. Eventually, I gathered enough courage and tiptoed to his bedroom. The window was knocking backwards and forwards from the wind. I secured it shut. The wolf from the poster glared at me.

Don't be ridiculous. My stomach felt like a tight knot. As I withdrew from Sean's room, the lights went out leaving me in total darkness.

'Sean?' I called out. Silence followed.

I heard a dull sound, as though an object had fallen on the carpet.

Someone was in the room. *What do I do? Where do I run?* I panicked as I felt cold, ferocious hands grabbing my throat from behind.

His grip was strong. We struggled. Although I couldn't see him in the dark, I knew that he was tall, towering over me. I fought back with all my strength. Pain. I was struggling to breathe. *Is this the end?* I thought of Dylan and my parents. *No, I have so much living to do.* More struggling I felt dizzy. *No air. Dear God, please help.*

I heard the sound of sirens. The tightness left my throat and I hungrily gasped for air, clinging to dear life.

I heard the front door closing. I sat in the dark, fighting hard not to hyperventilate. The rustling of keys distracted me, I knew I would be safe.

The lights came back on.

'Kathleen. What's the matter? Dear God, take deep breaths.' His voice sounded like the song of angels.

CHAPTER ELEVEN

'Another few seconds you would've been pronounced dead,' the intern informed me pragmatically. 'Just a few more bruises to add to your collection. Indeed you are a lucky woman.'

I thought I was very fortunate that the police cars and fire engines had rushed past Sean's place to attend to a house fire in the next street. The person who'd attempted to strangle me had failed in his objective.

Sean and I left the hospital at three in the morning.

Rain pelted down like machine-gun fire. The windscreen wipers worked frantically, their continuous movement reminding me of my mother's metronome on her beloved piano. The wind howled ferociously, affecting the balance of the car.

These were difficult conditions for driving, but he managed to carry on with expertise.

We were both lost in thought, neither inclined to communicate. Finally, I blurted out because I could no longer bear the sound of the natural elements, 'Was it a terrible case?'

'Are you referring to the homicide I attended?'

'Yes.'

He was silent for a few seconds. 'As it is with all homicides, this one was most certainly a tragedy.' He paused, 'Domestic case.'

We were silent again.

He made a sharp turn, almost skidding off the road in the heavy rain. The pain from my bruised ribs caused me to cry out.

'Are you all right? Do you have much pain?

'A little,' I replied. 'I'm sorry I've been causing you so much trouble.'

He gave me a quick side-glance and said, 'I enjoy rescuing

damsels in distress.'

This was obviously a game to him and I snapped, 'I'm eternally grateful to you, my knight in shining armour.'

He gave out a robust laugh, which put me in a worse mood.

We travelled for another twenty minutes or so. I assumed we were to head back to his apartment. How could I tell where we were going in such heavy rain? Instinct warned me we were travelling in another direction.

'Aren't you going too fast, considering the weather conditions?'

'Are you scared?'

'You might get a speeding fine.' I regretted the stupid remark considering he was a police officer, not to mention the fact there would hardly be any police patrol in such weather. I was sure he thought my comment was drivel. 'So where are you going to hide me now?'

'You'll soon find out.'

'Maybe you should lock me up in one of your cells at the station.'

He chuckled and I could just make out he raised his eyebrows in the light of an oncoming car. 'I might just do that. What a wonderful idea.'

His teasing irritated me.

'You're impossible.'

The car stopped suddenly and the electrical window on his side glided down smoothly. Sean reached over a gatepost and pressed a button.

'Yes,' a stern voice came over the intercom.

'Hello, Dale, it's me, Sean.'

'I'm sorry sir. I didn't recognise you or the car. What with the rain ...'

Large wrought-iron gates opened and we drove down a long pathway.

As we came to an abrupt stop, Sean jumped out of the car and opened the boot. He brought around to my side a large umbrella to shield me from the rain. We ran together to the large portico where a stocky man met us.

'Good evening or, more precisely, good morning Dale,' Sean

greeted the man cheerfully.

It was past four in the morning.

We entered into an impressive foyer. Everything there was Shiraz wine and gold colours. Fine Italian marble adorned the floor. I imagined myself in a Roman villa.

I was concerned we were making a mess with all the mud and water we brought in.

Sean thanked the man named Dale and grabbed my hand. We charged up the circular staircase at neck-breaking speed. The pain in my chest and back became unbearable. What was this mad policeman trying to do to me? We reached the dimly lit first-floor corridor. He led me into a pretty bedroom.

'Who's place is this? Where have you brought me?'

'You'll be safe here. Now, get some sleep,' he ordered and before I could ask where he was staying, he left the room, closing the door behind him.

I was exhausted, not even able to look around the room. What a difficult evening! I still felt those horrible hands around my throat squeezing hard and draining the air out of my body. Unrelenting. Determined. I glanced back to reassure myself no one was behind me. *I came so close to death tonight. I don't want to think about it anymore.* Without even bothering to get out of my clothes, I flung myself on the inviting bed and floated away into twilight.

***

The moment my eyes flicked open, panic set in. Nothing looked familiar. Then I remembered.

My day began with consternation, my clothes crumpled and my body feeling less than fresh. I left the room. My watch read 2:37. I couldn't believe I had slept for more than nine hours.

A young woman, slightly built, with hollow eyes went past me on the stairs. She held a stack of freshly ironed towels. It was as though she wanted to avoid me and forced a quick tilt of her head.

'Excuse me, could you tell me where I might find Sean Muldoon?'

'He is out on the lower terrace, Madame. Turn left at the stairs and enter the third archway, which will lead you to the pool area.'

She didn't even give me a chance to thank her. She disappeared up the stairs, as though she'd been a mere vision.

Following her directions, I stepped out of a large glass patio door. Sean sprang to his feet as soon as he noticed me. As he reached me, he said, 'I'm glad you were able to rest.'

My dishevelled state embarrassed me. 'I look terrible.'

'You look lovely.' He smiled.

'That's fine for you to say. You've had a shower and have obviously had time to iron your clothes.'

'After you have something to eat, I'll show you where you can shower. I'll get Miriam to bring you some fresh clothes.'

'Who's Miriam?'

'The housekeeper.' With that response, he took my hand and led me to an outdoor setting, where an elegant woman with snow-white hair sat serenely on a cane armchair.

'I want you to meet someone,' he said. 'Gran, this is Kathleen Kavanagh.' He turned to me and said, 'This lovely lady is my grandmother, Deirdra Muldoon.'

'Very nice to make your acquaintance,' said the old woman. She spoke softly, her warm smile lighting up her gentle eyes.

'Pleased to meet you too, Mrs Muldoon.'

'You must call me Deirdra, my dear,' she extended a fragile hand.

A robust, middle-aged woman served afternoon tea of various pastries and refreshments. I wondered if she was Miriam.

'Thank you, Francine,' said Sean. The woman gave a broad smile and retreated.

I felt hungry. The delicacies looked inviting.

'You've been through such an ordeal, my dear,' the old woman said as she held onto my hand tightly. 'My Sean told me all about it. There's so much wickedness in this world.'

I felt awkward. The enemy surrounded me. This was not part of the plan. I was here to find a way to remove the curse placed on the Kavanaghs by this family. Instead, I not only conferred with them but also sought their protection. *It's most bizarre. I can't believe I'm doing this.* I bit into another delicious quince pie.

The piping hot coffee was just what I needed to pep me up. On another large platter, delicately arranged pastries were a sure temptation. I appreciated the subtle spices of cinnamon and cloves in the rich fruit pie, reminding me of Christmas. Quite satisfied I lounged back, enjoying the breezy air caressing my skin.

Sean stepped inside to take a phone call. His grandmother was busy instructing the gardener on the best way to fertilise the hydrangeas when Donahl and Eliza made their entrance.

'Why cousin, what are you doing here?' Donahl asked. His expression was definitely one of surprise.

I was lost for words.

'I invited her over,' Sean said as he re-joined us on the patio.

'We'd no idea you were such good friends.'

'Yes, Ms Kavanagh is excellent company.'

Eliza Muldoon, petite and pretty, remained silent. She was very much in Donahl's shadow. She went over where her grandmother sat and the two women embraced.

'Tea or coffee?' Sean asked.

'We'll both have coffee, thanks,' said Donahl, speaking for his fiancée.

He took the seat opposite and gazed at me intently.

'You look as though you've been through the wars, Kathleen!'

'Ms Kavanagh met with an unfortunate accident,' Sean said. 'She'll be back to her usual self in a few days.'

'What accident?'

'She fell down some stairs.'

'Tell me, has she hurt her tongue as well?'

Donahl's scathing remarks didn't amuse Sean. I thought I noticed him giving my cousin a stern look. It was ironic Donahl had made that remark since he hardly let Eliza speak.

'So what have you two lovely young people been up to?' Grandmother Muldoon changed the subject.

Donahl folded his arms and said, 'Wedding arrangements, grandmother. Lots and lots of details for our grand wedding.'

Eliza looked away flustered, she seemed uncomfortable. *Interesting. Perhaps a lover's tiff?*

While Donahl and Eliza were there, I wanted to ask about Josh Abbott. However, in the light of Sean's recent remarks regarding my relationship with Josh, I thought it best to keep away from that subject.

As they spoke of the wedding plans, I looked out at the rose garden, which glowed in the misty afternoon sun. My mind drifted and I thought of Josh and remembered the evening, the same awful evening, when a callous driver had run over me, leaving me to die. *Surely, Josh knows what had happened that night. After all, it took place outside the pub. He doesn't even care to ask after me. Why should that bother me? He's just an acquaintance. So why does it bother me so much?*

Sean interrupted my thoughts when he came over and whispered in my ear, 'Are you all right?'

I smiled back and nodded sheepishly.

After Donahl and Eliza left, Sean suggested I go and freshen up. The hot shower comforted me, the droplets of water teasing my aching bruises. I enjoyed the sensation. Blue-crimson images, like clouds in a clear sky flashed before my eyes.

I was a little girl running in a sunburnt golden cornfield. I was happy. My mouth curved in a dazzling smile, reflecting my inner peace. The smell of the mother earth evoked experiences of freedom and wildness to my otherwise timid nature. The gentle wind frolicked wisps of my hair, exhilarating my senses. I was alive, full of energy. Was it possible to be so happy?

Like a bolt of lightning, all the warm emotions faded when I fell headlong into his powerful arms. His brooding, stern expression, so void of feeling, destroyed my frivolous mood. I knew he was about to punish me.

I opened my eyes and fell back into reality with a thud. I found myself under the steamy shower again. Who was this man – the stranger who haunted me – and yet he was so familiar? I knew where I must go to seek him.

***

Sean and his grandmother lavished a lot of attention on me while I lived under their roof. Total comfort and luxury surrounded me and I somehow lost sight of my mission. It was almost a week since I had even stepped a foot out of the grand estate. Christmas was fast approaching. I wanted to be with Dylan but I couldn't leave yet; nothing was resolved.

My bruises were mending, and on this particular morning, I decided to explore the vast grounds. I let my intuition guide me down a winding path, which led over a bridge to a tiny wood and clay-clad chapel.

Although the surrounding scenery was enchanting, the building itself exuded a haunting feeling. Climbing ivy and moss strangled the brickwork of the exterior. I slowly pushed the termite-infested wooden door and entered the disused chapel.

A sea of cobwebs and clumps of dried leaves hung from the vaulted ceiling. Someone had assembled chaotically broken pews on the dusty ground, leaving me with an odd impression of finality. It was a startling place. A musty smell overwhelmed the icy air that bound me like a burdened guilt. I couldn't shake the feeling that this small, ordinary chapel hid a deep, dark secret. The silence troubled me. Images of a garrotte around a woman's fragile neck flashed before my eyes. *I must leave. I can't handle this.*

I stepped out, taking deep breaths so I could come back to normality. I ran like a wild horse to get as far away from the chapel's decaying atmosphere.

The surrounding wilderness was breathtaking. In this remoteness, I felt a sense of peace and tranquillity. That sense of security was short-lived, however, when a powerful hand grasped my shoulder. I spun around, only to face Josh Abbott.

'What are you doing sneaking around here?' was all I could blurt out, startled as I was by his interruption of my reverie.

'I was hoping to bump into you. I wanted to reassure myself you were all right.'

'Why shouldn't I be all right?'

'A thousand reasons.'

'Name one reason!' I arched my eyebrows. I was angry with

him. I felt he had abandoned me.

'For one you're living with the enemy?'

'That's ridiculous'

'I can't believe your indifference. These people are out to harm you.'

'What?'

'You know what I'm talking about.'

'Are you implying the Muldoons have ill intentions towards me?' I fought to keep my cool.

'Have you forgotten the bad blood between your families or are you so blinded by your new boyfriend that you denounce this fact?'

'My boyfriend?'

'Yeah, the one you've been staying with.'

'If you're suggesting Sean Muldoon and I are lovers, you are grossly mistaken.' I made a snorting sound. 'For your information – not that it is any of your business – I'm in a relationship back in England. And, I don't make a habit of carrying on behind my partner's back.' I stopped to catch my breath. 'But if you must know, Sean has been a kind friend, helping me in difficult times. Why are you being so unfair?'

'Don't come running to me when it's too late. You'll soon find out what Sean Muldoon and his family are capable of.' His eyes were cloudy and grey like a murky pool of ice. 'One thing I'm sure of is that the Inspector has an agenda.'

'What nonsense! I find it ironical that one minute you're best pals with the Muldoons, the next minute you crucify them. Your accusations are absurd.'

'Then tell me why the mighty Inspector threatened me: he told me that I'd be in real trouble if I continued to be in contact with you.'

'What? When did he do that?'

'The night you were rushed to the hospital after you'd been run over.'

'You were there?'

'Of course I was there. Do you think I'd leave you to deal with what happened on your own? Have you any idea how worried I was for you?'

'But what happened?'

'The prodigious Inspector is what happened. He threw me out of the hospital, warning me not to come near you.'

'Why would he do that?'

A short, nervous laugh escaped his lips and he shook his head. 'Don't you find the whole scenario incredible? Haven't you questioned why the Muldoons are going out of their way to protect you, a Kavanagh, their mortal enemy?'

'You're wrong, Josh. Neither Sean nor his grandmother means me harm. In fact they've been extremely kind and hospitable towards me.'

'I've said my piece. If you don't want to take my advice, it's your prerogative. But I'm warning you, don't let your guard down or you shall pay a high price.'

With those dramatic words, he hurried away and disappeared into the fine haze.

It took a while for me to gather my thoughts. Josh's powerful words had upset me. *Could there be truth in what he's saying about the Muldoons? After all, only a few weeks ago Sean could barely compose himself to be civil towards me. Why has everything changed? Should I return to the house? The only thing I can do is be cautious of everyone around me.*

'Where were you?' Sean asked. His tone was harsh.

'I went for a walk.'

'Where to?'

'Around.'

It was evident he was annoyed with me. 'It's an 80-acre property. Exactly which part did we go exploring?'

'Why the interrogation? Or is it that I'm a prisoner here, not to roam about as I please?'

'Don't be ridiculous.' He locked his eyes into mine. 'Of course you're not a prisoner. But given the fact that there have been warnings and serious attempts on your life, it's only common sense to be cautious.'

He was, of course, right and I regretted my foolish outburst. It bothered me that I'd allowed Josh Abbott to influence me.

***

Over the next week, I continued to enjoy the Muldoons' hospitality despite my reservations about their intentions. I couldn't understand why Sean had become more preoccupied than usual and was avoiding my company at all costs.

On a particularly bleak afternoon, I was engrossed in a book in a reclusive part of the house, when Aggie Muldoon Doherty paid me an unexpected visit.

'You little witch, and you claim I'm possessed by the devil,' she squealed as a wretched rat would when caught in a trap. 'How dare you weave yourself like this in my son's life,' she raged on, 'oh, that boy has always been a fool, taken in by the wicked charms of a hussy like you.'

I could no longer tolerate her vicious outburst. Instead of coming to my defence, I took flight, running as fast as I possibly could, as though to save my life.

Once outside the steel & wrought iron-gates, I felt I could breathe easier and that was when I decided not to turn back. The woman's outrageous insults incensed me. I wondered whether Josh was right. Were the Muldoons cleverly deceiving me?

All my belongings, including my wallet, were back at the house. I didn't care. I couldn't bear to be around them for another minute. *How can I so easily forget the curse? I'm a fool.*

I must've walked for a long time because my legs started to feel really tired. It was as though I was on automatic pilot and found myself at Uncle Fionnbharr's estate. The place looked like an enchanted castle and despite my tiredness, I went exploring like a child mesmerised by the magical atmosphere. The Gothic architecture epitomised cruel passions and supernatural terrors in some medieval setting. It reminded me of Walpole's *The Castle of Otranto*.

Nothing had changed; the distinctive scent of the iris was nostalgic. I knew I had returned home. I had missed the place.

The gentle breeze wafted past my face, accompanied by the haunting tune of a harp. As I made a turn around the house, I heard boisterous laughter from the courtyard.

There she was with her long flowing hair and sweet

captivating ways. Her smile was broad, warming even the coldest day.

They were so much in love, the pair of them, young and frivolous. She was tall and beautiful, and he was youthful and full of energy. They played hide and seek as though they were a couple of children. Giggling in merriment, they chased each other as carefree kindred spirits. However, their vibrant mood was all too quickly shattered, when the young boy with his dark brooding looks entered the courtyard. His disapproving gaze was so powerful the lovely young woman looked at him terrified and ran back into the house, while the gangly young man took his leave by an archway. The boy lingered in the courtyard for a minute or two. He gave a cynical smile, satisfied he'd destroyed the happy mood of the young couple. He retreated into the house.

I stepped into the courtyard bewildered at what I'd just seen. *Am I really seeing these apparitions of my dead relatives, snippets of the mystery of my family's tragic past? Or am I imagining it all and have become that unhinged?*

One thing was obvious; I had to find out the truth.

Against my better judgement, I entered the house. The best place to start, I decided, was to head straight upstairs to the bedroom where I'd discovered some stacked boxes.

Each step of ascension was tricky as the wooden stairs creaked and groaned, moving under my feet, as though they were disturbed like the dead would be in their graves.

I hadn't yet reached my destination, when I felt his fiery yellow eyes following my every move. I turned around, but he was nowhere in sight.

My heartbeat accelerated.

I forced the brass door handle down and opened the door. The wood creaked, filling a void in the nerve-racking silence. As I reluctantly stepped into the dusty and damp smelling room, I immediately noticed someone had closed the curtains. I was sure I'd left them open when I was in here the other day.

The realisation the ghosts were not the only ones roaming about the house made me uncomfortable. Setting aside these gloomy thoughts, I began to unravel the contents of the twelve stacked boxes. The first few boxes were an assortment of trinkets and wares whose intrinsic value only their owner would appreciate.

It's amazing the bits and pieces we humans like to hoard as though we want to preserve a part of us. Nevertheless, I wasn't discouraged and continued optimistically to rummage through the rest, but there was nothing of importance in the boxes.

I was more determined than ever to find some clue, however small it might be, so I could free my family from the abominable curse of Aggie Muldoon.

I looked at the black chest; something of significance might be in it. After some physical effort, I lifted the rough, heavy lid. Hiding underneath some yellow stained sheets were five large, hand-painted portraits.

Tears welled up in my eyes. I was staring down into history, my family's history. A Marcus Burns had signed the portraits and dated them, 1845. Undoubtedly, he was the talented artist who captured the heart of this vital family. Four of the five were family portraits of a distinguished man with his young family. Here in front of me, portrayed on a piece of canvas, was my paternal Great-Great-Grandfather, Cormac Padraig Kavanagh. The beautiful woman next to him was my Great-Great-Grandmother whom I immediately recognised as the woman in my visions. There were four children. The youngest child with intense black eyes and a wild deportment looked vastly different from the other three siblings.

This must be Cailean. The apparition I encountered in the attic mirror, the man with the deep burning eyes and an untamed nature was undeniably Cailean. Cailean when he had turned into a man, no longer the young boy as in this sketch.

The fifth portrait both surprised and shocked me. It was as though I was looking at myself. *Who is this woman? My God, this is incredible!*

The only difference between this woman in the portrait and me was the time-period. She sat demurely on a chair and held a closed bible in her hand. She wore a long, grey dress down to her ankles and she wore her hair back, revealing a sad, defeated face.

My whole body went into frissons of shudders, as though I was hurtling through a time machine. *How can this be? Who is she?* A part of me was intrigued and yet I felt disturbed. A raucous laugh filled the room. I clutched onto the portrait as my face contorted with fear.

'Charlotte, my love, I knew you would come back to me.' A harsh voice surrounded me. 'You will never leave me again.'

A terrifying sensation struck like lightening through my brain into my chest; my head swam; it felt detached from my body, spinning around as though caught up in a cement mixer. All I wanted to do was to flee. He was here, hiding in a secret place but his yellow eyes followed my every move.

I must get out of here. I must run. He was after me, his strong voice inside my head. When I looked behind me, it wasn't the wolf but Cailean gaining on me.

Helplessness. Terror. *My God, I'm going to die.* At exactly the same moment I had thoughts of dying, my legs felt like jelly and all I could take in was the rolling sensation. I fell, pain followed. The trickle of light became dimmer and then, like a candle, it went out.

CHAPTER TWELVE

The pink lampshade seemed familiar when I opened my eyes and stared at the ceiling. The lampshade's tassels and translucent beads shimmered with the natural light. My head throbbed as though someone had hit me with a blunt instrument and had cracked open my skull.

Reluctantly and with considerable difficulty, I sat up in bed, looking around me. Disorientated. Perplexed. *I'm in the Muldoon's house. How can this be?*

I strained my memory. Images started flashing in front of me until I remembered everything. Maybe it had all been a nightmare and I'd not even gone to my uncle's house. 'That can't be,' I said aloud. I remembered my confrontation with Aggie Muldoon Doherty. What a horrid woman! I'd fled from this place. 'I'm not going crazy. I ran away from her.' Trying to get up, I felt as dizzy as a drunkard, unsteady on my feet. I looked back to the events of the immediate past and said aloud, 'Still, I think I'm losing it. Who's Charlotte? Is she the woman in the portrait who looks just like me? Is she a part of this mystery?'

A loud knock on the door disturbed my attempt at rationalisation. 'Come in,' I said automatically, without thinking who might be on the other side of the heavy wooden structure. When I spoke, my jaw hurt. I cradled my head in the warmth of my palms.

'How are you feeling?' Sean asked.

'I've been better.'

'What the hell were you thinking?' His concern dissipated into anger. 'Do you have a death wish?'

'You wouldn't understand,' I said, while groaning from the escalating pain in my head.

'No, you're right – I don't understand.' The concerned look that by now had become so familiar to me was back in his eyes. 'Look have a bath, try to relax and then come downstairs. We'll continue this talk later,' he said in a kinder tone.

He left hurriedly. I took a long bath.

By the time I left the room, I was desperate to question Sean about how I got back to the Muldoon's estate. The last thing I recalled was Cailean chasing me.

'Good morning, Ms Kavanagh,' said Miriam the housekeeper in her musical voice. 'Mrs Muldoon is in the dinin' room and is anxious to see you.'

'Thank you.'

It was a huge dining hall housed by a massive table with a gleaming French polish finish. Eighteen red and gold Louis XVI chairs surrounded it. Two female staff were busily setting the table for a late morning brunch. Deirdra struggled into the room via the French doors. The rhythmic thud of her intricately carved walking stick accompanied her. When she saw me, her gentle face irradiated like a cloudless Australian Summer's day.

'My dear child, come over here, so I can have a look at you myself,' she spoke with a lot of emotion in her frail voice.

When I reached her, the woman took my hand into her own trembling ones. That was when I noticed tears had formed in her eyes. A lump nestled in my throat. I realised my impulsive action to flee this house had upset this most gentle of women.

'Are you all right, Mrs Muldoon?'

Deirdra merely nodded her head and motioned me to sit at the table.

She was out of breath. Looking deeply into my eyes she said, 'Why did you run away from us, child? We mean you no harm.'

'I didn't mean to cause you all so much trouble, but Mrs Doherty's visit upset me.'

'Gran, could I have a private word with Kathleen?' Sean spoke with a stern voice as he stood behind my chair. He'd been listening to our conversation. Grabbing my elbow, he dragged me to my feet a little too roughly for my liking and we went out onto the patio, away from his grandmother and the staff.

'I would appreciate it if you didn't go upsetting my

grandmother.' His dark eyes were fiery, like the hot desert sun. I had seen the same look in Cailean's eyes. *Don't be ridiculous. Cailean was an ancestor who lived more than a century ago.*

'Are you listening to me, Kathleen? You seem to be away with the fairies.'

'There's no need to be rude,' I snapped as I brushed aside a lock of my hair, which insisted on annoying my left eye. 'I'm not deliberately trying to upset your grandmother. That's the furthest thing from my mind. Why would I upset a woman I've become very fond of? I was merely explaining to her why I'd left the house.'

He was quiet for a few seconds. 'Then explain to me too, why you ran away. I was worried sick something terrible had happened to you.'

'Well you don't have to be my keeper, you know.'

'Someone has to keep an eye on you, since you don't seem to have common sense.'

I ignored his jibe. 'Who found me?'

'I found you.'

'Why am I not surprised?' I pursed my lips. 'You were following me.'

'I wasn't following you. Lucky for you, I knew where to look. Tell me why did you go back there?'

'Where else was I to go? Your mother certainly made it clear how you all truly feel about me.'

'What the hell did she say to you?'

'I don't wish to talk about this anymore.' I turned around to leave when he pulled me back.

'You little fool,' he managed to say as he drew me into his arms and kissed me more passionately than I'd ever been kissed.

***

'How do I always manage to get myself in these situations?' I asked myself as I stared out of the bedroom window over a mass of fir trees. My handbag was on the chair near the window; I picked it up and searched for my mobile phone. I wanted to speak to Dylan. Dialling the numbers with a shaking finger, I was acutely aware of my nervousness. His voice came onto the message bank and I sighed with relief. I left a brief message saying I loved him and I would ring back later.

I didn't want to leave this room. *I can't face Sean.* After his whirlwind kiss, he'd murmured some incomprehensible utterances under his breath before scurrying off.

Pacing around the room like a caged bear, I decided to go out. 'I must go back to my uncle's house. The secrets lie in that haunting house. I just have to put the pieces of the puzzle together.'

With determination, coupled with apprehension, I sneaked out of the Muldoon's estate. I'd not even walked 50 meters when my mobile phone vibrated in my bag. *It must be Dylan.*

'Miss Kavanagh?'

'Yes.'

'This is Molly. Molly O'Rourke. You remember, we met at the Registrar for Births & Deaths where I work?' The woman sounded nervous.

'Oh, yes, of course. Hello, Molly. I must say this is a surprise. How can I help you?'

'I think I can help you.' I could hear Molly taking in a deep breath. 'Look I can't talk for long, my boss will kill me.' An abrupt pause followed, 'Meet me on the portico of your uncle's estate at 10 o'clock tonight. You will be amazed when you learn what I've discovered.'

'It will be dark by then I don't think it will be safe for either of us to go there.'

'Don't worry, we'll be safe. You must promise to be there.'

Against my better judgement, I made the unwise promise.

'I've to go now, my boss is heading this way.' The line went dead. Molly O'Rourke had hung up abruptly.

I turned around and headed back into the gates of the Muldoon estate.

***

'Make sure you stay put today. I'll be gone all day but I expect you, for your own safety, not to leave the grounds. Understood?'

'Yes, sir. Loud and clear, sir.' My attempt at sarcasm didn't impress Sean. He had a sour look on his face. I wanted to ask him if he had sucked on bitter lemons. *I mustn't be cruel. The man does get on my nerves even though he's trying hard to protect me. Or is he?*

He left without another word. I felt relieved, as I couldn't stand his interrogation or his scrutiny of my actions.

It was an unusually cold day. Winter had arrived suddenly, making the place mysterious and forbidding. Then when the sunshine bathed this little corner of the world with its warmth, the icy sheets on the landscape started to melt.

Feeling annoyed by Sean's condescending words, I found it difficult to concentrate on anything. It was going to be a long day, but I'd to make plans as to how I would break out of this impenetrable fortress, in the pitch of the night.

I stayed in my room to avoid any form of confrontation with a Muldoon. I felt guilty thinking this way, because Deirdra was such a nice person. She showed nothing but kindness towards me.

I decided to tackle the looming challenges.

Sitting on the plush Berber wool carpet, I began deep breathing exercises to connect with my inner goddess. I arranged oracle cards to guide me intuitively. I slowly turned the first card over and the image of Blodeuwedd came up. The Welsh earth goddess whom people associated with betrayal and treachery. The second card produced Kali, the Hindu goddess of destruction. *Is this card warning me of danger?* The third card I chose was Cerridwen, another Welsh card representing the mythical triple goddess. People associated her with prophecy, shape shifting, life and death.

I shuddered. These cards were negative, not what I'd expected. There was a lighter side to their meaning. Nevertheless, they didn't help my worsening mood. I paced the floor. Finally, I decided to go downstairs as it was close to dinnertime.

'Well hello.'

I turned around. It was Donahl.

'You startled me.'

'Why so jittery?' He laughed. 'What are you up to?'

'Nothing. Where is Eliza?'

'In with her grandmother. I don't know why but the old girl is apparently under the weather today.'

'It's bitterly cold, perhaps she has pain.'

'Perhaps. Tell me, have you had further run-ins with my father and grandfather?'

'Fortunately, not.'

'Glad to hear it. Not a nice pair.' From our previous conversations, it had become evident Donahl didn't have a high regard for his family. I couldn't say the thought perturbed me as I shared his sentiments.

There were only the three of us at the dinner table. Deirdra wasn't feeling well and remained in her room. Sean was at work. They didn't expect him home early, if at all. That was to my advantage. It would be so much easier for me to slip out of the house. I hoped my cousin and his fiancée wouldn't linger here.

It was about nine o'clock. We finished the last bites of the delectable dessert of Grandmother Muldoon's recipe of Irish Whiskey Cake, when I made excuses to retire for the night.

'It was a most enjoyable evening, we should do this again,' I said as I yawned. 'I must admit I'm exhausted, particularly after having such a feast. Guys, you have to excuse me, I need my beauty sleep.'

'It's not possible for you to be more beautiful than you already are.'

'Oh you tease,' I giggled and winked at him.

Eliza sat looking uncomfortable at our banter.

Donahl noticed his fiancée's sullen mood and said, 'C'mon old girl, lighten up.' Eliza became even more withdrawn after Donahl's unwise turn of phrase.

'Hope to see you both soon. Goodnight.' I escaped upstairs.

***

Back in my room, I hurried to change. Putting on a pair of jeans and a warm jumper, I glanced into the mirror. It felt like I was embarking on an expedition into the mountains. I double-knotted the laces of my joggers and zipped up my parka. The sliding door to the balcony creaked. *Hope nobody heard this racket. Why didn't I plan this breakout better?* The cold air was severe as I stepped onto the balcony. My nose felt as though it protruded like a chunk of ice, almost as though obstructing my vision in the dead of the night. I huddled in the parka and thought I should go back into my safe shelter.

What am I thinking? I can't possibly let down poor Molly. Besides, she said she could help me. I've to find a way to leave this fortress.

I checked my watch. *If I walk, it will take me about thirty-five minutes to get to my uncle's property. That's too long, I'd never make it. When I'm out of these gates, I'll call for a taxi.*

In the distance, an owl hooted – a haunting sound that made me shiver. The golden leaves on the surrounding tree rustled bowing to the force of the wind.

I looked around, taking in every detail of my hostile environment. I felt like a secret agent inviting danger.

Registering movement in the bushes below, I looked down. All was quiet. Although I was a fit person, even with my lack of stature, being only 5 foot 4, the thought of descending from the balcony was so daunting I felt my palms becoming clammy. *Why can't this be as easy as the situations depicted in the movies? Like Zena the warrior, why can't I leap onto the oak tree, which is so close to this balcony?* I looked again; the tree didn't seem so close anymore. I felt dizzy when I looked down from the balcony. There had to be a simpler way. I decided to go back into my room and figure out an alternative mode of escape.

I tiptoed out into the hallway but due to the abundance of polish wax on the parquetry, my joggers squeaked like a pair of mice. *Great. I'm going to be caught.* However, no one was in sight, which was a bit odd as most nights there was a flurry of activity in this massive house.

Maybe they all knew of my clandestine activity and were eager to pounce on me as I set foot out the door. Instead, and to my surprise, I found the front door slightly ajar and slipped out unnoticed, or so I hoped.

I couldn't believe my luck. The ferocious Dobermans were nowhere in sight.

CHAPTER THIRTEEN

'I'll pick up the cash tomorrow,' Dale uttered gruffly. 'Mind Dermot, you don't slip up in front of the boss, if you know what's good for you.'

I hid behind a bush when I saw the men approaching.

'Oh c'mon Dale, when have I let you down? I'll be careful, may Mary Mother of Jesus strike me down if I'm not.'

I frowned. *Am I about to witness some unsavoury business dealings? Should I mention this to Sean in the morning? What's the point? I don't even know what they're discussing.*

Dale disappeared back into the house and I could hear him locking the front door. Dermot veered toward the gates and opened a smaller side gate. This was my opportunity. I picked up a large stone and threw it near some bushes close to him.

Dermot pulled back and called out. 'Who's there?' He scratched his head.

I threw another stone, this time in the opposite direction.

'What's goin' on?' Nervous tension ran high in his voice. He picked up a heavy branch from the ground and with reluctance, headed in the direction of the noise.

I quickly got up and darted to the side gate without much effort. As I pulled the iron door backwards, it screeched.

'What the hell ...' shouted Dermot.

Wasting no time I fled, not looking back.

I congratulated myself. I had successfully made my escape. No footsteps followed me. At a safe distance, I stopped to draw in a deep breath.

The cold air swept past me like a bullet train. Swift and gripping, it demonstrated its clout. Descending fog cloaked me, making visibility difficult. Strangely enough, it gave me a sense of peace, as though I was at heaven's gate, gliding on soft cloud ready to meet my maker.

My sense of calm dissipated when I felt something brush past my arm. I was barely able to restrain myself from screaming.

I had no idea what it was. Did I imagine it? Possibly.

The incident disturbed me. For reasons hard to explain, it left me with the feeling the hand of death had just touched me.

While walking briskly, I kept thinking about the human mind, that it was a complex and intricate machine. Capable of assimilating thousands of thought processes, it created the realm of reality the conscious mind lived in. That same machine also created thoughts of fantasy, which could be destructive in the real world. In my case, I thought it was the latter. I had lost my rational senses.

My steps quickened even more. I felt increasingly uncomfortable. The fog intensified, but in the distance, I could make out a pair of yellow lights. Since it was the only thing that was distinct, I had no choice but let it guide me.

The approaching light headed straight for me.

It dawned on me what I saw were not lights. They were, in fact, powerful flaming eyes. Yellow eyes.

Fear gripped me. It was a conquering force. Bolted to the ground, my body felt encased in heavy steel. My limbs were rigid and heavy.

Was I breathing? I couldn't tell.

My throat tightened. Perspiration formed on my frozen brow. I shut my eyes but I couldn't escape the smell. The raw animal odour overpowered my senses, so dominant and so pungent. Should I scream or should I run? I couldn't do either. I desperately searched for my heartbeat, but couldn't find it. Had he torn me apart? Was that why I couldn't feel anything?

I opened my eyes. The ferocious beast's snout was touching my nose. Those huge round eyes, that nauseating smell. I wanted to scream for help.

'Are yer an angel?' a craggy voice asked.

I blinked and stared into a pair of hollowed eyes, which were deeply set into a furrowed old face. He held a halogen flashlight into my face. My terror was totally unfounded. I faced a man, an old homeless man. That explained the strong offensive smell. He was unkempt and was huddled in a shabby coat that was twice his size.

'Are yer an angel to take me away?' he persisted. Then he tugged at my sleeve and I wasted no time to pull myself up and take off at a rate of knots.

I ran, as though I was running for my life, even though I couldn't see where I was going. It didn't matter. All I could think was that I was alive.

One more leap and the fog lifted. It was as though I jumped out from a wormhole and found myself somewhere in another quadrant of the universe.

Where am I? I don't recognise this place. It isn't as though I've walked around for kilometres. This is so confusing.

The biting wind swept past, encouraging my bones to quiver yet again.

I put my foot off the kerb to cross the road when out of nowhere a car's blaring lights fast approached me. Time seemed of no essence, as I stood still, no strength of will to move away out of the car's path. It came within centimetres of hitting me. The screeching sound of burning tyres seized the still of the night as though the balance of nature had tilted.

'Get in,' his usual peremptory tone instructed.

I did what he told me to do.

He kept shaking his head as in disgust. 'You're just unbelievable!'

'I try hard.' Arms crossed, all I could do was look away as he manoeuvred the car around the bends of the steep road.

***

'Let me go!'

'Not until you behave like an adult and tell me where it is that you wish to go,' Sean growled as he pushed me into his grandmother's palatial foyer.

'That's none of your business.'

'I'm making it my business.'

'Well, I don't need you to be looking over my shoulder all the time,' I hissed. I resented him for ruining my plans. 'Now let me pass and go about my business. I have an appointment and I'm already running late, no thanks to you.'

'An appointment. Why didn't you say so?' Sean was deliberately sardonic. 'I should've guessed you had a midnight rendezvous with your lover.'

'You disgust me.' I bit my lip in anger.

'That's a turn for the books. Normally, I delight women with my charm and wit. I must be losing my touch.'

'Think again, this woman doesn't find you charming or witty. On the contrary I find you highly irritating.'

'That's a good sign. To be irritated by someone usually involves emotion.' He grinned.

It annoyed me that I found him dangerously sexy. Before I could open my mouth to hurl another insult at him he said, 'It's very late, I've had a hellish day and require peace and quiet. I suggest you contact Mr Abbott tomorrow and reschedule your date.'

Sean slipped his leather jacket off, flung it casually over his broad shoulder and marched upstairs.

***

Annoyed I had slept in I refused the tempting breakfast, which someone had left on the bureau when I emerged from the bathroom.

Thanks to the Inspector, I had endured a rough night tossing and turning. Hurriedly, I dressed and towel-dried the dampness out of my hair. After lacing my boots up and putting on my woollen beanie, I left the mansion without acknowledging anyone.

Umbrella in tow, I traversed the streets and entered the office of the Registrar of Births and Deaths.

Molly O'Rourke was not at her usual post. Instead, a scraggy young man busied himself keying data into a terminal.

'Good morning, I wish to see Molly O'Rourke.'

The young man went pale.

'One moment please.'

What's the matter with him? Like Molly, he's probably scared of the boss. I watched him shuffle his feet into the back room and closed it quietly behind him. Two minutes later, a woman with a despotic air about her emerged from the same room.

'Are you the one who's inquiring after Miss O'Rourke?' she asked.

Her authoritarian stance made me feel as though I should deny my request and abandon all knowledge of Miss O'Rourke.

Instead, I said, 'Yes, I am.'

'Are you a relative?'

'No, I'm a friend.'

'I see. Please follow me.'

The woman led me to her office. She pointed to a tatty chair for me to sit. Walking around the desk, she sat herself down on a bulky black leather swivel chair. She tapped her fingers on the table and cleared her throat.

'I regret to inform you that Miss O'Rourke is dead.'

'What?'

'Molly is dead.'

'Dead?'

'Yes, that *is* what I said.'

My mind couldn't cope with this most astounding and horrible news. How could Molly be dead?

'But that's impossible.'

'According to the police, her brother identified her body.' This woman, who hadn't even introduced herself to me, reported this awful piece of news dispassionately. I felt distraught. I'd spoken to poor Molly only yesterday. Stifling waves of guilt crept over me. Already thoughts of 'if only I'd been able to meet her last night' weighed heavily on my mind.

'How did she die?'

'Apparently someone strangled her.'

I flinched in horror. 'Strangled? Oh no, that's horrible. I can't believe this. There must be some mistake.'

The woman stood up. 'I'm afraid there's no mistake. I suggest you contact the police or approach her family for further details.'

'Yes, thank you for your time.'

'Goodbye then.'

Now I understood why Molly had been on edge at work. *I would be too, if this Gestapo chief breathed down my neck.*

***

Molly O'Rourke was dead.

Morosely I sat facing a mug of lukewarm coffee. The news of Molly's death had shaken me more than I could've imagined.

The blonde waitress gave me a cold stare. I had been occupying the table for the past two hours.

I didn't care. All I could think about was Molly's murder. *How could this have happened?* This question reverberated in my mind repeatedly, like the beat of a broken record never getting off its track. *Poor Molly. If only I had made it to our rendezvous.* I blamed myself as if I was the one who squeezed the life out of the woman.

I paid for the coffee, wandered through the streets, and entered the three-storey steel and concrete headquarters of the Garda Siochana. Sean's office was on the second floor. Two knocks and I entered his office.

I found him in deep concentration, looking over some files. From his expression I could tell I'd surprised him.

'To what do I owe this pleasure?'

'I need to talk to you.'

'Take a seat.'

'Where was Molly O'Rourke's body found?'

Sean's eyebrows arched up. 'What's your connection to Molly O'Rourke?'

'That's not important. I want to know where her body was found.'

'I repeat, how do you know Molly O'Rourke?'

I knew I had to cooperate or he wouldn't give me any information, so I replied to his persistent question.

'I met Molly on one occasion at the Registrar of Births and Deaths when I conducted research on my family's genealogy.'

'Yes, I remember that day.' He was silent for a moment and

then he asked, 'How did you find out about Molly? Her death hasn't been announced publicly.'

'Her employer told me. I just came from there.'

'And of course you're going to tell me it was pure coincidence you were visiting Molly today.'

'That's right.'

'No, that's not right, Kathleen.' He walked to the window and had his back to me for a minute. Then he spun around, his face grim. 'Why don't you tell me the truth?'

'This has been a tremendous shock to me, Sean. I feel responsible for her death.'

'What do you mean? What aren't you telling me?'

I hesitated.

'Oh, please don't tell me it was Molly you were to meet last night!'

'Yes, it was.'

'But why?'

'Molly contacted me and begged me to meet her at 10 p.m. in front of my uncle's portico,' I answered. 'She was adamant she had information for me.'

'But why meet at your uncle's, particularly at that time of night? It just doesn't make sense.'

'Nothing makes sense. It's all a mess. Molly has paid a very high price for her knowledge, for her kindness, for her willingness to help.' I was trying hard to hold back tears of desperation.

Sean told me some early morning joggers had found Molly's body in a park not far from my uncle's estate. I could no longer control my emotions, and tears flowed freely down my cheeks as I wept quietly.

'Your information throws a new light on our investigation.' Fortunately he had his back to me again, arms folded, as he continued to stare out of the massive glass window. By the time he turned around, I'd managed to bring my emotions under control. Anger blazed in his deep dark eyes. All he said was, 'One of these days you're going to find yourself in the cold of a grave.'

***

Back in my room I sat crossed-legged on the cameo-rose carpet. I was upset. My face felt swollen and flushed as though a swarm of bees had stung me. Sean's words were hurtful and ominous.

The gentle breeze swayed the dainty lace curtain. A pleasant smell wafted into the room through the half-open window. It reminded me of the autumn harvest, although winter had truly set in. At this point, even the great gifts of nature couldn't alleviate my torment. I felt responsible for Molly's death. Molly would still be among the living had she not sought to help me. Someone had strangled her, murdered her, in cold-blood. Did she know her assailant or was this a random attack on a defenceless woman?

Then a thought struck me. *Molly's killer might be the same man who tried to strangle me. What's the connection? What is at my uncle's estate that the killer doesn't want me to see? It's obvious Molly knew something. The killer is convinced of that too.*

'I shall avenge Molly's death. Justice must be served,' I told myself as I got up from the floor to lie on the bed. I'd taken some tranquillisers, which were beginning to take effect, calming my nerves.

CHAPTER FOURTEEN

'Can you hear the song of the wind trapped in these haunted walls, cousin?'

'Watch where you're going, Donahl.' My tone sounded terse to my own ears. 'You need to have your wits about you in this place.

'You have to spend a lot of money to restore this house to its original splendour. That is, when you inherit it all.' Donahl wheezed as he spoke.

'Are you all right?'

'A bit of the old asthma, otherwise fit as a fiddle.'

'Glad to hear it. I don't cope well with emergencies.'

We reached the second floor and headed to the attic.

'I appreciate you coming with me,' I said. 'There aren't many people I trust in this town.'

'What exactly are we looking for?'

'Clues,' I said.

'Clues?'

'Molly O'Rourke had some information. It's something she wanted me to see.'

'So, we're playing detective so that we can come up with clues about the identity of her killer?'

'No, that's for the police. We're here to unravel secrets hidden within these walls.'

'What do you mean by secrets hidden within these walls?'

'Figuratively speaking, Donahl.'

I lifted the latch and we entered the cramped room. 'Have you been in this attic before?'

He shook his head. 'Not since I was a boy.'

I pointed to the Edwardian oak dressing chest. 'If you want to contact your dearly departed relatives, you can meet them face to face in that mirror.'

'Jaysus, you're spooking me cousin!'

I tried to lighten the atmosphere. 'Fine time to tell me ghosts unnerve you! Big, strong lad like you, it's unthinkable. I thought you were here to protect me.'

'Give me an earthly adversary and I'll fight till the death. But if my path crosses that of a spook or a hobgoblin, I drop my shillelagh and run.'

I crossed my hands over my chest. 'Such valour.'

We laughed, mainly as a distraction from the eerie surrounds.

Thirty minutes later, we came out empty-handed. 'There must be something here, something your great-grandfather left behind to solve this mystery,' I said. I felt hopeless and frustrated.

'Ah, the clue.'

'It's more than that Donahl. As members of the Kavanagh clan, we need to work together. We have to find a way to reverse this curse.'

'I was wondering whether Eliza and I would be exempt from this curse. After all, she's a Muldoon.' A frown formed on Donahl's forehead and his childlike face started to irritate me.

'That's no guarantee. I was thinking along the lines of Molly knowing something about this curse.' Then I asked him bluntly, 'What are your thoughts on werewolves?'

'Werewolves?' He almost screamed in my ear.

'Yes, werewolves. You know, half-human, half-wolf.'

'Jaysus, you're teasing me. Shame on you.'

'This is no joking matter, Donahl. I believe your future mother-in-law is a werewolf.'

'You're not serious! Mary Mother of Jaysus, this is too fantastic,' he paused and added, 'sorry to say this cousin, but I feel you need to have your pretty head examined.'

'I'm serious. Anyway, don't worry about that now. Just keep searching for evidence.'

'If you ask me you're looking for trouble.'

'Someone has to save this family.'

'But who will save you from the great Inspector?'

***

I shuffled my tired limbs in the dark. My mind felt like a temple in ruin, desecrated. The racing sound of my heartbeat was my only companion. Finally, the moonlight shimmered through the dense foliage of the trees. It brought with it a glimmer of hope for my battered body. A trickle of my salty tear mingled with the tiny blood that festered at the corner of my quivering lip. I whimpered. It shattered the balance of the night. I knew I would pay the price for my weakness. His dark eyes were unforgiving ...

The shrilling sound of a siren aroused me from the nightmare. The flannelette nightgown glued to my body, I flung the duvet off and bolted to the bathroom.

The warm shower calmed my nerves. I felt exhausted, but although it was 4:13 in the morning, I didn't want to go back to bed. The dream had disconcerted me but Donahl's comment that I should fear Sean bothered me even more.

I looked out the window. The flashes of lightning dominated the sky, thunder followed. No living thing would want to be out tonight.

Electrical storms always agitated me. Quickly getting back to bed, I hid under the sanctity of the luxurious duvet and waited for daybreak to restore calm.

I left the room at 8 and made my way into the great dining hall, where Miriam and two maids were laying the breakfast table. Eight places were set.

'Are there guests coming this morning?'

Miriam looked up, inviting conversation with a generous smile. 'Aye and we're to have a fine feast.' She came closer to me as though she was about to divulge a secret, 'I'm not one to gossip, mind ...'

'Excellent, Miriam, that's what I like to hear, loyalty and discretion from my number one staff member.'

Miriam blushed. 'I'd better check on the kippers.'

'Did you have to embarrass the poor woman?'

'Good morning to you too. And the answer is yes. I expect loyalty from my staff. I don't pay them to stand around, wasting time in idle chatter or gossip.'

'Why are you so defensive?

Sean threw his head back and laughed. 'You'd love to find some scandal about me, wouldn't you? Just to convince yourself that I'm some hideous creature bent on destroying you and your precious family.'

'Don't be ridiculous.'

'Am I being ridiculous?'

Deirdra interrupted our conversation when she entered the room.

'Happy Birthday, Gran.' Sean wrapped her frail body in his arms.

'Why thank you, my Sean. With a hug like that I wish everyday was my birthday.'

'I didn't know it was your birthday. Deirdra, I feel so bad about not having a present for you,' I said.

'My dear child, one of your beautiful smiles warms up my old bones, that's the only present I need from you,' said Deirdra sweetly. 'Come here and give me a hug.'

Aggie Muldoon Doherty's piercing voice shattered our embrace. I felt the oxygen being drained from the room.

'Happy Birthday, mother.'

'Oh hello dear, thank you,' the old woman faltered.

'I'd like to speak to you Sean.'

Like an obedient child, Sean followed his mother out of the dining hall. The rest of us fell into awkward silence. Mother and son returned five minutes later, both looking very serious.

The three remaining guests arrived; Donahl, Eliza and a third person I had not met. He was older, distinguished looking, with silvery white hair. They introduced him as Uncle Seamus. Later I found out he was not a relative but a close friend of the family.

A Lucullen-like table was set. There were delicate bite sizes of smoked mackerel and kippers on Irish bread, scrambled eggs married with smoked salmon, herbed sausages and a selection of farmhouse cheeses. The black and white pudding was a bit daunting at first, but I was pleasantly surprised at its flavour. We finished with scones, blackcurrant preserve and with numerous cups of tea.

The conversation was light enough, but there was an underlying tension. My agnate cousin kept me busy with his colourful escapades. As usual, Eliza contributed nothing and looked melancholic. Perhaps the hostility between Donahl and his future mother-in-law explained the young girl's misery. I didn't envy her.

Uncle Seamus was a subdued character. He seemed preoccupied with his breakfast and the only interaction he shared was the occasional glances he cast at Deirdra. He seemed very fond of her.

It was almost midday when we left the dining room for the adjoining parlour. I quickly sought the warmth of the fireplace. Uncle Seamus followed me.

'I've heard a great deal about you, my dear.'

'All good things, I hope.'

A frown formed on his lined forehead. He looked around the room as if studying the characters on play. His breathing seemed to quicken as he whispered, 'Your life is in great danger. He's not to be trusted.'

'What are you two colluding about?' Sean said as he approached us.

'I have to be on my way, the dogs need attending to.'

The old man went over to Deirdra, kissed her on both cheeks and left the room without acknowledging anyone else.

'Are you all right?' Sean asked. 'Did Uncle Seamus say something to upset you?'

'No,' the word came out louder than I'd intended. 'I feel a bit out of sorts today.'

'You seemed fine at breakfast.'

'Why the inquisition? I was fine at breakfast and now I don't feel well.'

'I'm concerned about you.'

'Well you don't need to be.' I moved away from him and went over to Donahl and Eliza.

Unable to find anything to say to anyone, I went to my room, making an excuse that I didn't feel well. The truth of the matter was I wanted to escape them all, particularly Sean and the cold stare of his mother.

***

'I've missed you yet again. You must be very busy. I'll try my luck later on. Love you lots.' I hung up the mobile phone.

I dialled more numbers but couldn't reach my parents either. My heart sank. I had to find Uncle Seamus. I felt he had the answers I needed.

The house was like an empty shell when I came downstairs in the early afternoon. The employees had the afternoon off.

Sean must have gone to work. I opened the front door and stepped outside, only to face Oscar and Bonnie, the overzealous Dobermans. Surprisingly, instead of attacking, they received me as though I was the leader of the pack.

The buzzing of a chain-saw broke the silence. For some reason the noise didn't agitate the dogs. Instead, they lay down and went to sleep.

The buzzing grew louder, enticing me. I trailed the intermittent sound. It was coming from the old barn, behind the stables.

I found the wooden door bolted from the outside. *Odd.* I could swear the noise came from within. The buzzing started again. I circled the barn but there was no other entry. I lifted the heavy bolt.

'Ouch!' A splinter from the dilapidated wood lodged deep into the middle finger of my right hand. I sucked the throbbing area.

The barn was dark and smelt damp. Moving forward cautiously, I could just make out shapes from the sunlight, which streamed through the doorway. After I'd taken a few steps, the door slammed shut. I heard someone secure the bolt from the outside.

Only a small amount of light peered in from underneath the door, just enough so that I wasn't in total darkness. I shook the door violently and called out for help.

I froze dead in my tracks when the buzzing of the chainsaw started up again. This time I knew it was in the barn. *Does this crazy madman intend to slice me into pieces? Is it the same person having another attempt at destroying me?*

The grating sound stopped. There was no movement.

Although it was dark, I knew there was no one else in the barn.

The chainsaw started up yet again, causing me to jump back. After a few seconds, it stopped.

This pattern continued every few minutes. I took courage and moved towards the direction of the loud noise. I tripped and confronted my tormentor.

It was some sort of a recorder intermittently playing the sound of a buzzing chainsaw.

Someone is obviously playing a practical joke. Or maybe they wanted to scare me witless.

I hurled the machine towards the wall. I'm sure I smashed the machine into smithereens.

I went back to the wooden door and began a barrage of screaming and banging to invite some attention. After two exhaustive hours, Dermot, the young hired hand, rescued me.

***

Two days had gone by since the incident in the barn. It greatly distressed Deirdra when she learnt about the episode. Her grandson, on the other hand, had no knowledge of my plight. He'd left on the afternoon of his grandmother's birthday for County Meath, on the trail of a bank robber. I had not been aware of this, as he had departed without saying goodbye.

I was still determined to track down Uncle Seamus. I had to find out what he knew.

The following day, after breakfast, when I was alone with Miriam, I asked her some questions. 'Is Uncle Seamus related to the Muldoon's?'

'Oh no, ma'am, Seamus O'Grady and Mr Alan Muldoon, Mr Sean's grandfather, a grand fellow, Bejasus, bless his soul, were best of mates. They fought in the war together, you know. Seamus saved Mr Muldoon's life, you know. A grand gentleman.' She shook her head, came closer, and said in a whisper, 'There's much evil here. Mind, this family is a cursed one. Poor Alan, that evening he looked so shook up, so deathly. Folks around here have their own ideas about what happened that evening. Mind, I'm not one to blarney.'

'My God, tell me more, Miriam.'

The housekeeper fluffed up like a plumed bird, her eyes wide with excitement. Suddenly, she went pale and said in a defeated voice. 'Ah, Mr Sean will not be happy if I tell. Your man doesn't like blarney. I'm sorry. I have to get back to the kitchen.' She scuttled out of the room.

I took a deep sigh. A headache was forming at the nape of my head. I jumped back when I heard Sean's powerful voice.

'What's this I hear about you being locked up in the barn?'

I had no choice but to tell him everything.

**

It was 6 in the morning when I opened my eyes. I thought of Josh Abbott. *I haven't seen or heard from him for quite a while. He must've gone back to England. Maybe he's given up on his grandiose idea to acquire my Uncle's estate.*

The wind howled furiously, encouraging me to seek shelter in my warm bed. This sense of security didn't last. A thought struck me. *I should look up Seamus O'Grady in the phone book.*

Tiptoeing downstairs, hoping not to be caught out, I felt like a naughty schoolgirl. It was so cold that I regretted leaving my inviting bed. The extremities of my body were like frozen icicles. With stiff fingers, I managed to take hold of the white pages out of the desk drawer. Shuffling the delicate pages forward, I finally reached the letter O. To my disappointment, there were fifteen entries for Seamus or S O'Grady. *Great. That's a lot for the Wexford area. Now what do I do?*

Dismayed, I crouched down when I noticed a slim-line address book snuggled between two books. *Surely, Uncle Seamus' address and number must be in here.* I recognised Deirdra's flowing cursive writing. *Eureka!* Fortunately Deirdra had written, his name, phone number and address in the O section.

I quickly scribbled down the information on a piece of paper I found on the desk, my heart pounding the whole time. Then I tiptoed back to my room.

After breakfast, I sneaked out of the house and headed for the beach.

'Good Mornin',' an elderly man greeted me as I went past an old thatched cottage. He sat on a log, cradling a beautiful tortoiseshell cat, chatting to the passers-by.

'Good morning. What a beautiful cat you have there.'

'That she is, a regular vixen! I only have her left. Me missus passed away last year.'

'I'm sorry to hear that. Animals are such a comfort to us humans. I have a cat too. It's a Moggy, very feisty and rules the roost.'

'To be sure, they're cunning creatures. They love to have their way. Like a woman, I say.'

I giggled. *You're a character, aren't you? You'd be able to tell a yarn or two.* I smiled and said, 'I wonder if you could help me.'

'Always happy to help a lovely doll such as yourself,' replied the old man. In his younger days, I imagined he would've had his way with the ladies.

'I'd appreciate that. Do you know how I would set about to Captain Seamus O'Grady's cottage?'

'Seamus O'Grady, that sly dog, always has luck with women.'

'Do you know Mr O'Grady?'

'Everyone knows Captain Seamus O'Grady. Mind, us poor folk don't mix with them society folks. But he's a good sort. Always shares a drink with me at O'Hanrahan's. Never married, but talk was he was sweet on his best friend's wife. Oh the mighty Muldoons. You know them?'

'A little.'

'Weird lot. Possessed by the devil, if you ask me.' He stood up, dropping the cat from his lap and came right up to me. 'Those folks can eat you alive. They come from a cursed line of werewolves. Old Leary, he's seen with his own eyes that Aggie Muldoon woman turn into a wolf.'

'Do you know about that?' My heart missed a beat. 'Can you

tell me anything about the curse on the Kavanagh clan?'

'Well ...'

Suddenly, all colour drained from his face. He stared past me, as though he had seen an alien being. 'Stay away from here,' he warned. 'Mind yourself, pretty one. God Bless.' He turned around and disappeared in his thatch-roofed, white-washed cottage.

I stood there bewildered. I knew I was close to the truth. I looked around. It was obvious to me something or someone the old man saw had terrified him.

Just as I'm about to get closer to the truth, something weird happens! The old man knows something, if only he would speak to me. But he seemed scared. I bet so many people in this town know the truth. If only they weren't so scared. But what are they scared of exactly?

It seemed an impossible feat to track someone down to direct me to Seamus O'Grady's house. I found the street deserted, as though people hid behind closed doors, too afraid to come out.

With reluctance, I moved on. The sea air was bitter. Standing on the rocky beach, I looked onto the rippled waters of the sea. I felt a twinge, like a feeling of longing. The Emerald Isles, the land of my ancestors held much spiritual connection to me. Tears formed in my eyes.

'Have you had a quarrel with your lover?' a familiar voice asked.

I turned my head and gazed into his passionate ocean blue eyes.

'Josh!'

'I've risen from the dead, so to speak.'

'It's so uncanny to find you here. Only this morning I was thinking of you.'

'Oh? I'm flattered.'

'I thought you'd gone back to England.'

'I did. We had an emergency in the office. My father needed my help. I only got back here yesterday.'

We walked in silence for a while.

'Are you sightseeing this morning?'

'No, I'm trying to find someone.'

'Who?'

'Someone called Seamus O'Grady. He's a friend of the Muldoons.'

'Captain Seamus O'Grady?'

'Yes, do you know him?'

'I've met him several times. In fact, I think someone pointed out where he lives.' He stopped walking and asked, 'Why do you want to see him?'

'He warned me that I was in danger.'

'What?'

I told Josh the events that had taken place on the day of Deirdra Muldoon's birthday.

'You must see Captain O'Grady. Now you believe me?' His smile slipped away. 'I know the way to his place, I'll take you there.'

It was a good 20-minute walk along the coastline. We arrived at a jagged cove. Perched on top of a treacherous cliff was a grey stone cottage.

'How do we get up there?' I asked perplexed.

'Here, it looks like this trail leads up to the house. But I must warn you, it's a bit of a brisk climb.'

'I dare say. It looks hazardous.'

We were both out of breath when we reached the top. I looked below and felt dizzy. The huge waves looked threatening as they splashed on the toothed rocks beneath.

It would be horrible to slip and go hurtling down. You would meet a violent death as though pierced by thousands of spears.

The wind was powerful, making my hair fly around unruly. Josh softly brushed a wispy lock off my face. Our eyes met briefly locked in timeless space. Then he moved aside, not looking at me.

The scenery, although breathtaking, had the mark of betrayal. The uninviting cottage, coupled with the haunting environment made me feel sad. I was convinced I'd been here before. With each step, I gained on my past.

Josh walked slightly ahead of me. He had a dark aura about him.

'Does Captain O'Grady live on his own?' I asked.

'Apparently.'

'Lonely existence up here.'

'Perhaps he enjoys solace. Sometimes it's good to be away from the plastic world below.'

'Perhaps.' Only Seamus O'Grady knew his own heart.

After ringing the bell and knocking on the door several times, we concluded the Captain wasn't at home. My heart sank. Each time I had a lead, an obstructive force worked against me.

We circled the cottage, just in case the Captain might be working outside. There was no sign of him. We were about to give up and begin the arduous descent when I heard a whimpering sound. 'What's that noise?'

'What noise?'

'Listen,' I said. 'I think it sounds like a distressed animal, a dog perhaps.'

'It must be the wind.' Josh pulled up the collar of his coat. 'It's fierce.'

'No,' I insisted. 'I can definitely hear an animal crying.' I grabbed Josh's sleeve. 'Come on.'

We investigated. The feeble whimper continued repeatedly. We followed the sound. Some 20 metres from the cottage, we found a dog lying under a stone wall, someone had freshly dug the ground underneath him. The rain had drenched the poor animal; mud and dirt covered its black and white fur. It looked painfully weak from exhaustion and it appeared to have sustained injuries, like knife wounds.

'Oh, my God, The poor thing. Do you think this is Captain O'Grady's dog?'

'I don't know,' Josh said, as he caressed the stressed animal. 'It's a Border Collie. Look, there's a collar around its neck.' We looked at the round silver charm dangling from the leather strap. It was engraved "Misty".

'What do we do now?' I asked.

'We have to get her to a vet. She must be in pain. I don't think she can hold out much longer.'

It amazed me how Josh had formed a close bond with the dog so quickly. It was as though he understood the animal's suffering. The dog, in turn, seemed calmer, trusting herself to him.

A side door to the cottage was open and we let ourselves in.

Josh carried the big dog in his arms and we went around to the kitchen. I found a blanket and Josh placed Misty on it, near the hearth. He lit the fireplace while I rang a vet.

'I'm going to ring Sean Muldoon, Josh. Maybe he knows where his uncle is.'

'Good idea. I have a bad feeling about all this.'

I dialled Sean's number.

CHAPTER FIFTEEN

Rain drizzled throughout the funeral of Captain Seamus O'Grady.

The sky was oppressively grey, complementing the mourners' bleak mood.

Five to six hundred mourners attended. It was obvious Seamus O'Grady was a much-respected man in the County.

I stood in the background, aimlessly watching the procession. Josh was beside me. The preacher's eulogy became a muffled sound under the dreary sky as my mind went back to that dreadful day.

Sean had come around Uncle Seamus' cottage as soon as I had phoned him. When I'd related the story to him, he had looked upset.

'Who was he warning you about?' he had asked.

'I don't know. That's why I came here, to find out some answers.'

Sean had called for some back-up and had begun a search. 'I got one of my men to talk to the villagers. No one has seen him since Sunday afternoon,' Sean had said to me as he paced the kitchen floor.

Members of the Garda Sochiana had found two other dogs belonging to the Captain by the edge of the cliff, bludgeoned to death.

Then it had become apparent Seamus O'Grady had met with foul play. After exhaustive searching, they had decided to dig up underneath the stone wall where we had found Misty. Each cutting strike of the shovel's blade had brought closer the inevitable truth.

In the soggy mud, they had unearthed the Captain's body. The killer had slit his throat from ear to ear. Beads of blood had marred his pale skin, as though he wore a ruby necklace. His handsome face had been void of colour, almost ashen. Someone had buried him crudely.

Josh gently nudged me under the arm bringing me back to reality. The burial was over and the attendants slowly moved away.

'Curse you,' hissed Aggie Muldoon Doherty as she went past me. 'Poor Seamus died because of you.'

The woman's brutal words jarred me. Sean, who was behind his mother, tried in vain to repair the damage her words had inflicted.

'Don't take any notice of my mother. She was very close to him. We're all in shock, but no one blames you.'

'Your mother does,' I said. Her words hurt me deeply. I too blamed myself.

Sean moved away to escort his mother and grandmother to the car.

I burst out crying. Josh circled his arms around me.

***

'You don't have to take this abuse from the Muldoons you know,' Josh tried to convince me as we sat for a well-deserved cup of coffee. 'I'll go over and collect your belongings. I'll get you a room at the B&B where I'm staying.'

'You're right, Josh. I can't stay there anymore. Deep down I'm sure they all blame me for the poor man's death.' I wiped away a salty tear trickling down my face. 'I'll never forget the immense pain I saw in Deirdra's eyes. Did you know that Seamus was her husband's best friend?'

'I didn't know the connection. I thought he was a relative.'

'He might as well have been. Oh poor man. How ghastly. But, why Josh? Who could've done this cowardly act, killing a defenceless man?'

'I wish I knew. Tell me something,' he took a sip of his coffee. 'You said on Deirdra's birthday, when you met Seamus for the first time, he warned you to stay away from him, I think you said something like, "He means you harm".'

'His exact words were "Your life is in great danger, he is not to be trusted". How can I forget those words?'

'Didn't you ask him to whom he was referring?' Josh asked as he bit into a cream cake.

'I didn't get a chance. Sean came over asking us what we were colluding about. Next thing Seamus faltered and said he had to go and attend to his dogs.'

'This isn't looking good for the mighty Inspector. I'm definitely not allowing you to go back there. You're not to spend one minute more under the Muldoons' roof.'

'Oh, come on Josh, we've no proof Sean is connected with his uncle's death. He loved that man, as though he was his own grandfather. I'm sorry but what you're implying is absurd.'

'Is it? Think about it. Why did the Captain falter when Sean asked what you two were talking about?'

'I don't know. I suppose you do have a good point there. Still, I really have no idea what's going on.'

'Anyhow, I'd still feel more comfortable when you're out of that mausoleum. Besides, this way you can come and go as you please. Come on, while the family is at the chapel hall, we'll go and pick up your stuff.'

I gave out a frustrated sigh. 'Perhaps you're right. I should move out. It's for the best.'

Josh raced his Jaguar as though he was participating in the Grand Prix and we arrived at the gates of the Muldoon estate in no time at all. Dale let us in as soon as he recognised me. I quickly ran upstairs to the bedroom I'd been sleeping in for several weeks and gathered my meagre belongings. I scribbled a note for Deirdra and left it with Dale.

Once outside the gates I drew in a deep breath, feeling relieved like a bird set free from a cage.

***

Mulligan's Inn was like the Rolls Royce of the B&B world. It was almost as grand as a castle, hardly a village Inn.

Josh had no trouble getting me a room overlooking the sea. The woman who owned the place looked at me with disdain.

She was middle-aged and looked as though she belonged in a vaudeville act with her burlesque appearance and vulgar mannerisms, a total contrast to the elegant surrounds. I suspected the woman viewed me as unnecessary competition and was keen on Josh.

Josh and I dined together, mostly in silence. It was hard to be cheerful after such a difficult day. Both of us made a concerted effort to stay clear of unpleasant conversation. It was well past midnight when I withdrew to my room and had time to reflect over the day's events.

Thank God, I'm away from the Muldoons, particularly Sean. At least I feel safe with Josh. He has my best interests at heart. I went to bed with that thought.

Just before sunrise, I awoke. I felt a gentle kiss brush past my lips. It was excruciatingly soft but incredibly sensual. I suddenly sat up in bed feeling dazed. *Was that a dream or is my imagination playing a trick on me yet again?*

Fear gripped me. I saw him in the large mirror facing me. With his spellbinding yellow eyes, he stared at me. I dared not move. Instead, I looked at him mesmerised. Tears clouded his eyes.

Is he crying? I blinked. He was gone.

I touched my lips, hoping the tenderness would remain. I felt much longing. It was ridiculous. I buried my face in the soft pillow and took comfort in a soulful cry.

***

'Call me back,' his voice commanded on my voice mail. It was one of the half a dozen messages Sean had left on my mobile.

I had no intention of calling him back. Without mentioning anything to Josh about Sean's persistent calls, I agreed to accompany my friend for a drive in the country.

At breakfast, Josh had convinced me that we both needed to be well away from Wexford. I was eager for a spontaneous outing. Josh cajoled Mrs Mulligan with his playful ways to get her to organise a picnic basket for us. We left down the windy road in his sleek sports car, abandoning all our troubles, at least for the day.

The air was crisp and sharp but fortuitously there was not one cloud in sight. I enjoyed the burst of fresh air on my face as Josh lowered the hood of the convertible. I smiled at the thought of how with the first ray of sunshine, Europeans tended to lap it up. Being an Australian I took excellent weather for granted.

We left busy Wexford and headed for the Midlands, known for being the cradle of Irish civilization and the spiritual home of the Celts.

Josh deposited a large map on my knees and instructed me to navigate.

'Why do you need me, when you have your GPS unit to guide you?' I asked.

'Do I detect a bit of rivalry between you and Courtney?'

'Courtney?'

'My faithful GPS, of course.'

'Pardon me Josh,' I chuckled. 'After all, Courtney and I haven't been formerly introduced.'

'Ms Kavanagh, meet Courtney. Courtney, this is Ms Kavanagh.'

'Oh very funny, Mr Abbott.'

'You know you are much prettier than Courtney and much more fascinating.'

'Really? But I'm sure not as efficient at navigating.'

'I'm sure if you put your mind to it, you can lead me on as well or even better than Courtney.'

His smile was cheeky.

'I've no such intentions. I suggest you turn Courtney on and we shall be on our merry way.'

'Ah, alas you break my heart. Now I shall have to content myself with Courtney's mechanical charms,' he teased as he switched on Courtney.

'Life wasn't meant to be easy.'

We laughed.

After a couple of hours of high-speed driving, we reached county Westmeath. The landscape looked untouched and yet so rural in outlook that it made me homesick. It reminded me of growing up in New South Wales, when with my parents I used to go on long drives in the countryside to escape the chaos of the Big Smoke, which is what we affectionately call Sydney.

As the sleek sports car sped, I read the sign welcoming incoming traffic to Mullingar. Josh informed me our first stop was at Belvedere House. He said after a long drive, it would be nice to take a stroll in the beautiful grounds.

We pulled up in front of a magnificent Palladian villa overlooking the Lough Ennel.

'Sure is nice to stretch.' Josh flexed his long arms. Bolstered by a black, Italian cut leather jacket, he looked incredibly sexy and I felt guilty for admiring him.

'What's up?' he said as he took my hand. 'You look lost in thought.'

I smiled, hoping he wouldn't be able to read my thoughts.

We walked around the beautiful gardens, admiring the local flora. The setting was very romantic, perfect for lovers out on a stroll.

'This is the Jealous Wall, a Gothic folly built by the Earl of Belvedere in 1755.'

'Why is it called the "Jealous Wall"?'

'The story goes the Earl of Belvedere suspected his wife of having a torrid affair with his own brother.' He stopped to look at me, his expression hard. 'To punish her for her crime, the Earl imprisoned her for thirty-one years in a neighbouring house.' Josh's face looked almost wild as he asked, 'A just end, don't you think?'

'Well, if this Earl's wife did have an affair, then she'd have to live with her own guilty conscience. But to imprison her for thirty-one years is cruel and a crime in itself.'

'So you condone her actions?'

'I neither condone nor pass judgment on her. We don't even know the real circumstances. Besides, I don't understand why you seem so worked up about it?'

He hesitated and made excuses he needed to look for the public conveniences, leaving me at the Jealous Wall.

A strong burst of wind brought a whisper. 'Charlotte, you are just like my mother – a whore.'

Cailean stood in one of the archways of the wall, hatred consuming his dark, brooding eyes. The sky and the wall facing me became one. Each second ticking away felt as though my body disintegrated in tiny particles, like sand in an hourglass.

'My God, what's the matter, Kathleen? You look as though you've just seen a ghost.'

***

I was still shaking when we arrived in Kinnegad, a little town west of Mullingar. Left behind in the car was the picnic basket. Instead, we lunched in silence at a picturesque little pub.

My mood was grim and Josh was too busy with his own thoughts.

'I'd planned to drive along the River Shannon to Clonmacnoise, to a medieval monastery. Are you up to it?' he asked.

'No,' I uttered, as I focused on the small vase that bore pale pink and freckled Hellebore's, which had almost wilted.

'Right, let's go then,' he muttered.

That was the end of what had begun as a pleasant day.

***

'Men! And they call us women fickle.' I paced the floor as I looked back on the day's unexpected events. I couldn't work out Josh's attitude towards me. Maybe he had misunderstood our platonic friendship. *Great, that's all I need.*

I rang the studio. I hadn't spoken to Dylan for over a week, although I'd left several messages for him to ring me back. I was missing him. I tried convincing myself he was probably busy organising his trip to the States. On this occasion, he answered the phone.

'Dylan, darling,' I said. 'I've been worried. You didn't get back to me. It's been so long since we talked.'

'I've been busy.' His tone was detached.

'That busy you couldn't find a few minutes to ring me?'

'There've been new developments. I've been offered a

contract in the States, and I've accepted it.

'What? What contract? How long for?' My heart pumped fast.

'Indefinitely.'

'And you did this without discussing it with me? What about us?' I couldn't believe what he was saying.

'What about us? It was your choice to stay on all this time in Ireland.'

'That's not fair. I'm here for our future. I must find a way to remove this curse from my family.'

'What utter rubbish! Bloody curse indeed. It's all in your head.'

'That's unkind. You know very well what this means to my family.'

'So you keep saying. Look, I need to go now. It's pointless discussing this matter further. You're determined, well I'm also determined to go and make a future for myself in the States.'

'Dylan, talk to me. Please, we need to see each other. You can't just go off to the US without us resolving things.'

'Resolving what? Murders and curses – the whole thing is nonsense. You're obsessed. Well, I'm sick and tired of it all.'

'We can work this out. Just come here for the weekend,' I pleaded with him.

With a sharp tone he said, 'You've no idea what I'm going through. All you care about is your precious family. I'm under a tremendous amount of pressure. Do you think my work's easy?'

'Dylan, please.'

'I can't handle all this. I need some time alone.'

'What? This is unbelievable! Four years. Didn't it mean anything to you?'

'Cut the emotional blackmail crap.'

'I'm not emotionally blackmailing you. You're talking about throwing away our life together.'

'Everything is always my fault, isn't it? Perfect Kathleen – she never does anything wrong.'

'Dylan, we love each other. We can make it work.'

'Well it's not working for me anymore.'

'Just like that?'

'Yeah, just like that. I have to go now.' He hung up.

I felt dizzy. I just made it to the bathroom and retched. My lips quivered. My whole body quivered. I went back to the bedroom. I sat on the bed. 'He's stressed. He doesn't know what he's saying.' I wanted to cry, to release the pain. But I couldn't. I didn't want to believe this was happening. It was like being in a car accident. Trauma. Shock. Denial. So I picked up the phone and dialled his number. It went to message bank. I couldn't speak. No words came to mind. I hung up. I couldn't believe he had switched his phone off. It was as though he had anticipated my next move. 'Perfect Kathleen', he'd said. His sarcasm hurt. 'Am I that predictable? That naïve?'

A sinking feeling came over me. I knew I'd never hear his voice again.

This was unbelievable. The love of my life, my soul-mate and best friend suddenly had turned against me. *Maybe there's another woman involved. No. Not Dylan. He wouldn't do that to me.*

Then the tears came.

***

As I opened my eyes, the incessant ringing exacerbated the thumping ache in my head. *Did I scoff down that whole bottle of hard whiskey? Maybe I did. I feel crap.* I remembered going to bed on an empty stomach. I started to cry again. *Why is this happening? Dylan I love you.*

The ringing didn't stop. My heartbeat accelerated. I thought it might be him wanting to tell me it was all a big misunderstanding and that he loved me.

It was my lawyer.

'So glad I've caught you, Ms Kavanagh. We are instructed to meet the Judge in his Chambers at 1300 hours.'

'But I'm not feeling well,' I complained. 'Why didn't you give me prior notice?'

'I just found out about it myself. I'm sorry but we cannot reschedule. I'll pick you up at midday. Let's have coffee together. I need to go over some points with you.'

'Very well,' I said.

***

True to his word, Mr Kildare arrived exactly at twelve. I was waiting for him downstairs, under Mrs Mulligan's watchful eye. The woman had an expression of a Cheshire cat plastered on her heavily made-up face. She was happy my appointment was not with Josh.

After a quick lunch and an earful of instructions from my lawyer, we made our way to the courthouse. Everything looked bleak. A storm was swelling. I trotted along with him trying to keep up with his quick steps. My hands were in my coat pockets, nervously swirling around the tissues I'd stuffed into them just before leaving my room.

We entered the Judge's Chambers at exactly 1300 hours.

My eyes zoomed in around the room, like some eagle diving down a cliff, scrutinising its prey. Quick count, I confirmed all six of my family members were present. Donahl winked; it was his way of reassuring me; on the battlefield he was in my camp. Miserable as I felt, I couldn't help but smile at him.

I hoped this was the last time I faced this gruelling situation.

Judge Malone greeted me cordially. The crimson bow tie, which strangled his neck emphasised his ruddy complexion. His golden-flecked eyes held a hint of mischief on his round face. I had the suspicion when he was a young lad Judge Malone would have loved playing practical jokes, just as my Pop did.

'So nice to see you again, Ms Kavanagh. Please, take a seat.'

'Thank you, your Honour.'

I felt awkward crossing the room. Their scorching scrutiny stung me. Unwelcome heat bloomed on my face until I nestled down in my seat.

'Bah,' snorted old Conan, the huddled-up hunchback, looking like a wicked warlock. His son, on the other hand, bore a crooked smile, which displayed his yellow, stained teeth. I guessed he was a heavy smoker. Each time I saw him, he spurted out a barking cough and wheezed heavily. Donahl was the only one in the family who didn't wish me dead. At the first opportunity, the rest of them would destroy me – of that I had no doubt.

'Ladies and gentleman,' began Judge Malone, 'I've asked you all here today, as after much deliberation, I've reached my decision.'

For about fifteen minutes the Judge spoke in a monotonous tone. He said he'd evaluated carefully all facets of this case and came to only one conclusion.

'In the eyes of the law I cannot find any reason not to follow Fionnbharr Kavanagh's wishes. I thereby pass the motion that Ms Kathleen Kavanagh is the sole heir of Fionnbharr Kavanagh's estate to deal with it in the manner she desires.' He took in a deep breath and added, 'Of course, that is, once she removes the Curse of Aggie Muldoon.'

A scream engulfed the room as old Conan Kavanagh collapsed to the floor.

CHAPTER SIXTEEN

Slowly I put the phone down.

'Kathleen?'

I drew in a deep breath.

'Kathleen, are you OK?'

I straightened. The knock on the door got louder. I let him in. He looked childlike, his baby blue eyes void of the anger they'd held a couple of days ago.

'I've been worried sick for you. Where have you been?'

'In court.'

'In court?'

'Yes, I spent yesterday in court.'

'This is about your uncle's estate, isn't it?'

'Um ...'

'So?'

'What?'

Josh's questions were irritating me.

'So what was the outcome? Did you inherit it all, or did you lose?'

He was so wan with anticipation that I thought he was quite ill.

'I got lock, stock and barrel. Satisfied?'

His mouth gaped open. He was silent for a few seconds, then he blurted out, 'Hey, that's great. Congratulations.'

'I doubt congratulations are in order.'

'Oh, don't be ridiculous, Kathleen! Why aren't you out celebrating?'

'What's there to celebrate?' The death of Conan Kavanagh?'

***

'It was awful, Dad.'

'My poor darling.'

'He just dropped dead, like a frail bird falling off its perch. Next thing he was on the floor, lifeless. As soon as Judge Malone proclaimed I was the sole heir that was the end of Uncle Conan.'

'My God!'

'I mean I didn't want any of this to happen, Dad. Damn the fortune and everything it entails. I feel I'm responsible for yet another death.'

'What nonsense! What do you mean, yet another death?'

'Oh nothing, I'm just upset.'

'Your mum and I are going to the Central Coast for a few days, and then as you know I'm having my hernia operation at the end of the month.' He stopped to clear his throat. 'But I'm just as happy to drop everything and be with you, my princess.'

'Oh dad,' I said, all choked up. My selfless father was always there for me, always ready to protect me.

'Really, my sweet, I can be on the next plane.'

'I wouldn't hear of it. Honestly, I'll be fine. Promise me you will take that holiday with mum. Please go and have a good time.'

My father heaved a sigh and said, 'What about Dylan? Can he get away for a few days to be with you?'

'It's OK dad, he's very busy at the moment. I'll be fine, don't worry.'

We spoke for a while longer and then I chatted with my mother. How could I tell them about Dylan? Yet another thing for them to worry about. My father would be on the next flight over and I couldn't have that under any circumstances.

I dialled the number for our apartment in London. A recorded message informed me the telecommunications company had disconnected the service. I rang Dylan's mobile, the same result. I was stunned. *This is worse than a nightmare. He didn't even say goodbye to me. Why has he reacted in this way? I appreciate it hasn't been easy for him. I've been away for a while, but I thought he understood the circumstances. It's the weekend, so it's pointless ringing the studio.*

A knot formed in my stomach. Had he already left for the

Nadia Kehoe

States?

***

"To worship money is to worship the devil", my father always says. How right he is! A good example is Uncle Conan, lying cold in the morgue. And for what?

I sat morosely at the edge of the pond in Mrs Mulligan's garden and rehashed everything that had happened in the past twenty-four hours.

The doctor had attended Conan Kavanagh and had pronounced the old man dead. Later, I found out he had suffered a massive coronary. The shock that he wasn't going to be a part of the inheritance had proven unbearable for him.

Is it my fault he's dead? What a mess!

I hadn't asked to be the heir of Uncle Fionnbharr's fortune. The sad part was I had intended to share the inheritance with them. Their voracious greed wouldn't allow that to happen now. I certainly didn't take comfort in the knowledge I was soon going to be an extremely wealthy woman.

The water looked dark and murky, almost black. I flung a pebble into it, thinking this action might diminish my frustration. It didn't make any difference. I still felt miserable. I watched the pebble disappear as though an evil force sucked it down.

Feeling jaded, I moved down the garden path. I had only taken a few steps when I felt a presence behind me. Stopping dead in my tracks, I hesitated and then suddenly I turned around, to find Sean Muldoon approaching me.

'How did you know where to find me?'

'I make it my business to know everything.'

This repetitive statement ignited some hidden emotion within me. Jabs of shooting pain travelled through my head. I was in no mood for a confrontation. I was tired, the pain in my head started to intensify rapidly, as though it was a small ball of ice building up to an avalanche. I simply couldn't bring myself to have a conversation with him. Without saying a word, I sprinted in the opposite direction.

'Where do you think you are running off to now?'

I didn't care where I ran as long as I was far away from him. Scramming inside, I scuttled straight to my room.

'The nerve of that man, constantly hounding me! You'd think he would've got the message loud and clear by now, considering I haven't responded to his dozen messages.' I said aloud in a huff.

I felt nervous and vulnerable. Lies and deceit surrounded me. I could neither trust nor depend on anyone. Not even my own partner had stood by me.

I hardly slept that night. My body ached for Dylan. I wanted desperately to feel secure in his strong arms, to lose myself in him. I tossed and turned as though I was trapped inside a runaway train. I couldn't relinquish the memory of his burning kisses nor his sensuous lovemaking. Now it was all gone. I lay alone, in a cold double bed, only with the contemplation of my brusque altered future.

What a twist of fate! Things can't be worse than they are. When morning approached, an inspiration hit me. I had to work quickly to reverse the curse. Only then, might I still have a chance to win back Dylan. This would be the driving force to charge ahead. Once again the answers lay in my uncle's haunted house.

***

My tenacity impressed me. I wanted to confront Cailean today. This newfound determination was definitely a challenge, one I desperately wanted to conquer.

'Why do I fear him anyway? After all, he's just an apparition. He can't harm me,' I said out aloud after closing the door of the taxi, which sped away.

No one wanted to be near this forbidding place. I struggled with my umbrella. Any minute, the gust of the wind would sweep me away like Mary Poppins. I giggled at this silly image.

The storm raged, the dried leaves swirled around as though they were caught up in a tornado. The day's bleakness reminded me of Cailean's rage, his dark menacing look just as wild and uncontrollable as the tempest outside.

As soon as I stepped in the house from the back porch, I knew he was there. I could feel his presence watching my every move. I felt like a defenceless animal; any moment the beast would pounce on me. I wrinkled my nose at the distinct raw odour only a wild animal could produce. The crack of thunder swayed me back. That was when I heard a child sobbing. The sound came from behind the closed door. Do I dare open it? I asked myself.

The grandfather clock down the hall struck five times. I dropped my flashlight.

You're playing tricks on me, Cailean, winding up that clock. You want to tease me, entice me. You know what? I'm not going to give you the satisfaction of bolting out of here like a coward.

I stayed. Fearless. Determined. A woman very much in control. No ghost would stop me from solving this mystery.

Uncle Fionnbharr was onto something. People in this town gossip about my uncle. They claim the devil possessed him, and that he was involved in witchcraft. To be sure, he was an eccentric person, but people misunderstood him. Finding the truth was his only mission.

I turned the handle and opened the door. I flashed the torchlight around. The small room was empty. I half expected to find the young girl crouched on the floor, sobbing her heart away.

I walked around the room.

'Charlotte,' the voice moaned. 'Come here.' He sounded fiercer. 'You've been a bad girl, Charlotte. I have no choice but to punish you.'

I ran out of the room and stood in the corridor trying to catch my breath. *I'm imagining all this. I have to stay calm.*

The storm raged outside as though in battle with the forces of darkness and light. Just like the battle, I faced with the forces of good and evil.

The secrets lay in this great big house. Dark secrets. Hidden secrets. I had to find them at all costs.

I thought of Molly. *What was it Molly had seen and wanted*

me to find out? It was obviously something important. Crucial. A secret that got her killed. On that score, I'll never know. Who was this Charlotte? The only clue I have is her portrait. And in that she resembles me, as though I'd posed for the artist. The face, the eyes, the expression – her likeness to me is uncanny. Who was this woman in relation to the family but, more importantly, to Cailean? Was she a blood relative? That could explain why I look like her. Maybe I have to go back to the attic where I'd found grandfather Cormac's love letters to his wife. That tiny room has to hold answers for me.

Even though it was cold and damp, waves of fear rippled through my body. My face felt excruciatingly hot, as though the delicate skin was about to disintegrate from the intensity of heat. The fine blonde hairs on my arms stood upright, like the prickles of cactus plants jutting out in the hot desert sand. I wanted to imagine soaking in a cool stream but the damned inferno would not allow such thoughts.

'Am I experiencing hot flushes?' I murmured under my breath. Alarm bells rang. *Menopause. Change of life. Don't be ridiculous, I'm too young! Hadn't I read somewhere the sad phenomenon of the 21st-century woman undergoing the change of life as early as in her thirties? That's what happens when you're living in the fast lane. Fast pace. Fast cars. Fast foods. Fast careers. Fast sex.*

The words "fast, fast, fast" spun around in my head. My chest felt tight. *What if it's too late for me to have a baby? I want so desperately to be a mother. To have Dylan's babies. Dylan. My Dylan. He relishes, thrives on living in the fast lane. He is truly a product of the modern world. He goes about his daily life like a robot. Fast and incredibly efficient. If things don't match up with his pace he becomes frustrated, impatient, difficult to live with. Why am I even thinking of him after the way he has been treating me?* So I shut down the fast thoughts at the press of an imaginary button.

The ancient stairs croaked as I slipped upstairs. I had become confident roaming about only with a flashlight in hand.

I entered the attic. Heading straight to the boxes, I rummaged through them like a cat on a mission. At the bottom of one of them, I found a small lacquered box with an arched lid. Sprinkled on it was a wad of dust. An ornate clasp secured the lid shut. There was no key in sight. *Why does everything always have to be complicated?*

I looked around to find an implement to open the box. I came across a rusted screwdriver lodged among equally rusted nails in another box. *This is pure luck – obviously, someone up there likes me.*

It took a while but finally I forced the lock open.

Someone had packed the box with knickknacks: a black feather, a cameo brooch, an ice pick, a lock of hair. I went back to the ice pick. *Strange item to put in a keepsake box! I wonder what the story is there.* A gilded fountain pen bearing the Kavanagh crest and a gold ring with a beautiful blood red stone, perhaps a ruby were the next items I came across. My heart gave a flutter when I discovered a tattered notebook at the bottom of the box. *Can this be a diary? I hope so, it might help me out.*

To my delight, it was exactly that. *What beautiful, flowery writing, I'm sure it's a woman's handwriting.* With great care, I flicked through the delicate pages. The following was an amazing excerpt:

> *My heart is heavily burdened. Life has become a living hell. What am I to do? I know not but only ask the Almighty for mercy. Hatred has consumed him, he knows neither day nor night. Like a restless beast, he is triumphant in his treachery. I am so afraid. I saw him again yesternight, as I stood by my window looking out. He was naked, under the full moon. What he did next was the most abhorrent of sights. He hunted with his bare hands a fragile fawn that had wandered into our grounds. He drank its blood. When his thirst was satisfied, he gave the most chilling of howls and disappeared into the woods. Lord help us, I can no longer fight this evil.*

My hands trembled as I quickly turned the page. It contained only a few lines.

> *The end is near. I am so tired of his games. He*

denounced me by calling me a whore! His own mother! I believe he has no soul and that he is indeed mad.

These crumpled pages were from a personal journal kept by my great-grandmother. Her own son had terrified her. There was no doubt in my mind, my great-grandmother was referring to Cailean.

I wasn't able to read any more. Thumping footsteps fast approached the attic. Instinctively, I grabbed the ice pick and put the journal down on the floor. Turning my flashlight off, I hid behind a stack of boxes.

Footsteps echoed in the vast, uninhabited mansion. Then silence pervaded. I knew he was at the door; he was slowly tormenting me.

I clutched onto the ice pick so firmly my fingers ached. The sinews on the skin of my hands felt so prominent, bulging out as though they were about to tear.

Would I be able to plunge this sharp instrument into the person who was out to harm me? Such a drastic act! I decided I would in order to save my life. Self-defence. The thought sickened me. *What if it's Cailean? How will I fight an apparition?*

The door creaked. I closed my eyes. My auditory senses were sharper than usual. It was as though I could hear the perfect rhythm of my tormentor's heartbeat. He was in control and he enjoyed that fact. He came closer to the boxes and knelt down for a few seconds. He muttered something under his breath. He terrified me. Nausea took a strong hold in my abdomen. A few more seconds, and I was sure he would discover me.

He retreated and left the room, shuffling his feet like an old man would. The door closed and the footsteps diminished, leaving a distant echo in my petrified mind.

How can this be Cailean? Whoever was in here was very much flesh and blood.

Relief took over the fear. I was safe.

I didn't dare to move and stayed in this uncomfortable position, crouched on the floor until the bright light obliterated the blackness of the night. The crimson sun dominated the morning sky as the moon faded to return later to its nightly ritual.

The base of my neck throbbed with pain. At the same time, cowering like some terrified animal for hours had frozen my shoulder. With great effort, I got up from the floor. I felt like an old woman suffering from osteoporosis.

The small box lay where I'd left it. Bending down I searched for my great-grandmother's diary. I became frantic in my search as I realised slowly that it wasn't there. *I can't believe this, they've taken it! Why? Those fragile pages would've shed some light into this whole mystery. Who would want my great-grandmother's diary? I should've kept it with me.* There was so much material to go through in this attic alone that I gave up in exhaustion. I had no energy left after the weird happenings during the night.

Once I was outside the gates of the haunted house that was soon to be mine, I sighed with relief.

***

When I entered the hotel lobby, Mrs Mulligan motioned to me and told me I had a visitor. She informed me with her usual air of disdain a man was waiting for me in the adjacent lounge area. Although, I wasn't up to seeing anyone curiosity got the better of me and I redirected my steps to the lounge too see who it was.

As I turned the corner, my curiosity turned to irritation. Sean Muldoon stood near the fireplace, impatiently tapping his fingers on the mantle-piece. He seemed deep in thought. I wanted to escape unnoticed. But before I could act, he looked my way.

'Damn it woman, where the hell have you been?' he barked.

'Pardon me Inspector, what business is it of yours?'

His dark eyes intimidated me. They narrowed menacingly. 'Your welfare is my business.'

'Oh please.' I rolled my eyes.

'For someone as intelligent as you, sometimes you act very recklessly – almost like a moron really.'

'If you can't be civil Inspector, we have nothing to say to one another,' I started to retreat.

'Kathleen,' he grabbed my arm. 'Look, I apologise for my outburst, but we need to talk.'

'Let's see, what shall be the topic of our discussion?' Placing my index finger on my chin, I pondered theatrically, 'I know, the plight of the Efe pygmies in the forests of Congo dying of sexually transmitted diseases and other illnesses from the outside world. Perhaps, we can debate the dramatic effects of Niñò on the Galápagos, or wait, better still, the near extinction of sturgeon fish in the Caspian Sea.'

Josh walked into the room. A timely visit, I thought with great satisfaction. Sean stormed out.

'What did he want?'

'I'm not sure, Josh. Whatever it was, I'll never get to hear it. I'm glad he's gone.'

'How about coffee then?' He locked his arm around mine.

'Just what the doctor ordered,' I replied as we left the reception area arm in arm, under the perennial disdainful gaze of the vaudeville vamp.

***

As we sat enjoying the strong aromatic coffee, Josh entertained me with stories of his neurotic clients.

'Why don't you write a book on your experiences?' I suggested. 'Highly entertaining, might even become a bestseller, with any luck.'

'Nah, too much hard work. Besides there's no real money in it, considering all the effort that has to go into it,' he complained. 'I should've been a psychologist at least that pays better.'

We laughed. Josh always seemed to be there for me at the right time, bringing me welcome relief. 'By the way, where were you last night?' he asked, abruptly changing the subject.

'Resting.'

'Liar!'

'Do I have to account to everyone in this town? My actions are my own business. In any case, what makes you think I wasn't in last night?'

'I came by your room, it was obvious you weren't here.' His relaxed stance changed to a tense mode. 'Besides Darla said that she'd seen you leave the hotel and not return.'

'Darla, is it? On first name basis, are we?'

'Jealous, are we?'

'Just curious.'

'Um ...'

The pain in my shoulder brought back memories of the previous night. 'I need to get back to my room. I'm really tired.'

'You're not going to be let off so easily.'

'Is that right?'

'I won't let you leave this table without an explanation.'

Widening my eyes, feigning all innocence, I repeated his question, 'An explanation?'

'Absolutely. You have to tell me where you spent the night.'

'A lady never tells.'

A cloud came over his face. All his cheerfulness vanished. In fact, he reddened until his face became the colour of a tomato.

What is this all about? The fool must think I spent the night with Sean. If only he knew the truth. Let him simmer, he shouldn't pass judgement without knowing the facts. I wasn't going to give him the satisfaction of knowing what I was really up to. 'Well, thanks for the coffee and the chat, I enjoyed myself. See you around,' I said evasively and left.

I had so much on my mind. I wasn't in the mood for games.

Just as I thought things couldn't get worse, it did. As I headed to my room, Mrs Mulligan handed me a letter. It was from Dylan. I couldn't wait to get to the privacy of my room. I tore it open and began reading. Stifling a yelp, I scrambled upstairs and didn't venture out of No 5 for two whole days.

***

Outside the wrought iron gates, mothers loitered about waiting for the bell to announce the end of the school day for their children. In a few minutes, a torrent of energetic little folk would spill onto the pavement from opposite where I sat looking on morosely. A simple daily ritual for these mothers, something they probably didn't even think twice about. I felt a twinge of pain, for I would never experience what these people took for granted. It seemed I wasn't destined to have children.

In a matter of a few months, my world had changed drastically. It would never be the same again. My partner had left me, probably for good. My dreams and aspirations for a future with Dylan had vanished overnight. The whole situation seemed so bleak, I could hardly bear to go on. I clutched the aerogramme. *That's all he's sent me – an aerogramme! I didn't even know that they were still in use. That's how much he values me!* Bold letters stood out. The harsh stark words. Unfeeling. Threatening. It felt as though someone had plunged a dagger through my heart. Indescribable pain. Nothing made sense.

In a few brief lines, Dylan stated clearly that he wanted to end our relationship. No explanation, just a simple desire to explore a new life for himself – a life well away from me.

His only request was I wouldn't try to contact him. *How can I anyway? I don't even know how or where to reach you.*

I felt betrayed. The intense passion, the trust, the friendship, – had it all been a lie? I stared into space, numb from the pain. Suddenly a hand on my shoulder brought me back to the present.

'Please don't run away.'

Looking up, I felt the tears covering my face.

'Please leave me alone.'

Sean Muldoon was the last person I wanted around in my darkest hour.

'Sorry, no can do.'

I began to cry. He took me in his arms. For a short while, I felt protected. When he released me, the vulnerability returned. I felt fragile, about to shatter like delicate crystal.

He handed me a clean handkerchief and I mopped up the tears. Doused in freshly washed soap, the crispy cotton fibres reminded me of the washing powder my mother used. More tears, I desperately needed my mother; she always knew how to comfort me.

'Talk to me, I want to help.'

'I can't,' I said. My feeling of helplessness exasperated me. 'Look, I appreciate your concern but I just can't talk about it.'

'Why?'

'Sean, it's too personal.'

'Your tears, do they have something to do with the piece of paper you're holding? Is it a letter?'

I nodded sheepishly.

'Is it from your family? Some bad news?'

Typical policeman! He just couldn't help persisting with his irritating questions.

'I said I don't want to talk about it.' I blew my nose.

'Please, calm down.' His arm was around my shoulder. I was acutely aware of his raw masculinity. His strength was like a magnetic force. Deep down, I was even glad of his intrusion on my reality – a blessing in disguise to force me to go on.

***

He changed into first gear as he slowly merged into the heavy traffic on the highway. Each car methodically followed the other. No one dared to make a wrong move. No one wished to tilt the balance of conformity. The formality of the procession reminded me of driving in a funeral cortège. Sean, like everyone else, held that cooperative spirit.

Why can't someone have the courage to blow their horn, or make a gesture to show their impatience? The middle-aged man in the next car scratched his stubble. I watched his long fingers grimly indenting his face. That simple gesture shifted the harmonious balance. *Is this the way I'm going to vent my frustrations by being angry at the world?*

I was a stickler for rules, so why change now? It was simple. Cruel fate had slapped me in the face. I would never be the same naïve, trusting person. *I should've learnt my lesson after Jimmy.*

'You're hurting, aren't you?'

He had no right to be in my thoughts.

'Kathleen, I do care.'

I watched a small black bird dive. We almost hit it. *Maybe it wants to die. It might be tired of the endless struggle to survive in a difficult world. What's the point of its short life anyway? Stop it, Kathleen.* I heard my grandfather's voice from within. *Stop this self-pity. This pain shall pass too.*

Tears flowed from my tired eyes. My eyelids felt like they weighed a ton of cement, all swollen and gritty. I had to stop, stop this mindless self-destruction. I must get out of this negative mindset. Maybe I should allow Sean Muldoon to help me. What were the alternatives?

When he pulled up near a park, I retrieved Dylan's letter from my bag and handed it to him.

Now he would understand my heart.

***

'So wonderful to see you child,' Deirdra said. She was fragile and bedridden. Sean told me she had been ill since Uncle Seamus' death. I felt guilty I'd neglected her. Was that the way I repaid people's kindness these days?

'I'm sorry I wasn't there for you at this difficult time.'

'You have your own life to lead, I understand, my child,' she replied, inhaling with difficulty. She looked grey. I suspected everything was all an effort for her now. I held Deirdra's hand, which was cold to the touch. Even the little sparkle, I'd seen in her eyes not so long ago, seemed to have become extinguished.

A lump formed in my throat and I fought back tears. I understood the woman's pain. I too knew what it was to love so deeply – that unselfish love, so pure and untouchable and yet once taken would never return.

'Promise me something,' she whispered. 'Have faith my child. Do not judge him harshly. Believe in him, true love only comes once.'

She closed her eyes. Deirdra's words moved me so much that I felt tears forming in my eyes. I tried desperately not to cry so as not to upset the lovely lady lying in front of me.

'Who should I not judge harshly?' I managed to ask.

Alas, I didn't get a chance to find out as sweet, gentle Deirdra never opened her eyes again.

'My Angel sleeps peacefully now,' Sean whispered as he knelt by the bed and kissed his grandmother's lifeless hand.

CHAPTER SEVENTEEN

'You've had a rough week. You need to eat something.'

'I'm not hungry.' I dismissed any notion of food. Josh had brought some Thai take-away. He arranged paper plates on the small coffee table.

'Yum. This quail with fresh chilli and basil smells heavenly,' he said as he licked his fingers. 'I also got some water chestnut salad with fillet of pork, a green beef curry, and deep-fried tofu with peanut sauce.'

I continued to look out the window. The sun had mellowed. I wasn't looking forward to the night approaching. Since Deirdra's funeral, nightmares tortured me during the short bouts of sleep that I managed to catch.

Death surrounded me. I was a mess, both on a physical and an emotional level. Food was the last thing on my mind. Even the smell of it made me feel sick.

The phone rang. Josh picked it up. The caller hung up.

'What's their problem?' He shrugged and continued laying out the food. 'Come sit down, before it gets cold.'

'I'm not hungry,' I said again.

'I'll force something down your throat if you refuse to eat of your own accord.'

'Oh, all right.' I felt defeated and held out my hand. He passed a paper plate to me.

We ate in silence. Well Josh ate, rather voraciously, like a hungry animal. I, on the other hand, masticated a combination of bits and pieces, a formality to satisfy Josh so he would leave me alone. There was no pleasure in the ritual as everything tasted insipid to my dulled taste-buds.

'No wine?'

'No, thanks.'

'Pity to waste such a vintage, and it was a good year too.'

'So what was so grand about that particular year?'

'I discovered Ireland.'

'I see. A step closer to your past?'

'Small steps but soon it will be a huge leap.'

I hoped for his sake he would soon find what he was searching.

***

There was no peace in my heart. I sat looking at the tranquil ocean. The water's calm surface was a mere illusion, concealing its true violent nature.

Without warning, it would unleash such fury that it would destroy everything in its path. My own life felt like the ocean; on the surface I appeared calm but within I was ready to explode.

It shouldn't have ended like this. Dylan, why did you do this to us?

Not all is as hopeless as it seems. I could swear it was Deirdra talking. Jumping up, I looked around me, hoping to see the dear lady's kind face again. *I'm losing my mind.*

As I walked, a smile crept up my lips. Not all was hopeless. I was determined to regain my fighting spirit and get on with my life.

'No, definitely not all is hopeless.'

***

They were laughing like a pair of hyenas when I entered Mulligan's Inn. Donahl, draped on the counter, flirted with the fifty something Mrs Mulligan. They were engrossed in lascivious conversation. The word "cheap" sprang to mind.

I went up to collect my keys.

'Why cousin, finally, here you are. I've been waitin' since mid mornin'.' He smiled, beaming with his usual confidence. 'This fine lady has been keepin' me company.'

'I'm sure she has.'

Mrs Mulligan handed over the keys, disdainful as ever. The woman's abundant breasts spilled out of her tight shirt.

'Wait,' Mrs Mulligan spoke gruffly and handed over an envelope.

I took the envelope from her hands. My heart raced. Could the letter be from Dylan? Disappointment spread through my body as I read the return address. It was from my solicitor. I shoved it in my shoulder bag.

'I came to invite you out to tea,' Donahl said as he waved goodbye to Mrs Mulligan.

I welcomed the diversion. We walked out of the lobby arm in arm. I could feel Mrs Mulligan's malevolent stare lingering well after we left the inn.

Thirty minutes later, Donahl and I were huddled in a nearby pub to catch up on each other's news. I'd seen him briefly at Deirdra's funeral but he had been too busy comforting Eliza to take much notice of me.

'They're all dropping off like moths around us,' Donahl commented.

'How's Eliza coping?' I asked. 'I know she was very close to her grandmother.'

Donahl shrugged. 'Not too good, she's been in a bit of a mood.'

'That's understandable.'

'Yeah, I guess. But she's lucky I've infinite patience.'

His self-righteous words made me feel sorry for Eliza.

The noise level increased gradually as more and more people poured into the pub. Donahl sat there assessing the crowd. I studied the changing expressions on my cousin's face.

It was a long time before our food arrived. When it did, the dishes were both inventive and skilfully prepared from local produce. I realised it had been a while since I'd taken interest in food or, for that matter, anything around me. This was a small step to regaining my old self.

'You look down, Kathleen, what's botherin' you?'

I needed to open up to someone. Maybe it would be good to have a male opinion. I decided to tell him my troubles. 'So I still don't know what prompted my boyfriend to come to this decision.'

'Yeah, it's amazing. A girl like you – he must be out of his mind.' He shook his head as he looked down at the glass of beer in front of him and said, 'After everything you've told me, I can only conclude ...'

'What?' His pause had unsettled me.

'No, nothing, just forget it.'

'Forget what? You can't start saying something and then leave me in suspense!'

'Seriously, don't worry about it.'

'I'm not leaving here until I hear what you were going to say.'

'OK. I think your man has met another woman.'

'Oh please, Donahl.' I rolled my eyes. Typical. He didn't know anything about Dylan.

'You wanted my opinion.'

'And I'm telling you that you're dead wrong.'

'I hope for your sake you're right.'

***

My outing with Donahl set me back. My cousin's conviction there was another woman in Dylan's life played heavily on my mind. I sat on my bed and talked aloud, 'As they say, jealousy is a curse. What happened to good old fashioned trust? Is there some truth in what Donahl said about another woman in Dylan's life? How can I find out the truth? Dylan hasn't even bothered to let me know where he is. I have to come to terms my relationship is over. What's the point of pursuing a man who doesn't want me? It's clear he no longer has feelings for me.'

***

In the centre of the medieval town, the city archives' building stood in a prominent position. It was an imposing structure almost stoic in terms of its severe architecture. A late Victorian building, it was sombre in design but well suited to its purpose.

Displayed in the manuscript repository were neat rows of archived documents. They aligned methodically as though they were part of a military regiment. There was not a speck of dust or a slight disarrangement in any corner of the room.

It took some doing, but I managed to convince the overzealous young lad, Tomas, who was filling in for Mr Brogan, to let me gain access to the archival 'repository'.

On two other occasions, Mr Brogan had flatly refused to let me see any of the archived papers. The obdurate manager was a stickler for rules and he objected to my passionate pleas to provide me with documents dealing with the Muldoons' background history.

He claimed the papers were not for public knowledge and I would be breaking privacy laws. Even though I demonstrated I'd done my homework and was aware of the changes introduced since in the late 20th-century to Irish freedom of information laws allowing inspection by the public of private records.

Mr Brogan had continued flatly and unreasonably to refuse my requests. I became convinced this implacable man was on the Muldoons' payroll.

Half an hour later on the third floor of the archival 'library', I leafed through the Muldoon family's records, which went as far back as the 17th century. The information in front of me was so amazing I squealed in delight. Four sets of uninspired eyes scorned my happy mood. No wonder people often compare libraries to mortuaries.

The first set of papers I went through were preserved manuscripts of the early-recorded history of the family. The following were some excerpts in note form:

> *1689 – Eamon Oistan Muldoon, son of Diarmaid and Philomena Muldoon. At age 16, while on a hunt for game a pack of wolves viciously attacked him. Eamon survived the ordeal, although he sustained severe injuries and for many years, he battled bouts of depression. He married a local girl "Mella" from the O'Rourke clan. They produced five children. In 1720, the law sent Eamon to the gallows for murdering his wife of twelve years. The senseless crime was so serious in nature the Judge passed an*

immediate sentence. They certified him insane and hung him. The record showed Eamon had mutilated his wife's face to such an extent that she was almost unrecognisable. On a full moonlit night, in a moment of unprovoked rage, Eamon had perpetrated this vile deed.

I could scarcely believe what I read. Not just the abhorrence of the crime shocked me, but that Eamon had married an O'Rourke. Was it possible the murdered woman, Mella, came from our bloodline of O'Rourkes? I continued reading.

1745 – Breanain Uilfrid Muldoon, eldest son of Eamon and Mella Muldoon followed the same path as his father. Even as a toddler, the boy showed uncontrollable fits of rage. A peculiar desire for the hunt was apparent from young adulthood. Townsfolk gossiped on many occasions, saying Breanain often devoured deer and other game in the forest without cooking their meat. He had also married. His wife came from Gallway. Her name had been Blinne. They in turn had borne five children. Just like his father, Breanain viciously attacked and mauled his wife to pieces. They hanged him too.

History repeating itself.

1768 – Gilibeirt Muldoon, the eldest son of Breanain and Blinne Muldoon, went on a drunken rampage. Whilst drinking with two of his friends, he turned on them and like a wild beast mauled them to death. Thirty-two people in the drinking hall witnessed the attack. They hung Gilibeirt. His wife Richail and their three children survived him.

1798 – Ailfrid Cathbharr Muldoon, the eldest son of Gilibeirt and Richail Muldoon, joined the society of United Irishmen organised by Theobold Wolfe Tone, the brainchild of the Rebellion of 1798. As the peasantry took up arms in Wexford, Ailfrid was among the willing to fight for the cause. He died two weeks later – not honourably, as one would expect for the emancipation of suffering. Ailfrid Cathbharr's mates killed him. During the night before the battle at Vinegar Hill, in Enniscorthy, Co. Wexford, was to begin, Ailfrid shape-shifted into a wolf-like creature and turned on his fellow fighters. In a mad frenzy, he shred to pieces four hapless men. His co-rebels immediately surrounded the creature and hacked him to death with their implements. Ailfrid left behind a young wife and two baby twin daughters, Caitilin and Aggie.

My eyes immediately became transfixed on the page. My total focus was on that name. AGGIE. Aggie Muldoon, the mother of the gangly young man who'd captured the heart of my great-grandmother, Honora O'Rourke. Generations of Kavanaghs loathed and feared this same Aggie Muldoon.

This was the bloody history of my family's nemesis.

'Who gave you the right to go through my family's records?'

Sean's authoritative voice startled me and I jumped back, almost knocking the chair over. The pieces of paper fell to the floor, surrounding me in such a way that I imagined myself in a bridal gown. He stood over me. His breathing shallow, his dark piercing eyes more pronounced than ever.

CHAPTER EIGHTEEN

'Lycanthrope – half-man, half-wolf' is how the dictionary defined this term. I had to find out more about werewolves. I decided the Internet would be a good place to start.

To escape from my personal problems I immersed myself into researching this lycanthropic phenomenon. Even though the breakdown of my relationship was weighing heavily on my mind, this new diversion lessened the blow.

It took a few days to collate the information. I found it hard to believe the amount written on the subject, but most of it was not from a scientific viewpoint. Nevertheless, there were some interesting articles.

Since ancient times the creature described as half-human and half-wolf had haunted the imagination of many diverse cultures. Tales of werewolves striking terror into the hearts of good, honest people from northern and Western Europe, Russia and Asia were plentiful as examples.

After hours of reading, I was still sceptical. How could I place any credence to these tales and myths? Scientifically speaking it wasn't possible for species to shift magically their physiognomy to another species. Or was it?

At the same time, could I ignore the reports of village sightings of Aggie Muldoon Doherty turning into a wolf-like creature? Could I mock these incredible stories as fanciful imagination? After all, it was clearly recorded data that generations of Muldoons were shape-shifters. Witnesses had reported each gruesome and vicious attack as it had happened.

Science cannot explain paranormal phenomena. The paranormal is a state whereby rules of the natural world supersede the rules of another source of reality.

It was three in the morning. I kept on researching. I learnt more about bilocation shifting. This concept suggested that, while the human body was asleep or became unconscious, the etheric material, or spirit, as we know it, left the body and transcended itself into another form. This other form could be either a ghostlike figure or an animal teleporting itself to a different location. My understanding of this theory was that an individual could appear in two places simultaneously. Therefore, this phenomenon of bilocation indicated it was a projection of a double. The double might appear as a solid physical form or a ghost. *Can this be the answer I'm looking for? I have to keep an open mind.*

Rapaciously, I kept on reading about the subject. After all, Celtic legends often involved belief in shape-shifting.

Since childhood, my paternal grandparents had impressed me with stories of Scythians, who were ancient people living on the Steppes north of the Black Sea. According to the legends of the Lebor Gabala Erren (Book of the Taking of Ireland), the Irish were the direct descendants of Feinius Farsaid, a king of Scythia. I remembered my nana telling me stories of werewolves rampant in Scythian mythology and certainly plenty of stories circulated in Celtic folklore on the subject. How could I forget the story of St Patrick arriving in Ireland and discovering among his worshippers many families of werewolves?

'My God, what can all this mean? I think I'm beginning to lose sight of reality,' I said aloud. 'How can I possibly entertain the idea of werewolves existing in the real world?'

Even the great Greek Historian Herodotus, had mentioned a Scythian tribe called the Neuri who changed into wolves. I'd read Herodotus's works many times, and I clearly remembered his accounts of the Neuri.

The next day, I hurried to a local bookstore and bought a paperback copy of Herodotus. Back in my room, I skimmed through the pages. It was there in black and white on page 306 of the Penguin Classics of Herodotus: 'There is a story current amongst the Scythians and the Greeks in Scythia that once a year every Neurian turns into a wolf for a few days, and then turns back into a man again. I do not believe this tale: but all the same, they tell it, and even swear by it.'

Herodotus had reported what people had said around him. Naturally, he couldn't affirm he believed in this phenomenon, since he didn't witness it himself. Did people concoct these fanciful stories or hallucinations as real?

I desperately needed some sleep. But my mind insisted I needed to stay awake. *I've got to persevere. I must try to understand the pieces of the puzzle.*

I continued to read well into the night. The digital alarm clock went off, making me jump. It was seven in the morning and I was still huddled in front of my computer, reading articles on the Internet.

When I opened my eyes, it was eleven fifteen. I lifted my head off the desk and straightened up stiffly. *Damn. I must've fallen asleep. Ouch, my neck. I need coffee.*

I put the kettle on. I washed my face and brushed my teeth to remove the acrid taste in my mouth. I used all three of the sachets on the tray to make a strong coffee. The hot drink helped put things into perspective. 'Two whole days of research and what have I learnt? Theories, all theories and reported hearsay. Nothing concrete to go on.'

What bothered me more than anything else were the bizarre apparitions I'd been having at my uncle's haunted house. *What am I to make of them? Is it all part of my vivid imagination? How can I dismiss him? Those ubiquitous yellow eyes, their fixed stare never shifting, haunting me at every opportunity. Lunch. It might take my mind off things.*

I showered. Putting on a pair of jeans and a warm sweater, I went down to the dining room. *It would be a pleasant change if Mrs Mulligan isn't around. With some luck, it's her day off and I won't have to see her.*

The menu wasn't extensive but offered some good traditional dishes. I decided to have a substantial lunch, knowing all too well I would skip the evening meal.

The venison, cooked just right, was not at all gamey as sometimes this type of red meat could be. It was incredibly tender, practically melting in my mouth. The red-currant jelly and port wine sauce perfectly complemented it. Just as I wiped my mouth, Sean walked in.

'We need to talk.' His skin looked flushed. Maybe it was the cold air outside creating the distinct blush on his otherwise tanned face.

I shook my head, making it obvious I wasn't happy to see him. 'And here I was just thinking how lovely and relaxing my lunch has been. But now you're here. Do I need to say more?'

'Why do you insist on dishonouring my family?' An angry flash crossed his face.

'Excuse me, what have I done to dishonour you family? What are you accusing me of now?'

'Don't play games, Kathleen, you know damned well what I'm referring to.'

'Do I?'

I could hear his laboured breathing. 'I resent your methods.'

'My methods?'

'Yes, your methods. How dare you go upsetting everyone at the archival repository.'

'I beg your pardon, what *are* you talking about?'

'Remember young Tomas? The unlucky fool beguiled by your feminine charms? He is in serious trouble, no thanks to you. He might even lose his job. But I guess you don't care about that as long as you get what you want.'

'What? Lose his job? Whatever for?'

'As we speak the young man is in Mr Brogan's office and it's not for an afternoon tea party.'

'How did Mr Brogan find out about Tomas' involvement?'

'The truth always comes out.'

'How poignant that you talk about the truth – that is indeed what I'm after.' I could smell victory.

He stood up and leant forward, bringing his face close to mine and whispered, 'Take care, you're in way over your head. This is a dangerous game.'

He was gone, marching out in military fashion.

***

Is he trying to unhinge me? Is that his game? This proves he isn't to be trusted. The entire charade he's been concerned about my well-being is just that – a charade. To think I even stayed at his place under his so-called protective wing!

I shuddered when I remembered the night someone attacked me in his apartment. *Funny that. Uncle Seamus was right. I was sure the old man had tried to warn me about Sean. Look what happened to him. Ghastly. Shocking. Poor man!*

The more I thought about it, the more I realised Sean was always conveniently lurking about when a disaster had just taken place. *What am I thinking? I've no proof he's involved in trying to destroy me. But, I know there's much more to the mighty Inspector than meets the eye. I must watch my every step.*

I ordered a pot of lavender and marshmallow tea. It would certainly help my low spirits and nervousness. The cleared glass pot arrived, and as I admired the combination of the lavender's purple blossoms and the marshmallow's delicate pink flowers, Donahl appeared.

'Penny for your thoughts,' he said cheerfully as he pulled his chair close to mine.

'Donahl, have you observed anything unusual at the Muldoons' place?'

'What do you mean?'

'Don't worry, I'm just not thinking straight.'

'What? Tell me, something is obviously bothering you.'

'No really, my mind has just been in overdrive and I'm overreacting to things.'

'Things? Now you've got me really curious. I'm not going to let you off so easily.'

He hounded me for the next few minutes, so I confessed my concerns about Sean.

'You know, I've never liked that man with his condescending and pious ways. If it wasn't for my sweet Eliza, I would've given his arse a good hidin' a long time ago.'

'Definitely a brave move. I wouldn't be so bold.'

'You women are always scared, even of your own shadows. Bastards like Muldoon need to be put in their place.'

'Of course, you're just the man for the job, aren't you?'

The cacophony of our laughter created whispers among the patrons. I didn't care; my cousin had done wonders for my spirits, lifting the fog of misery that had surrounded me for far too long.

CHAPTER NINETEEN

Brittle bones. He looked forlorn, hunched up sitting cradled like a baby. His long, hoary hair was thin and sparse; his eyes, tired and hollowed – like his spirit. Bitterness swept his furrowed, hard face. He had had a long and difficult life. The end was near. He didn't fear it. It would be a relief. He knew he had to make things right. All his life, people called him a heretic, a man possessed by the devil. He didn't like it. He certainly didn't deserve such censure. Even his own family distanced themselves from him. Good riddance, he said to himself. They are a pack of vultures, all of them. Cannot have me dead and buried soon enough, so they can inherit my fortune. No, the truth must come out. It was high time to reveal the curse. He would show them all ...

I opened my eyes to discover I'd slept for thirteen hours. 'It's incredible! That dream was incredible. It's almost prophetic. I've to go to my uncle's house,' I talked to myself as I got out of bed.

I stopped to make a phone call.

'Hello,' a croaky voice answered.

It was 6:45 five on a Sunday morning.

'Hi, Donahl. Sorry to ring so early, but it's urgent.'

'It'd better be, cousin. Otherwise, I would have to say you're off your nut.'

'Well, that may very well be, Donahl, but you must meet me at your great-grandfather's place straightaway.'

'Arc ye headin'?' he asked.

'Yes, shortly.'

'Be Jaysus, as we Oirish say, a shave, a shampoo and a shite and I'm a new man.'

'Well then, hurry, Donahl I'll meet you at the gates in one

hour.'

***

Watching my white breath shield me like a soft cloud kept my mind off the freezing weather. Even the insulated leather gloves didn't warm my stiff fingers. My mind wandered and I thought about how everyone was saying it was unusually cold for December.

Christmas was fast approaching, my favourite time of the year. *What do I have to look forward to now? I'm not going to spend it with Dylan or my family.* Last Christmas, our third Christmas as a couple, we'd spent it in London, just the two of us. We'd bought a beautiful fresh tree and decorated it. We'd been like a couple of kids counting down the days to celebrate the festive season together.

It was such a special time. The day after Christmas, we'd left for that amazing ten-day trip to Spain. It was so exciting.

Look at me now, all alone hanging around outside a dilapidated haunted mansion. In a space of a few weeks, unexpected events have turned my life upside down – to be more precise destroyed. Life certainly has many twists and turns. Is anyone ever destined for eternal happiness? I used to think so. Fool, I say! I feel numb, I can't even cry. My tears have dried up like a desert well. Where's my crazy cousin? If he doesn't get here quickly, I'm sure I will freeze to death. I might even lose my nerve and abandon the whole thing.

There was a feeling of eeriness hanging in the air. The wind swept past me, making me shiver. *Cailean's here. I'm sure of it.* I could sense him, his intense eyes causing pain over my whole body. *Should I run? Run where? How can I entertain the idea? I can never escape him. He wouldn't allow that under any circumstances. He seems to be able to read my thoughts. My punishment is inevitable.* These irrational thoughts made me frantic.

'Boo.'

I screamed.

'What the hell is the matter with you?'

'Why would you be so stupid as to scare me like that? My mind was elsewhere. I'm just a bit jumpy, that's all,' I said annoyed at his childish behaviour. How could I tell my cousin about my ridiculous thoughts? I needed company today. I couldn't face being alone in that great big house.

'I'm sorry for being late and for frightening you. I was in a bad state. Too much alcohol last night – you know how it is.'

'Yeah, I know how it is.'

'Well, shall we go in or are we to freeze our arses?' he asked as he grabbed my elbow to guide me ahead.

I was still shaken up. However, I was determined Cailean's spirit wouldn't mar my day.

'You're very quiet. Has somethin' happened?'

'No, I'm just tired.'

'Then why are we here at this ridiculous hour?'

'We've a lot to do.'

'Yeah?' Donahl raised his eyebrows. 'We've been through the house before and haven't been able to find anythin'. What has changed?'

'My dream.'

'Are you saying you dragged me here on a Sunday mornin' because you had a dream?'

'This wasn't just an ordinary dream. He came to me. He wanted to tell me something. I know he wanted me to come to the house.'

'Who came to you? Cousin, I'm afraid you're losing it. Come on, let's get out of here. The place gives me the spooks.'

I headed upstairs, and despite his reservations, he followed me, muttering under his breath.

I continued talking, not taking any notice of my cousin's protestations. 'I know he had a message for me, I just know it. I can feel it in my bones.'

'Who the hell had a message for you?'

'Fionnbharr, Uncle Fionnbharr, your great-grandfather.'

'Fionnbharr? Why didn't yer say so?'

***

Up in the attic, we eagerly emptied boxes in the hope of finding a clue.

'We've been at this for an hour. I can't believe you talked me into it, just because you saw the old man in your dream. What was the message anyway?'

'It's a bit more complicated than a straight-out message. He didn't just appear and say, "Kathleen, this is what you have to do.' It's the whole dream put together. Don't you understand the symbolism here?'

'No.'

'Well, never mind. Just keep looking.'

'It would be helpful if you gave me a clue about what I'm supposed to be lookin' for.' Frustration ran high in his voice.

'Donahl,' I said with an exaggerated pitch, 'we're looking for a clue to remove the curse. This is just as important for you as it is for me. My God, you're to be married soon. How can you even contemplate having children when the damned curse is hanging over our heads?'

'Wow, cousin, calm down. Who's talkin' about having children?'

'I assumed Eliza and you would like to have children one day.'

'You assume too much. I'm not ready to be a father. To tell you the truth, I can't stand kids.'

It was best to change the subject. My cousin looked annoyed and I needed him to keep working away at finding a clue.

'Will you look at this ice pick?' he said as he picked up the sharp object and rotated it, as though he was piercing and twisting it through someone's heart.

I trembled as I recalled that awful night – the night I came close to being murdered.

'A few weeks ago that ice pick you're holding in your hand was my only means of protection.'

'What do you mean?'

I told Donahl about that night.

'Mary Mother of Jaysus, you're a brave one! I'm sure I would've given myself away. And you say you hid behind those boxes?'

'Uhum, I sure did. I've to confess, the horrible incident terrified me.'

'Any ideas who it might have been?'

'Well I know it wasn't the ghosts who freely roam about this house,' I said firmly.

'Oh, please, for God's sake, don't talk like that! I'll scramble down the stairs and I'll be out of here like a shot.'

'Shame on you Donahl! I never took you for a coward.'

'I've told you this before, I don't socialise well with people from the far beyond.'

'You don't have to worry. The person who was here that night was very much flesh and blood.' I stood up and brushed off the dust from my jeans. 'Now let's go and explore the rest of the house. We can come back here later.'

The musty smell was intensely dominant as we moved from room to room. We went back downstairs and hovered in the kitchen when I noticed through the window a detached cottage about 500 metres from the main house. A gigantic oak tree partially hid it.

'Do you know what that cottage was used for?'

'It was great-grandfather's retreat. I remember Grandfather Conan used to call it the old man's ivory tower. Apparently, he didn't allow anyone in there and if any of them kids ever snuck in, they used to get a good hidin'. Great-grandfather was renowned for his mean temper.'

'So you've never been in there?'

'No, we never came here. The old man had a falling-out with my grandfather, so my father didn't set foot in this house after that. I would confidently say great-grandfather was a weird man.'

'Doesn't it strike you odd he was so adamant he have privacy?' It made me wonder if great Uncle Fionnbharr had something to hide. 'Let's head out there.'

The biting cold hit us like a running freight train.

The locked door was not a surprise.

'It would be too easy for the key to be conveniently placed somewhere near reach,' I said. 'We'll have to break it down.'

Donahl frowned, obviously not happy with my plan.

'And how do you suggest we do that, my fair cousin? I'm no Arnie Schwarzenegger, you know.'

'Come now, you're a strong man. If we both give the door a nudge, I'm sure it will just fly open.'

'A nudge you say? Well you know what they say, ladies first.'

'Honestly, young men today have lost the art of chivalry. But, to prove I'm determined, yes, I'll go first. With no help from you, thank you very much.'

With great force, I thrust myself onto the door and as I hit the sturdy wood, I sprang back like a yo-yo, only to land in my cousin's arms.

He laughed.

'Okay, okay, I admit this wasn't such a brilliant idea,' I muttered while I massaged my sore arm.

'In fact, cousin it was a daft idea. Now watch the professional at work,' he said as he took out a Swiss army knife from his pocket. I pulled a face. He fidgeted with the lock for a few minutes and deftly opened the door. His elegant manoeuvre reminded me of Roger Moore in *The Saint*, although my cousin was neither as suave nor as dashing as my favourite English actor.

The light of our torches guided us in. Donahl walked to the window and pulled open the moth-eaten curtains.

It was a quaint cottage – compact with exposed beams and whitewashed stone-walls.

Typical of a worker's cottage and that's what it must've been in its heyday. It was a square room, not large, a bit like a box. The floor was dark slate, creating a sombre atmosphere. A coal-fire grate, flanked by a cast-iron range, occupied the main wall. Cluttered on the mantelpiece were miniature collectibles. Someone had positioned a solitary armchair near the fire. I surmised it had been a well-loved chair, with its worn material and the distinct indentation in its cushion. The only other objects were a footstool and a small side table, which housed several books. An ordinary room really, but its simplicity complemented country living.

A small door lay closed near the other wall. As I went to investigate, I had the most unfortunate accident. I lost my footing and tripped over the Oriental rug. I landed hard on my posterior.

'Ouch!'

'Are you OK?'

'No, I think I've hurt my coccyx.' Tears welled in my eyes, the pain was excruciating.

The slate floor was hard and cold. Donahl rushed over and helped me up. I flinched from the pain. 'I don't think I can stand up,' I cried out. I was angry with myself. I had ruined a very important day.

'We'd better get you to a doctor.'

'No – we've got so much to do here. Look, I'll be all right.'

'Don't be ridiculous! You can barely walk. The doctor will probably send you to have x-rays. Damn! What we need is some ice. That will bring down the swelling.' Donahl hovered around me with such concern I agreed to go to the hospital.

'This wouldn't have happened if it wasn't for this old rug. It's so worn and smells disgusting. Would you please throw it out?'

The heavy-patterned woven rug was rectangular and looked lightweight. He bent down and picked it up effortlessly. We stood there, mouths hanging open, eyes locked to the ground. The rug concealed an underground trapdoor.

***

The CT scan was just tolerable. Like most people, I detested these things. *Modern technology, but they still haven't worked out how to make the experience a pleasant one*. I got dressed, barely coping with the pain my movements were causing. The doctor informed me they found a hairline fracture on the coccyx.

'We can't do much for you, Ms Kavanagh. I suggest you take some painkillers and rest up.'

That's easy for you to say, I wanted to say. I was anxious to return to my uncle's 'cottage'. Even a fractured coccyx wasn't going to keep me away.

Donahl tapped his foot impatiently when I met him at the reception. *He's so sweet*. I sensed he was upset about my accident. I told him what the doctor ordered.

Donahl had his own advice. 'A bottle of great whiskey down at Selskar's will fix you up.'

'It will fix up my liver too.'

He took me back to the hotel, against much protestation. I knew it was the sensible thing to do, but I didn't have to like it.

We returned to the B&B and Donahl left me alone to nurse my aches and pains. A hot shower relaxed me slightly and I went back into the bedroom. Someone was banging on the door.

Mrs Mulligan stood there, a silver tray in her hands. She looked annoyed, as though I'd greatly inconvenienced her.

''Ere,' she shouted. 'Donahl said you wanted some sandwiches and a hot chocolate. I obliged only because he's so charmin'.'

Typical. With great pain I took the tray from Mrs Mulligan's hands and as I was about to thank her, she turned her back and waddled down the corridor, swinging her well-endowed hips as though she was doing an Irish jig. She really irritated me, being so unapproachable and gruff.

The sandwiches were unimaginative. 'This is downright awful,' I murmured under my breath. 'As they say, beggars can't be choosers.' I hadn't had anything since breakfast, so I struggled with the stale bread that sandwiched bits of grisly ham and wilted lettuce. *She's done this on purpose. I'm going to complain tomorrow. What a day! Everything happened so quickly. I wasn't banking on having an accident. That's life, always throwing something unexpected at you. At least we found the trapdoor under that stinky rug. What has my great-uncle hiding down there? We'll find out tomorrow.*

Donahl would pick me up after breakfast. It was going to be a long night.

***

I got up at sunrise, showered with great difficulty and got ready. By 7:30, I was downstairs, enjoying a continental breakfast of toast and delicious home-made boysenberry jam. Strong brewed coffee finished off the pleasant breakfast. As I perused over the morning Wexford Times, Donahl waltzed in, true to his word.

'Good mornin'. How's the patient today?' He kissed me on the cheek.

'Fine, I guess. Didn't sleep much.'

'Didn't think you would. I admire your stiff upper lip, I must say!'

'Let's go, I can't wait to get there,' I said. Not even a hairline fracture of the coccyx would stand in the way of my plans.

The sleek car purred and we were on our way.

***

We found the ground waterlogged – a pool of murky water mixed with mush. It had rained heavily during the night, making the grass sodden. We walked through the slush, crossing the neglected lawn to get to the other side of the house.

'Another freezing day,' I remarked. My scarf served as an effective barrier to the bitter wind. The sun shone brilliantly, emphasising the shimmering droplets on the surrounding trees. My heartbeat accelerated; its beat was like an old steam engine gaining momentum with each step.

Donahl was quiet, not his usual chirpy self. Even in the car, he hadn't participated much in the conversation. Perhaps he was having problems with Eliza.

The door to the cottage was ajar. 'Someone's in there,' I whispered as I held onto Donahl's jacket sleeve.

'Nah, the wind must've pushed it open.'

'But I remember you closing it firmly. Just be careful. Someone might be in there.'

My cousin pulled a face to indicate that he wasn't impressed with my theory. 'You stay here, I'll go in. If I don't come out in exactly one minute, you'll know I've been done in.'

'Don't be ridiculous, I'm coming in with you,' I said. I was not about to leave my cousin to go in there without support. Scared as I was, I wasn't going to be a coward.

'No, you stay out here,' he insisted. He looked serious. I had a bad feeling about this.

Donahl slid through the door as though he was a seasoned detective and disappeared from my sight. Cold and anxious, I kept looking at my watch. The minute was up and I didn't hear even a peep from Donahl.

My God, Cailean's got him! What if Donahl's dead? This is my fault. I sent him in there. These irrational thoughts kept churning in my head. I couldn't contain myself. I had to find out.

'Donahl?' I called out in a pathetic rasp. No answer. This was definitely not good. I walked in.

It was dark inside. Someone had closed the curtains.

'Shit,' I said. Donahl had drawn the curtains when we were here yesterday. 'Donahl?' Agitation rang high in my voice.

I knew he was behind me. If only I had a weapon in my hands, like a knife, something I could use to fight this fiend. I had to face him. I had to put an end to his goading, his evil games. I made a sudden turn and jumped back when Donahl cried out, 'Booh.'

'Oh, my back! That's a rotten thing to do. You're up to your stupid, juvenile games again!' His puerile behaviour really frustrated me.

My cousin laughed so hard his face was damp with tears.

'It's not funny. Sometimes I think you take great pleasure in seeing people suffer. It's narcissistic.'

'Oh, my poor cousin. How could you possibly entertain ideas like ghosts and dead ancestors are out to harm us? Did you think they were having a twilight shindig in this dismal room? Honestly, you remind me of my delicate fiancée – scared of your own shadow.'

I felt anger mounting. I'd just about enough of Donahl's immaturity.

'Just drop it, will you! Let's go and have a look at this trapdoor.'

***

It was rectangular. We congregated above it as though it was the most amazing discovery on Earth. My cousin bent down to pull the wooden door up; to our great disappointment, it appeared jammed.

'Oh for Christ's sake, not another complication,' Donahl muttered.

'Here, let me help.'

We both pulled the round iron-cast handle but it was of no use. The door was stuck.

'There doesn't seem to be a lock or anything,' I said.

'Maybe it's bolted from the inside.'

'Do you think so? Not likely, but maybe there is another access.'

'What a headache this is. It really pisses me off.' Donahl paced the floor.

The brilliant sunlight vanished and the dark clouds gathered as though they marched for battle. A storm was brewing.

'There's a shed at the back of the house. I might find a saw or an axe there. I'll go and see. You stay here.'

I didn't like the idea of being alone. It was ridiculous. On so many occasions, I'd been alone at the main house. That place was far more eerie than this solitary room.

'Did you hear me Kathleen? I said I'm going around to the shed to see if I can get an axe.'

'Sorry! Yes, I heard you. Please be careful.'

'Don't start that again,' Donahl said with a cheeky grin on his face.

No sooner was he out the door thunder struck. I jumped. The unnecessary movement made me wince. My lower back went into spasms. All this pent-up excitement had been masking my pain. Now it was back with a vengeance. I looked for some analgesics in my bag and managed to find a couple.

These are useless to me if I don't have water to wash them down with. Why can't I swallow pills without water? Grudgingly I put the pills back in my bag. *I just have to put up with the pain.*

I wondered what lay behind that closed door. Maybe it led to a kitchen or a bathroom. I went to investigate. I found the door locked. This place was like Bluebeard's castle – so many locked doors, so many secrets.

My body stiffened; his animal smell was evident. He was in the room. I was sure he was watching me. My temples throbbed. I felt my pulse quicken. I swung around only to scream uncontrollably. Donahl stood there, an axe raised high above his head, as though he was about to bring it down to crush my skull.

'Just a practical joke.'

I started crying. Donahl dropped the axe and held me close in his arms.

'I'm sorry. I'm such a jerk.'

'Don't worry, I'm on edge, but I wish you'd stop messing around.' I wiped away my tears. 'Look at you, all drenched. You'll catch pneumonia.'

'Nah, nothing of the sort, a little rain will make me hair grow.'

His infectious humour made me smile, despite my annoyance at his consistently foolish pranks.

***

It was laborious work breaking the trapdoor. Well, it was laborious work for Donahl. Perspiration flowed freely down his forehead and into his eyes. I stood there watching him and felt like a cruel overseer taking pleasure in my slave's arduous drudgery. The wooden door was sturdy. It was as though my cousin was cutting through steel. Finally, with the help of the axe, Donahl was able to create a big enough hole in the trapdoor and we made our way down the steep steps.

In the pitch dark, our powerful flashlights guided us down a spiral stairway. It gave me the impression we wound down a well. I counted thirty-nine steps until we reached flat ground.

'Oh, phew! What a stench!' my cousin remarked, as he wrinkled up his nose.

It was an unbearable smell of something decaying. I covered my mouth and nose with my scarf, which helped keep out some of the repelling odours.

Only a few metres away, we discovered the culprits of the offending smell. They were three dead rats, lined up in perfect symmetry, their corpses in fresh decomposition. I flinched. These vermin were enormous. At a distance, you could easily mistake them for small dogs.

We looked at each other and uttered, 'Ugh!'

'It's odd how they died side by side. I wonder what killed them?' I spoke first.

'Maybe they killed each other.'

'That might have been feasible, if there were only the two of them. How do you account for three corpses?'

'Beats me. Maybe they committed suicide. Let's move on, before I throw up.'

I couldn't blame him. The smell was truly sickening.

The bitter cold made my teeth chatter. We moved forward into a tunnel-like corridor, which appeared to go directly underneath the main house. It was a long corridor with walls constructed of large blocks of stone. Impenetrable, like some fortress.

The smell subsided and for that, I was grateful. Donahl and I kept moving along like a couple of miner's looking for gold, until we came to a wall. It was a dead end.

'Is this it?' my cousin shouted.

'Can't be. This has to lead somewhere.'

'Where to?'

'I don't know. It doesn't make sense why they would have built this underground tunnel if it just ends where it does.'

'Maybe it was like a hideout. I don't know. But it pisses me off.' He turned around and clicked his fingers, pointing to the direction of the exit. 'Come on, let's get back up. This place is givin' me the creeps.'

He was right. What was the point anyway? It was a dead end. The stench returned as we approached the dead rats. Donahl kicked one of them. The corpse rolled onto its back. That was when we noticed its face. Clawed. Torn to pieces. I gasped. Donahl kicked and rolled the other two over. We looked at each other. The other two rats had met the same fate as the first one. It was horrible. I knew who was responsible, and then I ran as fast as my feet could carry me to escape this horrible dungeon. I stumbled on the spiral staircase but kept pushing myself in desperation. The pain in my back was intensifying by the nanosecond.

***

'You don't actually believe this crap about the existence of werewolves, do you?' Donahl asked as he topped up his half-empty glass of beer.

I kept stirring the hot chocolate. The solitary blob of marshmallow floating at the surface started to melt from the heat. It looked like a deflated balloon, mirroring the way I felt about my futile attempts to find answers in this land where people regarded me as a foreigner, despite my ancestry.

I wondered how my cousin could enjoy that glass of beer on such a cold day.

'Well, are you going to grace me with your answer?'

'If you'd asked me that question a few months ago, I would've laughed at it. Then I would've said if a person claims they are a werewolf, then they were suffering from lycanthropic disorder, and if a person said they believed they'd seen a werewolf, I would have told them they were delusional.' My explanation came to an abrupt end when a waitress who was heading our way tripped and fell. An assortment of beverages hurtled towards us like a tidal wave.

'For God's sake, woman. What are you, daft or something?' Donahl shouted at the unfortunate girl who was quite mortified.

'For God's sake, Donahl! The poor woman's upset as it is, without you embarrassing her and exacerbating the situation.'

'They should train them better. Can't a man have a drink in peace?'

Dougal, the middle-aged manager of Mulcahy's bar rushed over. The pretty waitress who was by now in tears, collected the scattered glass from the wooden floor. 'Please accept my apologies,' he said, 'the girl is new. I don't know what happened.'

'That's no excuse. She's gone and ruined my jumper. This wine will stain.'

The manager said he would pay for the damage and offered

Donahl and me free cocktails.

'It was all an accident, Donahl. Anyhow, it was nice of him to offer to pay for the damage. Frankly, I think the stain will come off easily. Put some salt on it now and give it a wash when you get home and it will be as good as new.'

'Eliza gave me this jumper. I'm sure she's going to be cross.' His face softened and the boyish look was back.

'Eliza's a nice person and she's sensible. She'll laugh when she hears about the incident. So don't carry on about it.'

'The Muldoons aren't so forgiving,' he said and without warning sprang to his feet, dragging me along by the hand, 'Let's go back to my great-grandfather's place. There must be an entrance somewhere in that tunnel we've missed.'

***

Darkness swallowed us as we entered the pitch-black tunnel until we remembered to switch our flashlights on. The corridor looked longer than I remembered. We brandished the flashlights like swords in the hope of discovering a secret entrance. The stones on the walls were perfectly congruent; not one appeared out of its place.

After spending half an hour exploring, we were unable to find a secret chamber tucked away at this subterranean level. We gave up and decided to return to the cottage. As we were halfway down the corridor, approaching the dead rats, my scarf came undone and fell to the ground. I stooped down to pick it up, when I noticed several raised stones from the floor, not far from where I stood.

'Look at this Donahl!'

'What's up?'

'Look at the way these stones protrude, and this section is different from the rest of the floor.'

'Well, I'll be damned!' Was all Donahl could blurt out, with sheer amazement in his eyes.

He came over and helped me remove the stones.

There were about half a dozen of them. They were more like slabs; thin in height but deceivingly heavy. When we'd removed all the stones, we couldn't believe there was another concealed trapdoor. At least we were able to lift this one easily.

We went down another 39 steps, finally landing in an enormous rectangular room. I felt like I was a kid ensnared in a witch's den. The floors and walls were of plain stone and there were various charts, diagrams and mirrors on the walls. Four working benches, with a variety of alchemical apparatus cluttered on them took up the centre of the room.

'This place is amazing.'

'Yeah. It looks like the stories of great-grandfather being a wizard are no longer just stories.' Donahl picked up a dusty beaker and examined it.

'Don't touch that. Look how grotty everything is. This place simply *reeks* of the supernatural. I wonder how long it's been neglected. I hope there are no creepy crawlies about.' I made a quivering gesture. 'What was Uncle Fionnbharr doing with these flasks, pipes, bubblers, distillation columns and all the other paraphernalia?'

'I told you he was a weirdo.'

'Don't be mean, Donahl. It appears your great-grandfather dabbled in the occult and probably had an insatiable interest in the darker forces of life. I think Uncle Fionnbharr was a remarkable man, with an above average intelligence but he was highly misunderstood.'

The far wall housed a massive bookshelf, accommodating hundreds of books. This place was not only a wizard's laboratory but it was also a wizard's library. There was a long metal cabinet against the wall next to the bookshelves. Someone had locked it.

'You're not contemplating breaking this one down too, are you?'

'No chance! You've amply demonstrated you're the lock-pick. I'll leave it in your capable hands to open it up.'

Donahl set to work with his Swiss army knife and before I could count to ten, he'd opened it. Stacked full of loose papers and some tatty manila folders, it was a dusty cabinet. I sneezed noisily.

'Bless you.'

'Thanks.'

'So where do we begin?'

'This is as good a place as any,' I said as I carefully picked up a small frayed exercise book.

'What have you got there?'

'I think it's a journal.' I started to read it. It was Uncle Fionnbharr's journal. This was exactly what I needed. Finally, a lucky break!

I hadn't even finished reading a sentence when we heard a loud bang.

Donahl ran up the stairs to investigate.

'The bloody trapdoor has slammed shut,' he shouted down at me.

'I hope you're joking,' I shouted back as I ran up to help him but the trapdoor wouldn't budge. It was as though someone had bolted it from the outside.

'I think I know who's here. He is responsible for trapping us down here,' he slammed his fist on the wooden door.

'My God, it's Cailean, isn't it?'

'Don't be daft, it's not one of your illusory ghosts. Damn it – that bastard!'

'Who?"

'Sean. Sean Muldoon has locked us in.'

CHAPTER TWENTY

'Donahl, it's ridiculous what you're suggesting. In the first place, how would Sean know where we are?'

'I was tellin' Eliza of our plans when he walked in on us. He heard everything.'

'But what reason would he have for scaring us or worse, for harming us?'

'Come off it! You've had your doubts about him and know very well what he's capable of. I can't believe you're not arriving at the same conclusion.'

I paced the floor. 'But, really, why?'

'He's a Muldoon, isn't he? Who hates a Kavanagh more than a Muldoon? I'm convinced the lot of them are evil.'

'If you believe that, why in God's name are you marrying Eliza? She's a Muldoon.'

'She's different. You said so yourself. She's a sweet girl.'

'Look, there could be other plausible reasons why the trapdoor shut.'

'Yeah? Name one.'

'The wind.'

'If it was the wind, it wouldn't be locked from the outside, would it?'

My cousin had a point. Could his assumptions be right? A chill went through me as though an army of ants were crawling up my body.

'Now what are we going to do?'

'Damned if I know.' He grunted like a cantankerous old man.

I thought of the dead rats, Sean wouldn't have done that. Then an idea struck me. Was there a connection with the wolf and Sean? No, the notion was inconceivable. Preposterous. Or was it?

***

'I didn't think this was going to be my end,' Donahl complained. He was not much help and I was surprised how easily he gave up.

'Don't be so negative! We'll think of a way to get out of here. Besides you said Eliza knows we're here, she'll come looking for us.'

'How long is that going to take? May I remind you we have no water? How long can we survive?' He pulled a mocking face, which irritated me, then he said, 'Besides, what if she's in on it – to do away with us both?'

'Are you suggesting your fiancé is in collusion with her brother to murder us?' His allegations were absurd. I wanted to shake him, to knock some sense into him. 'Don't be ridiculous. What possible motive does she have? You're engaged to be married, for God's sake.'

'I told you a minute ago, expect anything from a Muldoon.'

I shook my head. My main objective was to work out a way to get out of this place. I left Donahl to sulk.

I looked around the room. There had to be something here to help us open the trap door, to loosen it. It was a simple bolt latch. I rummaged through the laboratory tables and found a bottle of aqua regia – an acid that dissolves metals. Many times I'd seen my Uncle Frank, who was a chemist, use the stuff.

'Donahl, come here. I know how to get us out of here.'

'Oh, sure Kathleen. What are you going to do? Perhaps summon your poltergeist friends to open the trapdoor or, even better, go through the walls with them?' he said with a derisive grin.

'Oh, shut up. Honestly, you're talking nonsense,' I replied. I held the bottle in my hand and brought it close to his face. 'See this? This bottle contains a powerful acid that's capable of dissolving metal. As the hinges to the trapdoor are from the inside, all we need to do is apply the acid to the metal to loosen it up and presto!'

He pulled a face. 'You make it sound so simple.'

'It is simple. You're not the only one who skilfully cracks

doors open.'

'You're not just a pretty face, are you?'

'I'll take that as a vote of confidence.'

Donahl beamed with happiness. I had the impression that it was the single most wonderful news he had received in all his life. His doubts had vanished and he was excited, as a child who was about to receive his first chemistry lesson. I hoped my plan would work. There was no reason for it not to. All I needed was a pipette or an eyedropper.

On the bottom shelf of the cabinet, we found an old wooden box, with numerous pipettes with bulbs of various sizes neatly stacked in it.

'Now this is too simple. It's scaring me.'

I ignored his incongruous remark and continued to look for a pipette that would best achieve my goal.

'Now I want absolute silence, and keep the flashlight steady so I can see what I'm doing. I've to make sure no acid drips back onto me. It's not going to be easy, but with a bit of concentration we'll be out of here in a few hours.'

We went to work, side by side, like a couple of industrious otters, in deep concentration.

With extreme care, I sucked up some acid in the bulb of the pipette and emptied the contents onto the metal hinges. I was in deep focus to ensure there was no spillage of the acid back onto any part of my body. The difficulty I faced was that the trapdoor was above me; it would therefore be easy for the acid to drip back down. To make matters worse, I had to reapply the acid to the metal several times to ensure a sufficient amount of coating. Then we would leave it to dry for about an hour.

'Wow, I'm exhausted.'

'Sit down, Kathleen. You need to rest.'

'No, let's look over these papers. We have to sort them out. There's so much material we must go through.'

The cabinets were full of old papers and journals. We would need several boxes to fit them all in. I took a handful to examine them back at the hotel.

'It's well over an hour; the acid should've worked,' I said. 'Let's see what we can use to pry that trapdoor open.'

'What about this metal rod?'

'Yes, that'll do. Be careful, it's very rusty. Hope you've had your tetanus shot.'

'Don't worry. It would take a lot more than an old rusty rod to put me off,' he boasted.

Yeah right, Donahl, an hour ago, you fell apart under the pressure, you big baby. 'I can use this wooden post. With both these implements the door has to come apart,' I said as I picked up the piece of sturdy wood. 'On the count of three ...'

The hinges of the trapdoor slowly gave way and came undone without much resistance. We were free at last!

As we left my uncle's property, I glanced back. I could swear for a fleeting moment Sean Muldoon stood at a window of the main house, coldly staring down at us. Or did I confuse him with Cailean?

***

At last, a bubbly heaven, the perfect relaxant as I soaked in the hot tub. I spiced it up with a few drops of Badedas, my favourite brand of bubble bath. Even when I was a little girl, I loved taking long baths, enjoying the abundant Badedas bubbles cloaking me with their soothing tickle. I would twirl my plastic princess Liadan perched on her dolphin Ferdy, together on their daily water adventures as I sang gleefully.

When I used to spend weekends or holidays at my grandparents' picturesque cottage in the mountains, I recalled my nana saying, as she would hurry me into the bathtub, 'My child, you can find self-knowledge soaking in the humble bath.' She would chuckle and continue, 'Damn sight cheaper than having hypnosis.'

As I lounged back, enjoying the gentle interlude of the whirling water unlocking the negative energy surrounding me, I reflected on the day's bizarre events. Not only was it extraordinary we stumbled across my great-uncle's secret hide-out, but we were now in possession of a lot of material that might be significant to understand the history of my family.

Uncle Fionnbharr had discovered something about the

curse, something quite extraordinary something that would amaze us all. Bit by bit, things were starting to fit in. It was like putting together the pieces of a complicated jigsaw puzzle. My uncle selected me, because of my background and training as a journalist to carry on his work. Fionnbharr Kavanagh wanted to expose the historical facts about the curse.

Those cold, dark eyes came back to haunt me. No mistake. I had seen him at the window, peering, observing, scrutinizing.

Transmigration was the druidic term; I knew it as shape-shifting. Could Sean, Cailean and the wolf be one and the same?

I got out of the bath. I was tired. I would sleep well tonight, even though my lower back still ached. I got into bed. All was quiet, the stillness so intense that I thought I would go mad. The phone rang sharply, lifting the heaviness.

'Hello.'

Silence, I couldn't detect even a hint of a breath.

'Is someone there?'

More silence. I hung up. *Probably a crank caller. How can it be a crank call? Whoever it was had rung on the hotel's landline.* I picked up the phone and dialled nine for reception.

'Hi, it's Kathleen Kavanagh from room 5. Did you just connect a caller to my room?'

'Yes, Ms Kavanagh, I did,' replied Gerry, the night porter.

'Was the call for me?'

'Of course, Ms Kavanagh. The man asked for you by name.'

'Did he say who he was?'

'No.'

'You didn't recognise his voice?'

'I'm sorry, I didn't. Is everything all right?' he asked.

'Well, it's just that whoever it was hung up. Thanks anyway, Gerry.'

It must've been Sean. I don't want to dwell on it. I have no proof. I'm only going by instinct. Is it instinct, or is it because Sean is a Muldoon? I could have sworn I saw him at the house.

The call perturbed me more than I cared to admit. I decided to read my uncle's journal to take my mind off the call. However, I remembered nothing more. I must have drifted off as soon as my head had hit the pillow.

***

His burning eyes penetrated her soul with their harsh stare.
Punishment was inevitable. She didn't even have to see his
face; he was behind her. He enjoyed being cruel, taunting her
like some helpless prey. His presence dominated her universe;
even her thoughts belonged to him – he possessed her very
being. It was as though he attached himself to her like an extra
appendage. Day and night, in darkness and in light he
followed her movements; he even knew the rhythm of her
heartbeat and every breath she took. What sort of life was
that? She must get away. The only way she could leave him
was in death, and even then ...

I opened my eyes. Charlotte was the woman in my dreams. I
still couldn't come to terms how much she resembled me.
Charlotte was the key to understanding Cailean. I was a step
closer to the truth. It would not be long now. A flutter danced
in my stomach.

***

The smell of freshly brewed coffee enlivened my dead senses. I
had been awake since 4 in the morning, not able to get back to
sleep after that startling dream. I needed some sustenance. I
hadn't eaten anything since the previous morning. A large plate
of hot cooked breakfast arrived on a copper tray. As I was about
to delve into it, Sean Muldoon walked in, casually strutting
towards me. There was a weird look on his face; it seemed that
he hadn't slept well either. He towered over me as I sat near the
window looking at me as though I was some exotic creature
trapped in a cage. A few uncomfortable seconds passed before
he made conversation. When he finally spoke, his voice cut
through the silence like a knife. 'Good morning, Kathleen.'

'Inspector.'

'Stop calling me Inspector. I thought we were past all that.'

I didn't reply. I was tired and in no mood to humour him.

His glum expression didn't falter, he simply said, 'I wanted
to know how you've been.'

'I'm touched. I suppose you wanted to find out whether I was dead or alive.'

'What is that supposed to mean?' An angry scowl crossed his face.

I was determined not to let him intimidate me. Sean was calculating. Just like Cailean, he was provoking me. He knew exactly what the state of my health was.

'I don't understand your attitude towards me, and frankly since my grandmother's passing, you've been downright hostile.'

'Might I suggest, Inspector that you reflect on your officious manner?'

His eyes narrowed. He looked so much like Cailean as if he was a carbon-copy, traced perfectly from his photograph. And I resembled Charlotte, I knew Sean would punish me like Cailean would.

'Kathleen,' he said my name so tenderly I felt a pang of longing. 'You shall soon find the truth you seek, but by God I hope your discovery doesn't destroy you.'

***

Does he mean to fluster me with that awful warning? The gall of the man! And only the day before, he locked us up in the dungeon. Why did he come to see me anyway? Perhaps to gloat? I'm not going to let him upset me.

Back in my room, I relaxed in the armchair huddled in a blanket, and began reading Uncle Fionnbharr's journal. The following was on the first page I picked up:

> *Astounding how I feel. Joy, it is to be my last hours in this damnable house. Freedom is so near my reach, I can almost taste it as though it's a sumptuous meal fit for a king! As I write, this withered, shrivelled hand does not mourn the passing of time, on the contrary, I rejoice in my greatest achievement, my finest hour. I welcome death as my rebirth. I shall soon rejoin my Teresa, who left me sixty-five years ago to this day. Sweet Teresa, she stole my heart with*

her bashful smile and tender ways that kindled my smouldering heart. She was the only human being on this wretched earth who understood me and showed me kindness. Yet God took her away from me. I look at my children and grandchildren and wonder how it is conceivable this gentle, unassuming woman could produce offspring such as ours. Each of our children and respectively their children are so contemptuous, so vile, like some black bile stagnating in a diseased system. Pack of vultures, the whole lot of them. They can't wait till I'm six feet under. But they shall soon find out what awaits them.

I know the first to read these pages will be young Kathleen Kavanagh, the great-granddaughter of my second cousin Aindriu. I have chosen her to complete the quest I began over seventy years ago. This quest took place the day our first-born of nine months, a sweet little girl whom we had named Siobhan, after my Teresa's grandmother, died as a result of the curse placed on our family by Aggie Muldoon.

There are ghosts who dwell in this house. But there is one who has survived, lives and breathes for over one hundred and fifty years, knows no remorse and only seeks revenge. A clever shape-shifter, he roams about as he pleases, knows your every move and thoughts till your dying day. He takes great pleasure in inducing suffering and terror in a Kavanagh's heart. I loathe him with every ounce of my weary being. I know in my heart the resilient and determined spirit of my grandniece; Kathleen Kavanagh will challenge this fiend. He sought her for eternity, for he thinks of her as his beloved Charlotte, and this mistake shall be his downfall. I have never crossed paths with my grandniece but I have every faith she will finally destroy the abominable creature, and she will be our family's final salvation.

Astounded, I felt my heartbeat accelerate as I completed

reading the last sentence. Uncle Fionnbharr had it all worked out. How did he know about Charlotte? And how did he know so much about me? Turning to the next page, I continued reading.

> *All the secrets you seek you shall find in this house. By now, you would have discovered 'them'. They roam about; they don't know day or night. In a way, they have kept me company all these years.*
>
> *I do not know how my side of the family came to inherit this house and all the wealth that came with it. I understand there was a falling out with members of family and my own father came to inherit it all.*
>
> *For a brief few years, all was peaceful and when I married Teresa, we were blissfully happy for the first three years of our marriage. But, when our precious Siobhan died, our world turned upside down. Teresa, in order to make me happy, gave me three more children. They were all boys. When the eldest was seven and the youngest just three, she slipped away from us to a world of dark melancholy. She never got over Siobhan and within a few years, she withered to practically a skeleton, until one morning she never got up. My grief was unimaginable and I swore I would avenge my wife and daughter's senseless deaths. It was then that I withdrew from the world. The boys, as they developed into young men, did not care nor had time for me. Their only mission was to grab as much of my inherited wealth for their own wicked pleasures.*

I jumped. The peal of the telephone threw me into confusion, as I was so absorbed in what I was reading.

'Hello.'

'Kat.'

'Dad.'

'We haven't spoken for a week, princess I was worried about you.'

'So nice to hear your voice.' I felt homesick. 'You've rung at a perfect time. I've so much to tell you.'

'Well, don't keep me in suspense.'

I told my father about Uncle Fionnbharr's hiding place, of being locked up there, of our escape and of finding his journal.

'This is amazing. He actually wrote it for you to find?'

'It seems that way. I've only read two pages so far but I know in my heart this journal is the key to dealing with the curse of Aggie Muldoon.'

'Be careful, my darling. I'll call in a few days to see how much you've progressed.'

'Thanks dad, I love you.'

'I love you too, my princess. I'll pass the phone to your mum now, she's just as anxious to talk to you.'

***

The following was on page three of Great-Uncle Fionnbharr's journal:

The problems of this cursed family go back almost one hundred and fifty years. It is said that my Great-Great-Grandfather Cormac Padraig Kavanagh murdered his wife and her lover. He tore their faces beyond recognition. The mother of the murdered young man was Aggie Muldoon. After hearing the horrible death of her son, she placed a wretched curse on Cormac Padraig Kavanagh and his descendants. No first born of ensuing generations of Kavanaghs would go past his or her first birthday. The child would die sometimes with no apparent cause, as was the case with our beautiful daughter Siobhan.

Records show Aggie Muldoon was born and bred in Wexford. She came from a long line of shape-shifters – to be more precise from a long line of werewolves. For centuries, townspeople were terrified of the power that this family held. People remember this damned family's thirst for human blood and their demonic bestowment.

When a child is begotten from a werewolf, people say it becomes immortal. Its sole purpose is to become a killing machine. This is true. The only way to fight this evil is to kill it, so that the pattern of reincarnating will finally cease.

I took a break. Too much to digest. I was visibly shaken. I could barely manage to pour myself a glass of orange juice. Carefully taking the half-full glass back to the desk, I settled back to continue with the fascinating account:

My sole mission after the pointless deaths of my beloved wife and baby daughter is to expose this damnation. I have discovered the truth but I'm an old man and can no longer fight this fiend. He lurks in the house and taunts me daily. He is not just a wandering spirit but I'm convinced he is breathing and very much flesh and blood. He knows no boundaries. His ultimate scheme is to destroy every living, breathing Kavanagh.

About five years ago when my now useless legs still held their own, I came across a small chest buried behind a wall. Ah, the arcane secrets of this haunted house are difficult to uncover!

The chest contains material, which will help reverse the curse of Aggie Muldoon. I have chosen young Kathleen Kavanagh for the task of unveiling the secrets and releasing this family of its tormenting pain.

Do not fail me. If you do so, you will be failing yourself. Use your skills, judgment and your investigative talents to find this chest. Then you can act upon so as to ...

The journal came to an abrupt end. Hurriedly, I turned the pages but not a single word followed. 'Is this a joke? What's this business about a chest that I have to find? The old man has implied my family's future depends on my finding it. Thanks Uncle Fionnbharr. Thanks a lot,' I said aloud. Maybe it was his way of getting back at my side of the family by making me a pawn in this bizarre game. What was going to be my next move?

***

As soon as I entered the welcoming bar of the timbered Westgate Tavern, I saw him, his eyes glued to the TV above the pub counter. Manchester United was playing against Irish League this weekend. It looked like a tight game, both sides boasting great talent.

'Hello there,' I said as I tapped him on the shoulder. 'We're going to make mincemeat out of you English.'

'Since when are you a Paddy, Ms from Down Under?'

'Since birth. I'm a Kavanagh. For your information I look at Ireland as my second homeland.'

'Is that so? Then as a local, you have every right to comment on a game of football. Although I've to warn you, we are going to thrash you,' he said as he winked at me.

'Huh. Such conceit, shall we make a wager?'

'That will be a pleasure. So what are we betting on?'

'If Manchester United wins I'll buy you a pub dinner. And if Ireland wins you'll take me to the finest restaurant in Wexford.'

'A deal. I better pick the pub that you'll be taking me.'

'Dream on,' I said and ordered a glass of chardonnay.

We chatted for a while and caught up on each other's news. Josh was away in England for the past few weeks. I realised how much I had missed his company. We'd developed a special bond since we met.

'So the mighty Inspector has been hassling you, has he?' Josh asked when I finished telling him about Sean's latest visit. 'The man's got a hide.'

'I don't care; he's not scaring me off that easily. But I must confess I don't begin to understand his angle.'

'You'd just better be careful. You never know his next move.'

'Anyway, I'm glad I've bumped into you.' I yawned. 'Now it's time for me to take myself to bed. I have an early start tomorrow at my uncle's house. Oh, I didn't tell you, I came across my great uncle's journal.'

'Really?'

'Yes, and the beauty of it all is that in this journal he's instructing me to search for a hidden chest, which supposedly contains vital information about the curse.'

'Wow. That's huge.'

'Isn't it just? But, of course, my uncle hasn't even given me as much as a hint as to where I'm to discover this hidden chest.'

'Come now, a fine journalist like you shouldn't have a difficult time of unearthing a hidden chest.'

'Huh, do you think it's that simple, Mr Abbott? I'm a journalist, not a clever magician or an insightful psychic.'

I said goodnight to return to the Inn. Josh was content to return his attention to the football match. He promised to let me know of the game's outcome, which he was convinced would be to his advantage.

Back at Mulligan's Inn, I prepared for bed. I put on my warm flannelette PJs and snuggled in the comfortable bed, intending to read my uncle's journal once more. No sooner had I turned the first page, the phone rang. It was 10:30 p.m. Who could be ringing at this time? Maybe it's mum and dad? Maybe it's Donahl returning my call. 'Hello.'

No reply.

'Hello. Is someone there?' I persisted. Whoever it was, hung on. After a few seconds, the line went dead.

The call made me uncomfortable. *Maybe it's Sean or perhaps it's just a prank call. Maybe I should ring Donahl. No, It's too late. He would've rung me by now if he'd received my message. He's probably with Eliza.*

The phone rang once more. Hesitantly I picked up the receiver. It was Donahl.

'Did you try ringing me a few minutes ago?' I asked.

'No, why?'

'Never mind.'

I told him about the hidden chest. 'You'll be amazed when you read your great-grandfather's journal. Do you want to come with me tomorrow to find this mysterious chest?'

'Sorry, I can't. I would love to be there, but I'm going to be out of town on business. I've got an early start, it's a bit of a drive to Limerick.'

'Ah well. I'll fill you in if I have any luck finding it.'

'Be careful, won't you? Our mutual friend might be lurking about.'

CHAPTER TWENTY-ONE

It was a blustery kind of day – the sort of day you would want to stay in bed. Although the alarm woke me at 6 it was 7:30 before I got out of bed. I felt rattled as I vividly remembered my dream.

I'd dreamt of Dylan who'd met a girl in America and had brought her to England to show her off to his family and friends. The woman was beautiful – a tall, blonde buxom bombshell, with exquisite bone structure. She was a fashion model. In the dream, Dylan had announced his lover was expecting his baby.

My heart sank when I analysed every aspect of this complex dream, embroiled with imagery. I desperately wanted to be the mother of Dylan's children.

It's just a dream. I'm being ridiculous with all this pent-up rage and jealousy I'm feeling. My God, how can I be jealous of a phantom woman? What if Dylan is involved with someone in the States? I shouldn't torture myself like this. Being negative isn't going to help me. I know I must just concentrate on finding this chest.

At 8:30, I was ready to leave the room to have a quick breakfast before heading out to the house when the phone rang.

'Hello.'

'Hey there. How are you this morning?'

'Oh, just great.' How could I be enthusiastic after a night of bad dreams?

'I see you're upset because you owe me a dinner.'

'Why is that?'

'You haven't heard then? I won the bet and you lost. You have to take me out.'

Josh was referring to the football match. I found it hard to come up with a light-hearted comment, so I said, 'That's life.'

'Oh come on, cheer up! I'll buy you coffee.'

'Thanks but I'll take a rain check. I'm off to my uncle's property. I told you I'm going hunting for the elusive chest.'

'Ah, yes, so you did.' He paused and then added, 'Would you like some company? You know what they say; two heads are better than one.'

I welcomed his suggestion and the company. Encountering Cailean was the last thing I wanted to do on my own.

***

The house was as creepy as ever. The grim weather created a dramatic background to the setting. Dressed warmly with low boots to give me support, I felt as though I was hunting for a chest in the depths of a frozen mountain.

'Where do we start?' Josh asked as he rubbed his palms together. 'Sure as hell cold today.'

I was about to agree with him when we heard a wretched howl in the distance.

A nerve in Josh's jaw twitched.

'What was that?' I asked.

'Probably some dog.'

'It sounded more like the howl of a wolf.'

'At 10 in the morning? Besides, there are no wolves around here.'

Fear gripped me, my stomach churning as though it was in a Mixmaster. Not wanting to scare off my companion, I'd to force myself to refrain from telling Josh about Cailean or werewolves lurking on the property.

I led him to the cottage outside the main house where we had found my uncle's secret hideout and where I'd discovered his journal. The underground tunnel that led to my great-uncle's lair amazed Josh.

'This place is incredible! Why would the old man have the need to keep such a place?'. He ran his fingers over the stonework.

'I told you he was renowned for being an eccentric.'

Josh walked around tapping the walls with almost childlike

wonderment.

He gripped each protruding stone as though he was about to create a sculpture. 'I'm just dumbfounded. Why on earth would your forefathers have built such an underground hideout?'

'No idea.'

We searched the cupboards like two famished wildcats but couldn't find anything of interest.

I went through the motions as if I was taking part in a ritual, but instinct told me Great-Uncle Fionnbharr hadn't hidden the chest here.

It was too easy.

'Let's go into the main house,' I suggested.

It was a relief to have Josh here with me. Quite fortuitous that he had rung. I no longer had the confidence to be alone in this house. I knew Cailean was out to harm me.

'Penny for your thoughts.'

'I was just thinking how good it is you're here with me I feel protected.'

'What is in this deserted old house that's making you so uncomfortable and on edge and that you think you need protection?'

'Oh, you know what these old places are like, a stair creaking, the antiquated plumbing playing up, rodents scurrying along to their respective hideouts – well, all this creates the perfect dissonance of eerie music to scare one witless.'

Josh made a shivering gesture as though he too was nervous being here.

I couldn't understand why my uncle had hidden the chest. I felt as though it was a grandiose game and I was a child let loose in a mysterious castle in search of a treasure chest. Would the treasure hunt culminate in disaster?

Old Fionnbharr was certainly having a good old laugh from his grave, but at my expense. People talked about his eccentricity, bordering on madness. He could have left the contents of the chest with Ambrose Kildare QC as he did with the will. So why the game? It didn't make sense.

We looked around. I'd to get into my uncle's mindset, the mindset of a 96-year-old whimsical man, to work out where he would hide the chest. Maybe a trustworthy servant or confidante had taken care of his business. How else would a frail old man get around?

'It's like looking for a needle in a haystack,' Josh commented, breaking the silence.

'That's what I've been mulling over. This property is so vast; I don't know where to begin. The strange thing is my uncle wouldn't have been very mobile at his age. I was just wondering whether he had someone who did things for him or helped him out.'

'That's possible. But who?'

'People around here seem nervous talking about my family.'

'Really? Why?'

'It's to do with the curse. Look at what happened to Mrs Whelan.' I shuddered as I reflected back on that night. 'It's no wonder people don't want to get involved. Remember the day we bumped into each other and you took me to Uncle Seamus' cottage? Well on that same day, I went past a quaint old cottage where an old man lives. To cut a long story short, when I got into conversation with him about my family and the Muldoons, he was quite keen to reveal something. Then, all too quickly, he appeared startled and couldn't get away from me quickly enough. I had the impression he saw something in the background that scared him witless.'

'What did he see?'

'I've no idea. But I'll tell you one thing, the poor man was scared stiff.'

We kept moving around the house almost aimlessly when I suggested we go up to the attic.

'Why up there?' he asked.

'Call it intuition.'

'A woman's sixth sense.'

'Stop teasing me.' I gave a dazzling smile. 'I've already found a few interesting things up there. It's a good place to start our hunt today.'

We went upstairs. I could tell Josh felt uncomfortable and perhaps regretted being here.

The first time I was in the attic, it was like déjà-vu. I knew I'd been there before. It was as though it was a secret hideout for me, to escape from Cailean's wickedness. Today, it felt different being in the attic. I felt naked, exposed, as though it was no longer my secret hiding place.

Josh looked around. I think the clutter fascinated him. He picked up a sword from a corner wall and brandished it about as though he was a valiant cavalier. 'This is a Scottish broadsword,' he enlightened me. 'It's from the 19th century.'

'Charlotte, Charlotte, come back here. I didn't mean to frighten you,' enticed Cailean. I knew not to fall for his trick.

I came back to reality to find Josh on his knees rummaging through a cardboard box, oblivious to my irrational thoughts.

'Josh, did you hear a man's voice?'

'No. What man?'

'Don't worry, I'm pulling your leg.'

'I hope so.'

What were these snippets of conversation or the scenes that appeared before my eyes? Were they part of my vivid imagination or was it like a sense of a past life? Was I Charlotte incarnate? Then who was Cailean?

I glanced at the Edwardian-oak dressing chest. It felt as if an invisible force pulled me towards it. The mirror was cloudy again. *I must clean it*. I yearned to look into it, to go back to who I was.

Gazing in the mirror, I felt safe. My sanctuary. He couldn't harm me. I wiped away a tear. I wanted to cherish the moment, a solitary moment without pain or suffering, to keep me sane. The feeling didn't last. He was behind me, his scowl tearing my heart out. My little attic was no longer my safe haven.

'My God, what's the matter, Kathleen? For God's sake, you're as white as a ghost.'

Choked up as though a fist-sized lump had formed in my throat, I rushed out the door, not sure, where I would run as tears blinded me.

'Kathleen, calm down, tell me, what's the matter?' Josh called out as he gained on me. He held me in his arms until I stopped crying. His embrace was comforting.

'Let's get out of here.' His voice sounded desperate.

'No.'

'Why the hell not?'

'We have to find the chest. I have to put a stop to this madness.'

'To stay here is madness, if you ask me.'

'You are free to leave, Josh, but I'm staying.'

A strange look came over his face, a mixture of fear and anger defined onto his fine lines. 'Very well, let's continue looking for this damned chest.'

***

I loathed this place I called the dungeon. The temperature was near freezing setting off the treacherous atmosphere.

We moved down the stone stairs, the kerosene light giving us much-needed warmth. We had our torches as backup.

'Why would he hide the chest in a place like this?'

'Because my uncle knew I'd come looking for it here. Besides, I have a strong premonition it's hiding somewhere in these chambers. Probably right under our noses. I can feel it in my bones, as it were.'

'That's what you said about the attic.'

'I'm not perfect. I'm allowed an error in judgment from time to time.' I patted his back and gave him a cheeky grin.

'You're allowed to make an error, but your sixth sense ...'

I punched his arm for teasing me. 'Hush! We need to be quiet down here.'

'Why? Are we disturbing the dead?' he chuckled.

'Believe me you wouldn't want to know.'

'That's reassuring.'

The kerosene lamp gave a comforting glow when we entered the first room. All seemed as it was on that day when someone had trapped me down here.

The glass eyes of the wooden horse stared at me. I wanted to tell Josh about this place but decided against it. My companion was already as uncomfortable as one would be in such a gloomy place. Even a hint of such revenant appearances would encourage him to a quick departure. I needed Josh for moral support.

'Now where would Uncle Fionnbharr hide this thing?'

'We don't even know the size of this chest.'

I shook my head. 'I don't imagine it to be a huge chest filled to the brim with priceless treasures. It would be fair to say what we're looking for is a smallish box that would be large enough to hold some documents.'

'Are you telling me we're going through this ghoulish place for a handful of documents?'

'Yes.'

'And you're to solve the mystery by the contents of these documents?'

'Yes.'

'I hope so, for your sake and my sanity.'

His comment irritated me. This man had no idea what all this meant to me and to my family. I lashed out at him, 'This is all a joke to you, isn't it? I told you an hour ago, you're free to leave. In fact, I insist. At least I'll have peace and quiet to concentrate on my mission.'

'Calm down, Kathleen. I meant no disrespect. It's just that we have no clues to go on.'

'I'm sorry too, Josh I'm at the end of my tether and all I wish is for this to be over.'

'It will be, I promise you that,' he said.

***

My watch read 10:30. Twenty minutes down in the dungeon felt more like two hundred minutes. Fear spread through my body. I was nervous being here, expecting an apparition to jump out at every corner. We went from room to room. Nothing happened.

'Maybe it's not down here,' Josh said apprehensively.

'It has to be. I really feel it.'

'Think about it, how would the old man come all the way down here to hide it? It's impossible.'

'Not if he had someone looking after him. I told you before, he must've had help.' I gave a light tap on his shoulder, 'We have come this far, let's not give up now.'

We entered the room where I'd witnessed the horrifying enactment of Honora O'Rourke dying a gruesome death, bound in shackles along with her lover. The rotten shackles lay on the floor. Undisturbed. Fixed. A shiver went down my spine at the exact moment as I felt immense pain on my own wrists, as though I was the one bridled with the cold metal of the shackles.

Josh was quiet and made no comment about the rusted shackles.

I tugged at his sleeve, guiding him away. Overcome by emotion, I was unable to speak.

The only other room left was the little room where the light streamed through the broken window above. I looked around. It looked larger than I remembered. The table, which had taken me so long to drag, remained in the middle of the room. The remnants of shattered glass reminded me of my frightening escapade. Looking at Josh, I noticed his fixed, stern expression. I took in a deep breath. I wanted to talk about that day. He looked sullen. Disappointed, I decided to keep quiet.

'This room holds such sentimental memories for me. I remember being almost hacked to death by a beautiful and feisty woman, hurtling around a hatchet twice her own weight.'

His teasing lifted my disappointment. 'I've just had a thought,' I said. 'What if my uncle hid this chest not in the house but outside?'

'What? You're not serious!'

'But I am.'

'What's the point of that?'

'Symbolism.'

'Symbolism? You're not making sense.'

'Don't worry. I think I know what this is all about,' I murmured and grabbed Josh's hand. We ran up the stairs and into the cold of the outdoors.

***

The dense cypress and pine trees shielded what daylight there was on this overcast day. We penetrated deep into the forest. I took in the powerful smells of the conifers.

'Kathleen, what are we doing here?'

'Trust me,' I said. Excited and feeling as though my heart grew little wings and was about to fly out from my body like a free spirit, I looked around.

'This is most bizarre.'

'Shush, now listen and meditate. The trees have knowledge and they will channel us to our destination.' I shut my eyes and concentrated until I was in a deep ruminant state. I visualised a small chest filled to the brim with documents. Vital documents the contents of which would set my family free. I felt relaxed as though I was in deep sleep. The trees, with their collective power influenced me to trust my inner knowledge, to look back on my time-line, to search my store of past memories and unlock the secrets of my ancient mind.

A petite woman, with auburn locks, carved her initials CLM on the hefty bark of the bishop cypress with a small metallic tool. A tear trickled down her pretty face, which looked forlorn from unhappiness. She liked these woods; she felt protected by the massive trees. Apart from the attic, this was the only other place where she found solitude and peace. He didn't like the forest in the daytime; he felt uncomfortable in it, so he avoided going in there. That fact made her happy and safe for just a little while. With a heavy sigh, she moved on, entering the thick of the wood where the majestic trees shunned even the natural light. It felt as though it was a place for a closed secret society. She felt humbled being there. She moved further in, until she reached a wishing well. It was not a deep well. It held pleasant memories for her. A sanctuary for many years since she was a little girl visiting the Kavanagh children and playing with Ursula for hours throwing petals of forget-me-nots down the hollow stone shaft. Those sweet years, how they wasted away. Now she lived here as a prisoner. Against her will, never allowed to leave. The only way to escape was by death's door and that would be the happiest day of her life.

I came back to reality. Josh was standing next to me. He too had his eyes closed and appeared as though he was in a trance. There was a disturbed look on his face as though some unexplained transformation was taking place. I wondered what part of his psyche he had tapped into.

His features had hardened; a pulse twitched at his temples and jaw. His light skin appeared insipid, almost ashen, void of healthy colour. The usual easy-going expression on his face had disappeared and a twisted look replaced it. I didn't wish to break the moment. I respected his way of dealing with an issue, to heal an internal dialogue.

Although his troubled metamorphosis made me uneasy, I waited patiently.

He opened his eyes and vacantly stared ahead. I put my hand on his arm. It felt hard as a steel bar.

'Are you OK?' I asked. He continued to stare ahead as though he was concentrating on the distant horizon, not even blinking as a natural process.

'Earth to Josh,' I said trying to sound cheery. He came back to reality and his harsh stance disappeared, making his features regain their soft and attractive appearance. The wind howled as the trees trembled against each other.

'So do you know where the chest is hidden?' Josh asked.

'Follow me.' We walked until we reached a crudely made wishing-well.

***

'You don't actually believe your great-uncle hid the chest at the bottom of this well, do you?'

'Yes.'

'And how did you arrive at this conclusion?'

'I visualised it on my time-line.'

'Your time-line? Right!'

'Don't act surprised. You were far away yourself a few minutes ago.'

He shook his head. 'What are you talking about?'

'Never mind. Look, I visualised this wishing-well. It's real and we're standing in front of it. That's good enough for me.'

He crossed his arms and asked, 'All right, Einstein, how do we get down there to find this chest?'

'This is an artificial well, built for the Kavanagh children. It's only a few feet deep.'

'This is beyond me. How do you know how deep it is and for whom it was built?' He cleared his throat and added, 'Besides what a ridiculous place to put a well. Why would anyone, in their right mind, build a well for little children in the thick of a wood?

'You have no imagination.' I locked my arm into his and we walked right up to the mouth of the well. 'A wood is a perfect place for children to play.'

'I thought a wood is a sanctuary for preserving the rights of wild creatures, not a playground for spoilt and careless children.' His serious tone surprised me.

'I didn't realise you were such a conservationist.'

'There's a lot you don't know about me.'

We heard the rustle of crushed leaves. *Is someone else here, perhaps watching us?* I hoped it wasn't Cailean. The sound stopped abruptly. *It must be the wind.*

Josh removed the guard-rail that someone had placed on the mouth of the well and he peered into it. 'My God, you're right! It's not deep and I can just make out something at the bottom.' He sounded surprised and bent over into the well. I held onto his jacket to make sure he didn't topple over. After a few attempts, Josh brought a small metal chest to the surface.

'I told you so; I was right all along.'

'Will you do the honours then? After all, it's your treasure chest.'

'This little box contains all the information I seek to rid my family of the confounded curse of Aggie Muldoon. Damn, it's locked!'

Josh tried to open the chest and had no success either. Fetching a small rock, he knelt down and went to work to break the lock. His perseverance impressed me. I watched his face as he worked quietly away in deep concentration as though he knew the importance of the contents hiding inside the locked chest. Finally, he broke it open.

My scarf swathed against the cold. With trembling fingers, I lifted the lid. Someone had arranged three small identical wooden boxes next to each other. Underneath the boxes was an envelope.

Carefully I opened the lid of the first box. The following items were its contents: a ruby ring encrusted with emerald cut diamonds, a large topaz pendant, a cameo brooch, a hand-crocheted collar for a young girl's pinafore, a sterling silver pocket knife, a white lace handkerchief bearing the initials H.M.O, a pair of delicate earrings, embedded with citrines, a pouch containing a handful of Roman coins, and a delicate 22-carat woven gold bracelet. Enclosed with the contents was a folded note. It read *Personal belongings of Honora Marie O'Rourke Kavanagh.*

English Sovereign gold coins filled the second box. A fortune on their own.

The third box was similar to the first one, containing more jewellery. This one included a marquisette fob watch, a sapphire and diamond ring encased by an18-carat platinum band, a black paste necklace, a pair of dress clips, a silver-cased comb, a lock of hair, a small leather-bound bible, and a gold pendant of seed pearl and peridot. Another folded note read; *Personal belongings of Charlotte Louise Muldoon Kavanagh.*

So, *Charlotte was a Muldoon and had married a Kavanagh.*

At the bottom of the chest was a white envelope. I picked it up with shaking hands. Funny how the decisive moment is often not a moment of triumph as you would expect. I hesitated, wanting to abandon the knowledge I was to gain. I was being ridiculous and cowardly; my practical side took over. I had to face the demons that lay dead for 150 years.

The wind was fierce. Josh stooped next to me, taking his cue from my silence. I'd dragged the poor man into this situation unwittingly. It was not his battle to fight. Secretly, I appreciated his company. It was not an easy thing to be alone in the heart of this desolate wood.

They say the eyes are the windows of the soul. Her eyes betrayed her torment. Her eyes couldn't conceal her unhappiness. It was like staring into my own eyes into my own soul. Incredible! On the back of the black and white photograph, someone had scribbled her name and the year the photo was taken: *Charlotte Louise Muldoon Kavanagh, 1880.*

The mysterious woman looking back at me was my carbon copy. She'd lived over a hundred years ago, but the resemblance between us was uncanny.

I almost dropped the second photograph, which displayed on its yellowed paper a handsome couple. It was Cailean. How could I mistake him for someone else? He had his arm possessively splayed across Charlotte's burdened shoulders. On the back it read: *Mr & Mrs Cailean Kavanagh, heir of Coamhanach's Estate.*

It occurred to me that when I'd researched the family tree, there was no official documentation about the marriage between Charlotte and Cailean. In fact, there was no mention of a Charlotte being part of our family.

Apart from this small box of jewellery and small items, the only other thing in relation to this woman was her portrait back at the house. *It's odd. And why was Cailean the sole heir? Our bloodline was from the second son Tiernan; in fact my long lost relatives came from Tiernan. Why did he not have a part of the estate? Then how did the estate revert to Uncle Fionnbharr?*

The third photograph was in colour. To my immense surprise, it was a picture of me taken sixteen months ago when Dylan and I were shooting pictures at a monastery, visiting nomadic Himalayan herders.

These were the only photographs in the envelope, along with some letters.

I almost fell over when I saw the letter addressed to me. I tore it open, unable to withstand the suspense.

To Kathleen Kavanagh,

Congratulations upon discovering the chest. I knew you would. I have been a great admirer of your work and followed your adventures around the world for many years.

Do not be alarmed at what I write. I am not a stalker but an old man who is proud to have a great-great niece who has tenacity, honour, courage and a sense of adventure.

That is why I chose you for this task, which I began sixty years ago. My aim was to destroy the treacherous fiend who has lurked in the hearts, minds and souls of every living member of our Kavanagh family for one hundred and fifty years. If you are successful, which I have every confidence that you will be, in destroying the enemy, then you shall not only inherit my vast estate and fortune, but you will save the ensuing generations of Kavanaghs by removing the abominable curse of Aggie Muldoon.

Kathleen, what you are about to embark on is the most challenging and difficult task of your life. From this moment on, you have to pull your wits about you to conquer your adversary, the monster who is relentless until he has sought his revenge. The monster I refer to is Cailean Kavanagh. He is cunning, clever and comes in many forms.

He seeks you out in particular, as you represent his soul's redemption. By now, you would have worked out that you resemble – an understatement if there ever was one – his love, Charlotte Louise Muldoon Kavanagh. Many years ago, in a secret hideout, I found letters written by Cormac Padraig Kavanagh, Charlotte and Cailean himself. When you read these letters, you will come to understand it all. Believe me when I say, you are the only one who will be able to destroy Cailean, but beware that he doesn't get to you first.

Fionnbharr Kavanagh

With shaky hands I gave my uncle's letter to Josh and picked up the next one.

To my beloved son Cailean,

I take up my pen to write my last words. I sleep

THE CURSE OF AGGIE MULDOON

but little. The perplexity of my wounded heart augments rather than it diminishes. I must confess that though my beautiful Honora deceived me and committed the ultimate sin of adultery, the abhorrent sight of her mutilated body torments me. The only course for me to take now, my son, is to confess as the slayer of my wife and her lover.

I write in haste, as I know the servants will shortly discover the two bodies in the cellar. They've been dead now for several days but we can no longer conceal their bodies. Already, too many people are asking questions and it is only a matter of time before they come looking for them down here! Oh, my boy, my youngest child, what have you done?

I shall not bring shame to this family by bringing to public your crime of matricide. I know you did it for my honour; I understand and forgive you. Nevertheless, rest assured the law will not be as forgiving.

Hence, my decision to notify the constabulary and give myself up is of the utmost importance. You are young and have a full and long life ahead of you. I, on the other hand, no longer have anything to look forward to. I pledge to you not to admit publicly what you have done and grant me the wish to take your place to face punishment. Promise me you will abide by my wishes; you must, you will, as you are a dutiful son who has put his own life at risk in order to avenge his father's honour.

I have always loved you even above your siblings. Be brave, my boy, for the unpleasant days ahead. They will hang me from the gallows, but you must swear to keep your silence. This shall remain our secret for eternity.

Your father in life and in death.
Cormac Padraig Kavanagh

'My God! This is incredible,' I cried out as I pushed back a lock of my wind-swept hair. 'Great-grandfather was innocent.'

'Fionnbharr?' Josh interrupted.

I looked at him but my thoughts were all muddled up, like some odd bits of patchwork haphazardly sewn together.

'No, I mean Great-Grandfather Cormac.'

'What do you mean he was innocent?' Josh asked.

'This letter was written to his youngest son, Cailean. Cormac wasn't the one who had killed Great-Grandmother Honora.'

'Well, that's only natural he would deny his crime to his children. They must've hated him and what better way to cast doubt than to deny the whole thing.'

'No you've got it all wrong. Here, you read it. Great-grandfather Cormac deliberately put the blame on himself in order to save his son. It was Cailean, who committed the ghastly crime. I should've known,' I said. 'Cailean was the murderer.'

***

The wind picked up tenfold. The leaves rustled as though they were partly to blame for keeping this secret and having shielded a monster. Josh couldn't take his eyes off great-grandfather's letter, and I sat on the mossy grass, deep in my own thoughts.

Cailean had been a monster, a shameless monster who had allowed an innocent man to hang at the gallows for a crime, which he hadn't committed. Not only had this monster of a man had murdered his own mother, but also he had condemned his father to death by keeping silent. Not only did I fear Cailean, but also I loathed him. His presence was everywhere, his evil soul alive in every square inch of this vast property.

What a morning it turned out to be! I unveiled a significant portion of the truth. I drew out the third letter from the envelope.

It was a single page. It appeared as though someone had torn it from a small diary. The handwriting was childlike.

> *Fear, my constant companion; freedom, an unobtainable luxury. Loss of youth and the degradation of my soul are too much to bear. The*

slightest look from his burning black eyes silences any hope I harbour for an ounce of tenderness. In my grief and my childlike faith, I persist to exist and to endure. But soon no more, I shall shed my own blood to gain back my dignity, and all I ask of the Lord is that he spare me my tormentor, my husband on earth not to follow me into eternity.

By tomorrow, I will be on my way to conquer my new Kingdom, somewhere I have never travelled, but a place where I shall experience for the first time the love and self-worth I lacked in my old life. Sweet death, my salvation, take me to your dwelling place.

'I don't believe this. It's a suicide note,' I cried out. I felt as though someone was squeezing the breath out of me. 'Scribbled on this paper are desperate words, by an unhappy and tormented woman. Poor Charlotte. She took her own life to escape Cailean.'

CHAPTER TWENTY-TWO

Just as I finished that statement, a pool of blood surrounded me, staining the lush moss. Josh had slumped over; his bloodied head nestled awkwardly on the soft ground. It all happened so suddenly that there was no chance to feel fear. Another gust of frosty wind rushed towards me. I looked at Josh again. He seemed peaceful, like a sleeping child. Was he breathing? I couldn't tell.

Long, solid legs stood over me. I felt like an insignificant insect about to be trudged by a cruel giant. I kept looking up at the man, who wore a khaki-coloured ski mask. He held a sturdy log in his hand; the brown bark carrying splatters of burgundy wine marks. After a few seconds, it registered in my numb mind those marks were Josh's blood.

The masked man stood still, not making a move.

This was no game, nor was it one of my fanciful illusions. This was real – very real, very threatening. I expected that at any given moment the log would come down cracking my skull. Looking deep into the ski mask, I could see beyond it. The man who stood over me was not Cailean. An apparition would have no need to mask his face. This man was very much flesh and blood.

Why hide behind the mask? He's going to kill me anyway. No, I think the bastard's taking great pleasure in my vulnerability. Should I acknowledge I know his identity? Will it make any difference? I can run for my life. What foolish ideas are you harbouring, silly woman? He's taller and stronger, so he'll be able to outrun me in no time. Besides, this is all fun and games for him; he'll quickly anticipate my next move and thoroughly enjoy the chase.

The masked man turned his head when he heard leaves

crunching in a nearby tree. This presented the perfect opportunity for me to flee. No sooner had I begun to run, I could hear him gaining up on me. A sense of hopelessness nestled in the pit of my heart. I ran around in circles with no idea where I was heading. My sense of direction had abandoned me completely. Each turn I made, he was a step ahead of me. He was cunning and clever. He knew these woods. He was the seasoned hunter, fearless and shrewd, and I was the fragile prey, entirely at the mercy of this sadistic killer. Realising the hopeless situation, I came to a sudden halt and turned to face him with as much courage as I could muster. All I could think of doing was to ask him to stop this game, but my throat was so parched that I feared I wouldn't be able to utter a sound. Suddenly my chest heaved and I was astonished to hear the clarity of my own words.

'All right Sean Muldoon, you've got me exactly where you want me to be. Go on, finish what you started. Put an end to it. I'm sick of your games.'

He started to come towards me, the sturdy log in his hand, high up in the air, ready to strike me down. As he came closer, I could hear the distinct wheezing.

'My God, Donahl, is that you?'

This time it was he who came to a sudden halt, a few inches from me. He whisked the ski mask off his head with such power it was as though he was proud to show his face.

'But why?' I heard my voice asking feebly.

He grabbed my arm and gruffly pushed me to the ground.

Confusion. I thought I had worked it out. *Cailean is Sean Muldoon, who shape-shifts into the wolf. Can my cousin Donahl possibly be Cailean? But how? He's a Kavanagh, not a Muldoon.* With these thoughts still whirling through my mind, I said aloud, 'I don't understand.'

'Her ladyship doesn't understand,' Donahl mimicked me derisively.

My thoughts raced so furiously that I thought my head would explode. *This must be a joke. In true form, Donahl is playing a practical joke on me.* How I wished this was theatre and we were actors in a play. No, this was real and my cousin's

231

expression broiled with contemptuous expression was unmistakable.

A strong headache accompanied the nausea that I could feel rising to my throat. Perhaps the best thing was to vomit; not only would it make me feel less terrible, but it might divert Donahl's attention and give me a chance to escape.

'Please, Donahl, I really don't understand what's happening.'

'What part don't you understand, you bloody slag?'

I was speechless. I couldn't believe Donahl was serious. Did he hate me that much to want to kill me?

'It's the inheritance, isn't it? You're upset that your great-grandfather has left it all to me.'

The loud clapping sound was absurd, as I lay crouched on the muddy ground watching my cousin's hands going through the motions of derisive applause. It reminded me of cymbals crashing in an orchestra. 'Aren't you the smart one, working it all out by yourself? But, the truth is you're daft, you know. I mean how could you have contemplated the idea that I liked you and welcomed you in my family? You, an Australian slut, a stranger to us all, and you're to inherit what is rightly ours? I don't think so.'

'You're willing to commit murder for money, for the inheritance?'

Donahl's cynical laugh sent a chill through my body. 'You're too much. Are you serious or just plain stupid?' He shook his head and said, 'I've already committed murder; number four ain't gonna make a difference to my conscience.'

'Number four?'

'Well, you already know about the noble Englishman, dead as a door knob, on the grass over there ...'

I gasped, shivering from head to toe. I thought of Josh, his lifeless body slumped on the green moss surrounded by his own blood. Could he still be alive? I wondered whether I could save him if I were able to get away from this monster. My cousin interrupted my thoughts as he made a disgusting, gurgling sound in his throat and callously spat out the remnants.

'That bastard was a meddling fool. He deserved what was coming to him. If you ask me he was hittin' on you so he could swindle you by getting this place at a bargain price once it was handed to you. Oh yes, your gallant prince was nothing more than a shyster, out to make a buck for himself. I know the type only too well ...'

I hated the lies that poured from Donahl's uncouth mouth. His false accusations regarding Josh appalled me. Josh had been a good friend during the difficult times I'd had in this country. Donahl was being mendacious, no doubt to appease his own guilt and justify his horrid crimes.

'So aren't you going to ask me who else I have done in?' He spoke as though he was proud of his evil deeds. 'No? Cat got your tongue, huh, cousin?'

He poked me in the leg with the bloodied log. 'Oh, come on, I know you're dying to know, pardon the pun. Go on, take a guess.' He took great pleasure in taunting me. Suddenly he thrust the log at my right arm.

I was still in shock. I wanted to say so much, to make sense of this craziness. No words came. He shook his head and let out a forced laugh. He sounded like a wretched hyena. Another spit flew out of his vile mouth, narrowly missing me.

'Go on, slag, say somethin'. You're startin' to get on my nerves. You know that other stupid slag, your friend – four eyes, as I used to call her. I took particular pleasure in squeezing the life out of that one,' he said as he continued his high-pitched laughter. 'That moron couldn't keep her trap shut, so naturally I had to shut it for her.'

This time he swung his leg and struck a great wallop on my thigh. I cried out from the pain. His barrage of abuse was relentless. 'You know, four eyes, she was a leech. She used to make me sick, the way she looked after that foolish old goat. She was always here at his beck and call, somethin' funny was goin' on there, if you ask me. Great grandfather had been a bit of a ladies' man and that ugly slag, Molly, well she was desperate. Only a 90s plus old hag would look at her. I vomit at the thought of those two together, disgusting and the worst part was she was related to us – after all she was an O'Rourke.'

'You killed Molly?'

'What a delight that was, putting an end to her pathetic life.

Yes, I remember that night clearly, the slag was waitin' for you, but you never showed up and the rest as they say is history. I'll say one thing though, she put up a good fight. I enjoyed seeing those puny slits for eyes open up like saucers as I kept squeezing that scrawny neck of hers. I wanted to make her suffering longer but never mind, soon you'll be screamin', but no one will hear yer hollers, not in this secluded wood. Yes, sirie, I'll make you holler so much that you'll wish you'd never been born, and that you can bet on my grandfather Conan's grave. You know who I'm talkin' about, the poor old sod whom you drove to his early grave.'

'I'm not responsible for your grandfather's death.'

'No, of course you'd deny it. But we witnessed it all, the old man just curled over and his ticker stopped tickin' and all because of you.'

'That's absurd.' I managed to utter in a feeble voice, barely coping with the severe pain he'd inflicted on me.

The blustering wind stopped and just as though someone had turned on the water for a shower, it began to rain furiously. Donahl threw his hands high up in the air and howled like a lunatic.

My God, could it be that he's the werewolf? But that's impossible, he's a Kavanagh. I'm confused. How can Cailean be the wolf? He too was a Kavanagh.

Donahl interrupted my thoughts. 'You know what this reminds me of, my pretty cousin? Go on ask me.' He kicked me.

'What?' I asked. My voice sounded even weaker, I felt like I was running on batteries and they were about to die out.

'I'll tell you, since you're so keen to know. This rainy day reminds me of that day, let me think what date it was, yeah, I remember it was the 6th of December. How can I forget? It's the day I came into this world. And you know, my little one, on that day I got the best gift of my life. Go on, ask me what gift?' This time he knelt down and pulled me back by my soaked hair.

In tears, I mumbled, 'What was the gift?'

'Can't hear you cousin, better speak up.' He pulled my hair back so much I thought he would scalp me.

'What was the gift?' This time I yelled out with all the energy

I could muster. He released me and took a few steps backwards.

'That's better. You know, with all this rain I can barely hear you. Now let's see, what was it that you wished to know? Yeah, I remember you wanted to know what the gift was, which I received on 6 December.' He knelt down again and cupped my chin in his large hand as he whispered, 'The gift was the blood of Captain Seamus O'Grady. Imagine that.'

I stretched forward and without warning, retched all over my cousin. He sprang up like a yoyo and slapped me so hard I fell backwards. He was furious. As he cleaned himself up, he uttered one unspeakable profanity after another.

The rain pelted down drenching us despite the shroud of the majestic trees.

The cold was penetrating my bones. We were both soaked to the core. My clothes clung to me like ice packs. Donahl didn't flinch. He was happy to continue revealing his horrific deeds.

'I knew that day at the Muldoon's place, the day you met the old Captain. Actually, before anything else, I must tell you some juicy bit of tittle-tattle,' Donahl spoke as though we were two old friends having a good gossip session over a cup of coffee.

'You know that old horn-bag was a kept man, yes sirie, he was sweet on old Mother Goose Muldoon. Her lothario, but I'm sure you would've guessed that. On more than one occasion, I've heard the servants whispering tales of how unexpectedly the old man Muldoon was done away with. What do you reckon, cuz? Mother Goose Muldoon and her gigolo Captain took care of the old boy, if you know what I mean. And fancy that, Muldoon was O'Grady's best mate. Shows you, you can't trust anyone in this world, can you, cuz?'

I bobbed my head in agreement.

'Anyway, back to December 6, my birthday. I went to pay the old codger a visit. I suspected he tried to poison your mind about me. Now I couldn't let that happen, could I? He would have spoilt the fun, and we wouldn't be enjoying ourselves so much today if he had. Huh, what do you say?'

'You're sick.'

'Cousin, I'm offended. No, worse – I'm mortified that you've formed such a low opinion of me,' he shouted with exaggerated gestures. 'Fancy you thinkin' like that, and all along I thought we'd become good buddies. Didn't we discover the old man's secret hide-out together?' He used the log again to poke around my thigh, which was throbbing where he'd kicked me.

I yelped even though I tried desperately to contain myself. I didn't want to show this heartless murderer how much pain I was suffering or how frightened I was. I didn't want to give my crazed cousin the satisfaction, but the pain was too intense and I could no longer control myself.

'You distracted me, cousin with your unfounded insults and I never got to finish me story about good old Captain Seamus O'Grady.' He paused and cleared his throat as if he was about to address an audience. 'On the 6th of December, I paid a visit to the seaside cottage of Seamus O'Grady. No sooner, the old man opened the door; I could see plainly he wasn't at all happy to see me. Damn inhospitable, don't you think? We argued a bit. He accused me of using Eliza to get to the family and so forth. He threatened to go to the mighty Inspector Sean Muldoon with 'evidence' about me. Damned fool! He thought he was onto something. I think he thought himself as a bit of a sleuth, like Hercule Poirot. Do you know of that famous Belgian detective Down Under? Anyway, one thing led to another, and I slit his throat.' Donahl's nonchalance astounded me. Could he possibly believe that was the most natural course to take? 'Then those mutts of his got in the way, so I got rid of them too. Unfortunately, as I heard later, one of them survived. But it's of no consequence to me. A dog is hardly a good witness, huh? You're awfully quiet there ...'

Panic. Confusion. Stomach pain. Nausea. I retched again.

'Come on, cousin, you're a real weakling, aren't you? I thought being a journo, or what's your fancy title? Oh yeah, miss photojournalist and all, you'd be used to tales of blood and guts.'

Hot tears rolled down my face. I used my sleeve to clean up my nose and cheeks.

The rain continued, but it didn't deter Donahl one bit, he relished the fact that he was in control.

'Now you know the whole story, I've poured out my heart to

you, dear cousin. Now that's called trust. See, I trust you, I came clean. But it hurts right here.' He made an exaggerated gesture towards his heart. 'Yes, right here. It hurts that you don't trust me.'

How could I have been so wrong about this man facing me? A relative whom I had become fond of over the weeks, thinking he was the only family here in Ireland who didn't harbour ill feelings towards me. Donahl had misled me with his charm and innocent, boyish ways. He'd certainly won my trust. Totally fooled me.

However, underneath the sweet beguiling exterior lay a dangerous man. Stark mad. I didn't see any warning signs of his malicious character. It dawned on me it was Donahl who on occasions was at my great-uncle's property, and my mind built up this phantom ghost in the form of Cailean.

All along, it was my cousin. Then what of this curse and the tragic way that the Kavanagh babies had died over the years? An inexplicable feeling of loneliness took hold of me. I started to sob like a child.

'Shut your fuckin' gob!' Donahl yelled. 'That wailin's beginning to really irritate me.'

I calmed down and for some reason said, 'Poor Eliza.'

'What did you say?' He sneered like a dangerous snake. 'You're about to die and you're feeling sorry for that slapper? You're too much. Highly amusing actually.' He paused for a moment. Was he churning ideas in his evil head? 'You want to know why I'm carrying on this charade with Eliza Muldoon? OK, I'll tell you. Two reasons. One is to take over the Muldoon's vast fortune once I get rid of the loving brother and sister. Two, in the process, I'm enjoying torturing that weak excuse of a woman. My darling fiancée has no backbone. She's so besotted with me that it's going to be a cinch to take the ultimate revenge out on the Muldoons. It's going to be such a pleasure to strangle my sweet, stupid fiancée. The old bat is dead; all that remains is the high and mighty Inspector and boy, have I got plans in store for him! To let you in on a little secret, I have mapped out the details to frame him for your death. In fact, for all the other deaths. Pity you won't be around to witness it all. I think you'd be quite impressed by my ingenuity.

'You need help, Donahl. It's not too late you know …' Before, I could finish my sentence, he slapped me so hard that I fell back onto the wet moss.

'You whore, you're goin' to get your just desserts,' he screamed as he started to unbuckle the belt on his jeans.

Oh sweet Lord, no, this can't be happening to me! This crazed maniac is going to rape me.

With one leg, he pushed me down and manoeuvred his solid body around my hips, and at the same time, he yanked the skirt off me. I fought back with all my strength. To no avail. Another slap. No, it was more like a punch and I lost my senses for a few seconds.

'You're a feisty one! I'm goin' to enjoy this and then more …' he said as he spearheaded my legs to force himself into me. I closed my eyes but did not give up the struggle until I heard the most terrifying shrill coming from Donahl's mouth.

***

When I opened my eyes, I saw a magnificent white wolf, like the one in my visions, dragging my cousin off me. Donahl's cry for help was pitiful. The wolf didn't relent for even a second and mauled his victim with ferocity. I screamed. The scene was too horrific to witness.

I ran for my life. I ran, not knowing where I was going. My chest heaved so much I thought my heart would explode like a grenade. *I should go to Josh.* I decided against it. *He might be already dead and I can't risk going back there. The house. I'll be safe there. At least for now.*

CHAPTER TWENTY-THREE

Like a water-slide, droplets of water slid down my freezing body. I stood shivering in the dark corridor. Terrified and bewildered, I found it hard to think what to do next.

Damn, I have left my handbag in the woods. I could've used my mobile to call the police. I must find somewhere to hide. It's going to be OK. Donahl couldn't have possibly survived the wolf's clutches. Where shall I go? What shall I do? I can't think clearly. It's not like me to be so indecisive.

The image of the wolf tearing Donahl to pieces wouldn't leave me. I remembered Donahl's blood gushing like water surges from a busted water pipe. Scarlet red. Flowing like an angry river. It seemed to surround me.

I was convinced the wolf was Cailean. *But Cailean was a Kavanagh. Hang on a minute, his mother was an O'Rourke. And weren't the O'Rourkes related to the Muldoons? One thing I'm sure of is that this creature is real, not a figment of my imagination. My worries are far from over.*

I thought of Donahl again. As insane as it sounded, I felt for my crazed, greedy cousin. The sight of the wolf tearing his limbs apart would turn the coldest heart to soft jelly. I also felt immense disappointment, for I thought I'd found a soulmate in him.

'Charlotte, are you hiding from me?' I could swear I heard that unmistakable voice uttering those words.

No, God, please, I just got away from one maniac, only to face a vengeful apparition? I wanted to run, to hide. Whatever I chose to do, he would find me.

'I knew you would be back. You can't hide from me, my sweet. You know you have been a bad girl. Come here at once, surrender to me and confess your wickedness. Otherwise you know the consequence of your disobedience.'

It was his voice; I had heard it countless times before.

I was exhausted. My throat was parched. It reminded me of the time when with some friends I went crossing the Nullarbor Desert in Australia and the four-wheel drive broke down, leaving us stranded for days, with very little water, until some Aborigines came to our rescue. At the time, we'd faced a certain death. In comparison, that episode was not anywhere as startling as what I was going through at that moment.

These memories distracted me from the severity of my dilemma. I even contemplated to darting out of there and running for my life. The risk of facing the wolf was too great, so I leant against the cold wall and stared blankly into space, having no clue what action to take next. *Am I deluding myself, thinking I'm safer in here? Wherever I hide, he'll come looking for me.*

The throbbing pain in my head intensified and my eyes felt like a couple of lead balloons. To make matters even worse than was possible, my abdomen cramped into spasms. Soaked to the bone I was practically half-naked.

Thanks to Donahl, who'd managed to tear off my coat and skirt, I walked around in my wet blouse, my underwear and stockings. Even my shoes were lost in the woods, along with my handbag.

I must dry off. I'm freezing. The attic. That's where Charlotte had felt safe. That's where I should go. The nagging feeling skulked back in my mind. *How long am I going to hide from him? I should run for my life through the grounds and into the outside world.*

That world seemed a long way away. The estate was set on some 60 acres and the closest neighbour's property was a considerable distance away. Maybe 20 minutes or more of walking distance. To be out there for that length of time, with the wolf in tow, would leave me no chance for survival. Perhaps a little rest in a safe spot would give me an opportunity to think things through, to come up with a sound strategy to get out of this den of insanity.

I ran upstairs, into the cramped attic and carefully closed the door behind me, turning the old-fashioned key to a locked position. For a moment, I felt safe. But how long could this feeling last? Tiptoeing over to one corner, I lowered myself down slowly to the floor and looked around the semi-dark room.

Draped on one of the boxes was a large, purple robe. *I swear I hadn't seen that here before. It's of no consequence.* With great difficulty, I dragged myself up again, grabbed the robe and brought it back to my corner. Every inch of my body ached from the brutal treatment my demented cousin had subjected me to. Taking off what remained of my wet clothes, I wrapped my body in the soft material and placed my shirt and underwear onto the box to dry.

***

Opening my eyes, I found the attic much darker than when I'd first come in. I must have dozed off. My body felt like a rock, cemented to the ground. I could just make out the time on my watch. It read 7:15. For a few seconds I felt disorientated. Was it morning or evening? Then I realised it was still Wednesday, so it must be 7 p.m. Soon it would be pitch black outside and the darkness would trap me.

A pale glow from the rising moon filtered through the small porthole. It was deathly quiet. I had a barmy urge to break the silence.

I remained in this uncomfortable position all night long, too afraid to sleep. I must've floated off into a dream state a couple of times. *I was in a small square room with more than a dozen doors. Only one door led to my freedom. The rules were I could have three goes. If I opened the wrong door, I would be eternally stuck in the little room. Which one was I to choose? So much confusion! It would be catastrophic if I made the wrong choice. I followed my instinct and opened the first door, only to find a wall behind it. The second choice was not much better; another wall presented an obstacle. I felt tense and afraid. I had forfeited two chances. This was my last opportunity to gain my freedom. I closed my eyes and turned in a circle then walked with my eyes shut towards one of the remaining doors. My heartbeat pounded loudly in my ears. I felt my heart was beating like a mullet on a piece of meat. I slowly turned the knob –* I never found out if I made the right choice as I came around only to realise it was nothing but a dream.

I reflected for a long time on the symbolism of the dream and realised there were many doors open to me in my lifetime and the choices I'd made of my own free will had led me down the path of this adversity. A few months ago, a door had opened for me to come to Ireland, and through my own choice of pursuing this path, I'd altered my future. Did I now have a future?

***

The rays from the early morning sun reflected through the porthole onto the wall opposite where I sat. Struggling to my feet, I stretched my bruised and exhausted body.

The few pieces of clothing I'd put on the box were still damp. I decided to put them on, the velvet cloak wrapped around me.

I thought of Josh. I felt sullen. *Poor man, what a terrible end to his life!* I felt responsible. Not that I was the one who drew the fatal blow to his head; nevertheless, it was because of me he was at my uncle's property. 'Talk about being in the wrong place at the wrong time,' I said aloud.

Then I thought of Dylan, my parents, my relatives and friends. *Will I see any of them ever again?*

My thoughts went back to Dylan. *If only he knew of my predicament. Where is he now? I hope not in the arms of some sleek American beauty.* I felt a pang of jealousy. *Why did Dylan give up on our relationship, on me?* It was all too much. With those depressing thoughts going through my head, I started crying. *I mustn't wallow in self-pity. There must be a way out of this hell.*

My underwear and blouse felt like bundles of icicles.

A strange feeling came over me. I was grateful Cailean had left me alone through the night. That raised fresh questions in my head. Why had he kept his distance? I tried to make a joke out of it, by thinking even ghosts needed to sleep. But I knew him all too well. He was up to something. All he needed was the right moment. It was like playing a game of chess. He was the master at it. He anticipated my every action, all he needed to do was to wait for my next move and then he would accomplish what he set out to do. The final showdown, call it the grand finale.

***

Like a frightened mouse, I snuck down the first set of stairs and landed on the second floor where most of the bedrooms were side by side. Even though it was daylight, it was dark and dingy when I approached the landing. I felt a bit more confident as I made my way towards the other side to take the stairs nearest to the front door, when I heard a loud bang like a door slamming.

Intense heat channelled through my veins as it made its voyage to my head. My cheeks felt as though they were on fire. Strange sensations took place in my body, from racing heartbeat to electric shocks in my head. D*eep breaths. Yes, I must breathe in deeply, hold my breath for four seconds, let the air out, hold it for another four seconds and exhale totally.* Gradually I calmed down and breathed normally.

No mistake. It's Cailean up to his old tricks. He's waited all night, so he can have the whole day to torture me. This is insane. I'm terrified of a ghost. But it's more than that; I have a live wolf to contend with. I don't particularly relish the thought of the beast ripping me to pieces.

My anxiety resurfaced when the image of the wolf mauling my cousin, from limb to limb, took hold in my mind.

A quick check around the hallway, I darted into the first bedroom, which was nearest to me, and closed the door securely.

It was the smallest room, with bare furnishings and a bayonet mantled on the wall that had left me with uneasy feelings the first time I'd explored the house. The Victorian mahogany breakfront three-door wardrobe covered the north wall. I went over to see if there was anything in the wardrobe, which I could use as a weapon to protect myself. The right hand side door was slightly ajar. Flinging it open, I was surprised to find a floor-standing wooden boot rack. Placed on it was a shabby-looking pair of boots, with the soles sopping with fresh mud and grass. *It's obvious someone has worn these recently. I think I know who it is. It all makes sense. Cailean is a shape-shifter, turning himself into the wolf.*

The Muldoons were notorious shape-shifters. Honora O'Rourke, my great-great grandmother had been related to the Muldoons. *Perish the thought! This meant all Kavanaghs have O'Rourke blood and are potentially shape-shifters. No, I have to change my train of thought. Yes, best to think about the Muldoons.*

The only male Muldoon alive today was the son of Aggie Muldoon Doherty, the descendent of Aggie Muldoon who lived 150 years ago. This man was the wolf and indeed Cailean. The mystery was solved, the man who was out to destroy me was none other than Inspector Sean Muldoon. No surprise there; I'd already worked that out ages ago.

I opened the centre door of the cupboard. It was empty. The third door, on the left-hand side, however, was not. Another single item occupied the confined space, an item not kept in an average cupboard. *Why am I not surprised?*

This object was a large crossbow.

Is it a coincidence? Has my uncle put it here in the event of a confrontation with the wolf?

I tried lifting it out but it was too heavy for me. The crossbow was finished in Realtree hardwood; it looked impressive and had in bold writing 'Deluxe version, Exomax, an Excalibur crossbow'. Someone had loaded it with a single bow, its head being of pure silver.

I remained in this small room for a good ten minutes, never taking my eyes off the crossbow. It was as though the powerful object was to be my saviour, something I must guard as though my life depended on it. I had unwittingly stumbled across the only weapon that could save my life. In my research on werewolves, I'd read the only way to kill a werewolf was to strike a blow to its heart with a silver-tipped bow or a silver-tipped bullet.

I plucked up all the strength I could muster and left the room holding the weighty crossbow in my hands, ready to defend myself.

CHAPTER TWENTY-FOUR

As soon as I left the room, I was aware of a presence, not that there was anything or anyone in my line of vision. Something intangible, some form of energy or spirit essence surrounded me. *Damn that Cailean! He's playing games with me, but this time I'm ready for him.*

A new form of confidence rose up in me. Holding the crossbow somehow manifested a belief I was no longer the kill but I was the one in control. Although I faced a supernatural force at that moment, I was self-assured, prepared for a confrontation with my adversary.

No sooner was I downstairs then I found myself staring at my cousin, Donahl. The front door was open; the gust of wind was twirling his limp body in a slow anti-clockwise swing. His corpse dangled from the ceiling, a tight noose around his neck. The wolf had clawed and torn his face beyond recognition. Raw flesh hung loosely from what was once a handsome face. In reality, I could only assume it was Donahl because of the clothes he was wearing, although copious amount of blood had almost totally covered the cream woollen turtleneck and tan corduroys. You could easily mistake the abhorrent sight for a large animal carcass in an abattoir, freshly slaughtered.

I couldn't grasp reality. I just stood in the same spot, devoid of emotion, looking at the dead body as though I was in an art gallery studying a sculptured form.

The shock of the disgusting sight had dulled my senses. The only thoughts going through my mind were how light my hands felt. The crossbow lay 10 metres away from me. I must've dropped it at the first glimpse of my dead cousin and hadn't realised what I'd done.

I must get to the weapon. My survival instinct was at an all-time high.

As I took a step forward, I saw him sitting gingerly next to the crossbow. He looked splendid, his yellow eyes in perfect harmony with his snow-white coat. He had the look of an obedient pet, waiting for instructions from his master. He didn't at all look like a vicious predator, which he was.

The more I looked at him, the more I imagined the animal to be the fine work of a world famous taxidermist as it sat so stiffly, his paws in perfect symmetry. He looked elegant, almost regal.

There was only one thing that marred the beauty of the beast. Its mouth was blood red. He had accomplished the first part of the ritual; he had enjoyed a taste of revenge in preparation for completing the full circle.

The law of the jungle states: do not run if you're facing a wild animal. I remembered reading this somewhere; a nature magazine explained most wild animals wouldn't attack if they weren't threatened. More often than not, the animal would retreat if no one challenged it.

Was I fooling myself by this counsel? This was no ordinary wild animal. This was Cailean. He had me exactly where he wanted me to be. I could stand still, at this exact spot for a whole day and it wouldn't make a difference. He would wait. He was patient. He enjoyed the diversion.

Slowly, I ebbed towards the door, when my back brushed the cold, limp arm of the hanging corpse. The unimaginable horror finally sank in. I was convinced I would endure the same fate.

This realisation sent me over the edge, and like a crazed woman, I stood screaming at the top of my lungs. Without thinking of the dire consequences, I started running. Then everything kept spinning. Was I falling? I couldn't be sure. I floated in blackness.

***

It was a queer sort of a sensation when I opened my eyes. It felt I'd travelled for a long time in the dark. But, it wasn't dark; in fact there were dozens of little flickers of light, the whole room illuminated by their faint rose colour. All kinds of thoughts went through my head, but I couldn't even describe one, or put my finger on one and say yes, this was a definite thought going through my brain. It was as though I was a feather floating in air.

Something about a hunt came to mind. *What was it? Oh yes, a horrible carcass, it must've been a deer.*

Tiredness – another thought I concentrated on. *Maybe it's night and I'm dreaming. If I'm dreaming, why do I feel so tired?*

Pain – yet another thought just crept in. *I feel pain, but where? What part of my body is aching?* I couldn't tell nor could I explain why I didn't know.

I guess that's the trouble with mixed-up dreams. It can't be a dream; I feel pain, a lot of pain, and I can't move my arms. Oh my God, I think I'm paralysed and I'm lying in some hospital room. It can't be, because it's too peaceful.

The little flickers of the rose light soothed me, whereas hospital rooms were stark and there were always people in and out; no one left you in peace.

There was a horrible pounding in my chest and ears; I felt frightened. I thought it was because I couldn't remember my name. This revelation was so incredible and ridiculous I started to laugh. 'How can one not know who they are? But I don't. I simply can't remember my name, where I come from, or where I am. Am I an old person or young? Am I married or single?' I simply didn't know the answers. The funny thing was I sensed I should know these simple facts.

'Have I always not known?'

My throat felt dry as though I hadn't had water for a long time. *Water – that's something I remember as being important. Now why can't I think of other things that are important?*

My eyes remained open and I stared at the high ceiling where the dancing lights flickered. *Maybe I shouldn't just look up there. I should be able to turn my head. At least I think I should.* My mind kept saying I should.

Just as I was about to turn my head to the left, I saw a golden face glaring at me from the top. I felt no fear. The golden face kept coming closer, almost touching my face.

'You are awake, Charlotte,' the voice behind the golden face said. 'This is what happens when you run away from me.' He sounded annoyed.

Have I run away? Where have I run to? I wanted to ask him, but for some reason I couldn't bring myself to do so. I couldn't explain why. The face moved away and disappeared altogether.

I still lay on my back, facing the ceiling. The flickering lights fascinated me. *Where am I? Am I lying in my own bed? If I am, it's damned uncomfortable. Besides, do I own a bed? I can't remember that either.*

I closed my eyes, thinking it might make a difference. All that achieved was it created a new emotion. Fear. But that was good; I'd added another word, another emotion to my limited world. What was fear? I guess it was what I couldn't explain, like my identity. Pain was back again, I thought it was my head but it was more than that. I lay facing up, my arms stretched all the way to my head. I thought it was best to change their position. It might make the pain disappear. I tried but I couldn't move my arms. That was when fear stepped in.

The golden face was back. *It doesn't look like a face should be. Is my face golden too?* As I continued to look at him, I felt his face should display at least some form of expression – be it happy, sad or angry. I didn't know why but I pulled a face, just so he might react and I could see an expression. No result.

'Do you mock me, Charlotte?' The man with the expressionless golden face demanded. I couldn't produce an answer.

I closed my eyes and counted to 10 in my head. I obviously knew numbers. It was getting better and better. I opened my eyes. The face was no longer there. That pleased me.

Surely I have a name. What is it though? Do I even know names? Laura. Is that a name? Is that my name?

'Oh, wait a minute, I remember now; the man with the golden face had called out my name. I'm sure it wasn't Laura. Now what is it? Think!' I got angry. Another emotion, there was no end to these emotions.

Anger, brought about frustration. *How wonderful.* I could

now remember some of my responses and emotions; fear, pain, tiredness, anger, frustration. These were many words. It pleased me. *Now if only I could remember my name …*

***

'Damn you, woman, wake up!'

I forced my eyes open. The golden face was back. He frightened me. I couldn't forget the pain he'd inflicted on me, slapping my face with such force. I wished he said my name, instead of calling me 'woman'.

'If you think you shall escape punishment by playing games with me, you are sadly mistaken. You whore, how you have tortured me for over a hundred years, but I'm back …'

I closed my eyes but the picture of his face wouldn't leave me. I started a string of short conversations in my mind. *It's not a face. It's a mask, a golden mask, with a thick black line painted over the eyes. It's a mask like in a colourful procession at the Venice Carnival. It's hiding reality in a world of fantasy. How can I know such things? I don't even know my own name. He called me Whore. Is that my name? Surely not, it doesn't sound right to my ears. Although I think I remember someone calling me that a thousand times.*

Here we go again, that number, thousand. Do I know how to count to a thousand? I think not. But I did count before. One, two, three …

Wetness. Cold and wet, and there was a different smell about too. It was hard to describe – a funny sort of sensation on my face.

I opened my eyes, and instead of the golden mask, I stared into a pair of yellow eyes. The face was distinct too, long and pure white, as if he wore a fur coat. An odd sort of black nose complemented the long face and the cherry ripe red mouth was striking.

It's a strange-looking face, somewhat mean looking. I prefer the face with the golden mask. It's becoming clearer; the face belongs to an animal. But, what type of animal? That much I couldn't tell because thinking was too much of a strain.

250

I must think of names, like when I was trying before to think about my own name. It's so irritating. My lack of memory, I mean. What's it doing circling me and sniffing as though it's the normal thing to do? How strange.

I wished the pain in my head would go away. *That's probably why I can't think straight or remember things. I'll ask the masked man, if he comes to visit me again. I hope he does. There's no point talking to the animal. Right? Everybody knows you can't talk to animals. I mean I can't very well say, 'Excuse me Mr Animal, I don't know what type of animal you are, or if you have a name'. The problem is I can't even remember my own name.*

This time I didn't close my eyes but the snow-white animal just disappeared and the masked face returned.

'Please can you help me?' I asked.

He brought his face really close to mine and whispered, 'You're beyond help, my love. I'm surprised you're even asking. After all you've put me through, you dare ask for my help? I've been to hell and back, it took me over a hundred years to find you and it sure wasn't so that I could help you!'

The masked man was furious. Maybe it would have been better if I'd asked the animal. I felt confused. Another emotion.

'Stop this at once Charlotte! You know, I had hopes you had changed, but no, you're still the conniving whore you always were, just like my mother. Lies, lies, lies!' The masked face shouted. I couldn't comprehend what he was saying. The only thing that stood out in my mind was that he'd called me Charlotte.

I felt happy. Now I had a name. It was very important to have a name. At least I think it was. And mine was Charlotte.

Silence followed. I watched intently the little rose-coloured flickers on the ceiling. They were beautiful, like flower petals dancing in the wind. I asked myself whether I liked flowers. I couldn't say; I had no memory of it.

I felt angry and confused when the masked man had shouted at me. *I think he said terrible things. Of course he did – he called me a liar. I know what that means; that I'm not telling the truth and I don't like being called a liar.* I felt like shouting at him, 'Stop that! I'm not a liar.' I decided I would tell him that when he came back. *It's important to me that he doesn't call me liar. It's most important, although I can't quite work out why.*

Blast! That animal's back. Maybe he's my pet. No, I don't think so; if he were, I'd know. There doesn't seem to be a bond between us. All he does is circle around me, quite annoying really. What's the purpose in that?

'I want to talk to the man with the masked face.' I sounded decisive. It had a result. The man with the golden mask appeared almost immediately.

'What game are you playing?' he asked. He was angry again.

'I'm not playing games,' I protested.

'Why do you call me the man with the masked face? Can't you bring yourself to say my name? Of course not, after what you've done to me – tortured me for eternity – you dare not speak my name.'

I was just about to say I didn't have a clue about his identity when he burst into an even wilder temper.

'Say it, whore, say my name!' And that's when he came close to my face and kept screaming, 'Say sorry, say I didn't mean to be bad, I didn't mean to be disrespectful, say that you belong to me.'

I cried from both the shock and the pain. He hit my face again. 'Spineless, weak whore,' he hissed. 'So typical of your sex. Pretending to be scared, vulnerable – lies, all lies.'

Who was this man and why was he so upset with me? I continued to whimper and he continued his abuse. 'Shut up, Charlotte, you trollop, or I'll shut you up. You're not going to make a fool of me this time, you slut. You think you won the last round by shedding your own blood. I have news for you, my sweet, I'm back, and this time I'm going to finish the job with my own hands.' He slapped me again and then disappeared.

This was madness. I had no idea what was going on, nor did I know who I was and who was this madman. 'He's nuts! All he does is hurl insults and inflict pain on me.'

His pet was back again, circling me, his yellow eyes transfixed on me and never leaving me in peace. *Maybe, if those two leave me alone, I can think and start remembering my past. At least, I have a name now. Charlotte. It's a graceful name; I like it.*

Nevertheless, something inside me awakened and it didn't feel right. Charlotte for one, I didn't think that was my name, but I still couldn't explain why I thought that.

This new awakening made me bolder and I dared move my head from side to side and realised I lay on a cold floor, barely dressed with my hands above my head, tied up in metal chains. Now I realised why I was in pain. An avalanche of words rushed through my brain. It felt as though I was building this grand machine to store knowledge. *Shackles. Yes, that's what they're called. They're the metallic instruments that are holding my arms in prison. More words, prison, prisoner. That's what I am, Charlotte, the prisoner to the man with the golden mask who also has a regal-looking pet.* 'It's not good to be a prisoner.' I shouted aloud. Then I went on, murmuring to myself: 'Obviously, I'm guilty. Maybe I've committed a terrible crime. Yes, I must've. This place looks like a dungeon and I'm being kept a prisoner. Maybe I'm dangerous. Now I remember, the man said something about shedding blood.'

My heart thumped so hard that I thought it would explode. I felt nervous as mental pictures of deer carcasses, hanging from ceilings, kept pouring through my mind. The more I became agitated, the more the images of dead animals and flowing blood intensified, until I lost control and screamed with such force that anyone within hearing range would've thought someone was slaughtering me.

The man was back. His severe black eyes instilled great fear in me even though they hid behind the shield of his mask. I stopped screaming.

'Nobody can hear you down here Charlotte. We're all alone, just how it used to be. Just the two of us, in this great big house. Nothing has changed.'

'Please tell me my crime,' I pleaded.

He let out a loud roar. 'So you finally admit your sins. It's taken you a century for absolution.'

'I'm sorry,' I cried out, although I was not sure what my crime had been.

The vortex of confusion made my head spin. I felt as though a washing machine was whirling me around. *Maybe I am in hell and this is the devil judging me. My God, I must really be guilty to be in this horrible place. Of course, it makes sense. The creature is a dog, no, more like a wolf and is the guardian of the underworld.* I remembered names like Dormarth, the dog that guards death's door or maybe it was Fenris, the giant wolf, or Geri, the hound of hell, or Cerberus who was the hound of Hades, the king of the underworld. *No, it can't be Cerberus – that one has three heads. This one has only one head.*

How do I know all these creatures? Have I met them? Greek, Norse, Irish mythology. What does it all mean? Mythology, that means something. I couldn't think what. I strained my memory. *Mythology means the study of supernatural or imaginary persons or creatures. Maybe I'm just imagining all this. But why? Both the man and the animal are real – that's a fact I'm sure of. This is no dream.*

My thoughts turned to more immediate matters. *I'm being kept a prisoner against my will. It's possible I haven't committed a crime at all, and that I've been kidnapped and am being held for ransom. Maybe I'm a wealthy woman and this madman is demanding money for my release. So many possibilities.* I just couldn't think clearly.

Perhaps the man with the golden mask is a psychopath; he's enjoying torturing me and then he's going to kill me. This final thought got my heart racing and I felt unwell. *Why can't I just know who I am, where I am and why am I to endure all this torment?*

I both feared and hated this man with the golden mask. *Only if my memory would come back, maybe then I would know how to escape from his torturing.*

A broken shell was what I felt I had become. I was like a sea creature out of my shell in a new world, a cruel world, a world without reason or sense. I was lost, but I thought it was because my soul was lost. Maybe I was dead, this was purgatory and God had put me to the test, a kind of purging of my soul.

I closed my eyes and tried imagining a different world, a happier world. *Have I ever been happy? Maybe that had been an illusion too. Do I know other people? No one comes to mind. Surely, I have parents, but I can't remember them. Maybe they are dead. Who am I and what is my purpose in life?*

An intense need to scratch an incredibly itchy spot on the nape of my head erased all these consuming thoughts. I could not move my hands. I started panicking. It was as though spiders were crawling up my neck. I remembered hating spiders. A huntsman had bit me when I was seven. *How do I know that?*

My panic suddenly turned into triumph. I remembered something about myself. It was a victory, however small. It opened up fresh hopes. I was on the road to regaining my memory.

Huntsman, that's the type of spider that bit me, I'm sure of it. Think, Charlotte. I don't like calling myself that because I don't believe that's my name. I want to go back to the huntsman. More information poured into my mind. *The huntsman is found on the continent of Australia. I think I know a lot about that big island. Yes, of course, it's called Down Under. Surely this means I come from there.* I got more excited. *The horrible huntsman bit my eyelid, making it swell like a balloon.* I could visualise it all, the beautiful woman with auburn hair and huge laughing eyes. She put a soothing lotion to make my eye better. She looked so familiar, her warmth and generous laugh always comforting me. She called me *hokis. That means something. It's a different language. What language though? Think! Find the answer before he comes back. Armenian, that's it! That's a language I know well. Hokis means my darling, my soul.* Another triumph. The beautiful woman was back again hugging me and my sore eye felt better. Mummy, I hate spiders. She nodded, she understood my pain, she always knew how I felt, what to say to comfort me. *Hokis,* mummy will never allow a naughty spider to harm her little Katushka ever again. *Katushka, Katya, Katig, Kat, Kitty, Kathleen ...* My mind was about to explode again. *Kathleen, that's my name.*

'That's it,' I said with conviction.

He was back once again.

'I'm Kathleen, not Charlotte,' I said with the resolution of a child challenging an adult's authority. I felt very pleased with myself.

My momentary pleasure turned to horror when the snow-white wolf opened its mouth to exhibit long, sharp, bloodstained teeth. Like a rabid dog, its fetid breath conquered my nostrils like uncontrollable bacteria multiplying.

The creature circled me, its fervent gaze following every little move and twitch of my body. Its gawping attention made me feel naked and violated. The consistent grunt-like noises coming from the creature's throat broke the eerie silence. It sounded like a squashed toad about to expire.

Then it came on top of me and placed its wet nose onto mine. The smell of decaying blood was too much for me to bear and I started to scream uncontrollably. The creature retreated and the masked man returned. He knelt down to adjust the shackles.

'Charlotte, Charlotte,' he repeated the name as he shook his head. 'For a moment you made me believe you had changed, you had become obedient.'

His voice rang higher decibels with each word he spoke.

'I told you, my name is not Charlotte; I'm called Kathleen.'

'You dare speak?' he shouted. 'How many times have I told you that you shall only speak only when I tell you to do so? Now, say "Sorry, Master Cailean".'

He pinched my arm so forcefully that I had no choice but to acquiesce, and I cried out. 'Sorry.'

'There you go again, never following instructions. I said to say "Sorry, Master Cailean", not just "Sorry",' he growled. He didn't release his fingers from my bruised arm.

'Sorry, Master Cailean.'

'That's better, whore. Now you are beginning to understand your place. I think you know very well what happens when you disobey me, don't you?'

I nodded as I sobbed.

He shook his head and said, 'What was that? Did I hear you say, "Yes master"?'

I complied with his wishes and repeated his words

submissively. At least, he seemed satisfied and disappeared. If that's what it took to get rid of him, at least temporarily, it was worth it.

It was time to think again, until this crazed man came back. I didn't know why but I remembered the term 'werewolf', where a human transformed himself into a wolf. *Is this something that regularly happens to humans? Will I be turning into some abhorrent creature?* These thoughts obsessed me to the point where I felt like a vast river of tears. My desperate search for my identity compelled me to question everything. *Think, Kathleen. What's my surname? I have to have a surname, I know that much. My mother – I remembered her a few minutes ago. She's such a striking woman with huge liquid amber eyes and long black eyelashes. Thick dark hair cascading to her shoulders in contrast with her milky-white skin. I established before she was Armenian. Yes, I remember the tiny country in the Caucasus, with a turbulent history, embracing the Christian faith for almost two thousand years. How do I know all this? I can picture her now, with her intricately carved cross on her delicate neck. She always smells fresh, like a valley filled with tuberose.* My heart accelerated as more memories flooded in. *Talar. That's it. That's mum's name. An Armenian name, meaning Green. Verdant, like an emerald. Emerald. What's so significant about that? It's a gemstone. Why am I thinking of the word 'emerald'?* I thought some more. Emerald Isles. *That's it, I'm in Ireland. Now I remember, my mother is Armenian and my father is of Irish descent. His name is the same as that of one of the saints. He is like a saint, all goodness. An honourable man, my mentor, I know I adore him. Stephan, that's my father's name.*

I could see clearly a white business card.

Mr & Mrs Stephan & Talar Kavanagh

15 Lotus Crescent

Lavender Bay, NSW 2060, Australia

Why am I in Ireland? I started to get a headache. Too much information bombarded my head.

Kavanagh's my surname, I know that's Irish, the Gaelic is Caomhanach, meaning follower of St Caomhan. I remember my father telling me Caomh translates into gentle or tender.

I felt elated at last, as though I was just born, looking into my world from fresh eyes. Then my joy turned back to the nightmare, when the crazed man walked back into my life. I immediately stopped receiving more information just in case this horrid man could read my mind.

'So Charlotte, did you miss me while I was gone, or were you scheming ways to leave me again?'

I couldn't think of a reply and stared straight up to the ceiling, ignoring him as though he wasn't there. My action ignited fury in the hateful man and he deluged me with a torrent of obscenities. He was indeed evil, the devil incarnate.

Yoga. Meditation. These were what I used to practise in order to relax. So I started to block out his shrilling voice and withdrew into my own world, a world where I created a safe place, a beautiful lush green meadow, a natural stream bubbling pure water from its banks. I felt carefree and alive.

A handsome man's face appeared in this emerald green meadow. His skin was smooth and his complexion fair, piercing green eyes captured me as though he had hypnotised me. He was striking. He looked like a hero or an ancient god. He had strong shoulders, proud of his ancient heritage but at the same time, he was kind and compassionate, gentle and wise. He brought his face next to mine and kissed me. He whispered his name. I think he said Dylan. *What a gallant name! Surely he must be a prince or a great warrior.*

My prince disappeared as the crazed man placed his hands over my neck and tightened his grip. My life force was depleting fast. I had to fight. I could hear my inner voice crying out for help. No help came. I started to choke. He released his grasp from my throat and roared, 'That will teach you to ignore me.'

The dungeon started to darken gradually, like a theatre in which a play was about to start, as each flicker of the rose-coloured glow wavered until everything turned black. I could hear my shallow breathing. It gave me comfort.

'Kathleen,' I spoke to myself. 'Close your eyes and go back

into your safe green meadow.'

***

The rose-coloured glow was back. Turning my head from left to right, I realised the glow came from the dozen pillar candles that surrounded my body. I lay flat on my back on a cement floor, my hands tied to some rusted shackles above my head. The realisation I was this crazed man's prisoner overwhelmed me. The partial return of my memory was at least some consolation.

Damn that Cailean, he's captured me and is keeping me prisoner in my Great-Uncle Fionnbharr's dungeon. I finally knew the truth. My brain collated every single detail, like some charted ancient route. I knew exactly who I was, where I was, and where I came from. My mind had cemented the horrific events that had taken place on the previous day.

My heart sank when I thought of my friend Josh. *Poor man, he's lying dead out there in the woods, exposed to the elements.* I even felt compassion towards my greedy, murderous cousin, Donahl. I couldn't reject the memory of discovering his mauled body, swinging from a rope, a floor above where I now lay. My stomach felt raw and nausea gained momentum in my exhausted body, like pistons moving up and down in a diesel engine.

Curse that Cailean. He was a point of contention in my tired mind.

As though I prophesised his presence, he waltzed into the room and towered above my head.

'This will be your greatest day, Charlotte,' he said. 'Today, you shall meet your maker. The devil himself has come seeking your tortured soul. All those who take their own life commit a cardinal sin. You must pay your redemption, to me and to Lord Lucifer, you shall enter his Kingdom because I have decided it's time.'

'You're stark mad,' I cried out. To my surprise, he didn't react to my outburst.

'You've become bold, my sweet Charlotte. The passage of

time has done much to improve your previously pathetic and weak character. I'm beginning to even admire this self-assured young woman who lies before me, but this new-found confidence will not alter your fate. You see, my sweet, I'm not the horrible beast you make me out to be. You never understood me. Do you think I'm proud of the way I am?'

I was lost for words. I didn't know how to reply to this question.

'I thought not,' he continued. 'You see, my darling Charlotte, the minute you draw your last breath, I shall take my own life too. It's like a double-edged sword. My guilt and my pleasure will mingle. I'll finally take my revenge on you but make amends to the Kavanaghs by reversing the curse of Aggie Muldoon. It's the only way.'

'Please, Sean, I understand the turmoil you're in. Killing me or yourself, or even both of us, is not going to alter anything.'

'What did you call me?' he snarled like an annoyed bear.

'I know it's you, Sean. You don't have to hide anymore.'

'Just because I said I admired your new-found self-assurance doesn't mean you can speak out of turn, woman.'

He was back to the old Cailean. He pulled my hair back as if he was about to tear it off my scalp. As usual, he seemed to relish inflicting pain. He was the master and he wanted to make sure I knew my place. 'Typical woman, you give them an inch and they take a mile. Do you think I have wiped all those memories of my mother and her deceit? Then history repeating itself, my cherished wife deceiving me. Do you take me for a fool?'

'Listen to me,' I pleaded, 'I'm not Charlotte, my name is Kathleen. Kathleen Kavanagh.'

'Silence!' I think I did prefer you when you were your old self, meek and mild, like a scared mouse.'

'This is madness,' I insisted. The clunking noise from the shackles defused his anger as I thrust myself from side to side.

Cailean stood above me. I am sure he took pleasure in watching me struggle.

'You know what's amazing?' He waited for me to say, 'What's amazing?' I was determined not to give him that satisfaction. 'It's gratifying seeing you in the very same shackles my mother was restrained in, the day she died. On that day I exposed her deceit and treachery to the world.'

'My God, is this what it's all about? It all makes sense now. You witnessed your father slaying your mother and her lover. Oh my God, now I understand what you felt ...'

He let out a raucous laugh. 'You're too much. You know damn well Cormac Padraig Kavanagh didn't slay his whore of a wife nor her pathetic lover, who was her first cousin.

Old man Kavanagh was too weak to do anything so noble to avenge his honour. I took care of it all; I couldn't put up with her deceit any longer. I was the one who put an end to my mother's meaningless life. Yes, I killed both my mother and my father. You're cunning, only a few hours ago you had in your hand the written confession of Cormac Padraig Kavanagh. You already know he was not guilty of the crime he was meant to have committed.'

'Yes, I know the truth and you were responsible for sending an innocent man to the gallows.'

'He sure did go to the gallows. That fool of an old man thought he was being honourable and sacrificed himself to spare his son's life. What a joke.'

'How can you stand there and mock your father, when all he did was destroy himself to let his son live. To let you live,' I said hotly.

'His son. Yes, the prodigal son. My so-called dear father was so busy accumulating money and fortune, he had no idea it was his wife who mocked him. Cheated on him. And he claimed he loved me more than his other children. How pathetic! I wasn't even his offspring. I was the product of his beautiful wife and her cousin, who begot me.'

'Are you saying Cailean is not a Kavanagh?'

'Precisely, but you surprise me by feigning disbelief. You know all this, Charlotte. You knew from the beginning I tore my parents to pieces. You witnessed it all. That's why you tried running away from me, refusing to marry me although you were with child. My child. You remember? Our unborn child, who never had the chance to be born when you decided to take your own life. For over a hundred years, I've roamed the earth, planning and plotting for the time when our paths would cross. And finally here we are, together again.'

He got up and left the room. I quickly tried to gather my thoughts.

What a twist to the story. I didn't expect this, although I should have. It all made perfect sense now. My great-great grandmother had an affair with her first cousin who was a Muldoon, and her youngest child Cailean was the biological son of her lover. That was the reason why Cailean looked so different from his siblings. The jigsaw finally took shape.

Cailean's words struck me. He had said something vital. Crucial for what I'd come to Ireland to discover. The only hope for my family. The salvation the Kavanagh's sought for all those years was now in my hands. Cailean had clearly said he wished to die with me. *Can this end the wretched curse? Will this stop the senseless deaths of the Kavanagh babies for ensuing generations?* These thoughts buzzed in my head like bees around a honeycomb.

Maybe I had to die to put it right. My death would remove the curse. *But is it really a curse?*

A few weeks ago, I'd done my research on the Muldoon family. Let me think. *Yes, I remember, the business about the Muldoons becoming werewolves went back to the 1600s. What was his name? Think! Yes, I recall the story of the young man named Eamon. At age sixteen, a pack of wolves viciously attacked him. He was the one who married an O'Rourke. I can't think of her name. Mea ... Melea ... Amalie ... Mellanie. No, it was Mella. Mella O'Rourke. Somehow, the young man carried a virus or something similar, which mutated into the gene pool of generations of Muldoons to shape-shift into wolves. So where's the magic involved? There's no magic. Therefore, there's no curse. It's the first-born male in each generation of a Muldoon who becomes a 'killing machine'.*

From the research I'd conducted over the past few weeks, it was evident that, even though the women carried this gene, they didn't have the ability to shape-shift; they never became aggressive or had the need for human blood. The violence only affected the men. So, if there were no more male Muldoons, the violent werewolf gene would stop. As far as I knew, there was only one male Muldoon left. And that Muldoon was Sean.

From all the evidence I gathered in my mind, Cailean was the only son born to the next generation of Muldoons. When Cailean's grandmother Aggie Muldoon invoked the curse, she was really only creating a dramatic showdown to appease her broken heart for losing her own son. Cailean would've gone on to be a shape-shifter whether he liked it or not. It was not because of some curse but a gene he had inherited through his birth-line.

The wolf was back again, circling me, sizing me up. *What's he waiting for? Why doesn't he just attack and be done with the business of taking his revenge?*

He left as abruptly as he'd appeared. Cailean was back. 'You think you've worked it out, don't you, Charlotte? You think you're so clever. You think you can keep secrets from me? I knew even when you carried my child, my first-born, your heart belonged to my eldest brother Muiris. Half-brother really. God, I hated him, he was my mother's pride and joy. It was the greatest day for me when I drowned him and everybody thought the poor young man lost his balance and fell into the river. And how you cried; you were inconsolable. But even with your loss, you turned to me. Like my mother, you were a whore. You didn't fight to bed me. But you shall pay now, pay for what you've done to me.'

He stopped talking and looked at me. Even with his masked face, the intensity of his emotion burnt on my skin.

'I also take credit for killing my dear sister Ursula. You remember, you two were as thick as thieves? She was a tart too, flirting with any man who crossed her path. She even flirted with me, her own brother but one day she went too far. We were in the woods and the whore practically jumped me, begging me to make love to her. I obliged, then squeezed the last breath out of her. No one ever knew. I buried her near your favourite oak tree and everyone just assumed she'd run off with some man. Tiernan, the only other living relative just got up and left. Practically everyone in our pathetic family was dead; it was just you and me in this great big mansion. Until you decided to trick me and when my guard was down, you shed your own blood. God, how I despise you!'

'You think you despise me? Then take your revenge on me and stop this bloodshed of innocent people. How long are you going to go on like this, Sean?

'Why do you keep calling me Sean? My name is Cailean, as you are Charlotte.'

'No, you're not Cailean. Cailean doesn't exist. He's only a ghost, a painful reminder of the past. Sean is the present, the physical being. It's who you are on this earthly plane. Cailean is only your repressed memory, your past,' I said in one breath. 'You said before that your only purpose for existing was to avenge me. Then do so. Finish what you started, and let future generations live in peace. I know there is goodness in you, Sean; I've seen it. If this is what it takes to put an end to this madness, I'm prepared to die. To die with you, alongside you. Charlotte and Cailean side by side, they need to rest in peace, finally. I'm not afraid to die, but I'm afraid to go on living if you continue your hatred towards my family. To destroy innocent lives, like you have, because they cross your path and you're blinded by hatred. I think you know, you said so before, you feel remorse, you feel guilt but that other part of you, the part when Cailean takes over, demands revenge. Well let him seek his revenge. I beg of you, Sean, let's put an end to this horrible guilt that has plagued us for over a century.'

***

For what seemed like an eternity but must in fact have been only about ten minutes, I didn't get a visit from Cailean. I started to wonder whether he'd disappeared. Panic started to grip hold in my mind until he finally returned, carrying two large pewter goblets. He appeared changed, almost subdued.

I still lay in the same position. My hands above my head, trapped in the icy-cold shackles. He knelt near my head and with care undid the metal instruments.

Silence cloaked us. I was lost for words and Cailean was lost in his own world. *Do I dare move my arm?* I didn't have to wait long. He took my arms and guided them down to the side of my body.

'Rise,' he spoke softly. I obeyed. With some effort and help from him, I sat up.

'Thank you,' I murmured as I massaged my aching wrists.

He didn't say anything but continued to look at me. It was hard to describe the change that had come over him. He was almost tender, loving, in his own way. At that moment, I understood the passion he had felt for Charlotte. Despite his outbursts, he genuinely believed she'd wronged him and perhaps she had.

'The time has come now,' he whispered as he handed over one of the goblets. 'This is how it has to be Charlotte. This is how it should have been over a century ago. We will die together and I promise all the suffering will end. Let's drink to our blood in unity. Let's drink to Charlotte and Cailean, and to Kathleen and Sean.'

Guiding my hand, he brought the goblet to my lips.

'Don't drink that!' an all too familiar voice yelled.

Turning my head to the left, I noticed Sean Muldoon standing in the doorway. He was aiming the Excalibur cross bow at Cailean. I was astounded.

'Kathleen, move away from him.'

What on earth is going on? I'd been convinced that Cailean was Sean. How could he be in two places at the same time? I looked from one man to the other in utter astonishment.

'We must make it right,' Cailean pressed on guiding the goblet to my lips.

'He's tricking you, Kathleen, put the goblet down!'

'But I want it all to stop,' I said as a torrent of tears started to flow down my face. I seemed to have no control over my emotions anymore. 'I just want it all to end ...' was all I could whimper pathetically.

'Don't listen to him. Let us take the drink together,' insisted Cailean with equal urgency in his voice as Sean's had had a few seconds ago.

Was this another trick? Despite my reservations, all I could utter was, 'I'm so confused ...'

'Trust me, Kathleen. Put the goblet down.' Sean said as he moved closer to us. 'And you, move away from her and put your hands up.'

'Gally!' called out the masked man.

On that command, the snow-white wolf rushed into the room.

The masked man raised his arm and pointed at Sean, 'Gally, kill!'

The arrow from the Excalibur travelled at the speed of light through the air. At exactly the same moment the snow-white wolf leapt towards Sean, the arrow pierced the animal's heart. A final whimper echoed in the room as the magnificent but terrifying beast fell to the ground.

'Put your hands up,' Sean commanded. 'Otherwise you'll have the same fate as your pet.'

The man with the golden mask slowly raised his arms in the air and surrendered to Sean. 'It's all over, Kathleen,' Sean said as he handcuffed Cailean. He then removed the golden mask from Cailean's face.

'Josh?'

His ocean blue eyes, as cold as the arctic ice, turned towards me as he cast a look of loathing.

'Cailean is no more. You can safely say the curse of Aggie Muldoon is finally reversed,' said Sean as he led us out of Fionnbharr Kavanagh's dungeon.

CHAPTER TWENTY-FIVE

'Come on, aunty Kati, I wan' some fai foss.' How could I resist those gorgeous emerald green eyes?

'You know what Annie? Aunty wants a giant, pink fairy floss too,' I said as I hugged my cousin Laura's gorgeous five-year-old daughter. The little girl is breathtakingly beautiful, with dark locks of hair to her waist, the cutest button nose and pale milky-white skin. Like me, Annie's mum is Armenian and her dad is Irish. *What's the attraction of these Irish men?* I chuckled. *Trouble if you ask me ...*

'Led's go,' Annie pulled my arm.

The phone rang. 'Hang on honey, I need to answer the phone.'

'Hello.'

'Hello, Kathleen.' It was three months since I'd heard his voice.

'Oh, hi. This is a pleasant surprise.'

'The pleasure is all mine.'

'So what do I owe this honour to?'

'Wanted to check up, see how you're getting along.'

'Grand, just grand, as you Irish say.'

We chatted for a while.

'How's Eliza?' I finally asked. We were both circumspect of the past.

'Getting stronger, everyday. It will take time to heal the wounds.'

'Yes, I know how she feels.'

'Everything will work out, you'll see Kathleen. Have faith and believe in the power of love.'

I felt choked up, unable to speak. I remembered Deirdra's words before she'd passed away.

'Eliza often asks about you.'

'Say hello to her. She's such a nice person,' I said.

'There's someone else here who wants to have a word with you, I'll put her on.'

'Hello, Kathleen.'

Hearing Aggie Muldoon Doherty's forceful voice jolted me.

'Hello, Mrs Doherty.'

'I didn't get a chance to see you before you left for Australia. I wanted to apologise for my behaviour. I treated you shabbily, and for that, I'm truly sorry. I just wanted to say I hope the Kavanaghs and the Muldoons can bury the animosity and hatred of the past once and for all.'

Silence, I was too surprised to speak.

Aggie Muldoon Doherty continued, 'This whole affair has been a nightmare for us all. Especially finding out the baby boy I gave up so many years ago hunted me down to take such unimaginable revenge on me and my family. It was unfortunate you got caught up in all of that.'

'Thank you for saying that, Mrs Doherty. No one could have predicted what Josh was about to do. He had us all fooled. I understand now what you went through. But you have two wonderful children who love you very much.'

'I know. I'm lucky to have Sean and Eliza. Speaking of Sean, he has this impatient look on his face, telling me I've to hand the phone back to him. Goodbye Kathleen.'

'Goodbye Mrs Doherty. I appreciate your call and I can safely say there'll never be bad blood between the Kavanaghs and the Muldoons.'

Sean's baritone voice was on the line.

'That wasn't so bad, was it?'

'No, Sean, that wasn't so bad. I really appreciate your mother's kind words. It takes courage to say sorry.'

'And it takes great temperance to accept the apology. Anyway, I'd better get back to the office – a tonne of papers to shuffle.'

'Thanks for calling, Sean. Thank you again, for everything. I owe you my life.'

'Don't mention it; I'm always there to rescue a damsel in

distress,' he laughed. Emotion overcame me, as I recalled the events of the past few months.

'Bye then ...' he said.

'Bye ...'

'C'mon, aunty. You pwomised.'

I locked the door behind us and together Annie and I, we walked downhill towards Luna Park, hand in hand, like two carefree children.

***

My mother was busy stuffing vine leaves with a mixture of rice, mincemeat and pine nuts. My father sat at the kitchen table, newspaper in hand, attempting to keep his wife company by reading to her from the *Sydney Morning Herald*, when Annie and I walked in.

'Look, look, aunty Kati won dis for me,' the child held a small but shabbily made bear, which I had the amazing luck to win at one of the side-shows at Luna Park. 'Its name is Bozo. Like aunty Kati's bear!' My niece insisted naming the bear after my much-loved one. When I was about Annie's age, my grandparents had bought me a bear at a church bazaar and I had called it Bozo because it had a frilly collar around its neck and my grandma had said it reminded her of Bozo the clown.

'I see you girls have been busy,' my dad remarked as he winked at me.

'We sure have, and guess what, dédé Stephan? Annie and I went on the Ferris wheel and saw Sydney from the sky.'

Annie made a cooing noise and said with pride, 'And I wasn' scarr' at all.'

'Now you two,' my mother interrupted. 'Go and wash up. I've got chocolate chip cookies just about done in the oven and I'm just about to pour some milo.'

'Yeah...' squealed Annie as she ran to the bathroom.

'That must've been exhausting,' my father commented as I finished yawning. He was right; Annie was a bundle of energy. She kept my parents entertained once a week, when they babysat her to give my aunt a break, as she looked after little

Annie as her daughter Laura worked full time.

'So, anything exciting happened when we were away at the markets?' my father inquired.

'You mean apart from the fairy floss, hot dogs, the Ferris wheel and the merry-go-round?'

'Yeah, apart from all that.'

'I had an unexpected phone call.'

'Who?'

'Sean.'

'Oh?'

'And I spoke to his mother too.'

'Aggie Muldoon Doherty? That must've been unnerving!'

'She apologised and wants to mend fences between the families.'

'Yes, I think it's high time our families put the bad blood to rest. What else did Sean say?'

'He just wanted to see how I was getting along. It was very nice of him. You know dad, he saved my life.'

'I know, sweetheart, we have a great deal to be thankful for to that man.'

'We sure do,' I said as I thought of my ordeal in the dungeon. Sean had saved me from the clutches of death.

'I still can't come to grips with the terrible experiences you went through; it's inconceivable.'

'That's putting it mildly. I just get goose bumps each time I think of the charade Donahl Kavanagh and Josh Abbott played, the lengths they went to destroy me. At the end they destroyed each other, both as greedy as the other.'

My father shook his head as he took a bottle of orange juice from the refrigerator. 'They had it all worked out, right from the beginning when you first arrived in Ireland. It makes my blood boil, how immaculately they had planned to drive you mad, to the extent that you began to believe in nonsense like werewolves and ghosts of ancestors coming back to take their revenge.'

'I still shudder when I think back on the shenanigans of those wicked two. The money they'd wasted combining holography and cinematography to create scenes of dead relatives to make me think I was having "visions". Down in the dungeon, as I moved from room to room, they played these three-dimensional holographic images, which felt so real that I was tempted to reach out and touch them. Those two villains did the same thing when I was up in the attic, when they projected Cailean's figure onto the mirror. I thought I was seeing a real ghost. Combined with the speakers they wired all over the house, to make eerie sounds and whisper conversations of Cailean to Charlotte, the illusion was complete. They hoped to have me carted off to a mental asylum in no time at all.'

'They didn't bank on your persistence, or your insatiable curiosity.'

'Too right. That's when the bastards thought the only way out, was to get rid of me.'

'My brave girl, you've been put through so much.'

'I know this sounds strange, Dad, but I wasn't terrified of the "visions" of our dead relatives. You know my thoughts on the paranormal. What really got to me was the deceit and malice of two people whom I trusted and respected. The worst part of it was the deaths of Molly and Uncle Shamus. They died because they had found out the devious plan of Abbot and cousin Donahl.'

'My poor darling, put it out of your mind.'

'I'm trying Dad, I really am trying.'

'How's Sean's sister?'

'He said she was getting better each day that goes by. It's not easy being betrayed by someone you love.'

'Of course, it's not.'

***

It was three in the morning. I was wide-awake. My conversation with my father in the afternoon had brought back a flood of painful memories. It was still implausible for me to believe how close I came to losing my life.

Right from the start, when I had arrived in Wexford, my cousin Donahl had conspired with Josh Abbott. Donahl's objective was to murder me, so the fortune and estate of

Fionnbharr Kavanagh would automatically revert to his family. My greedy and vindictive cousin had attempted to take my life three times. He was the callous hit-and-run driver; he was the one who attempted to strangle me in Sean's flat; and of course, he was the one at the final showdown, which culminated in his own death when he attempted to rape me. However, Josh gained consciousness and realised Donahl had double-crossed him and set into motion the wheel of revenge.

After his arrest, Josh Abbott confessed to the diabolical and elaborate scheme the pair had painstakingly planned and carried out.

A year before uncle Fionnbharr's death, Josh Abbott had made his way to Ireland because he had found out his biological mother lived in Wexford.

Most adopted children who desire to reunite with their biological parent or parents do so to discover their ancestry. Josh Abbott's reasons to track his biological mother were different. He was a man obsessed with taking revenge. Revenge on his biological mother who'd given him up from the day he was born. That woman was Aggie Muldoon Doherty.

At age thirteen, young Aggie went to a boarding school in London, to escape the vicious local gossip that she had inherited the werewolf gene. At fifteen, Aggie had fallen pregnant after a liaison with a boy of similar age. She had kept the news of her pregnancy from her family. Terrified of rebuke and condemnation from her parents if they discovered her plight, Aggie, with the aid of some close friends guarded her secret and gave her baby boy up for adoption. Years later, when she was back living in Wexford, she adopted a brother and sister, Sean and Eliza who had lost their parents in a tragic car accident, making them orphans at a very young age.

Josh couldn't comprehend how his biological mother, after giving him up, could adopt and love children who were not even her own.

When he learnt about his biological mother, he devised an elaborate plan to destroy her and anyone else who stood in his way. He firmly believed it was his birthright to inherit the Muldoon wealth, not some adopted kids, Sean and his sister

Eliza.

Within a month of his arrival in Wexford, he'd met Donahl Kavanagh. The two men fast became friends when Abbott confided in Donahl his real identity.

Donahl jumped at the chance to be part of Abbott's plans to destroy the Kavanagh's nemesis, the Muldoon family.

Both men agreed to weave their way into the life of the influential Muldoons. The easiest way to meet their objective was to win the heart of the shy and retiring Eliza Muldoon. With his boyish charms, Donahl accomplished that without much effort, and Eliza Muldoon fell in love with him. Once the marriage took place, the deplorable duo would get rid of each member of the Muldoon family and then share the spoils of the Muldoons' vast fortune.

When Fionnbharr Kavanagh passed away, he left his immense fortune and estate to me, a grand-niece many generations far removed from his own family. According to my great-uncle's lawyer, Ambrose Kildare, the reason Fionnbharr chose me to inherit his wealth was because over the years he'd followed my journalistic triumphs and had been impressed by my adventurous spirit. Despising his own avaricious children, grandchildren, and their respective families, he wanted to have his own sweet revenge and cut them out of his will. This had set into motion the extraordinary events that I had the misfortune of being involved in when I'd gone to Wexford to unravel the mystery of the 'curse'.

My arrival in Wexford had presented an unnecessary complication for Donahl and Josh. After deliberation, they'd decided to kill me. They used to their advantage the local gossip, embedded in the psyche of village mentality, of the Muldoons' being descendants of werewolves. Even the archived records they researched about the incidences of the Muldoons' coming from a long line of werewolves were sketchy and based on hearsay, fuelled by people's vivid imagination.

After the whole saga was over, Sean explained to me the story of the Muldoons being werewolves might have stemmed from a congenital disorder known as hypertrichosis or werewolf syndrome. This is a rare genetic condition that affects one in ten billion people. Throughout centuries, experts couldn't explain this mutative gene and the unfortunate victims of the disorder were coined evil shape-shifters, particularly werewolves.

Mrs Whelan and others were prejudiced against the family because of fabled gossip and innuendoes that had passed down from generation to generation. It was no wonder everyone in Wexford feared the Muldoons and stereotyped the family as being heretics and shape-shifters. When a tragedy struck in Wexford, people immediately placed the blame on the Muldoon family.

Josh and Donahl preyed on these false tales about the feared family. They had months to prepare an elaborate charade, a scheme so fantastic that until this day I can't come to terms with the deplorable chain of events. Sometimes, I think it was but a nightmare.

The disturbing past of the Kavanagh family had indeed been a tragedy. Fionbharr Kavanagh had come across many letters and a plethora of documentation to prove the true history of his ancestors. He had all the proof that Cailean, the youngest of the Kavanagh children, was in fact the illegitimate son of Aggie Muldoon's youngest son. Cailean himself had left behind a journal that described in detail his emotions and grim deeds. He'd been a cruel and vindictive child and became a monstrous person as an adult.

He'd murdered his own parents and sent an innocent man to the gallows for that heinous crime. He'd also been responsible for killing his eldest brother and older sister, and had sent his wife Charlotte to an early grave. That was 150 years ago, and what I'd witnessed in the 'haunted' house certainly hadn't entailed any magic or ghosts.

There never was or will there ever be any trace of tortured souls roaming about on the Kavanagh Estate.

The fiendish games Josh and Donahl subjected me to were the product of two very sick minds. The eeric voice of Cailean calling out to his unfortunate wife Charlotte was the trickery of Abbott when I was at the 'haunted' house. The aim was to scare me witless to the point of making me believe I was Charlotte. They'd gone to incredible lengths to achieve their evil ends.

They'd commissioned a portrait depicting a woman who looked exactly like me. They'd created photographs, courtesy of modern technology, representing Charlotte as my double. Thus had begun a fantastical play in which I'd been an unsuspecting actor.

Historically, Cailean had forced a woman named Charlotte to marry him. She'd committed suicide some years later. However, this woman, who lived over 100 years ago, had looked nothing like me. Josh Abbott and Donahl had the original photographs of the Kavanagh ancestors and letters from a bygone era. They'd forged letters to suit their needs, like the one supposedly Fionnbharr Kavanagh had written to me. How naïve I was! How could an old man have known that I would definitely find the letters he'd written to lead me to a wishing-well? It was too perfect. They'd subtly planted in my mind clues to track the treasure chest.

'Of course, I fell for it hook, line and sinker,' I said aloud. 'Poor Molly, that's why she'd implored me to meet her at my uncle's property. She'd discovered of Josh and Donahl's diabolical mind-game and was going to foil the pair's evil master-plan. Unfortunately, I never got a chance to keep the rendezvous with Molly, Donahl had made sure of that.

And what of the so-called visions I had in the dungeon? It was the trickery of holographic brilliance. In some ways my own mind had started to play tricks on me because I'd allowed superstition, gossip and the story of a curse that had plagued my family for scores of years to influence me to such an extent that I'd completely lost all sense of reality.

The affirmation from my own father that I'd had a baby brother and a cousin who'd died unexpectedly further sank me into the belief of the Curse of Aggie Muldoon.

Josh and Donahl's clever tricks had entrenched in my mind the images of the wolf. I recently discovered my great-uncle Fionnbharr had kept a large wild dog resembling a regal-looking wolf on the grounds. Naturally, as I had glimpses of it whenever I was on the estate and as I have a propensity for dramatising situations, I'd started to believe the ghost of Cailean shape-shifted from wolf to man. Sadly enough, and to the delight of my wicked cousin and his equally iniquitous friend, I wrongly surmised Cailean, the wolf and Sean were one and the same. Sean, who wasn't even the bloodline of the Muldoons.

And what of that incredible final showdown? Josh had gone through the charade of convincing me to make the ultimate sacrifice and die side by side with Cailean by drinking poison in order to rid the curse from our families' bloodline.

Naturally, Josh never had the intention of dying; he was only planting evidence for those who found my body after I'd drunk the poison and died, ridding the Kavanagh Family of the Curse of Aggie Muldoon. No-one would suspect he was involved in this bizarre ritual, as no-one knew of his true identity.

He'd set up security cameras recording my imprisonment in the dungeon by the golden masked man, so that when the police searched the premises after my death, they would find videotapes that would implicate Sean as my killer.

This elaborate scheme was the way Josh Abbott had decided to get rid of Sean, so he could take over the estate which he thought was rightfully his, not Sean's or Eliza's.

***

'Why don't you come with me, love?' my mum suggested, referring to the outing she'd organised with her friends at Mosman. 'We're just going to potter around and have lunch at The Rower's Club. Come on, you love the clay-pot of the mixed seafood ...'

'Thanks, but I just feel like doing nothing and soaking up the sun, Mum.' I was lazing on the deckchair on the upstairs balcony, taking in the breathtaking view of the bay. And what a view it was! *Sydney is truly one of the most beautiful cities in the world.* I was lucky. My parents owned a three-storey mansion in the fashionable suburb of Lavender Bay, on the North Shore. The scenery from every vantage point was just breathtaking. My father, a renowned architect had designed their palatial house, supervising the building work to ensure the finest quality and craftsmanship.

'Well, mind that you don't get sunburnt,' my mother fussed. I chuckled. My mother was not the outdoor type; summer or winter, rain or shine, she donned herself with one of her numerous colourful hats. She was the Imelda Marcos of hats.

'Oh well, if I can't convince you – now don't forget to eat, I've made a tuna-and-corn quiche. It just needs heating up.'

'At this rate, Mum, the way you're feeding me, I won't even be able to move off these chairs. Maybe you're plumping me up to be the pig on the spit for the family fare at Easter.'

'Very funny, young lady. Anyway my sweets, I have to run. Your father should be back from his golf game by four. See you later.'

'Bye, Mum and say hello to Zevart and Anahid for me.'

'Will do, though it's a shame you won't be joining us.'

'Next time I promise.'

Mum left and I enjoyed my own company for a few hours, reading a charming novel by an Australian writer, Frank Coates, titled *Tears of the Maasai. What a glorious day it is*. Even though it was April, the air was still pleasantly warm and the strong Australian sun saturated the bright blue skies. April was one of my favourite times of the year, as usually Easter fell in that month. My family, particularly my mother's side, being Orthodox, celebrated Easter with reverence. Apart from the religious aspect, since I enjoy going to our Church in Chatswood. The foods my mother and my aunts prepared with their culinary creativity, the baking of sweet Easter breads and biscuits, colouring and decorating eggs is a strong tradition in our family and dear to my heart. It's wonderful the way everyone gets together not to mention passing down from generation to generation the traditions we hold of our culture but still assimilating to and mingling with the Australian way of life.

Then as though a dark cloud marred the day, a sudden sadness descended upon me. Although everything was perfect, one important aspect was missing – Dylan, who meant the world to me. He'd been my best friend, my lover and my soulmate. I began to cry.

***

'So, tell us the truth, Kathleen. Do you prefer living in Ireland, England or Australia?' my uncle Arto asked as he cracked the bright red Easter egg with my own blue one.

'That's a hard one, pardon the pun,' I replied truthfully, as I peeled the shell off the boiled egg. 'Each country has its pros and cons, like everything else.'

'But you can't beat our good Aussie weather, can you? Look, it's supposed to be autumn, but it's a glorious sunny 26-degree day,' my uncle Arto, continued as he finished putting the last bite of his second Easter egg in his mouth.

'I totally agree. We Australians are spoilt by wonderful weather for most of the year, although I don't enjoy the 40-degree days.'

'Oh – they're far and between. What I don't like is the incessant rain you get in Europe.'

'That's what I love. I thrive in cold, wet weather. I always say when one day I come back home to retire, I'm going to settle in Melbourne.'

'God forbid! Do you enjoy having four seasons in the one day?' my uncle laughed.

'So, how are you doing Katya?' Mrs Sarian, a family friend of my grandmother's, asked, interrupting our conversation about weather.

'I'm well, thank you.'

'My dear, poor girl,' Mrs Sarian said as she shook her head. 'Terrible, terrible business. I pray for you every day, my child, and light a candle when I'm in church. I was saying to our Archbishop the other day ...'

'Mrs Sarian, I've saved you the best seat. Come, the pig on the spit and all the kebabs are well cooked, just as you like them.' My father rescued me and guided the woman to her seat where some of her friends from church were already enjoying their food.

'Aunty Kati,' Annie pulled on my skirt. 'Mummy don' want me to eat too much chocolate. But I wan' the bunny on the table, you give me in secret.' My niece was pleading with her gorgeous cajoling eyes. The little minx had worked me out and could wrap me around her little finger every time she gave me that look of helplessness.

'I'll make you a deal; you eat all the veggies your mum has put on your plate and I'll make sure you get the bunny, OK?'

Annie laughed, lighting up my heart and gave me a big hug as she said, 'I wuv you aunty Kati.'

I fought back tears as I watched the precious child run to her mother.

'It's so good to see you,' my cousin Haig said as he planted a kiss on my cheek.

I hugged him. 'You've no idea how good it is to see you all, to be with my family. So, what's this I hear about the new lady in your life? She's the fourth one this year, and it's only April,' I teased my cousin. He was my favourite of the male cousins and the youngest.

'This one's serious.'

'That's what you said about the last one.'

'Enough talk about me, how are you doing Katya? Seriously.'

'I'm OK. Some days it's easier than others. A bit more of a struggle at times. But heck, I'm lucky to have you all around me.'

He followed me indoors away from prying ears. 'Tell me, have you heard from Dylan?' Haig asked.

'No, and I have absolutely no idea where he is.'

'I thought he was in America.'

'Well, yes, as far as I know, but America is a big place.'

'Things will work out, you'll see. Have faith and believe in the power of love.'

'You're the third person to tell me that. But I love you for it. Besides, to tell you the truth, I'm not sure I want Dylan back.'

'Plenty more fish in the sea, I say. Come on, Katya, let's get some more of my aunt's delicious lemon pie.'

***

The 8th of July, I couldn't believe six months had gone by since my return to Australia and practically nine months since I'd seen Dylan. I still asked myself the same questions. What had happened to our relationship? What had gone wrong? In those short few months I was in Ireland, busy chasing clues, ghosts and werewolves, something had happened to change my partner's view of our relationship.

But what? Another woman? No, I won't believe that. Our love is, pure, sacred, at least on my part. I think I've been romanticising the past.

I was tired, even though most days I did relaxing things. I walked on the beach, went boating with my father, shopped with my mother, dined with family, caught up with friends – all pleasant activities, and yet I felt empty. And what of my career? I asked myself.

Even little things, mundane things, which I did on a daily basis, reminded me of Dylan. Now, I understood the pain my grandmother went through when my grandfather passed away. She'd said a part of her had died with him, never to return.

That was how I felt.

Nevertheless, a part of me faced the reality my relationship was not perfect. Not really, my mind insisted. I was the one that had held it together. I loved being in love, although I didn't think Dylan felt the same passion for me as I did for him. In fact, he ended it so easily, so clinically. Not even bothering to face me. So why did I feel this way?

Was it because he bruised my ego? I guess I was most upset that there was no closure. What was the point of pining over a man who didn't care for me? I had to move on, close that chapter of my life. I made a pact with myself to get on with my life, regain my old confidence.

***

'Your mother and I will miss you, princess.'

'I'll only be gone for three weeks. Besides, it's only a two-hour drive to the Blue Mountains. You can both visit any time you like.'

'Just teasing you. You'll be glad to have some peace and quiet away from your old man,' my father said as he picked up the suitcase to take downstairs.

'Now let me do that.'

'What, you think I'm already so feeble that I can't even carry a little case downstairs? Besides, this suitcase feels as though it's empty. You haven't taken after your mother, love; now she packs the whole wardrobe in her case, even if it's just for a weekend away.'

'Shame on you, Stephan Kavanagh talking like that behind my back.'

'Now I'm in trouble,' my father laughed practically bolting out the door to avoid my mother's teasing rebuke. *What a pair. The both of them, still as much in love as the day they'd met. That's how I'd thought my relationship would have worked out. No, I'm not going to cloud my mood by such thoughts, besides I don't want to worry my mum; she does enough of that even without encouragement.*

'You know your Nana and Pop are delighted you're going to look after their cottage, and the menagerie they keep, while they're away in Queensland,' my mother said as she put some of the clothes hangers back into the cupboard.

'I love going up there, Mum, it reminds me of school holidays when I was a kid.'

'Make sure you eat properly though.'

'Yes, mum. Stop worrying. I know how to look after myself.'

'I know you do, my darling, but mums always worry ...'

We hugged and kissed. I felt instant calm. 'You're the best mum a girl can have.'

***

My champagne-coloured Toyota LandCruiser purred gently as it ascended the mountain in four-wheel-drive mode. I made my way to the township of Leura to my grandparent's property. The cottage was set on 10 acres, surrounded by bushland. My pop had migrated to Australia with his parents when he was a young boy. He'd grown up in inner-city suburbs. At age 18, much against his parents' wishes, he'd joined the army and had fought courageously for his country in the Korean War. Captured by the enemy, my pop had spent several years as a POW. The story goes that years of torture and imprisonment in confined spaces had given rise to feelings of claustrophobia. When he returned to his homeland in his mid-twenties, he'd met and married my nana, a country girl from Tamworth. He'd vowed to move to the country to enjoy open spaces. He acquired a 75-acre property at Singleton, north of Sydney and turned the arable land to a successful horse stud farm.

All that was before my time. Ever since I can remember, my paternal grandparents were retirees and lived in a picturesque cottage in the Blue Mountains. Of course, they still keep some horses and even now, my pop, who is in his early eighties, is a keen rider. In fact, they are quite self-sufficient, raising their own chickens, and growing a wide variety of vegetables and abundant fruit trees.

They asked me to be in sole charge of the precious animal and plant-life for a few weeks. I felt a little nervous. This was a blessing in disguise, I convinced myself. I desperately needed to escape the city and to a degree from the family, even though I adored them.

Nevertheless, it was evident that everyone treated me with kit gloves, as though I was a delicate piece of china, waiting to be shattered.

***

'What's the matter, boy?'

Buster, the blue cattle dog, who was like a grandchild to my pop, barked a couple of times. He jumped on the sofa. He whimpered as he placed his snout on my legs. 'You're a bit restless tonight, aren't you? Missing your master, no doubt. I'm not so bad, am I?'

Buster whimpered again and nuzzled further into the couch.

A cold feeling went through me. It was a chilly night and I had the fire going. I was quite content sitting in front of it and reading a romantic novel my nana suggested. I turned the cover and read inside the pocket about the writer Monica McInerney, who is a successful Australian writer and has set her stories in

Australia and Ireland. *This should be interesting. One day I'll return to the land of my ancestors. It's a magical place. Literally, it was magic for me.* I still thought a lot about the ordeal and all I had endured. Goose-bumps tingled my body. *I'm safe here; the past is truly behind me. It's the present I have to deal with. I have to heal myself.*

The phone rang. Buster sprang to his feet and barked.

'Heel, boy. It's OK.'

After six rings I answered the phone. 'Hello.'

'Hi, Kathleen. It's Sean Muldoon here.'

'Hi there. How did you get this number?' I wondered how he found out I was at my grandparent's property since my father was at a conference in Melbourne and my mother had accompanied him.

'I keep telling you, I make it my business to know everything.'

'Yes, I'm beginning to see you are indeed well informed. You know, Sean, you could always quit the force and run your own, and I'm sure very successful, Private Investigation agency. Yes, I can really picture that.'

'Can you, now? Well, perhaps you can quit journalism and we could become partners. You're a bit of a sleuth yourself, always seeking danger and adventure. I think we would make a good team, don't you?'

'I don't know about that. I think we would kill each other. We are both headstrong and stubborn ...'

'Well, always leave your options open, I say.' An awkward silence followed for a few seconds. I wondered where this conversation was going.

Sean changed the subject. 'So I hear you're quite the farmer these days ...'

'And who might have told you that?'

'Oh, a reputable PI never breaks the confidence of his sources.'

'Aha, is that so? I think you've been misinformed. I'm a city girl through and through and am quite happy to get back to the mayhem and chaos city life offers. If I wasn't responsible for the gorgeous animals here, I'd go stark mad in all this solitude.'

'And I'd give anything for peace and tranquillity; maybe we should trade places.'

'Sounds like a good deal to me. There's nothing like chasing criminals and bringing their crimes to justice.'

'Frankly, I thought you had enough adventure to last you a lifetime and more ...'

'Oh, please don't remind me.'

We spoke for a good hour and Sean informed me he recently went to see the renovations at my 'haunted' house. He said everything was going according to schedule. I'd decided to donate the estate to a charitable organisation as soon as the builders refurbished the place. An orphanage would be set up at the estate and funded for many years to come by the rest of the fortune, which was in a trust fund.

As our conversation came to a close, Sean said, 'It's a very generous and selfless thing you have done, leaving the estate and vast fortune to charity.'

'For generations, that place never brought peace or happiness to my family, but now it will be put to good use. So you see, Sean, I don't think it's a selfless act, but something I just had to do.'

***

In the kitchen, the tap was dripping. Each droplet sounded louder than the previous one. Maybe there was truth in what I'd just said to Sean about going mad here.

The tranquillity and utter peace was beginning to irritate me. *How ridiculous, I've only been here a week. Or is it because I'm starting to become a bit scared? Scared of what though? I think I'm scared because I'm lonely. It's strange how it doesn't hurt as much when I think of Dylan these days – I'm not bitter, just annoyed at his callousness. Not one call, not one form of correspondence from him. Doesn't he care? Doesn't he want to know whether I'm dead or alive? I know Dylan's the sort of guy who's self-absorbed and his needs come first, but even for the sake of human decency, wouldn't he want to know where I am? How I am?*

I had my parents, extended family and supportive friends, but it seemed as though there was something lacking in my life. I had a strong urge to plunge myself back into the field of journalism – for adventure, knowledge and excitement. *I think it's time I start making plans to go abroad again. Not back to London, no, I couldn't face that! But I have contacts world-wide. Tomorrow, first thing, I'll call Jasmine.*

Jasmine Sanderson, who'd been a loyal friend since university days, had moved to Toronto some years ago and ran a successful magazine directed at female executives. *Good time to be there, being summer and all in Canada. Besides, I've some relatives and a few friends with whom I would love to catch up there.*

The front doorbell rang. Buster was up again, barking, circling around my feet, and furiously wagging his tail. I went to the door wondering who on earth could be calling on me at 11 p.m.

Switching on the porch light I opened the door, feeling safe behind the locked security door. I stood there, in disbelief.

CHAPTER TWENTY-SIX

'May I come in? It's freezing out here.' His voice carried down the corridor.

I was dumbfounded, but in the confusion, I tried to hold down Buster as the dog kept barking to ward off the man as if saying, 'Watch out Mister, one wrong move and you're dead meat'.

'I'll just put Buster in this room.' Was that my voice? I sounded more like a croaking toad than a self-assured woman. Self-assured? Hardly, as ripples of excitement, confusion, and amazement simultaneously went through my body.

The dog was safely out of reach, although he continued to bark frantically behind the door. The visitor walked in, and closed the door behind him. He just stood there, staring at me. The word awkward came to mind. It was as though we were strangers, almost cautious of one another. This was so unexpected, but I felt unusually keyed up.

'I can't believe this. How?' I asked.

He looked shy, withdrawn, like a teenage boy, self-conscious and unsure of himself.

All I could come up with was another stupid question. 'Are you hungry?'

'No, but thanks, I've already eaten,' he replied with a faltering, nervous voice.

I couldn't believe, I sounded like my mother, always worried everyone around her was starving and it was her duty to feed the world.

'How long have you been in Australia?'

'Since 6 o'clock this evening. I took a taxi from the airport.'

'Oh.'

'Do you think you should attend to the dog? It seems quite

distressed.'

The dog, what dog? Buster, of course, the poor thing's still barking away.

'You're right,' I blurted out. 'Just give me a moment.'

Do I have to leave him? Even just for a minute? Pull yourself together, Kathleen. Just deal with the dog situation and then you have all the time in the world.

*** *

Peace reigned once more as Buster settled on his favourite blanket in my grandparent's bedroom. 'Good boy, now go to sleep, mummy's fine. That man out there is a friend. Hush, no more barking, OK, Buster?'

The dog whimpered and closed his eyes, ready for sleep. *This is easy, too easy. Now I've to face a much harder challenge.*

Gently pulling the door behind me, I left it ajar so as not to distress Buster, who might have felt abandoned behind a closed door. I drew in a deep breath. My heart fluttered. When I realised that he wasn't in the hallway, or anywhere else for that matter, disappointment nestled in my body. Or was it fear? *Oh God, have I just woken up? It must've been a dream. Yes, of course, I just came out of the bedroom. I must have dozed off near the dog and had that weird dream.*

My stomach felt queasy; there was a hollowness inside that I couldn't identify.

'It didn't take you long to calm him down,' his voice said behind me. Startled, I swung around, not sure whether the man facing me was an apparition. He stood there, tall and handsome. This was not a dream. It was real, very real. 'I just ducked into the bathroom,' he explained.

'I'll make us some tea,' I said as I walked away, my heart pounding hard. He followed me, quietly, like an obedient dog.

I fiddled with the tea making paraphernalia as though I completed the motions in a ritualistic tea ceremony. Nerves. Sheer nerves. I almost dropped the glass teapot, my fingers feeling clumsy. I didn't know how to use them, as though they were these obtrusive bits of stick just jutting out from my hands.

'Let me help you.'

I smiled. It seemed the right thing to do. It was one way of acknowledging his help. Otherwise, the glass pot full of tea would've been all over the floor. He poured some tea in the delicate china. My fingers felt useless again. I felt it was best to fold my arms, that way they would be out of the way.

'You look well,' he said as he placed two lumps of sugar in his cup of tea. Had he always had two lumps of sugar? I couldn't think. I just kept looking at his long fingers, which were busy mixing the cup of tea. The sugar seemed to take forever to dilute.

'So have you been having fun, up here in the mountains?'

I stared blankly at him. *Fun? What does he mean by fun? I've been damned depressed for most part of the days and he has the audacity to suggest I'm having fun. What's the matter with me? The poor man's just making attempts to talk. He's as awkward as I feel.*

Anger. That was what I was experiencing. Anger towards Dylan, towards myself and everything else, which happened in the past year. But, especially anger towards my cousin Donahl and Josh Abbott for going to such lengths to serve their evil.

***

'I hope you don't mind I've come here.'

'No, of course not. I'm speechless, that's all.' I blushed. My stomach felt like it was this incredible sphere of tension like a tightly strung ball of wool. Admittedly, I felt more than happy he had come.

'I wanted to make sure, you are indeed well and coping with the memory of all the horror you went through. You know, I thought seeing you in person would be the best thing.'

'I am well, but I'm very glad you have come.' I smiled and thought to myself that I was more than glad.

There was a sparkle in his dark, intense eyes, which made him irresistibly sexy.

'This is unbelievable,' I said as I stared into his handsome face. 'Not in my wildest dreams would I've guessed you would come here, to Australia.'

'A bit naughty of me, wasn't it? Coming unannounced, I just wanted to surprise you.'

'Well you certainly did that.'

'To think, with what you've endured, it's remarkable you're functioning so well.'

'Thanks to you, Sean. The curse of Aggie Muldoon no longer haunts my family. We will forever be indebted to you.'

He gave a cheeky grin. 'It was about time us Muldoons and you Kavanaghs put the awful past behind us. Besides, as I've said to you before, I like rescuing damsels in distress.'

The familiar banter, I loved it. 'What other damsels have you been rescuing, lately?'

'No one as memorable as you.'

'Memorable? That's a novel way to be described. I always thought, Inspector, I irritated you.'

'I have to admit you were at times testy, but I guess that was one of your many attributes, which made me fall in love with you.'

Did I hear him right? He was in love with me?

He cupped my chin and said, 'I know you think I'm a self-opinionated, grumpy policeman, but do you think you have it in your heart to give me a chance to prove to you that deep down I'm a nice guy?'

I nodded. My eyes filled with tears and a knot formed in my throat. His candid words overwhelmed me. I was unable to speak.

'Have I told you before how irresistible you are, particularly when you're not angry with me?'

I shook my head.

He took my face into his warm palms and his lips left a soft imprint on my mouth. 'I wanted you from the moment I laid eyes on you at Mrs Whelan's house.'

I didn't get a chance to respond as he took me in his strong arms. I lost myself in his hot, passionate kiss. When he pulled away, I couldn't bear to be apart.

'So what do you say, Kathleen Kavanagh, would you like to come back to Wexford, to keep a trying policeman in check?'

I stretched up to plant a soft kiss on his lips. 'I think it's a splendid idea.'

There was a chilling howl and as we turned our heads toward the hallway, we both cried out, 'Buster, be quiet.'

About the author

Nadia was born in Addis Ababa, Ethiopia, of Armenian parents. Her grandparents had moved from the Armenian Highlands to Ethiopia in the late 1920s. She had a blessed childhood growing up in the Horn of Africa. In 1973, the family migrated to Australia as civil unrest became imminent. They settled into a new life in Adelaide, South Australia.

From a young age, Nadia loved reading, especially the Classics. Her late father was her mentor; he was an avid reader with an extensive library. He taught her that books are man's most precious possession. During her teenage years she started reading genre fiction, particularly thrillers, murder mysteries and romance novels.

In 1996, her husband's work took the family to Sydney where she joined the NSW Writers' Centre and began her life-long ambition of writing fiction. She writes mainly romantic suspense, combining her favourite fiction genres. Nadia lives in Sydney with her husband, mother, daughter, cat and cute guinea pigs.

Printed in Germany
by Amazon Distribution
GmbH, Leipzig